VOLUME 3: SHORE OF THE DYING LIGHT

IMAGE COMICS, INC.

Robert Kirkman - Chief Operating Officer
Erik Larsen - Chief Financial Officer
Todd McFarlane - President
Marc Silvestri - Chief Executive Officer
Jim Valentino - Vice-President
Eric Stephenson - Publisher
Corey Murphy - Director of Sales
Jeff Boison - Director of Publishing
Planning & Book Trade Sales
Jeremy Sullivan - Director of Digital Sales
Kat Salazar - Director of PR & Marketing
Branwyn Bigglestone - Controller
Drew Gill - Art Director

Jonathan Chan - Production Manager
Meredith Wallace - Print Manager
Briah Skelly - Publicist
Sasha Head - Sales & Marketing Production Designer
Randy Okamura - Digital Production Designer
David Brothers - Branding Manager
Olivia Ngai - Content Manager
Addison Duke - Production Artist
Vincent Kukua - Production Artist
Tricia Ramos - Production Artist
Jeff Stang - Direct Market Sales Representative
Emilio Bautista - Digital Sales Associate
Leanna Caunter - Accounting Assistant
Chloe Ramos-Peterson - Library Market Sales Representative

IMAGECOMICS.COM

JEFF POWELL
Collection Design

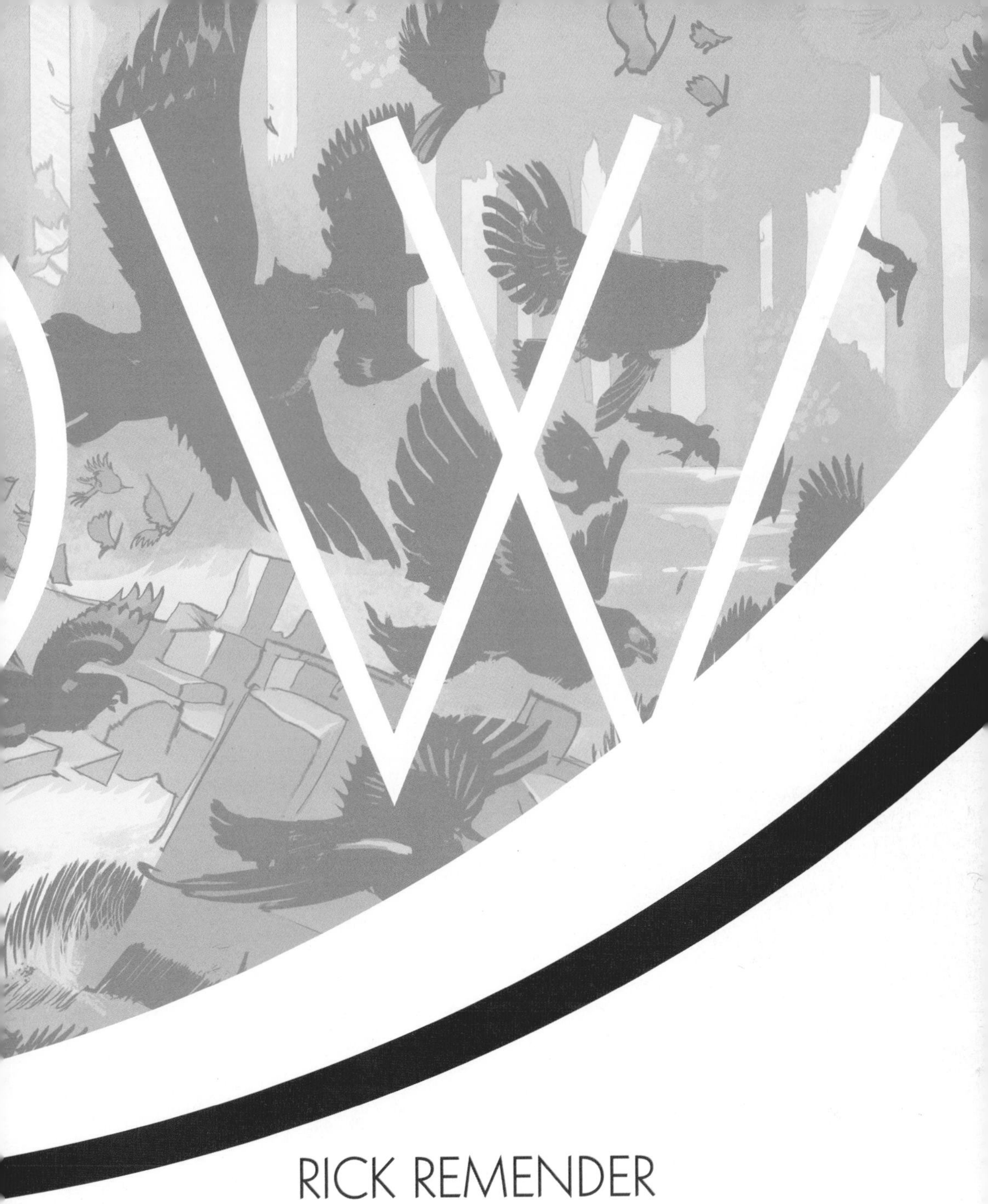

RICK REMENDER
writer

GREG TOCCHINI
artist

DAVE McCAIG
colors

RUS WOOTON
letterer

SEBASTIAN GIRNER
editor

Created by Rick Remender & Greg Tocchini

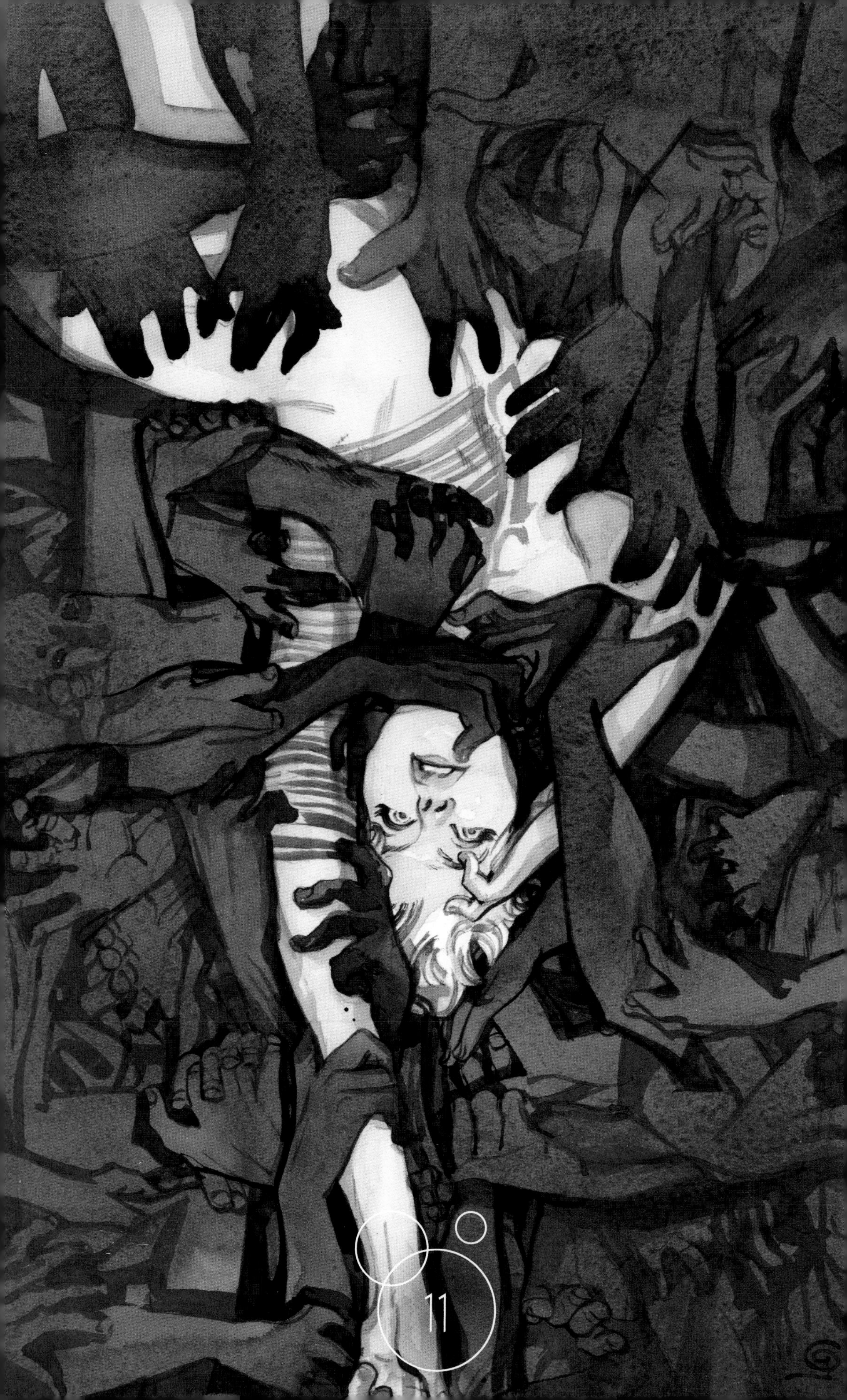
11

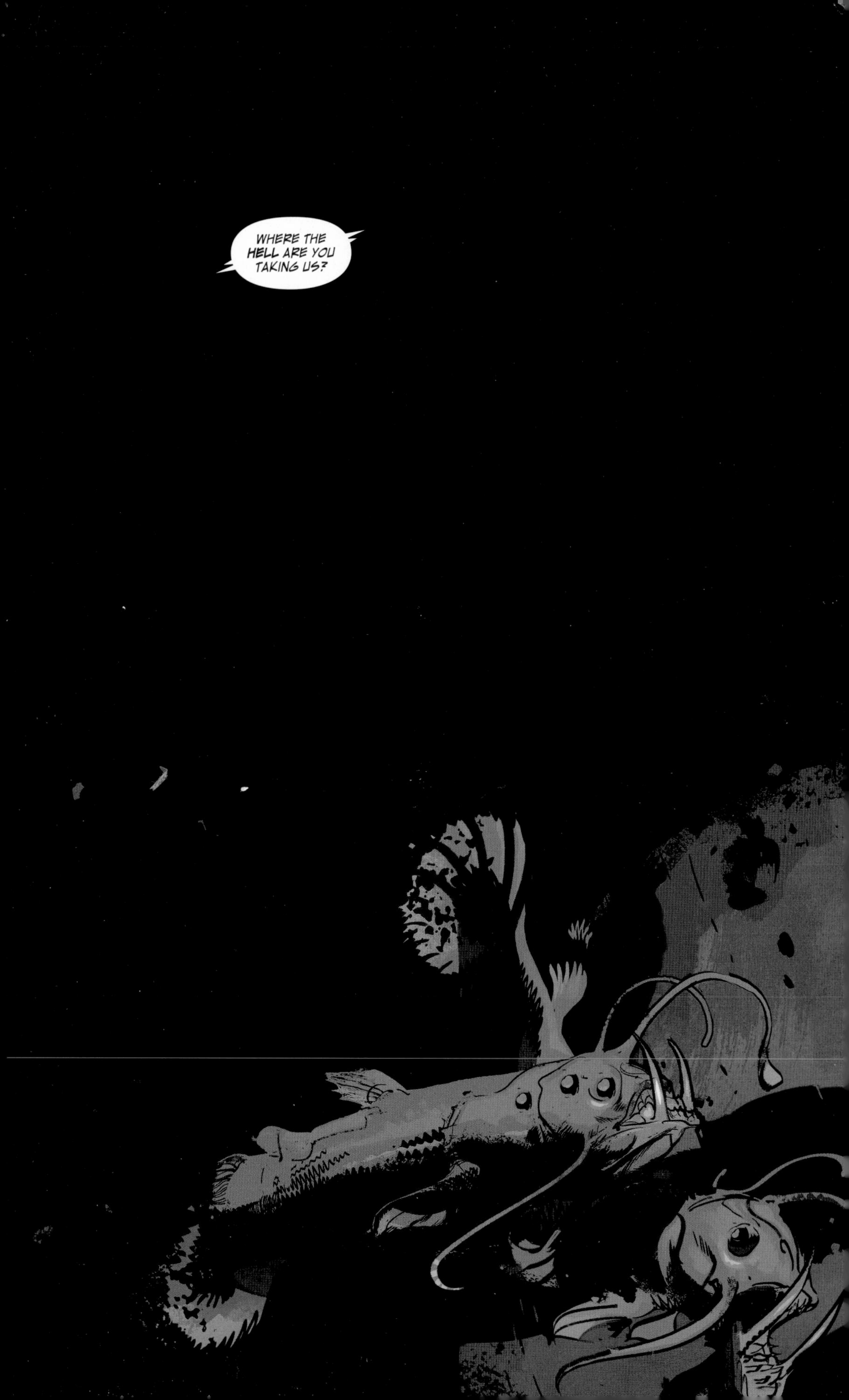
WHERE THE HELL ARE YOU TAKING US?

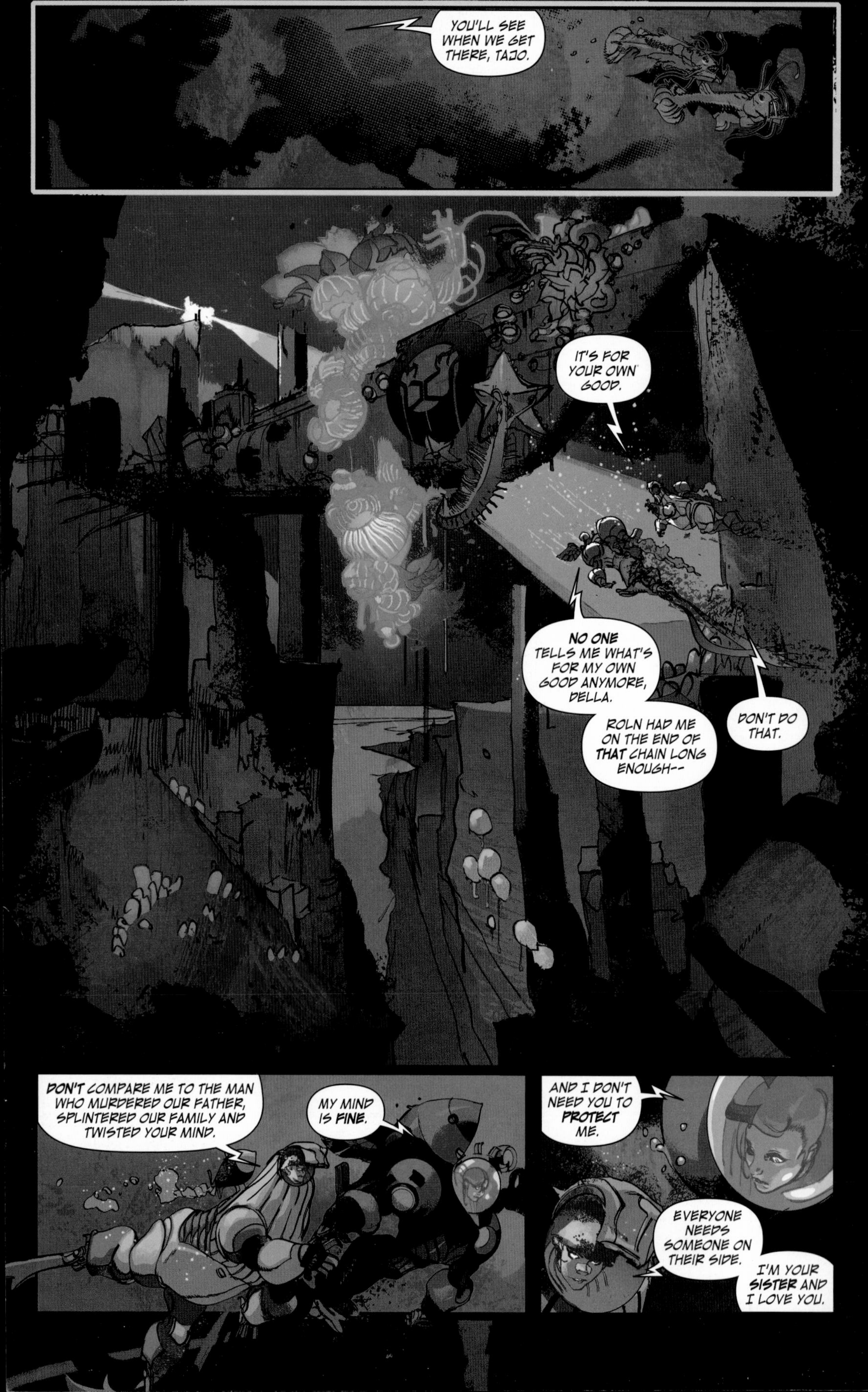

YOU'LL SEE WHEN WE GET THERE, TAJO.
IT'S FOR YOUR OWN GOOD.
NO ONE TELLS ME WHAT'S FOR MY OWN GOOD ANYMORE, DELLA.
ROLN HAD ME ON THE END OF THAT CHAIN LONG ENOUGH--
DON'T DO THAT.
DON'T COMPARE ME TO THE MAN WHO MURDERED OUR FATHER, SPLINTERED OUR FAMILY AND TWISTED YOUR MIND.
MY MIND IS FINE.
AND I DON'T NEED YOU TO PROTECT ME.
EVERYONE NEEDS SOMEONE ON THEIR SIDE.
I'M YOUR SISTER AND I LOVE YOU.

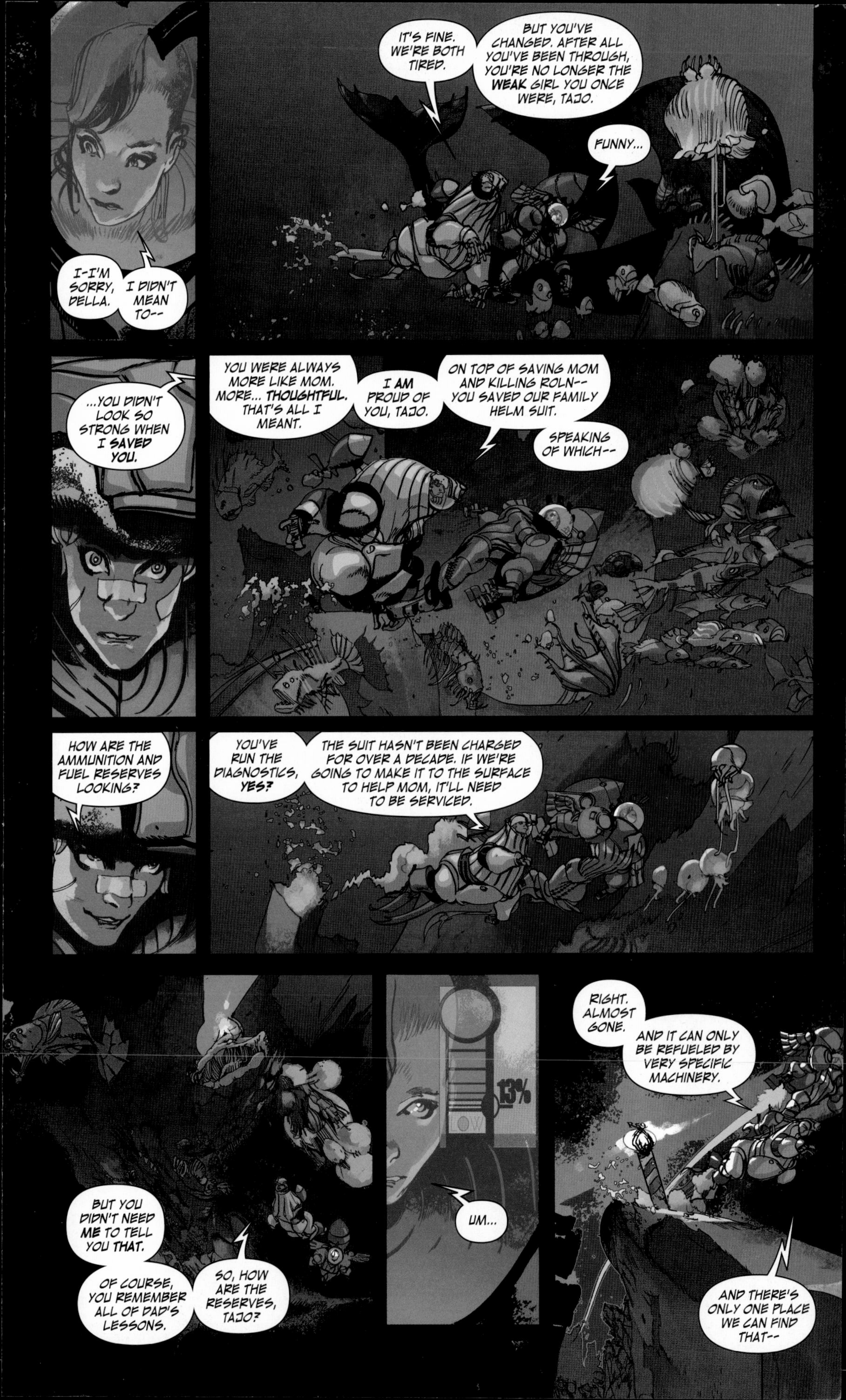
I-I'M SORRY, DELLA.
I DIDN'T MEAN TO--
IT'S FINE. WE'RE BOTH TIRED.
BUT YOU'VE CHANGED. AFTER ALL YOU'VE BEEN THROUGH, YOU'RE NO LONGER THE WEAK GIRL YOU ONCE WERE, TAJO.
FUNNY...
...YOU DIDN'T LOOK SO STRONG WHEN I SAVED YOU.
YOU WERE ALWAYS MORE LIKE MOM. MORE... THOUGHTFUL. THAT'S ALL I MEANT.
I AM PROUD OF YOU, TAJO.
ON TOP OF SAVING MOM AND KILLING ROLN-- YOU SAVED OUR FAMILY HELM SUIT.
SPEAKING OF WHICH--
HOW ARE THE AMMUNITION AND FUEL RESERVES LOOKING?
YOU'VE RUN THE DIAGNOSTICS, YES?
THE SUIT HASN'T BEEN CHARGED FOR OVER A DECADE. IF WE'RE GOING TO MAKE IT TO THE SURFACE TO HELP MOM, IT'LL NEED TO BE SERVICED.
BUT YOU DIDN'T NEED ME TO TELL YOU THAT.
OF COURSE, YOU REMEMBER ALL OF DAD'S LESSONS.
SO, HOW ARE THE RESERVES, TAJO?
13%
LOW
UM...
RIGHT. ALMOST GONE.
AND IT CAN ONLY BE REFUELED BY VERY SPECIFIC MACHINERY.
AND THERE'S ONLY ONE PLACE WE CAN FIND THAT--

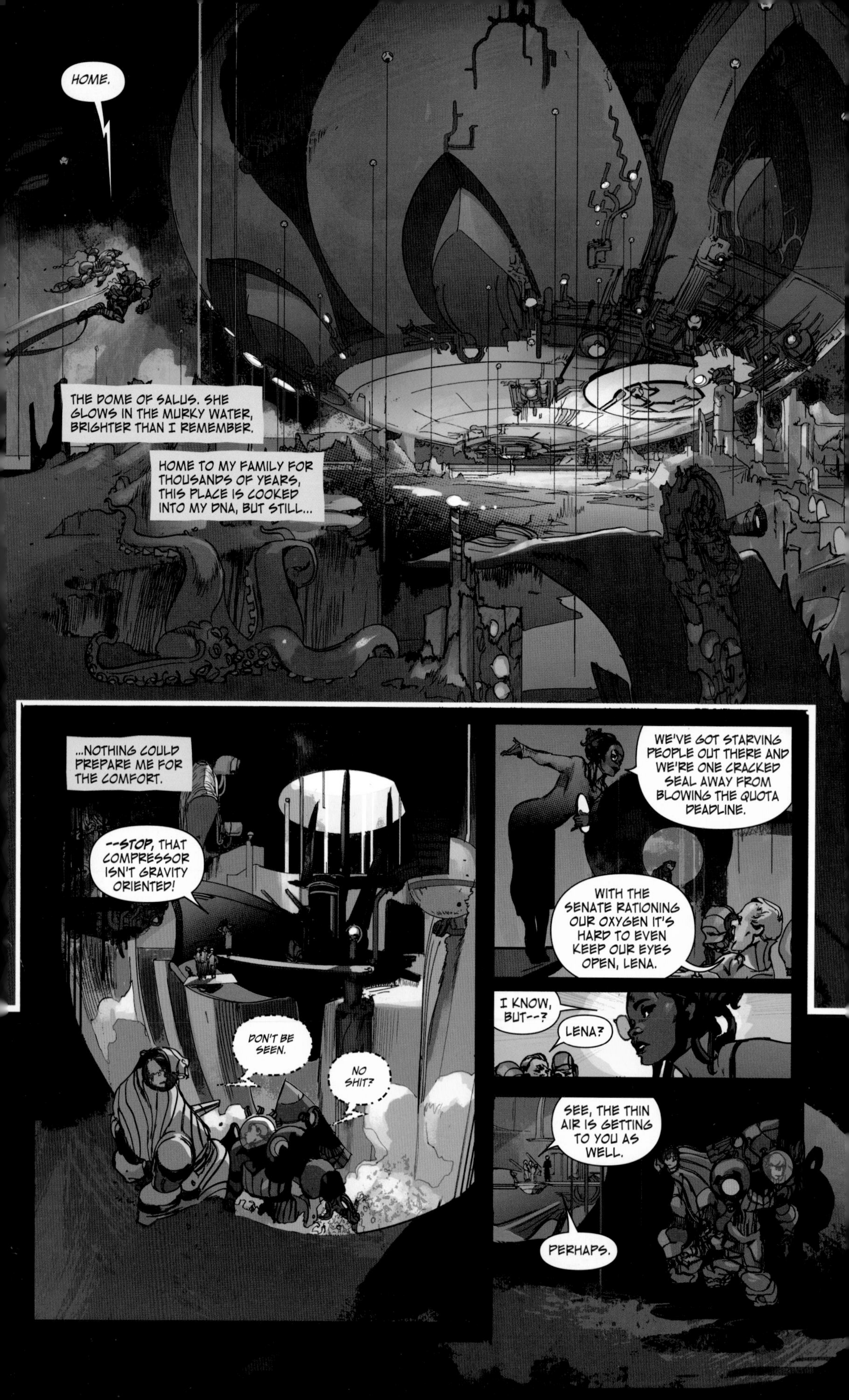
HOME.
THE DOME OF SALUS. SHE GLOWS IN THE MURKY WATER, BRIGHTER THAN I REMEMBER.
HOME TO MY FAMILY FOR THOUSANDS OF YEARS, THIS PLACE IS COOKED INTO MY DNA, BUT STILL...
...NOTHING COULD PREPARE ME FOR THE COMFORT.
--STOP, THAT COMPRESSOR ISN'T GRAVITY ORIENTED!
DON'T BE SEEN.
NO SHIT?
WE'VE GOT STARVING PEOPLE OUT THERE AND WE'RE ONE CRACKED SEAL AWAY FROM BLOWING THE QUOTA DEADLINE.
WITH THE SENATE RATIONING OUR OXYGEN IT'S HARD TO EVEN KEEP OUR EYES OPEN, LENA.
I KNOW, BUT--?
LENA?
SEE, THE THIN AIR IS GETTING TO YOU AS WELL.
PERHAPS.

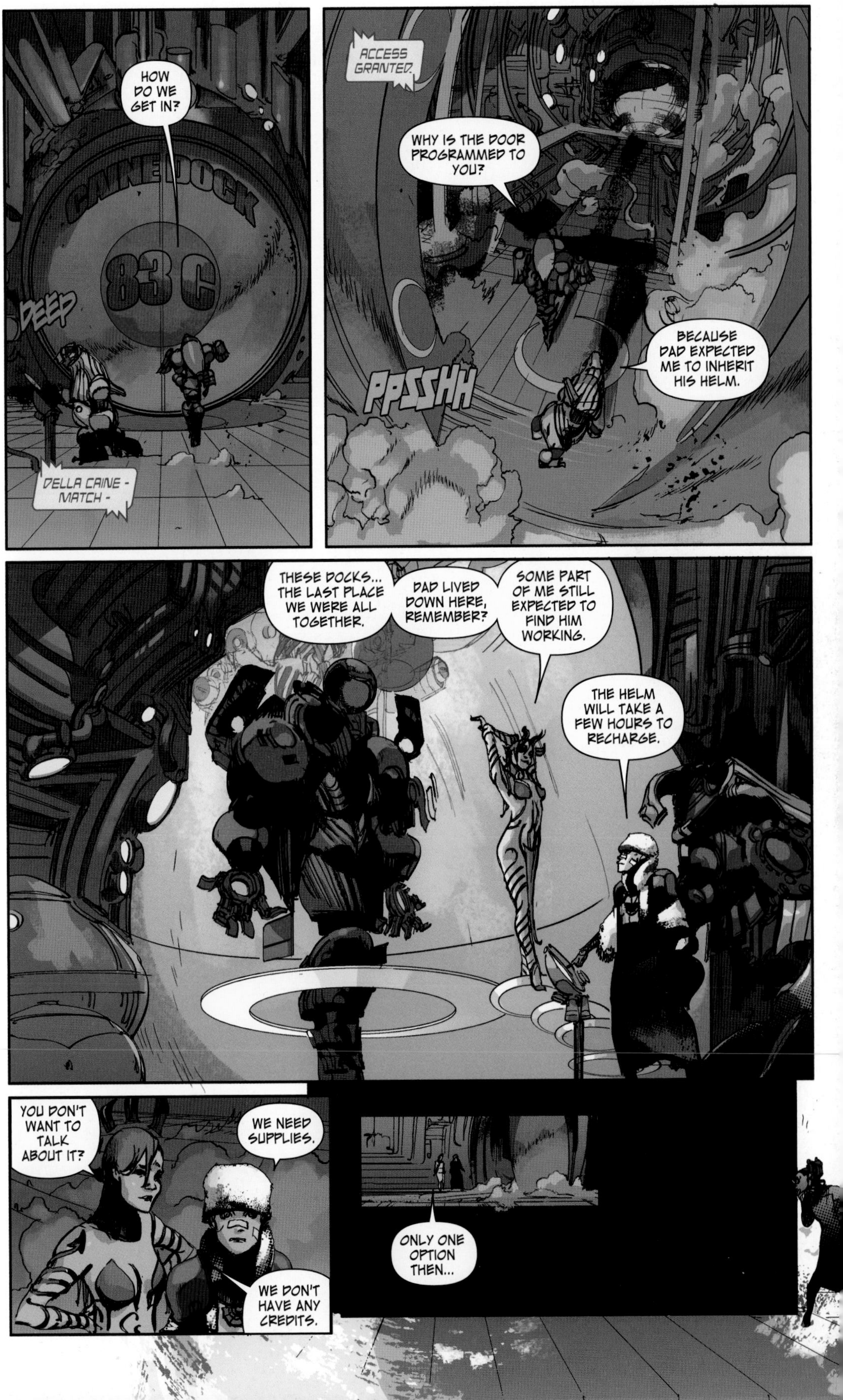
HOW DO WE GET IN?
CAINE DOCK
83 C
DEEP
DELLA CAINE - MATCH -
ACCESS GRANTED.
WHY IS THE DOOR PROGRAMMED TO YOU?
PPSSHH
BECAUSE DAD EXPECTED ME TO INHERIT HIS HELM.
THESE DOCKS... THE LAST PLACE WE WERE ALL TOGETHER.
DAD LIVED DOWN HERE, REMEMBER?
SOME PART OF ME STILL EXPECTED TO FIND HIM WORKING.
THE HELM WILL TAKE A FEW HOURS TO RECHARGE.
YOU DON'T WANT TO TALK ABOUT IT?
WE NEED SUPPLIES.
WE DON'T HAVE ANY CREDITS.
ONLY ONE OPTION THEN...

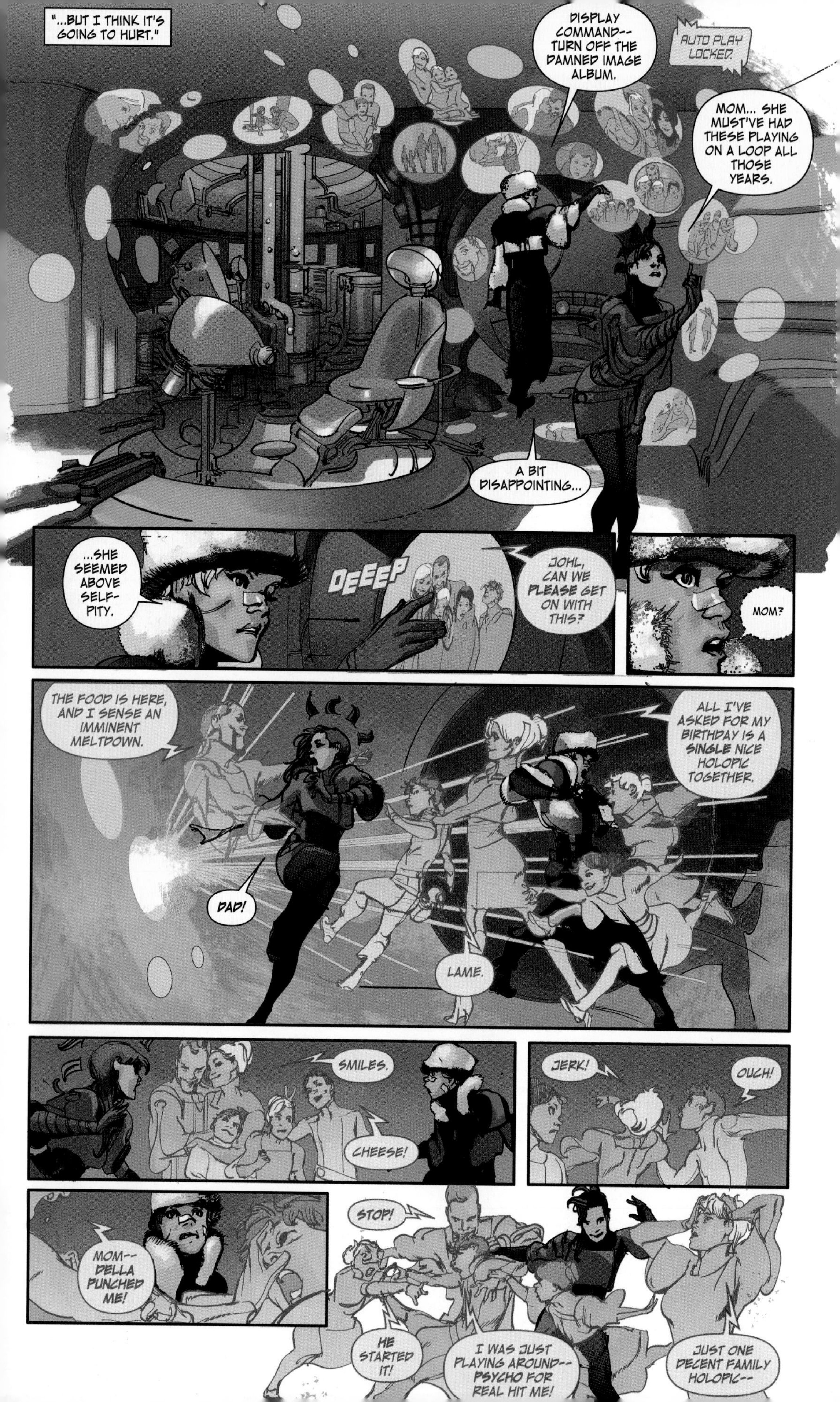
"...BUT I THINK IT'S GOING TO HURT."
DISPLAY COMMAND-- TURN OFF THE DAMNED IMAGE ALBUM.
AUTO PLAY LOCKED.
MOM... SHE MUST'VE HAD THESE PLAYING ON A LOOP ALL THOSE YEARS.
A BIT DISAPPOINTING...
...SHE SEEMED ABOVE SELF-PITY.
DEEEP
JOHL, CAN WE PLEASE GET ON WITH THIS?
MOM?
THE FOOD IS HERE, AND I SENSE AN IMMINENT MELTDOWN.
ALL I'VE ASKED FOR MY BIRTHDAY IS A SINGLE NICE HOLOPIC TOGETHER.
DAD!
LAME.
SMILES.
CHEESE!
JERK!
OUCH!
MOM-- DELLA PUNCHED ME!
STOP!
HE STARTED IT!
I WAS JUST PLAYING AROUND-- PSYCHO FOR REAL HIT ME!
JUST ONE DECENT FAMILY HOLOPIC--

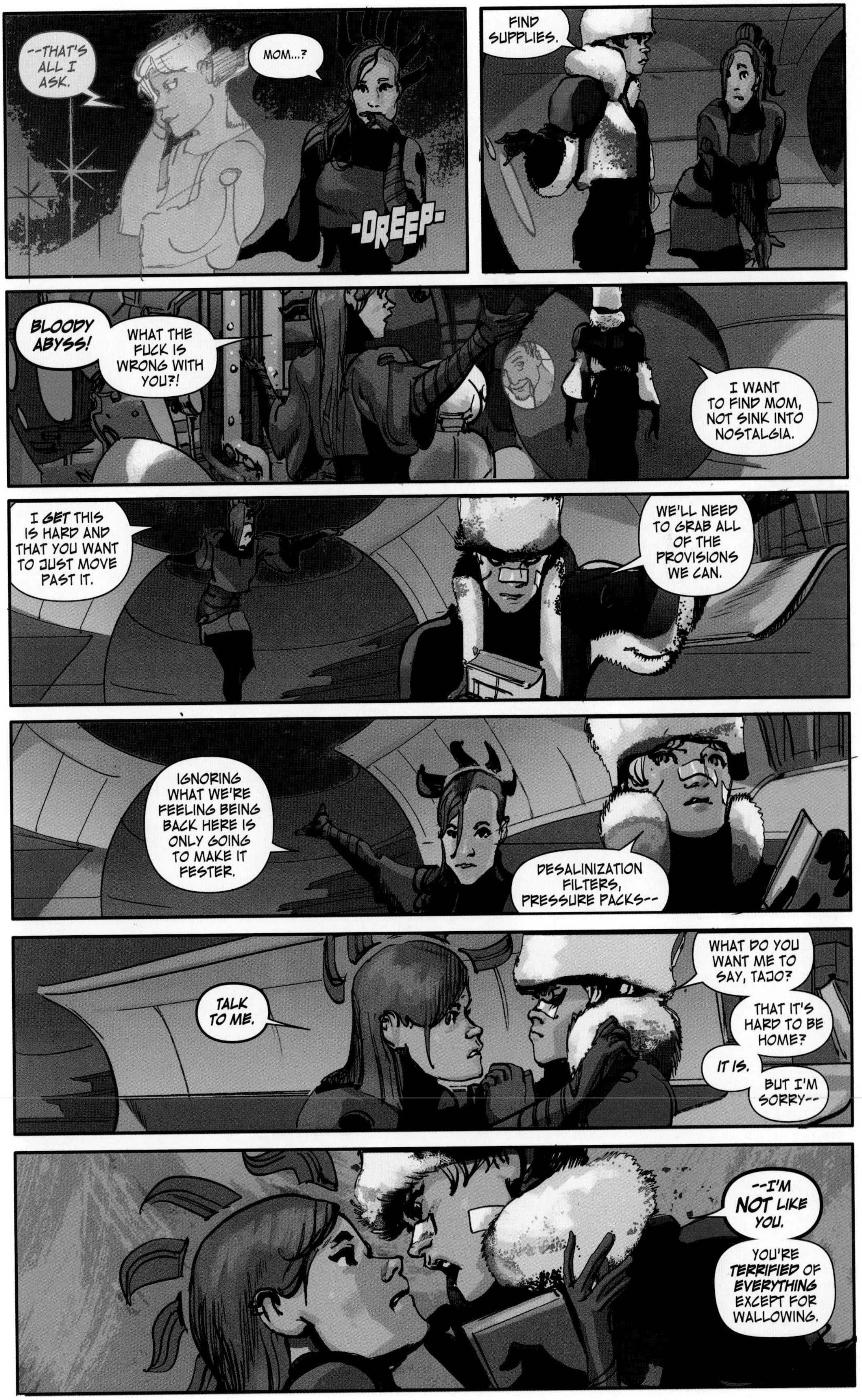

--THAT'S ALL I ASK.
MOM...?
-DREEP-
FIND SUPPLIES.
BLOODY ABYSS!
WHAT THE FUCK IS WRONG WITH YOU?!
I WANT TO FIND MOM, NOT SINK INTO NOSTALGIA.
I GET THIS IS HARD AND THAT YOU WANT TO JUST MOVE PAST IT.
WE'LL NEED TO GRAB ALL OF THE PROVISIONS WE CAN.
IGNORING WHAT WE'RE FEELING BEING BACK HERE IS ONLY GOING TO MAKE IT FESTER.
DESALINIZATION FILTERS, PRESSURE PACKS--
TALK TO ME.
WHAT DO YOU WANT ME TO SAY, TAJO?
THAT IT'S HARD TO BE HOME?
IT IS.
BUT I'M SORRY--
--I'M NOT LIKE YOU.
YOU'RE TERRIFIED OF EVERYTHING EXCEPT FOR WALLOWING.

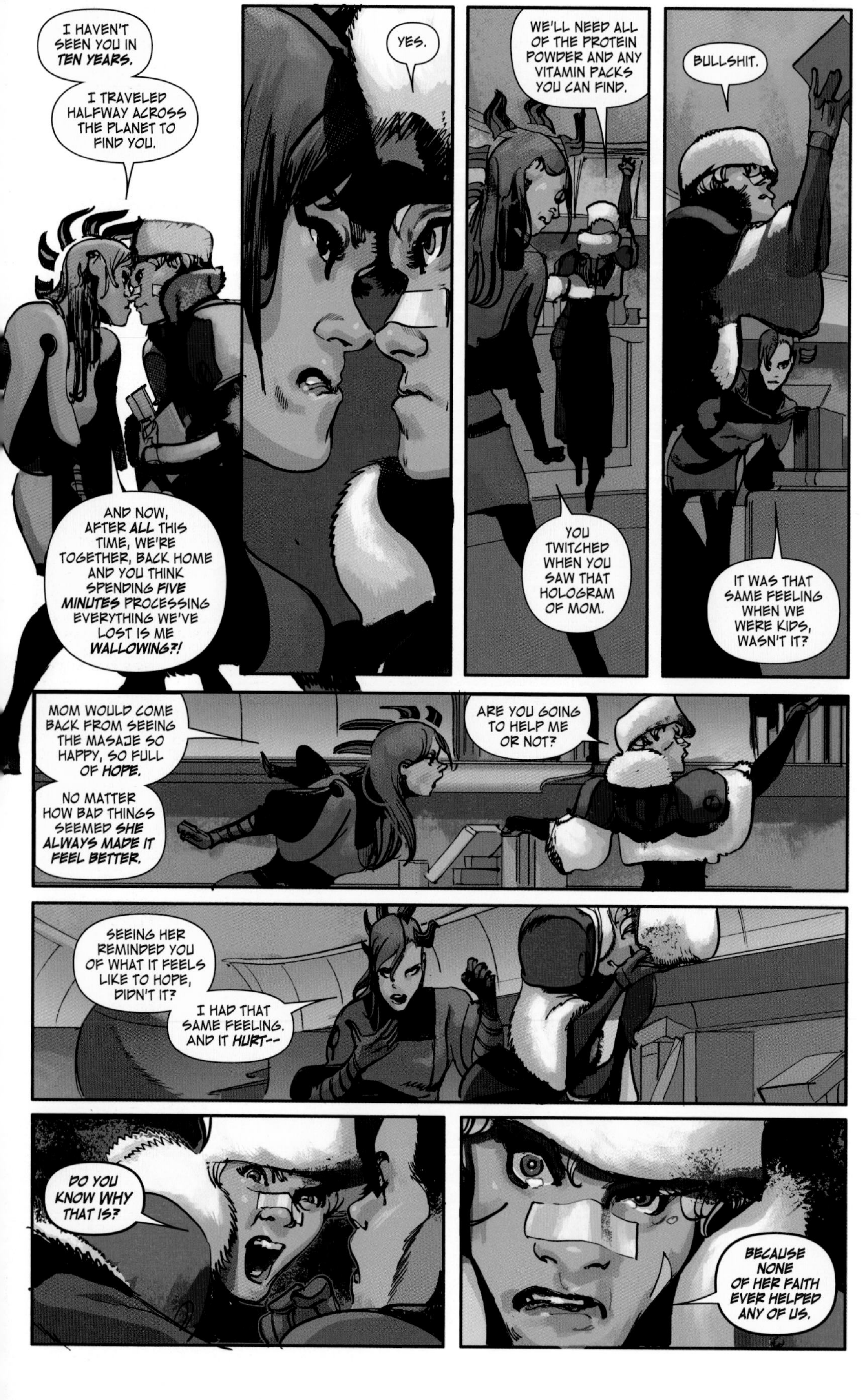

I HAVEN'T SEEN YOU IN TEN YEARS.
I TRAVELED HALFWAY ACROSS THE PLANET TO FIND YOU.
AND NOW, AFTER ALL THIS TIME, WE'RE TOGETHER, BACK HOME AND YOU THINK SPENDING FIVE MINUTES PROCESSING EVERYTHING WE'VE LOST IS ME WALLOWING?!
YES.
WE'LL NEED ALL OF THE PROTEIN POWDER AND ANY VITAMIN PACKS YOU CAN FIND.
YOU TWITCHED WHEN YOU SAW THAT HOLOGRAM OF MOM.
BULLSHIT.
IT WAS THAT SAME FEELING WHEN WE WERE KIDS, WASN'T IT?
MOM WOULD COME BACK FROM SEEING THE MASAJE SO HAPPY, SO FULL OF HOPE.
NO MATTER HOW BAD THINGS SEEMED SHE ALWAYS MADE IT FEEL BETTER.
ARE YOU GOING TO HELP ME OR NOT?
SEEING HER REMINDED YOU OF WHAT IT FEELS LIKE TO HOPE, DIDN'T IT?
I HAD THAT SAME FEELING. AND IT HURT--
DO YOU KNOW WHY THAT IS?
BECAUSE NONE OF HER FAITH EVER HELPED ANY OF US.

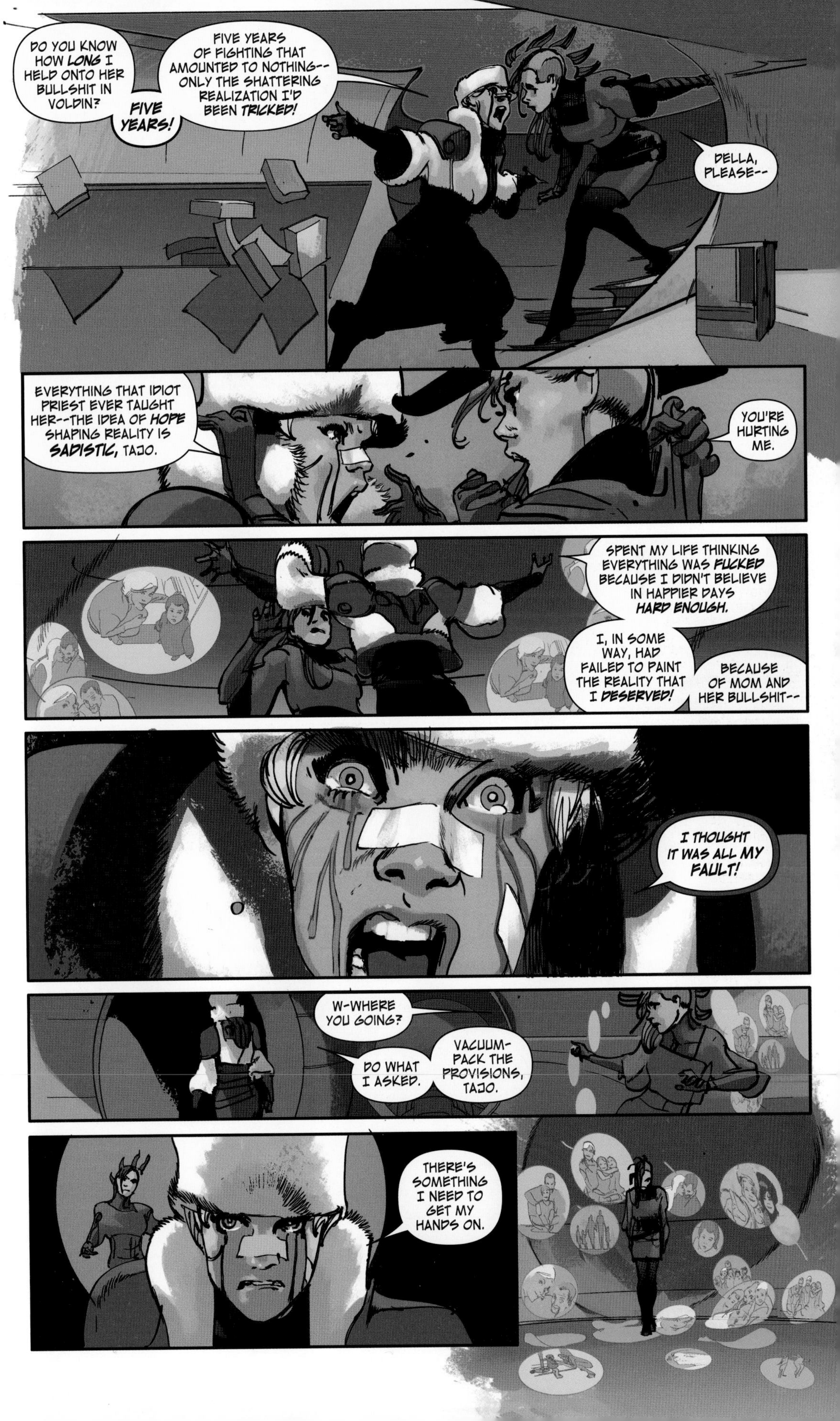
DO YOU KNOW HOW LONG I HELD ONTO HER BULLSHIT IN VOLDIN?
FIVE YEARS!
FIVE YEARS OF FIGHTING THAT AMOUNTED TO NOTHING--ONLY THE SHATTERING REALIZATION I'D BEEN TRICKED!
DELLA, PLEASE--
EVERYTHING THAT IDIOT PRIEST EVER TAUGHT HER--THE IDEA OF HOPE SHAPING REALITY IS SADISTIC, TAJO.
YOU'RE HURTING ME.
SPENT MY LIFE THINKING EVERYTHING WAS FUCKED BECAUSE I DIDN'T BELIEVE IN HAPPIER DAYS HARD ENOUGH.
I, IN SOME WAY, HAD FAILED TO PAINT THE REALITY THAT I DESERVED!
BECAUSE OF MOM AND HER BULLSHIT--
I THOUGHT IT WAS ALL MY FAULT!
W-WHERE YOU GOING?
VACUUM-PACK THE PROVISIONS, TAJO.
DO WHAT I ASKED.
THERE'S SOMETHING I NEED TO GET MY HANDS ON.

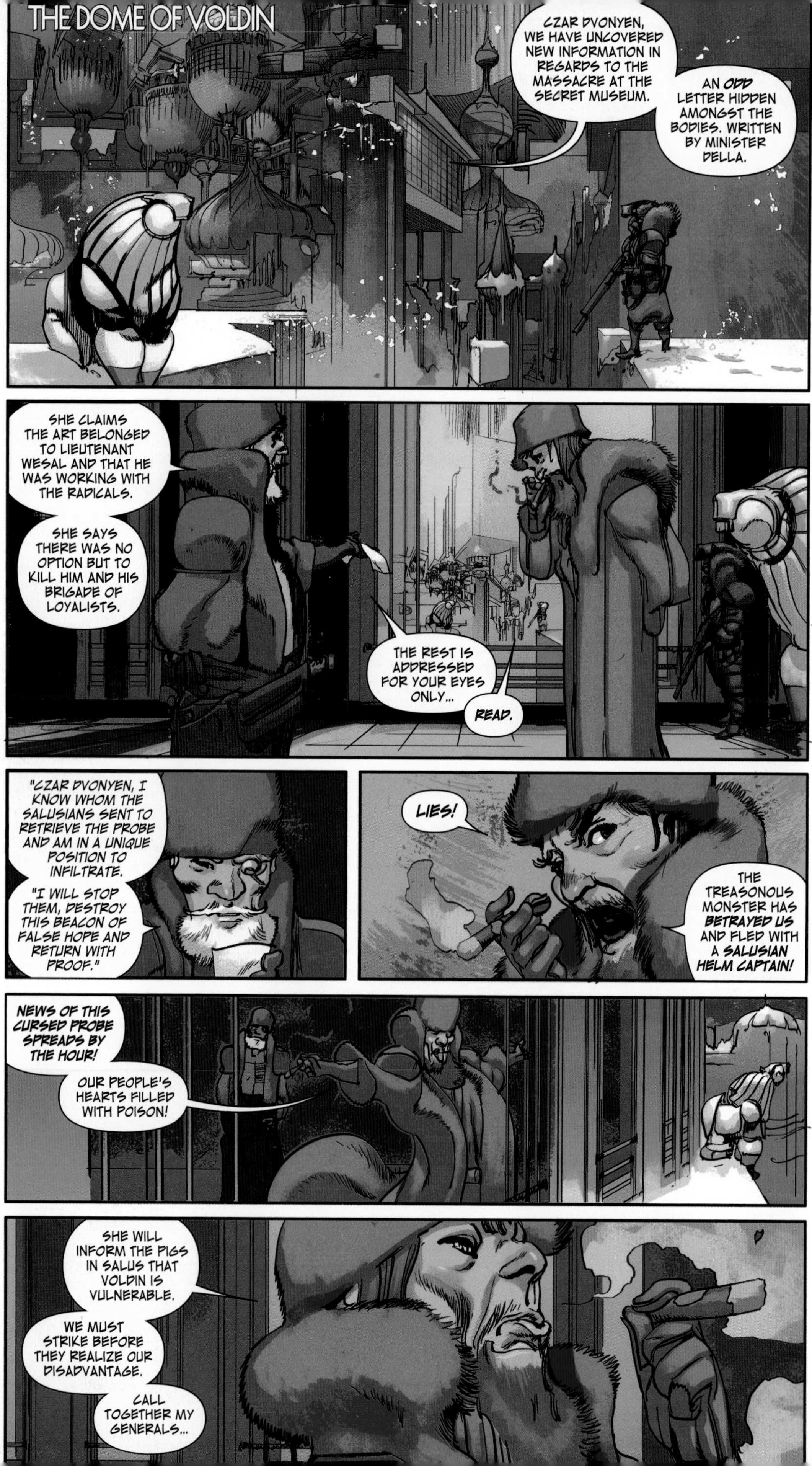
THE DOME OF VOLDIN
CZAR DVONYEN, WE HAVE UNCOVERED NEW INFORMATION IN REGARDS TO THE MASSACRE AT THE SECRET MUSEUM.
AN ODD LETTER HIDDEN AMONGST THE BODIES. WRITTEN BY MINISTER DELLA.
SHE CLAIMS THE ART BELONGED TO LIEUTENANT WESAL AND THAT HE WAS WORKING WITH THE RADICALS.
SHE SAYS THERE WAS NO OPTION BUT TO KILL HIM AND HIS BRIGADE OF LOYALISTS.
THE REST IS ADDRESSED FOR YOUR EYES ONLY...
READ.
"CZAR DVONYEN, I KNOW WHOM THE SALUSIANS SENT TO RETRIEVE THE PROBE AND AM IN A UNIQUE POSITION TO INFILTRATE.
"I WILL STOP THEM, DESTROY THIS BEACON OF FALSE HOPE AND RETURN WITH PROOF."
LIES!
THE TREASONOUS MONSTER HAS BETRAYED US AND FLED WITH A SALUSIAN HELM CAPTAIN!
NEWS OF THIS CURSED PROBE SPREADS BY THE HOUR!
OUR PEOPLE'S HEARTS FILLED WITH POISON!
SHE WILL INFORM THE PIGS IN SALUS THAT VOLDIN IS VULNERABLE.
WE MUST STRIKE BEFORE THEY REALIZE OUR DISADVANTAGE.
CALL TOGETHER MY GENERALS...

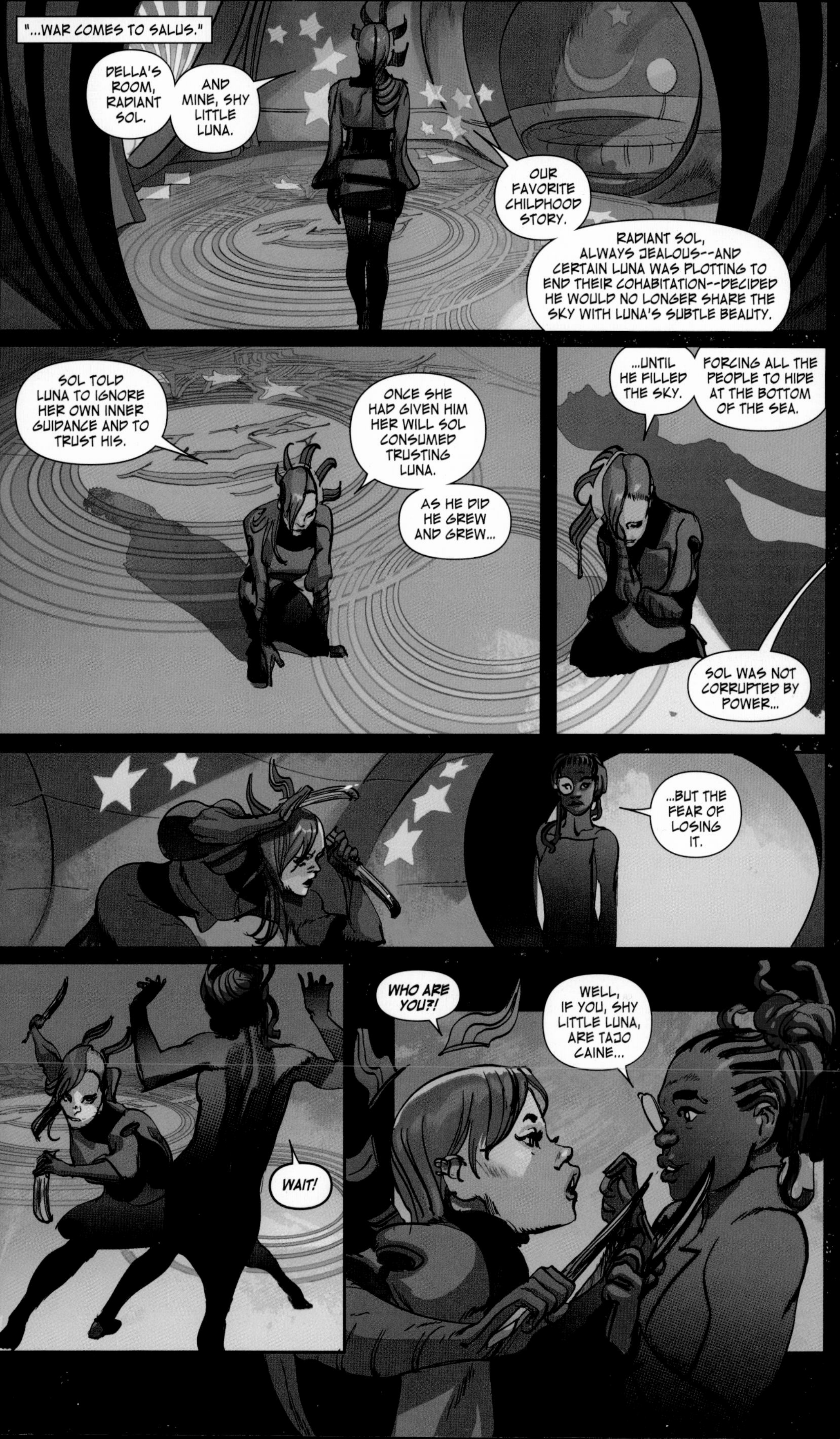
"...WAR COMES TO SALUS."
DELLA'S ROOM, RADIANT SOL.
AND MINE, SHY LITTLE LUNA.
OUR FAVORITE CHILDHOOD STORY.
RADIANT SOL, ALWAYS JEALOUS--AND CERTAIN LUNA WAS PLOTTING TO END THEIR COHABITATION--DECIDED HE WOULD NO LONGER SHARE THE SKY WITH LUNA'S SUBTLE BEAUTY.
SOL TOLD LUNA TO IGNORE HER OWN INNER GUIDANCE AND TO TRUST HIS.
ONCE SHE HAD GIVEN HIM HER WILL SOL CONSUMED TRUSTING LUNA.
AS HE DID HE GREW AND GREW...
...UNTIL HE FILLED THE SKY.
FORCING ALL THE PEOPLE TO HIDE AT THE BOTTOM OF THE SEA.
SOL WAS NOT CORRUPTED BY POWER...
...BUT THE FEAR OF LOSING IT.
WAIT!
WHO ARE YOU?!
WELL, IF YOU, SHY LITTLE LUNA, ARE TAJO CAINE...

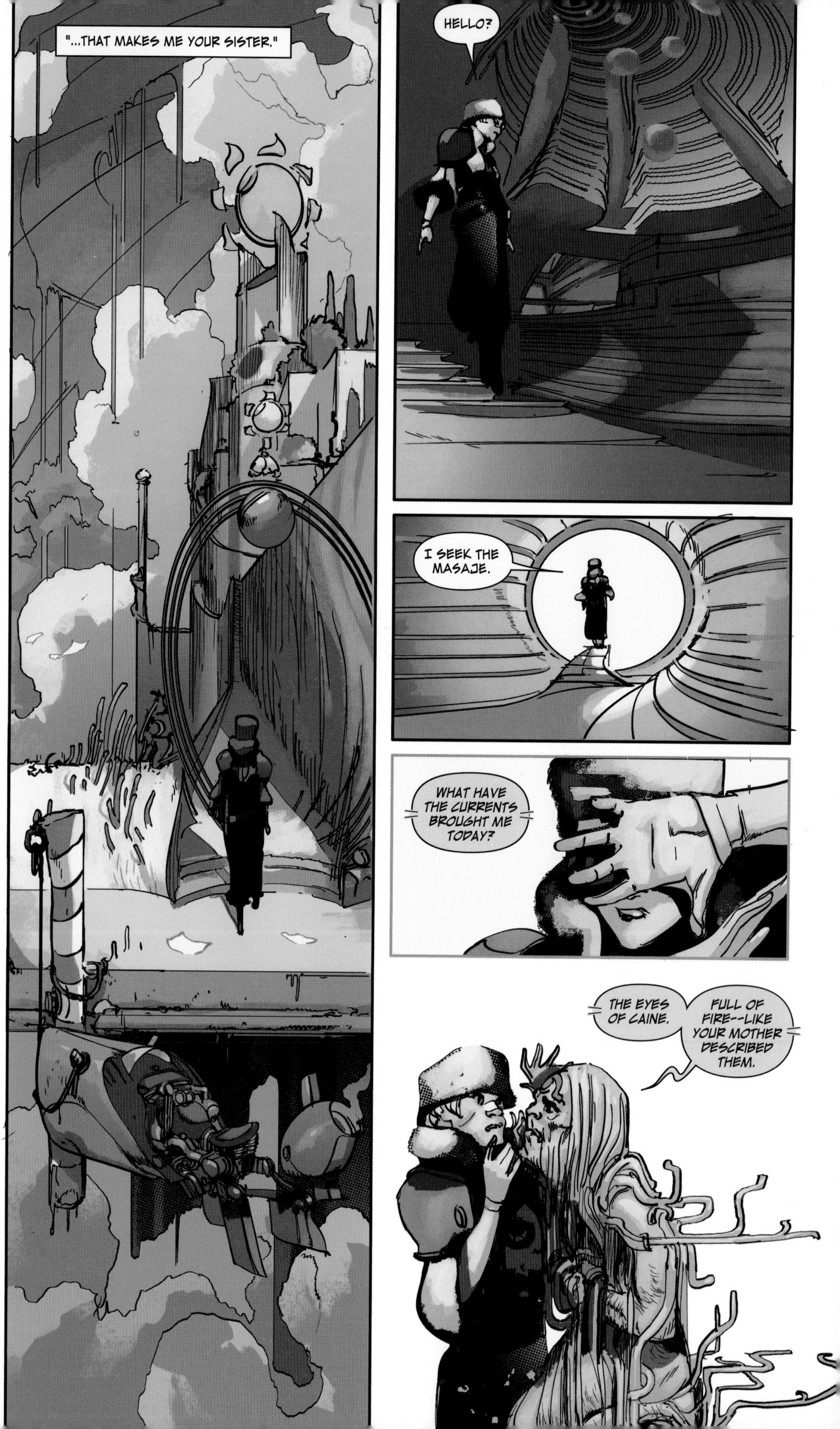
"...THAT MAKES ME YOUR SISTER."
HELLO?
I SEEK THE MASAJE.
WHAT HAVE THE CURRENTS BROUGHT ME TODAY?
THE EYES OF CAINE.
FULL OF FIRE--LIKE YOUR MOTHER DESCRIBED THEM.

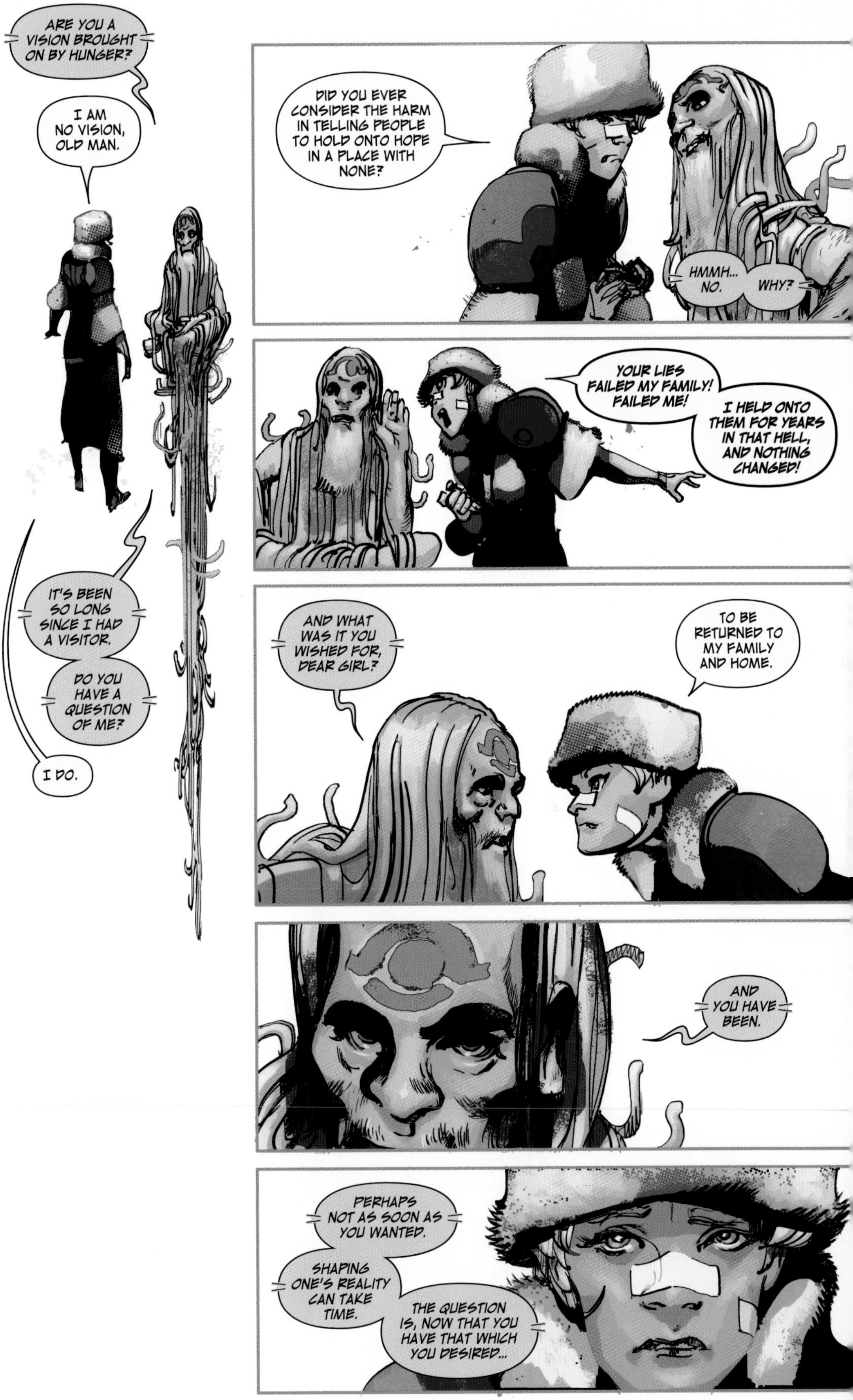
ARE YOU A VISION BROUGHT ON BY HUNGER?
I AM NO VISION, OLD MAN.
IT'S BEEN SO LONG SINCE I HAD A VISITOR.
DO YOU HAVE A QUESTION OF ME?
I DO.
DID YOU EVER CONSIDER THE HARM IN TELLING PEOPLE TO HOLD ONTO HOPE IN A PLACE WITH NONE?
HMMH... NO.
WHY?
YOUR LIES FAILED MY FAMILY! FAILED ME!
I HELD ONTO THEM FOR YEARS IN THAT HELL, AND NOTHING CHANGED!
AND WHAT WAS IT YOU WISHED FOR, DEAR GIRL?
TO BE RETURNED TO MY FAMILY AND HOME.
AND YOU HAVE BEEN.
PERHAPS NOT AS SOON AS YOU WANTED.
SHAPING ONE'S REALITY CAN TAKE TIME.
THE QUESTION IS, NOW THAT YOU HAVE THAT WHICH YOU DESIRED...

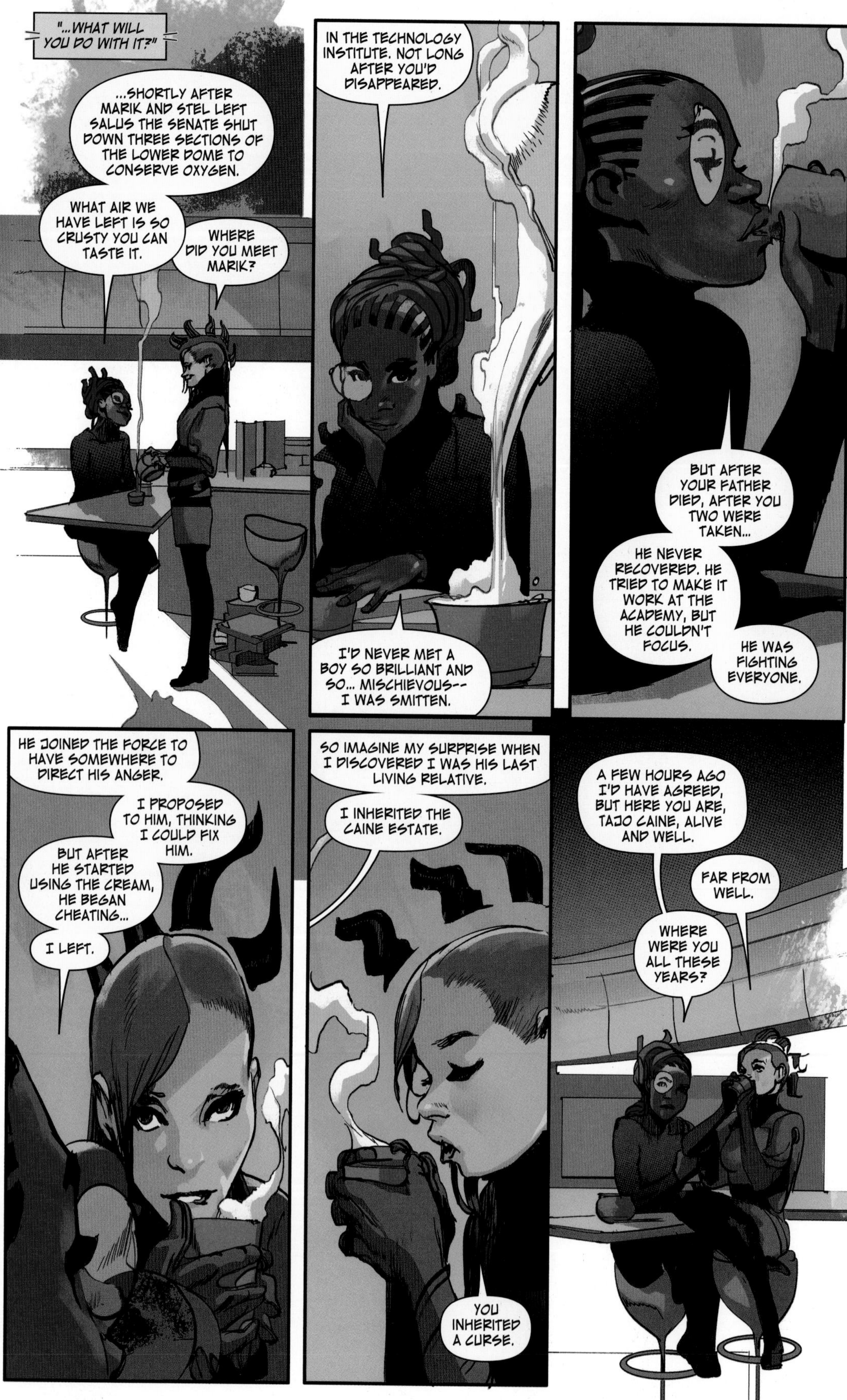
"...WHAT WILL YOU DO WITH IT?"
...SHORTLY AFTER MARIK AND STEL LEFT SALUS THE SENATE SHUT DOWN THREE SECTIONS OF THE LOWER DOME TO CONSERVE OXYGEN.
WHAT AIR WE HAVE LEFT IS SO CRUSTY YOU CAN TASTE IT.
WHERE DID YOU MEET MARIK?
IN THE TECHNOLOGY INSTITUTE. NOT LONG AFTER YOU'D DISAPPEARED.
I'D NEVER MET A BOY SO BRILLIANT AND SO... MISCHIEVOUS-- I WAS SMITTEN.
BUT AFTER YOUR FATHER DIED, AFTER YOU TWO WERE TAKEN...
HE NEVER RECOVERED. HE TRIED TO MAKE IT WORK AT THE ACADEMY, BUT HE COULDN'T FOCUS.
HE WAS FIGHTING EVERYONE.
HE JOINED THE FORCE TO HAVE SOMEWHERE TO DIRECT HIS ANGER.
I PROPOSED TO HIM, THINKING I COULD FIX HIM.
BUT AFTER HE STARTED USING THE CREAM, HE BEGAN CHEATING...
I LEFT.
SO IMAGINE MY SURPRISE WHEN I DISCOVERED I WAS HIS LAST LIVING RELATIVE.
I INHERITED THE CAINE ESTATE.
YOU INHERITED A CURSE.
A FEW HOURS AGO I'D HAVE AGREED, BUT HERE YOU ARE, TAJO CAINE, ALIVE AND WELL.
FAR FROM WELL.
WHERE WERE YOU ALL THESE YEARS?

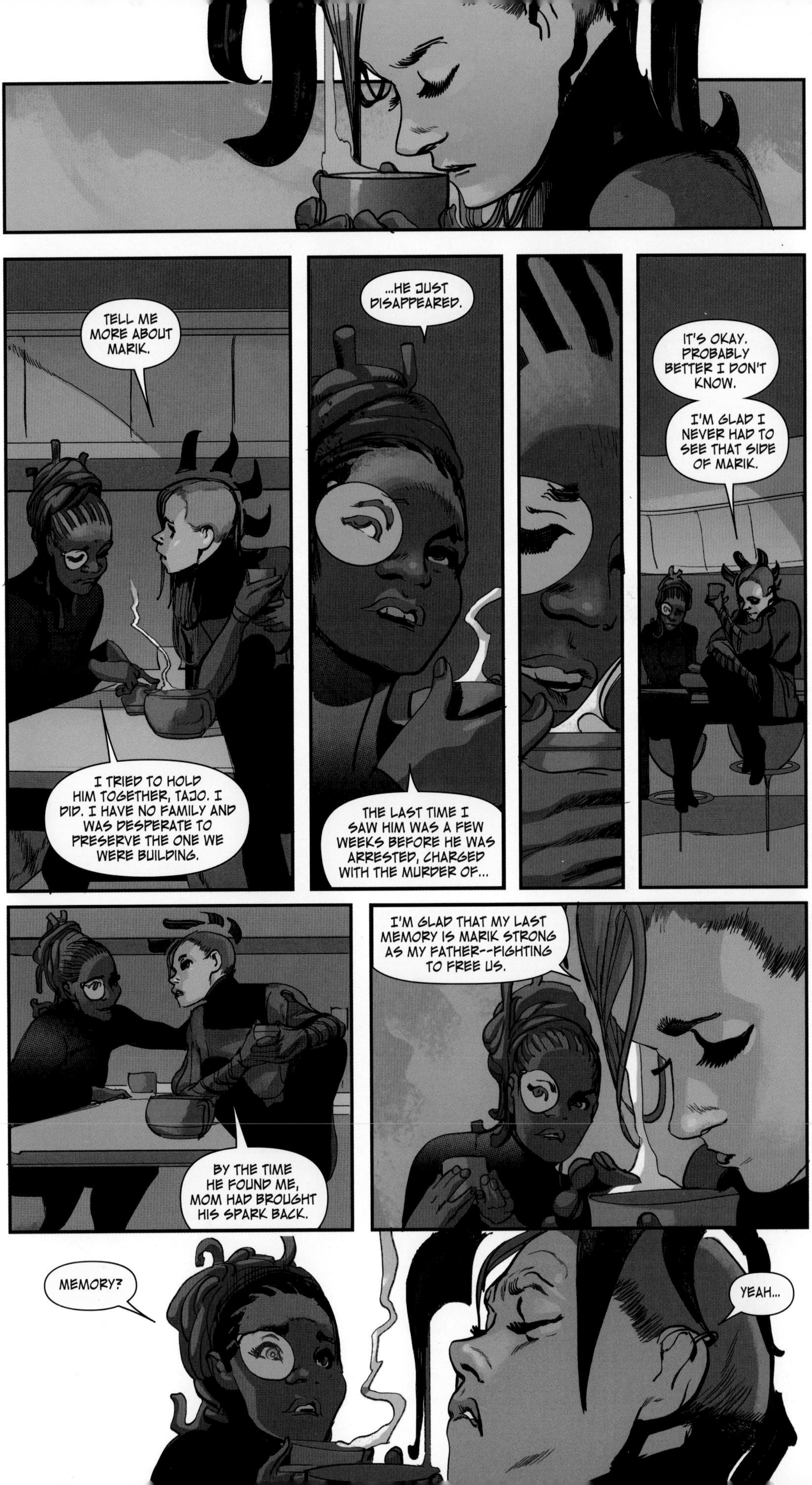

TELL ME MORE ABOUT MARIK.
I TRIED TO HOLD HIM TOGETHER, TAJO. I DID. I HAVE NO FAMILY AND WAS DESPERATE TO PRESERVE THE ONE WE WERE BUILDING.
...HE JUST DISAPPEARED.
THE LAST TIME I SAW HIM WAS A FEW WEEKS BEFORE HE WAS ARRESTED, CHARGED WITH THE MURDER OF...
IT'S OKAY. PROBABLY BETTER I DON'T KNOW.
I'M GLAD I NEVER HAD TO SEE THAT SIDE OF MARIK.
BY THE TIME HE FOUND ME, MOM HAD BROUGHT HIS SPARK BACK.
I'M GLAD THAT MY LAST MEMORY IS MARIK STRONG AS MY FATHER--FIGHTING TO FREE US.
MEMORY?
YEAH...

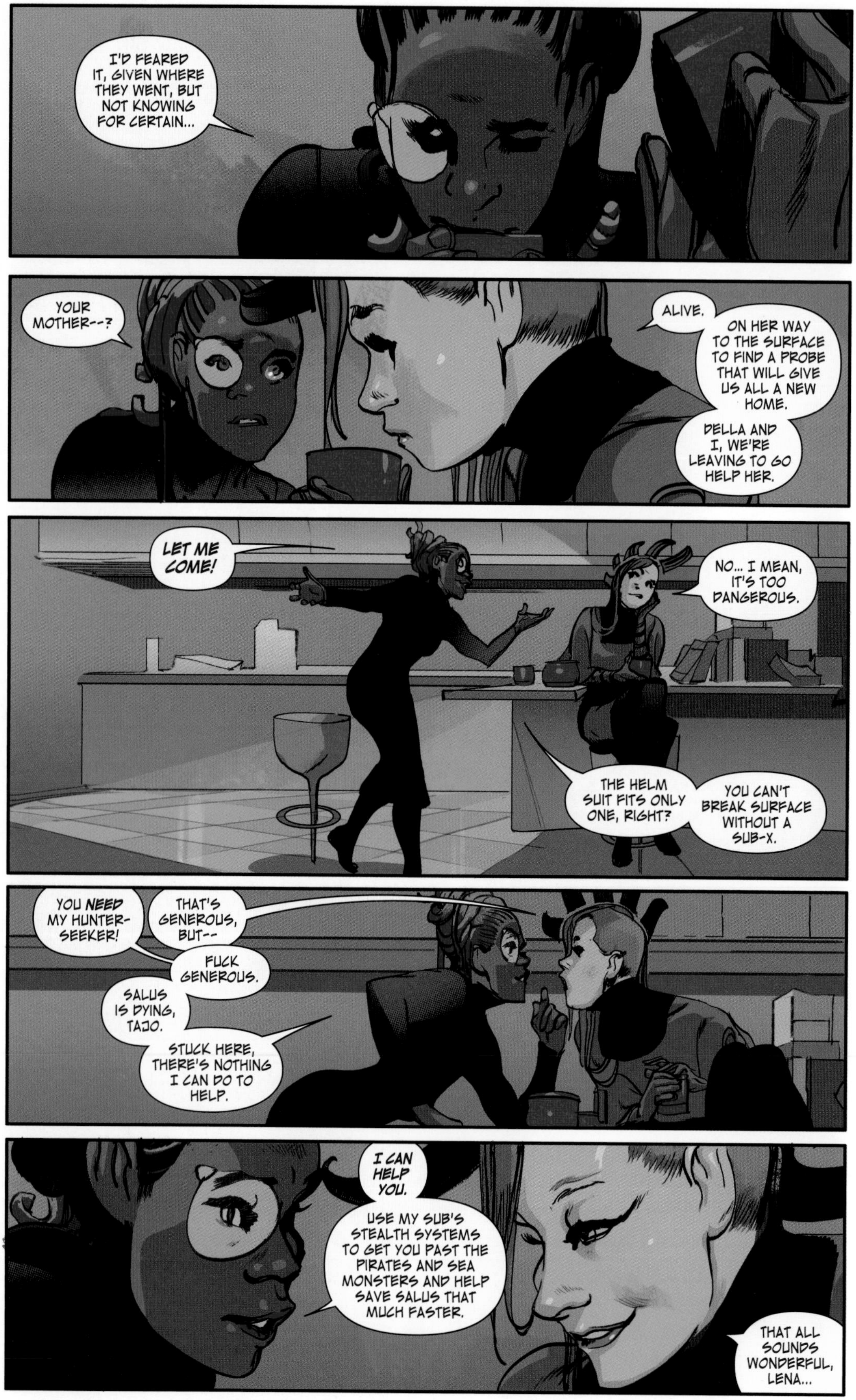
I'D FEARED IT, GIVEN WHERE THEY WENT, BUT NOT KNOWING FOR CERTAIN...
YOUR MOTHER--?
ALIVE.
ON HER WAY TO THE SURFACE TO FIND A PROBE THAT WILL GIVE US ALL A NEW HOME.
DELLA AND I, WE'RE LEAVING TO GO HELP HER.
LET ME COME!
NO... I MEAN, IT'S TOO DANGEROUS.
THE HELM SUIT FITS ONLY ONE, RIGHT?
YOU CAN'T BREAK SURFACE WITHOUT A SUB-X.
YOU NEED MY HUNTER-SEEKER!
THAT'S GENEROUS, BUT--
FUCK GENEROUS.
SALUS IS DYING, TAJO.
STUCK HERE, THERE'S NOTHING I CAN DO TO HELP.
I CAN HELP YOU.
USE MY SUB'S STEALTH SYSTEMS TO GET YOU PAST THE PIRATES AND SEA MONSTERS AND HELP SAVE SALUS THAT MUCH FASTER.
THAT ALL SOUNDS WONDERFUL, LENA...

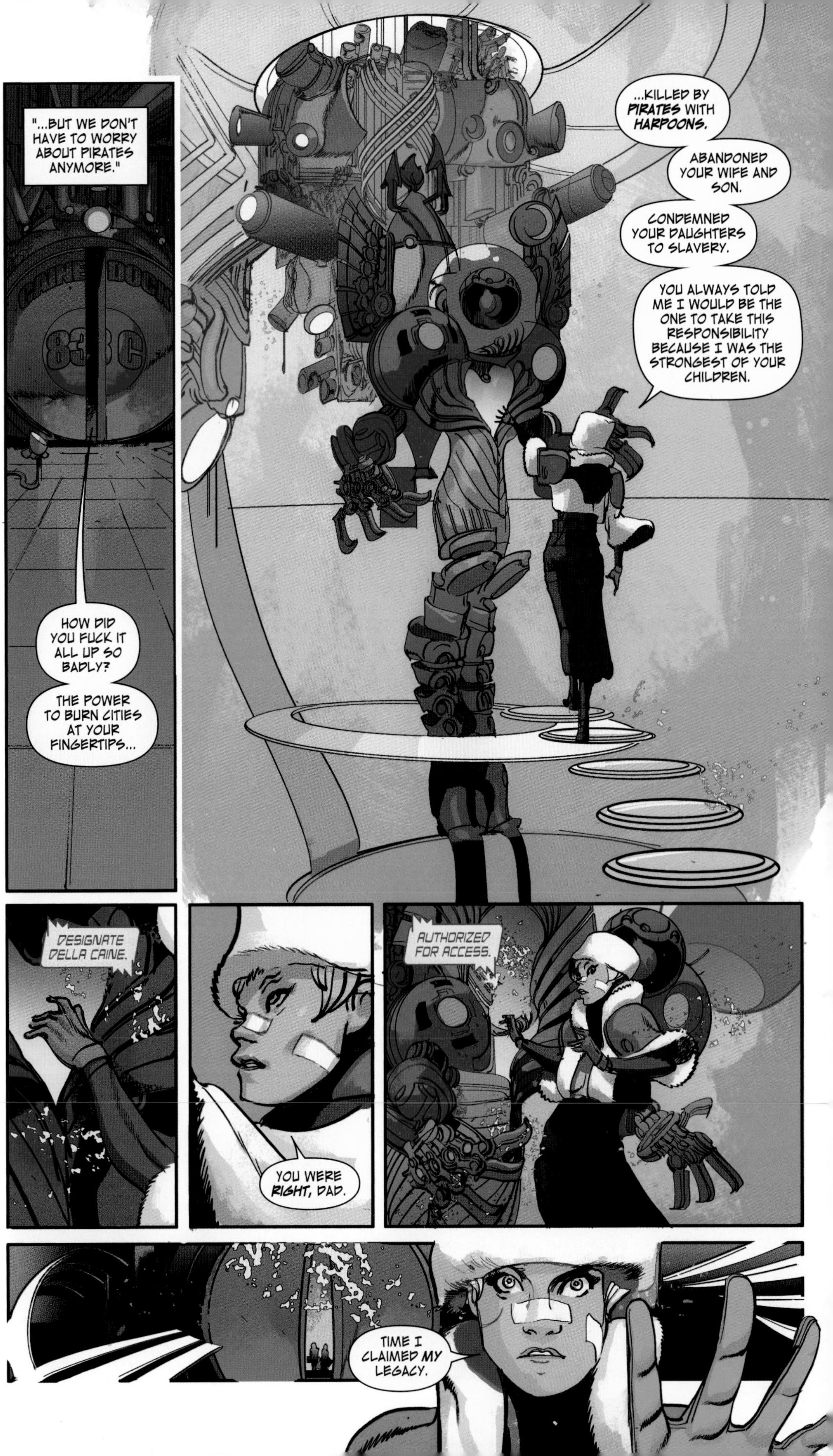
"...BUT WE DON'T HAVE TO WORRY ABOUT PIRATES ANYMORE."
HOW DID YOU FUCK IT ALL UP SO BADLY?
THE POWER TO BURN CITIES AT YOUR FINGERTIPS...
...KILLED BY PIRATES WITH HARPOONS.
ABANDONED YOUR WIFE AND SON.
CONDEMNED YOUR DAUGHTERS TO SLAVERY.
YOU ALWAYS TOLD ME I WOULD BE THE ONE TO TAKE THIS RESPONSIBILITY BECAUSE I WAS THE STRONGEST OF YOUR CHILDREN.
DESIGNATE DELLA CAINE.
YOU WERE RIGHT, DAD.
AUTHORIZED FOR ACCESS.
TIME I CLAIMED MY LEGACY.

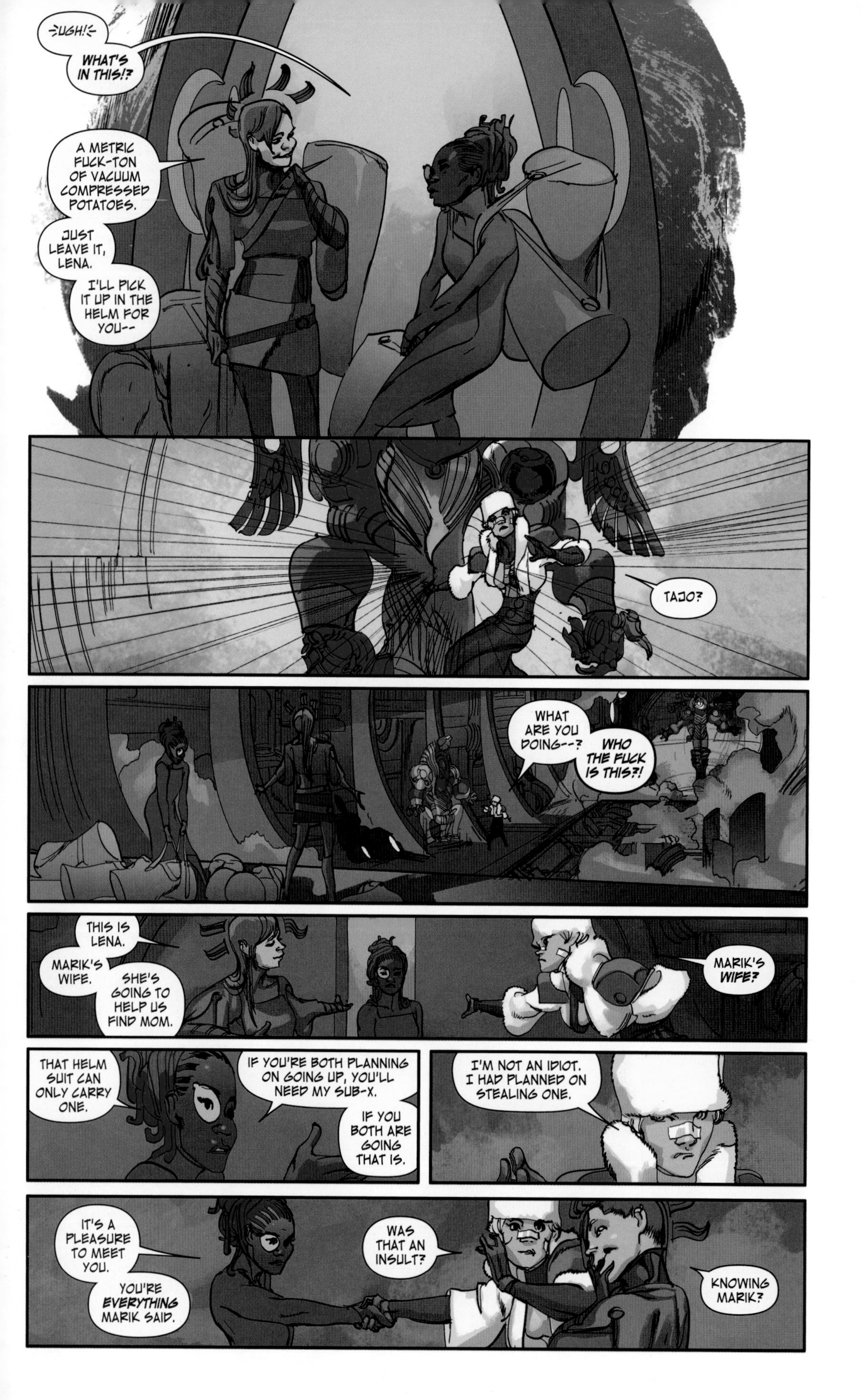
UGH!
WHAT'S IN THIS!?
A METRIC FUCK-TON OF VACUUM COMPRESSED POTATOES.
JUST LEAVE IT, LENA.
I'LL PICK IT UP IN THE HELM FOR YOU--
TAJO?
WHAT ARE YOU DOING--?
WHO THE FUCK IS THIS?!
THIS IS LENA.
MARIK'S WIFE.
SHE'S GOING TO HELP US FIND MOM.
MARIK'S WIFE?
THAT HELM SUIT CAN ONLY CARRY ONE.
IF YOU'RE BOTH PLANNING ON GOING UP, YOU'LL NEED MY SUB-X.
IF YOU BOTH ARE GOING THAT IS.
I'M NOT AN IDIOT. I HAD PLANNED ON STEALING ONE.
IT'S A PLEASURE TO MEET YOU.
YOU'RE EVERYTHING MARIK SAID.
WAS THAT AN INSULT?
KNOWING MARIK?

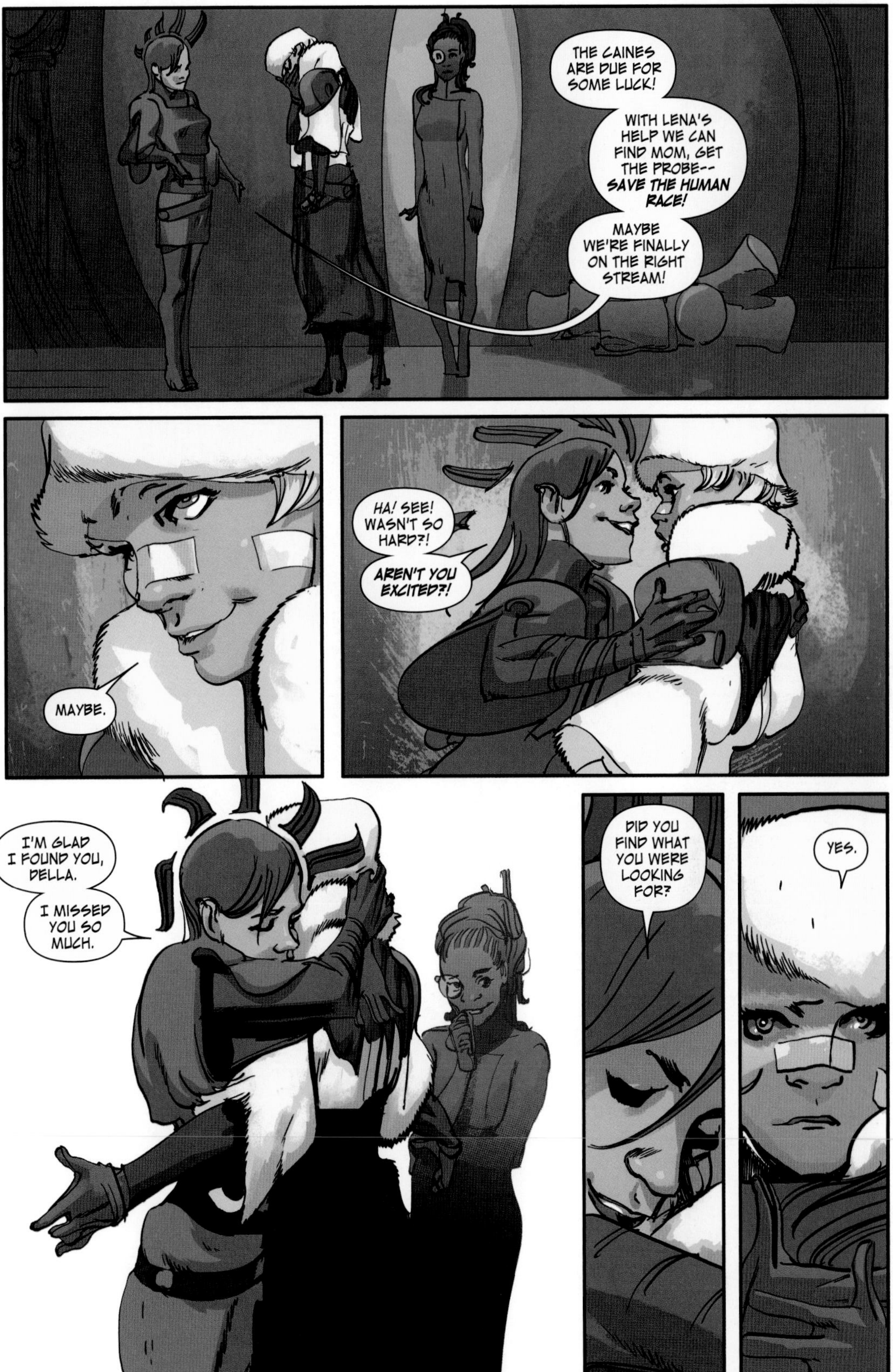
THE CAINES ARE DUE FOR SOME LUCK!
WITH LENA'S HELP WE CAN FIND MOM, GET THE PROBE-- **SAVE THE HUMAN RACE!**
MAYBE WE'RE FINALLY ON THE RIGHT STREAM!
MAYBE.
HA! SEE! WASN'T SO HARD?!
AREN'T YOU EXCITED?!
I'M GLAD I FOUND YOU, DELLA.
I MISSED YOU SO MUCH.
DID YOU FIND WHAT YOU WERE LOOKING FOR?
YES.

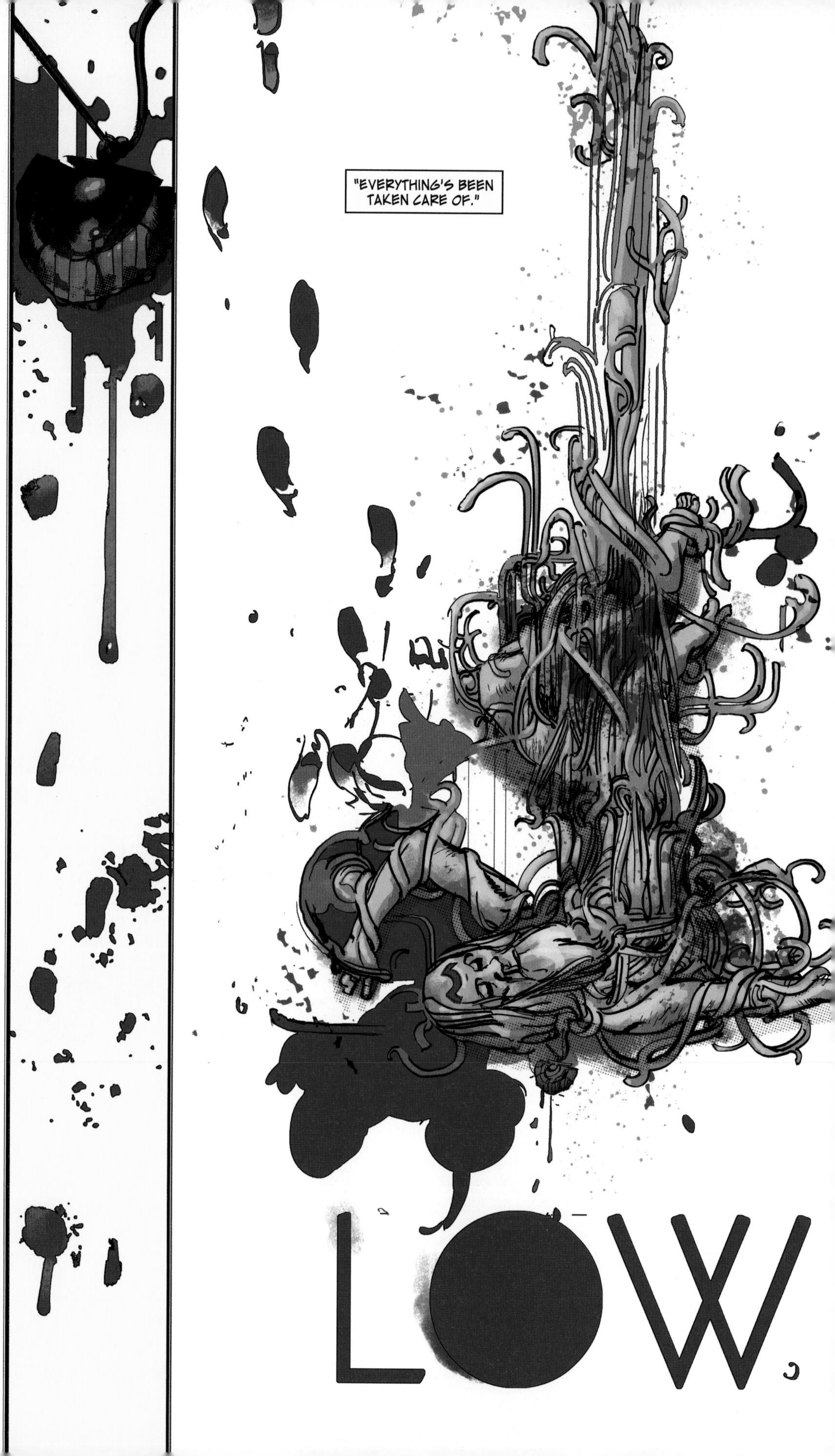
"EVERYTHING'S BEEN TAKEN CARE OF."
LOW.

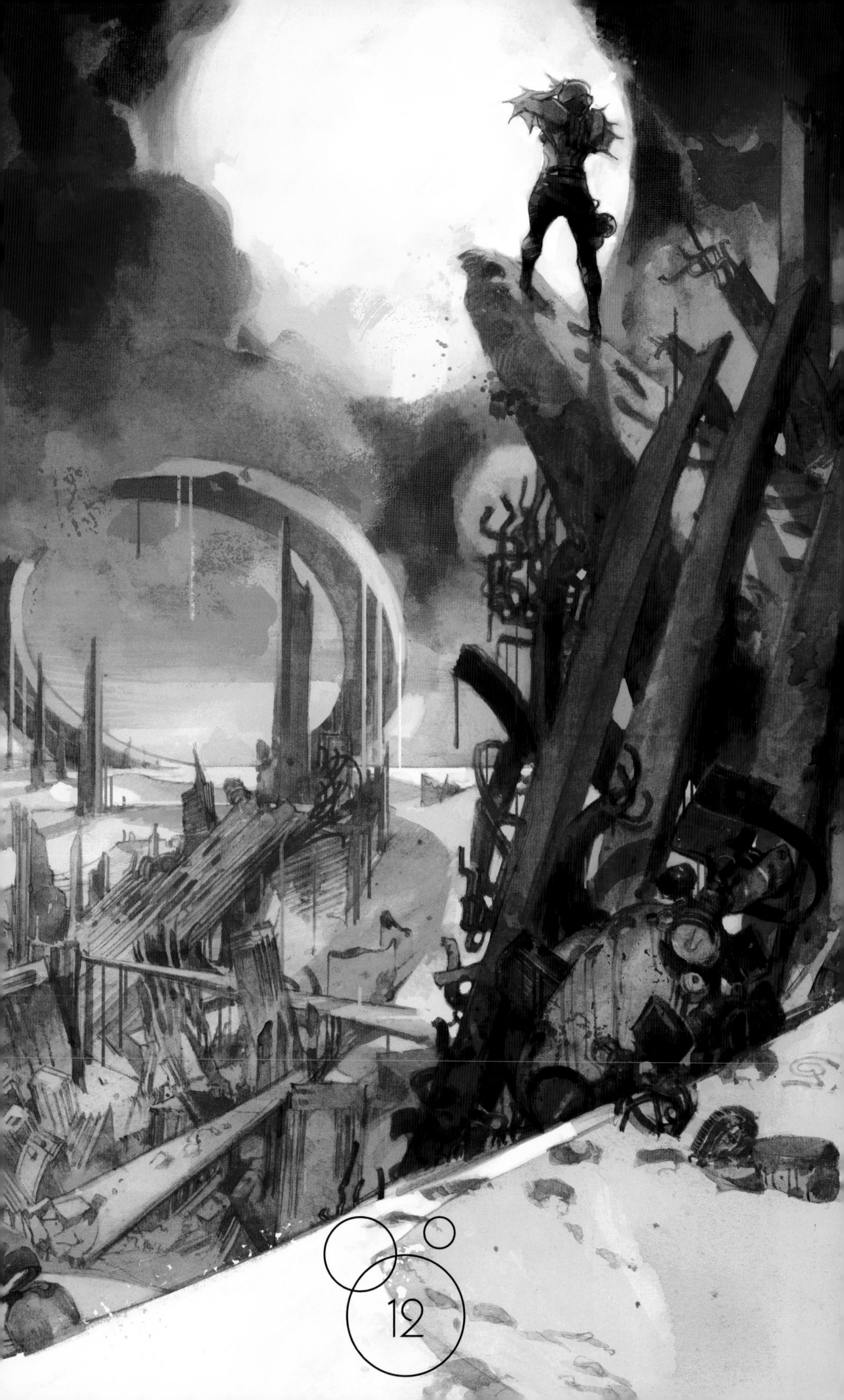
12

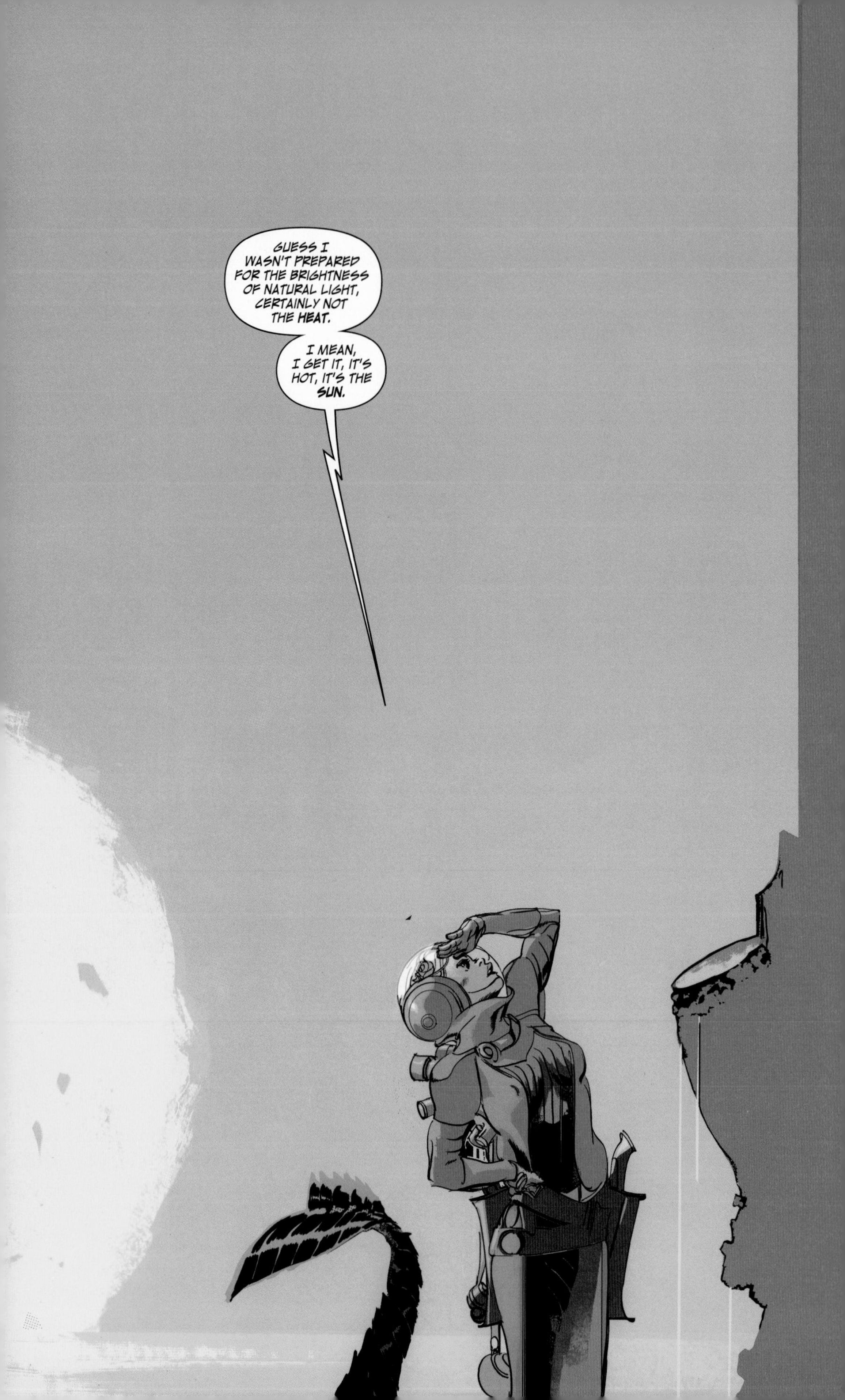
GUESS I WASN'T PREPARED FOR THE BRIGHTNESS OF NATURAL LIGHT, CERTAINLY NOT THE HEAT.
I MEAN, I GET IT, IT'S HOT, IT'S THE SUN.

BUT YOU CAN'T **REALLY** GET YOUR HEAD AROUND THAT CONCEPT UNTIL YOU EXPERIENCE IT.

THOUGH, IF I'M HONEST, I'M SORT OF GLAD I CAN'T FOLLOW YOU ON THE NEXT PART OF THE TRIP.

I EXPECTED THE OCEANS TO HAVE RECEDED...

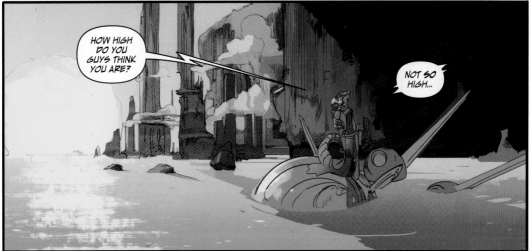

HOW HIGH DO YOU GUYS THINK YOU ARE?

NOT SO HIGH...

....JUST A TWO-MILE DROP BELOW US.

COULD YOU BOTH **PLEASE** BE QUIET.

PLEASE.

HEAD SPINS, HEART POUNDS.

ABOVE IT ALL NOW.

THE FILTERED AIR, RICHER IN OXYGEN THAN ANY I'VE EVER BREATHED, HITS LIKE A CHEAP DRUG.

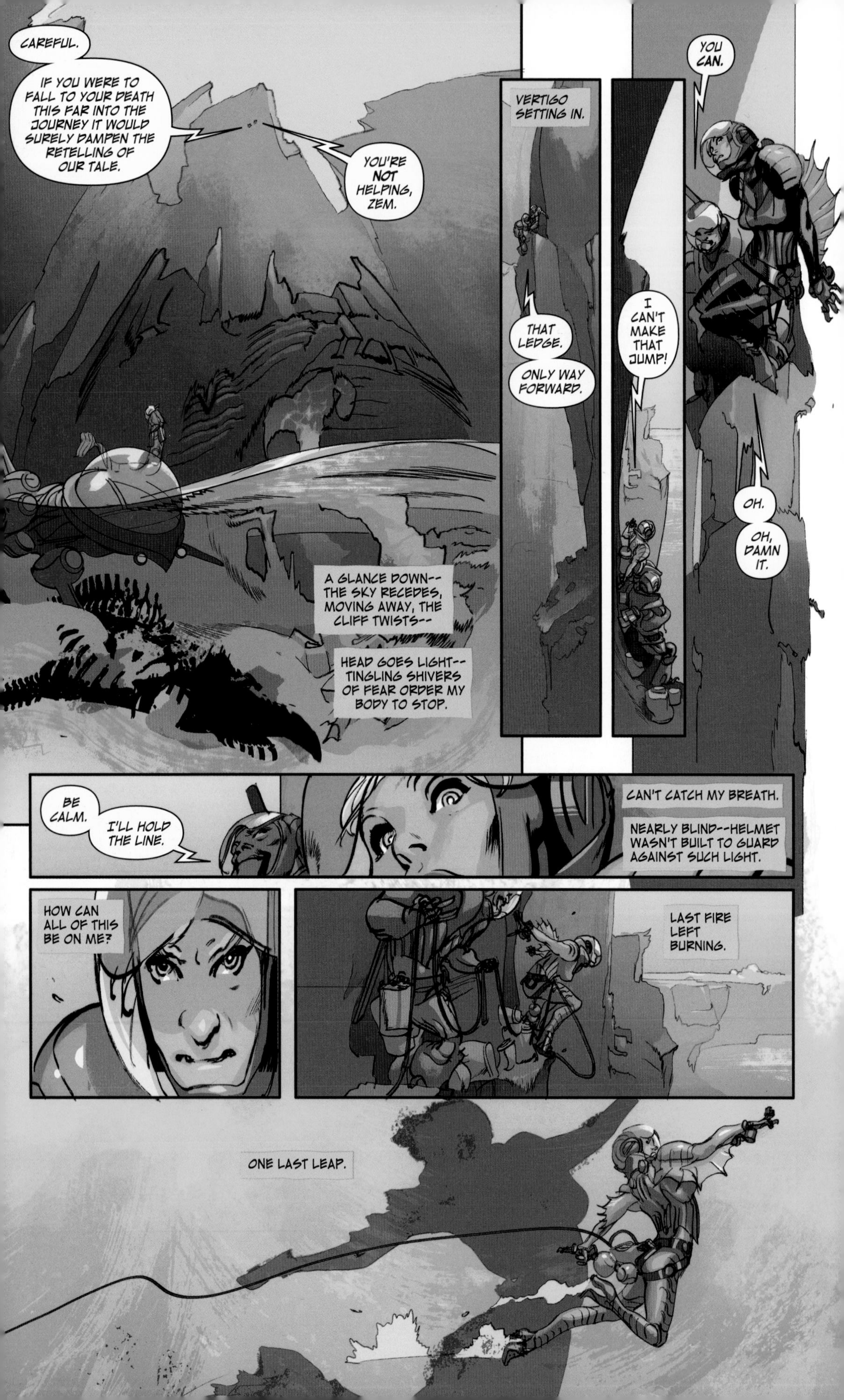
CAREFUL.
IF YOU WERE TO FALL TO YOUR DEATH THIS FAR INTO THE JOURNEY IT WOULD SURELY DAMPEN THE RETELLING OF OUR TALE.
YOU'RE NOT HELPING, ZEM.
A GLANCE DOWN--THE SKY RECEDES, MOVING AWAY, THE CLIFF TWISTS--
HEAD GOES LIGHT--TINGLING SHIVERS OF FEAR ORDER MY BODY TO STOP.
VERTIGO SETTING IN.
THAT LEDGE.
ONLY WAY FORWARD.
I CAN'T MAKE THAT JUMP!
YOU CAN.
OH.
OH, DAMN IT.
BE CALM.
I'LL HOLD THE LINE.
CAN'T CATCH MY BREATH.
NEARLY BLIND--HELMET WASN'T BUILT TO GUARD AGAINST SUCH LIGHT.
HOW CAN ALL OF THIS BE ON ME?
LAST FIRE LEFT BURNING.
ONE LAST LEAP.

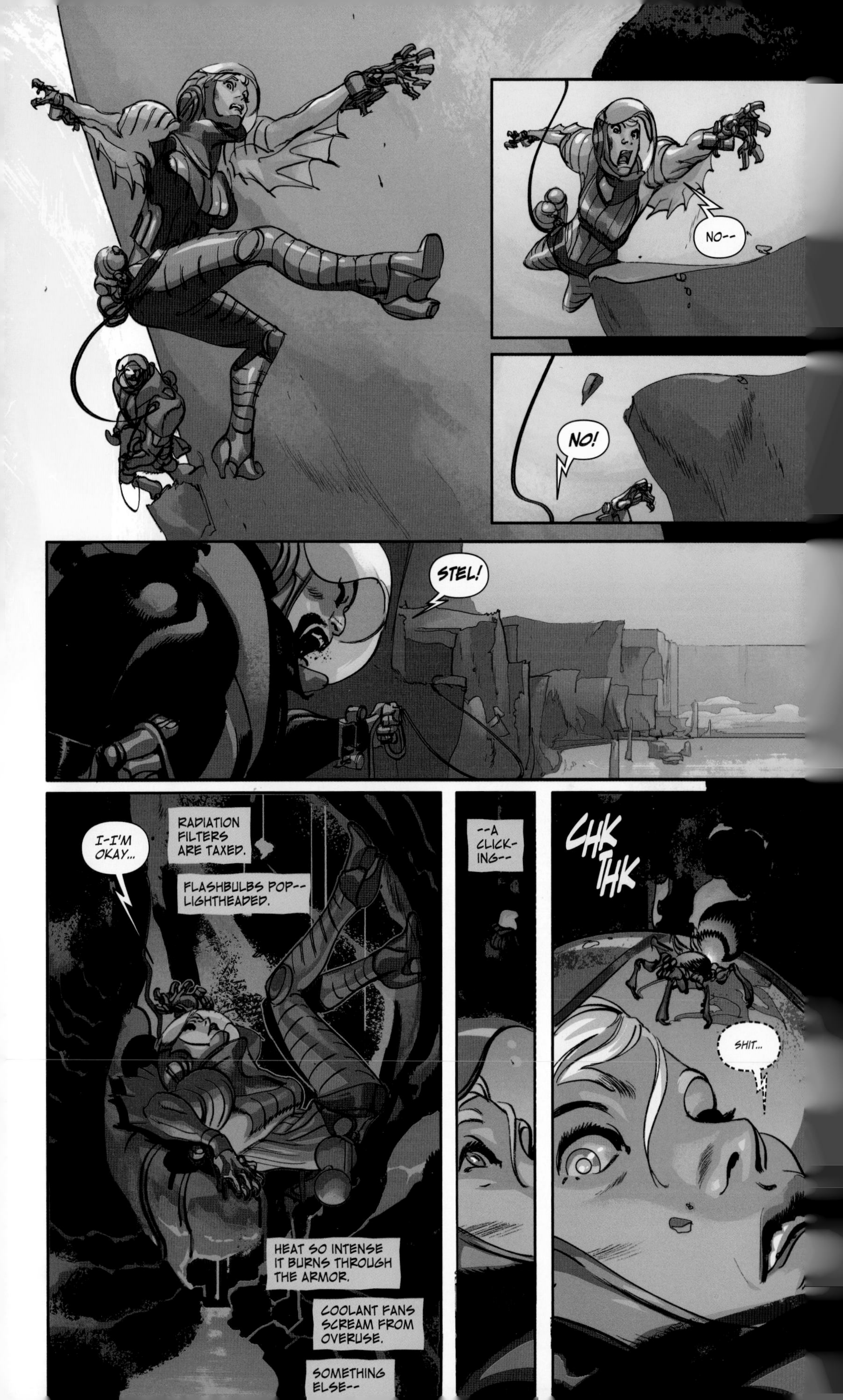
NO--
NO!
STEL!
I-I'M OKAY...
RADIATION FILTERS ARE TAXED.
FLASHBULBS POP--LIGHTHEADED.
HEAT SO INTENSE IT BURNS THROUGH THE ARMOR.
COOLANT FANS SCREAM FROM OVERUSE.
SOMETHING ELSE--
--A CLICKING--
CHK THK
SHIT...

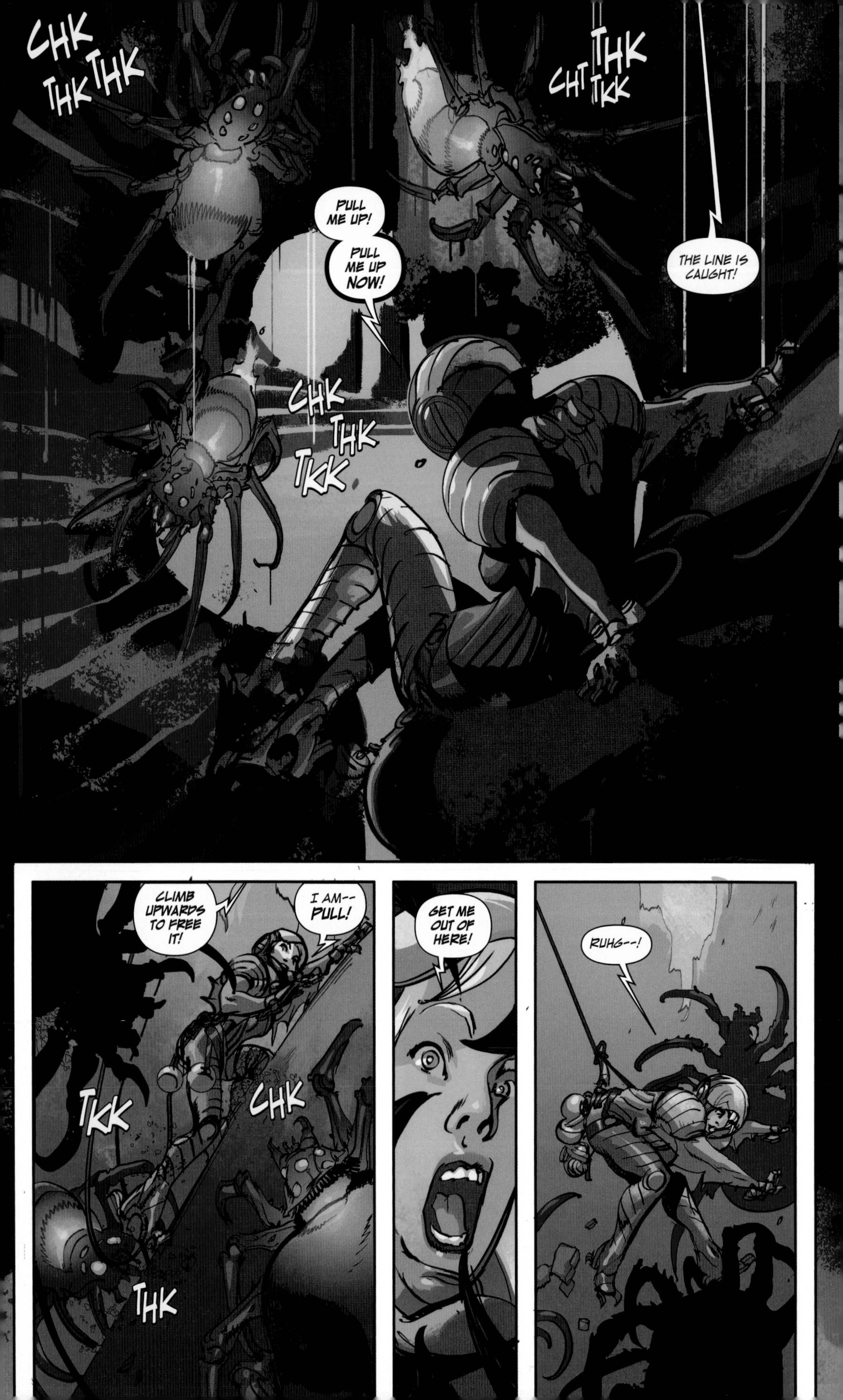
CHK
THK THK
CHT THK
TKK
PULL ME UP!
PULL ME UP NOW!
THE LINE IS CAUGHT!
CHK
THK
TKK
CLIMB UPWARDS TO FREE IT!
I AM-- PULL!
TKK
CHK
THK
GET ME OUT OF HERE!
RUHG--!

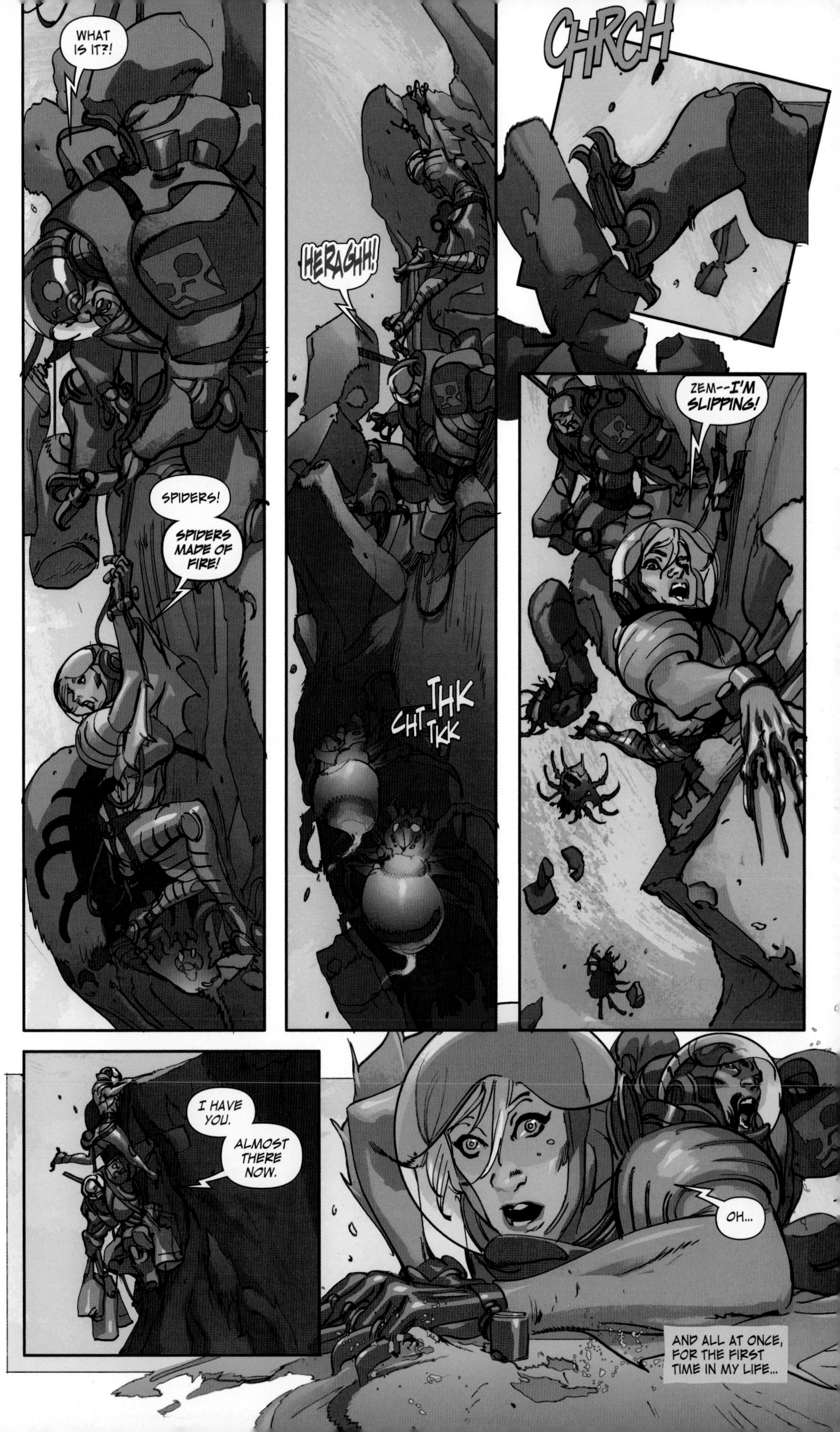
WHAT IS IT?!
SPIDERS!
SPIDERS MADE OF FIRE!
HERAGHH!
CHT THK TKK
CHRCH
ZEM--I'M SLIPPING!
I HAVE YOU.
ALMOST THERE NOW.
OH...
AND ALL AT ONCE, FOR THE FIRST TIME IN MY LIFE...

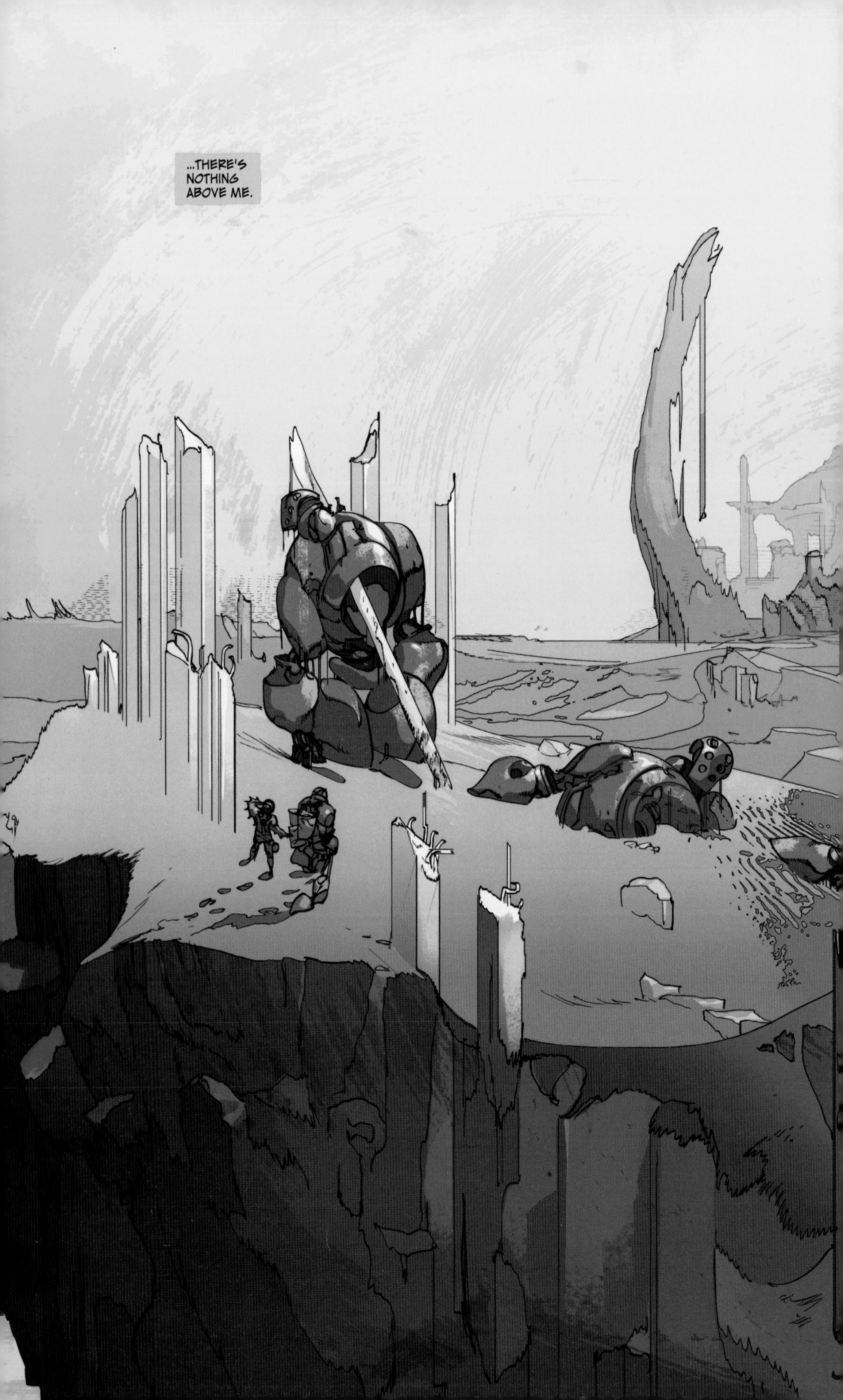
...THERE'S NOTHING ABOVE ME.

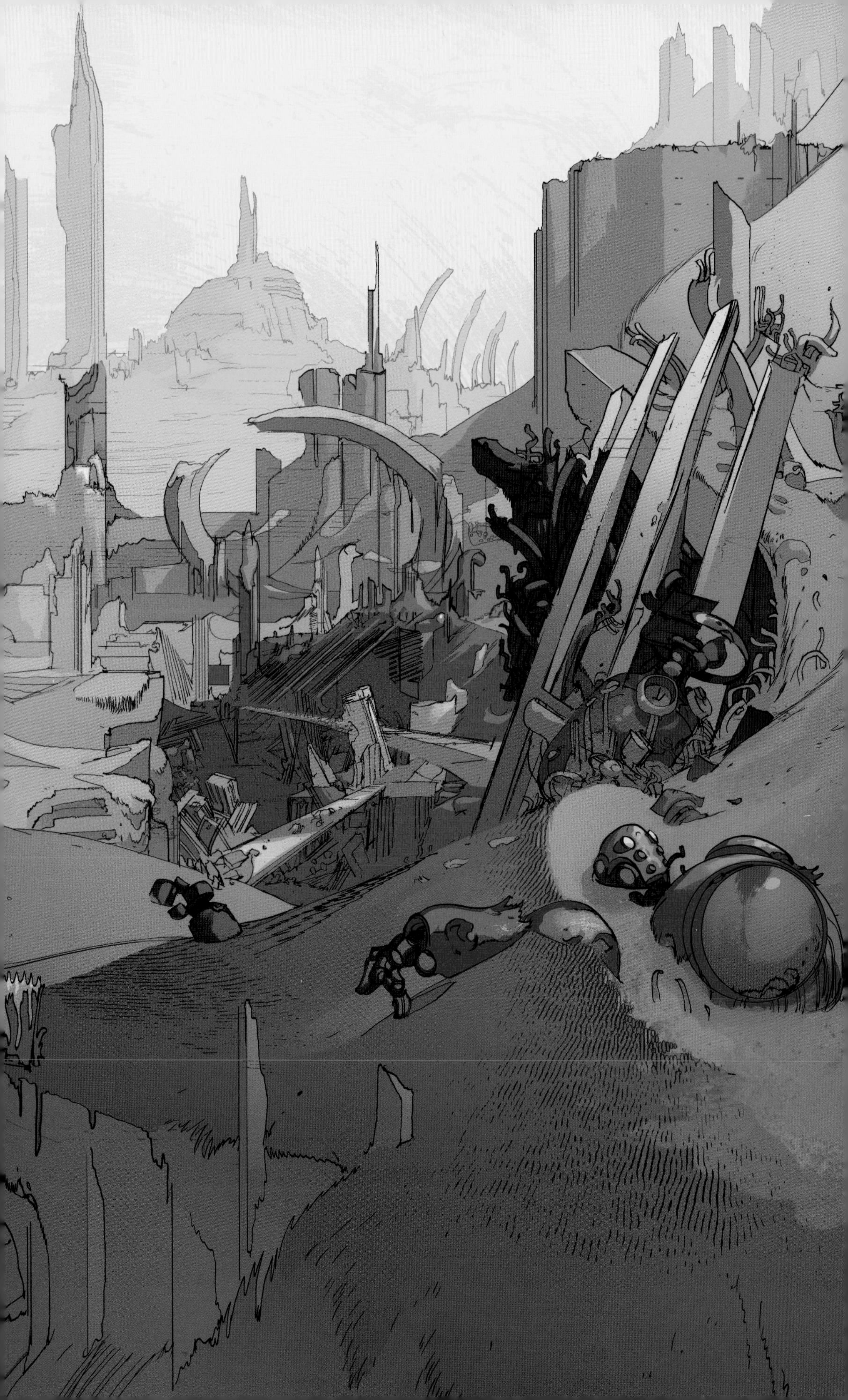

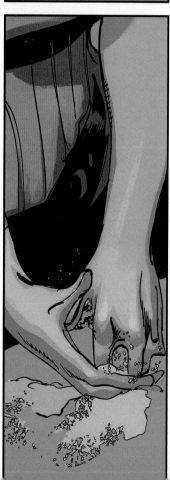

YOU DID IT, MARIK.

YOUR FRIENDS GOT ME HERE.

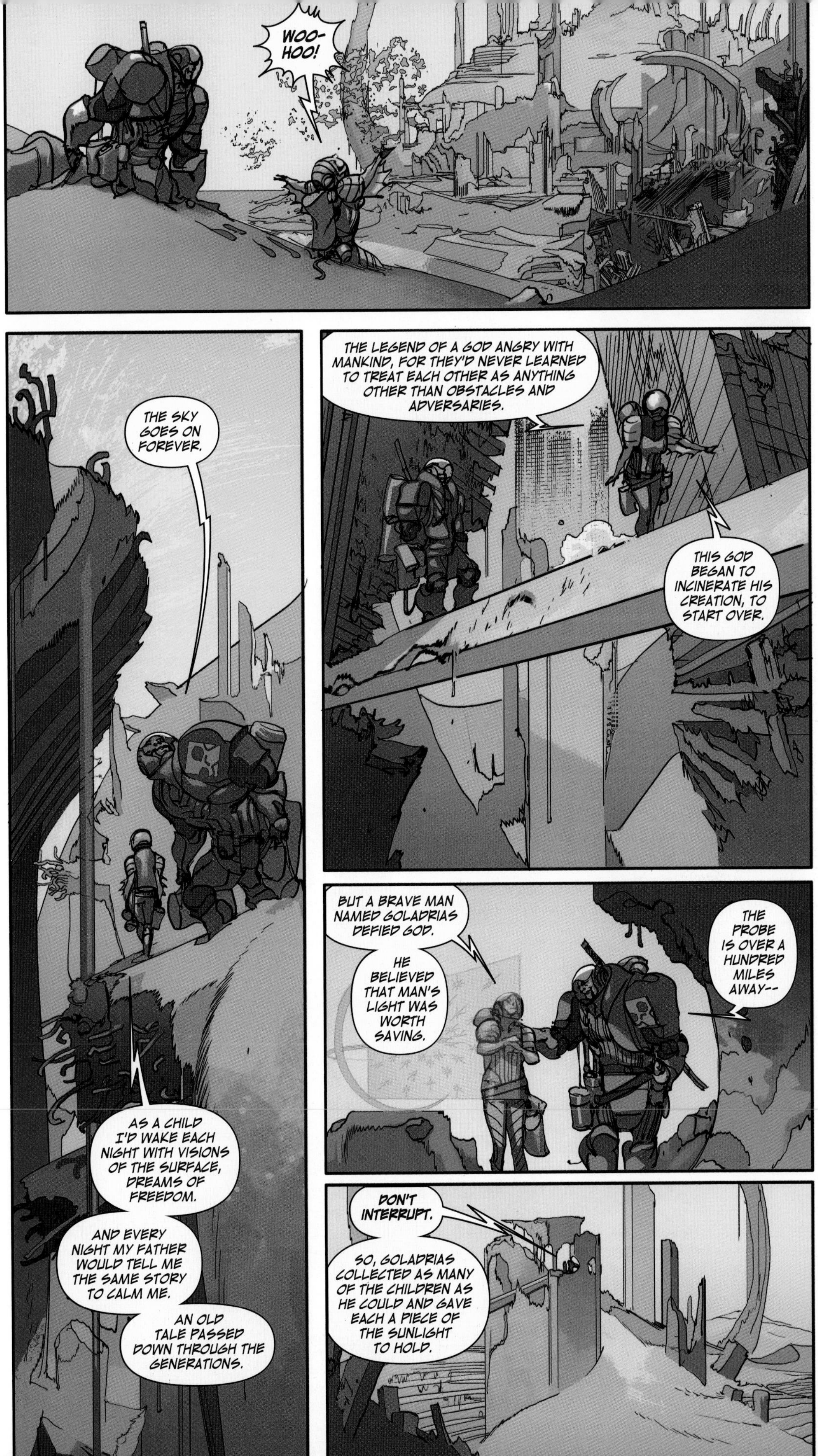
WOO-HOO!
THE SKY GOES ON FOREVER.
AS A CHILD I'D WAKE EACH NIGHT WITH VISIONS OF THE SURFACE, DREAMS OF FREEDOM.
AND EVERY NIGHT MY FATHER WOULD TELL ME THE SAME STORY TO CALM ME.
AN OLD TALE PASSED DOWN THROUGH THE GENERATIONS.
THE LEGEND OF A GOD ANGRY WITH MANKIND, FOR THEY'D NEVER LEARNED TO TREAT EACH OTHER AS ANYTHING OTHER THAN OBSTACLES AND ADVERSARIES.
THIS GOD BEGAN TO INCINERATE HIS CREATION, TO START OVER.
BUT A BRAVE MAN NAMED GOLADRIAS DEFIED GOD.
HE BELIEVED THAT MAN'S LIGHT WAS WORTH SAVING.
THE PROBE IS OVER A HUNDRED MILES AWAY--
DON'T INTERRUPT.
SO, GOLADRIAS COLLECTED AS MANY OF THE CHILDREN AS HE COULD AND GAVE EACH A PIECE OF THE SUNLIGHT TO HOLD.

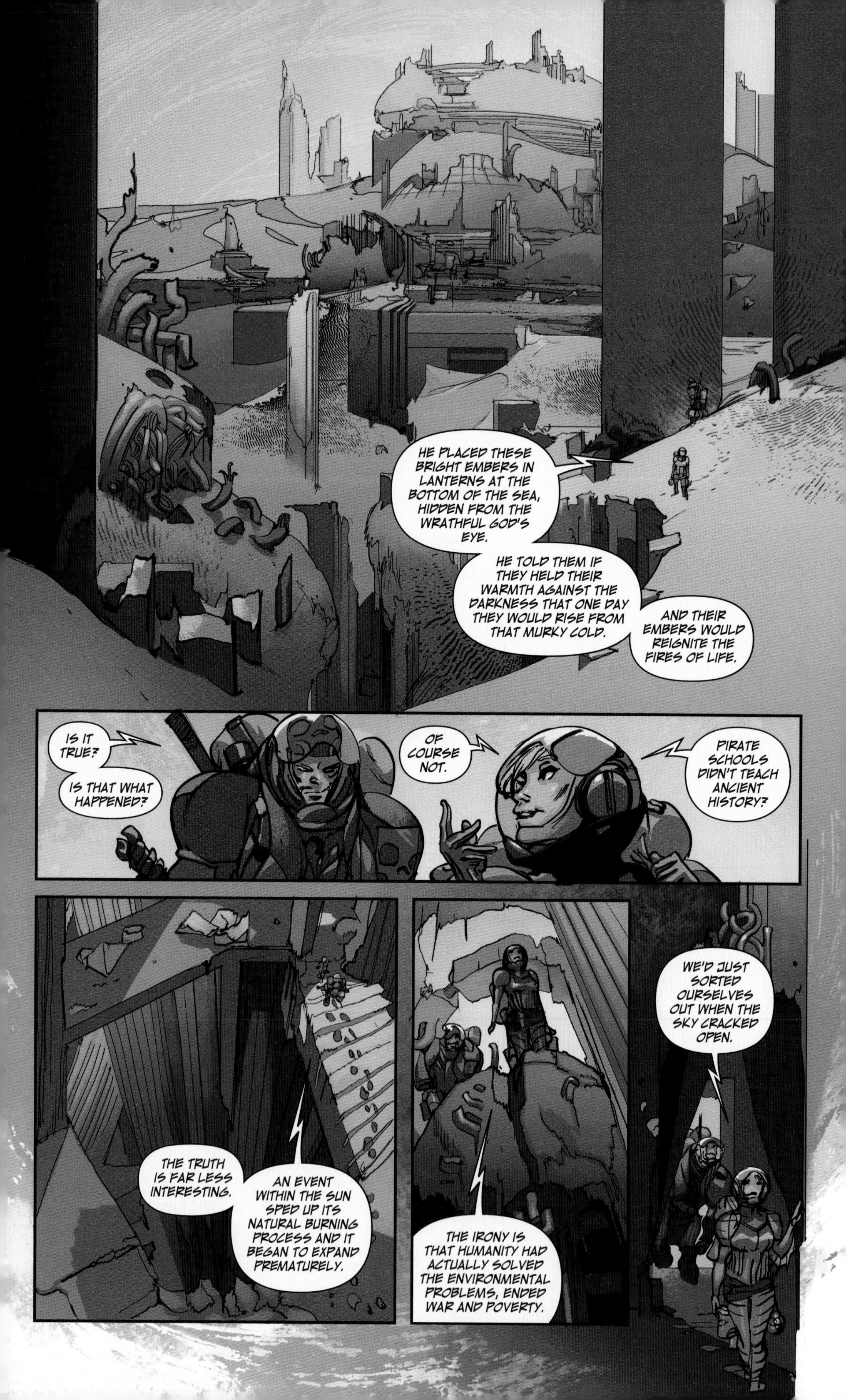
HE PLACED THESE BRIGHT EMBERS IN LANTERNS AT THE BOTTOM OF THE SEA, HIDDEN FROM THE WRATHFUL GOD'S EYE.
HE TOLD THEM IF THEY HELD THEIR WARMTH AGAINST THE DARKNESS THAT ONE DAY THEY WOULD RISE FROM THAT MURKY COLD.
AND THEIR EMBERS WOULD REIGNITE THE FIRES OF LIFE.
IS IT TRUE?
IS THAT WHAT HAPPENED?
OF COURSE NOT.
PIRATE SCHOOLS DIDN'T TEACH ANCIENT HISTORY?
THE TRUTH IS FAR LESS INTERESTING.
AN EVENT WITHIN THE SUN SPED UP ITS NATURAL BURNING PROCESS AND IT BEGAN TO EXPAND PREMATURELY.
THE IRONY IS THAT HUMANITY HAD ACTUALLY SOLVED THE ENVIRONMENTAL PROBLEMS, ENDED WAR AND POVERTY.
WE'D JUST SORTED OURSELVES OUT WHEN THE SKY CRACKED OPEN.

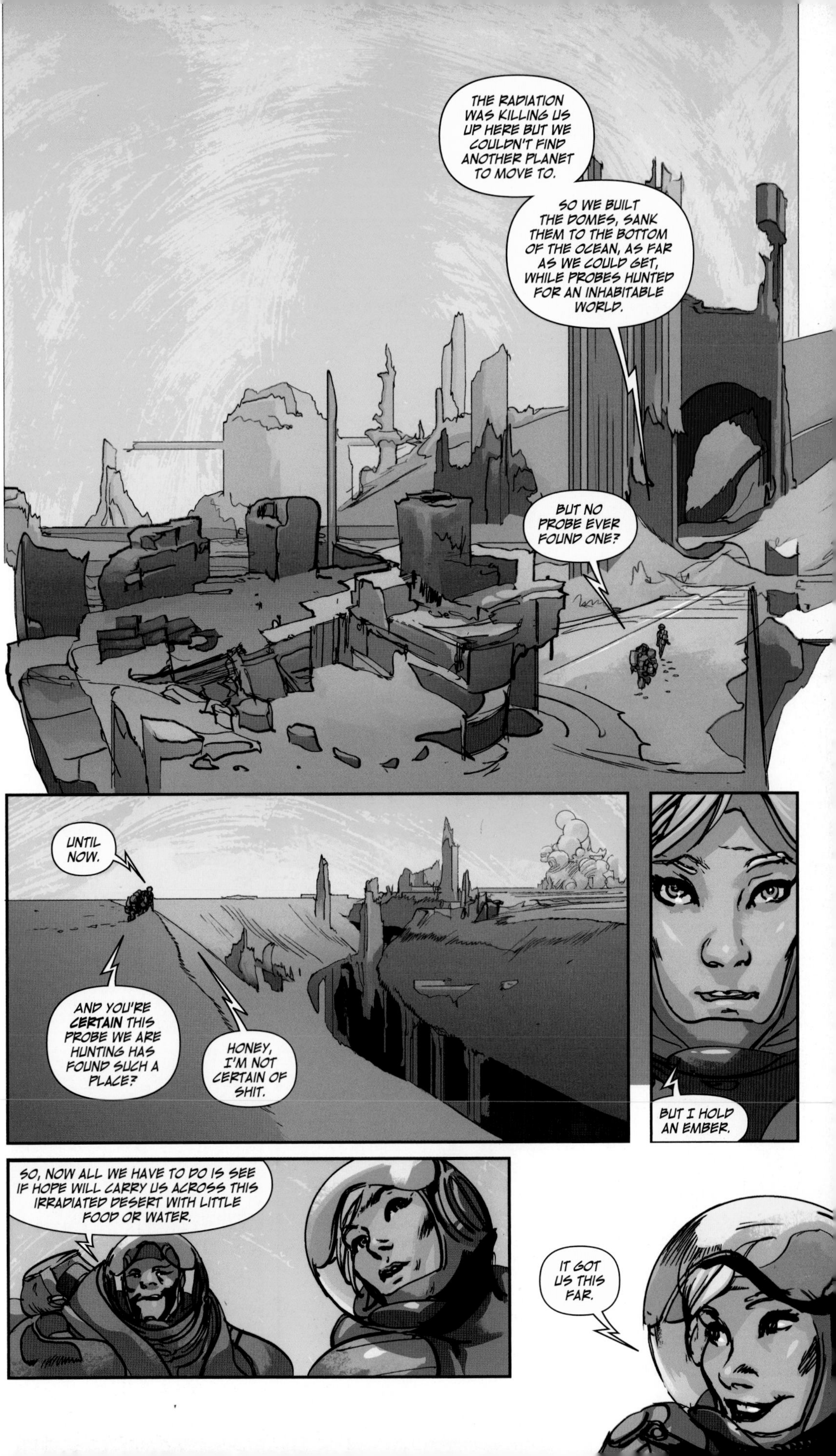
THE RADIATION WAS KILLING US UP HERE BUT WE COULDN'T FIND ANOTHER PLANET TO MOVE TO.
SO WE BUILT THE DOMES, SANK THEM TO THE BOTTOM OF THE OCEAN, AS FAR AS WE COULD GET, WHILE PROBES HUNTED FOR AN INHABITABLE WORLD.
BUT NO PROBE EVER FOUND ONE?
UNTIL NOW.
AND YOU'RE CERTAIN THIS PROBE WE ARE HUNTING HAS FOUND SUCH A PLACE?
HONEY, I'M NOT CERTAIN OF SHIT.
BUT I HOLD AN EMBER.
SO, NOW ALL WE HAVE TO DO IS SEE IF HOPE WILL CARRY US ACROSS THIS IRRADIATED DESERT WITH LITTLE FOOD OR WATER.
IT GOT US THIS FAR.

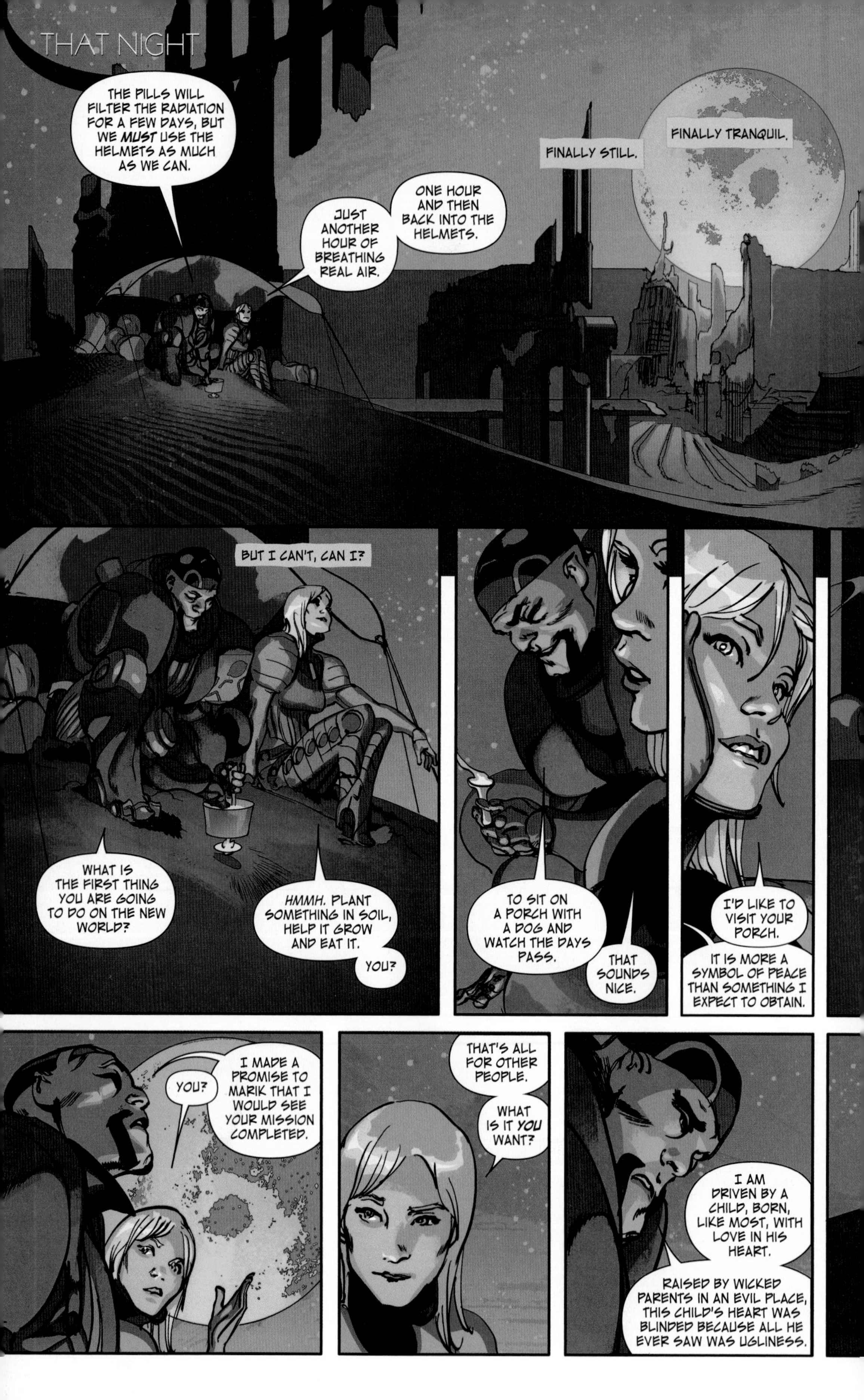
THAT NIGHT
THE PILLS WILL FILTER THE RADIATION FOR A FEW DAYS, BUT WE *MUST* USE THE HELMETS AS MUCH AS WE CAN.
JUST ANOTHER HOUR OF BREATHING REAL AIR.
ONE HOUR AND THEN BACK INTO THE HELMETS.
FINALLY STILL.
FINALLY TRANQUIL.
BUT I CAN'T, CAN I?
WHAT IS THE FIRST THING YOU ARE GOING TO DO ON THE NEW WORLD?
HMMH. PLANT SOMETHING IN SOIL, HELP IT GROW AND EAT IT.
YOU?
TO SIT ON A PORCH WITH A DOG AND WATCH THE DAYS PASS.
THAT SOUNDS NICE.
I'D LIKE TO VISIT YOUR PORCH.
IT IS MORE A SYMBOL OF PEACE THAN SOMETHING I EXPECT TO OBTAIN.
YOU?
I MADE A PROMISE TO MARIK THAT I WOULD SEE YOUR MISSION COMPLETED.
THAT'S ALL FOR OTHER PEOPLE.
WHAT IS IT *YOU* WANT?
I AM DRIVEN BY A CHILD, BORN, LIKE MOST, WITH LOVE IN HIS HEART.
RAISED BY WICKED PARENTS IN AN EVIL PLACE, THIS CHILD'S HEART WAS BLINDED BECAUSE ALL HE EVER SAW WAS UGLINESS.

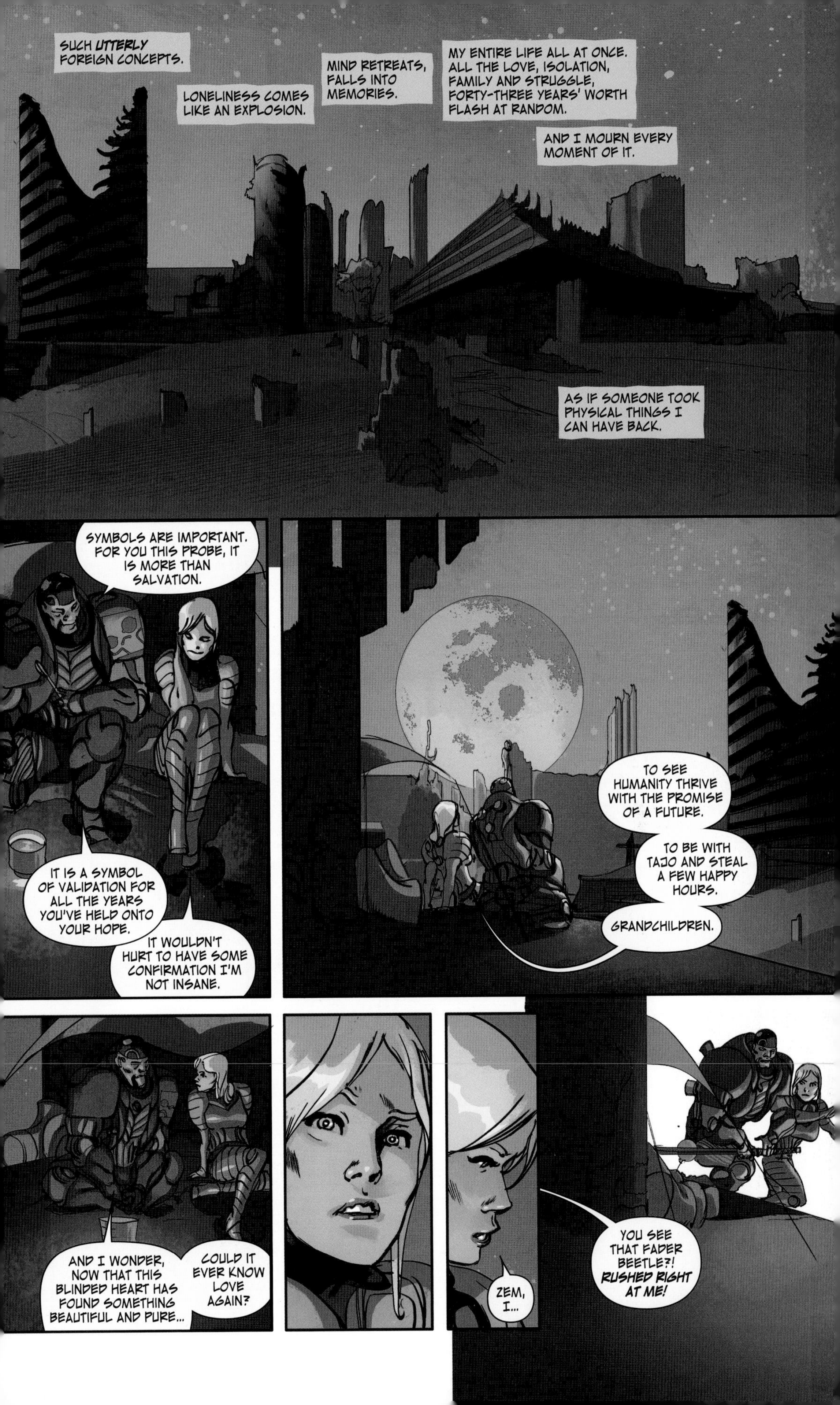

SUCH UTTERLY FOREIGN CONCEPTS.
LONELINESS COMES LIKE AN EXPLOSION.
MIND RETREATS, FALLS INTO MEMORIES.
MY ENTIRE LIFE ALL AT ONCE. ALL THE LOVE, ISOLATION, FAMILY AND STRUGGLE, FORTY-THREE YEARS' WORTH FLASH AT RANDOM.
AND I MOURN EVERY MOMENT OF IT.
AS IF SOMEONE TOOK PHYSICAL THINGS I CAN HAVE BACK.
SYMBOLS ARE IMPORTANT. FOR YOU THIS PROBE, IT IS MORE THAN SALVATION.
IT IS A SYMBOL OF VALIDATION FOR ALL THE YEARS YOU'VE HELD ONTO YOUR HOPE.
IT WOULDN'T HURT TO HAVE SOME CONFIRMATION I'M NOT INSANE.
TO SEE HUMANITY THRIVE WITH THE PROMISE OF A FUTURE.
TO BE WITH TAJO AND STEAL A FEW HAPPY HOURS.
GRANDCHILDREN.
AND I WONDER, NOW THAT THIS BLINDED HEART HAS FOUND SOMETHING BEAUTIFUL AND PURE...
COULD IT EVER KNOW LOVE AGAIN?
ZEM, I...
YOU SEE THAT FADER BEETLE?! RUSHED RIGHT AT ME!

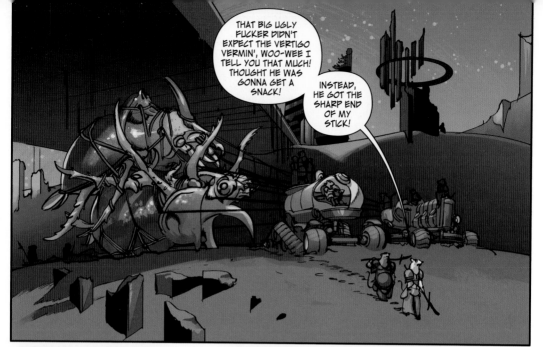

THAT BIG UGLY FUCKER DIDN'T EXPECT THE VERTIGO VERMIN', WOO-WEE I TELL YOU THAT MUCH! THOUGHT HE WAS GONNA GET A SNACK!

INSTEAD, HE GOT THE SHARP END OF MY STICK!

YOU SMELL THAT SWEAT? SOMETHIN' COOKIN'!

THAT'S JUST THE MISSUS GETTIN' THE BROTH READY FOR THE SWEET STEW WE GONNA SUCK DOWN.

WE DONE GOOD TODAY, BOYS.

WE DONE REAL GOOD.

TATALA, OPEN THIS GATE!

GOT A SURPRISE!

TOOM

BARYL, YOU WERE GONE SO LONG, I WAS FRIGHTENED!

A LONG JOURNEY, BUT TAKE A LOOK AT WHAT WE GOT.

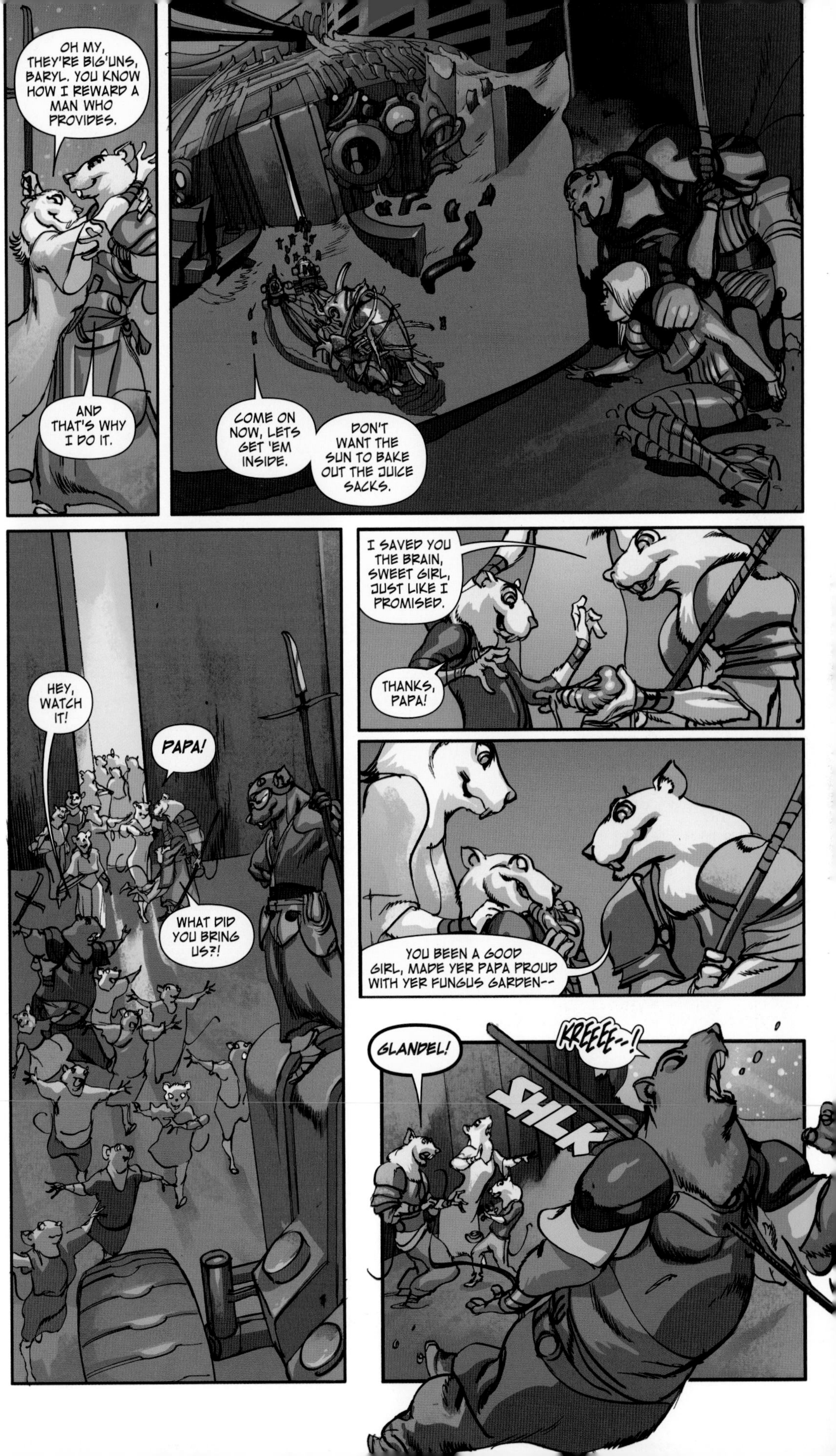
OH MY, THEY'RE BIG'UNS, BARYL. YOU KNOW HOW I REWARD A MAN WHO PROVIDES.
AND THAT'S WHY I DO IT.
COME ON NOW, LETS GET 'EM INSIDE.
DON'T WANT THE SUN TO BAKE OUT THE JUICE SACKS.
HEY, WATCH IT!
PAPA!
WHAT DID YOU BRING US?!
I SAVED YOU THE BRAIN, SWEET GIRL, JUST LIKE I PROMISED.
THANKS, PAPA!
YOU BEEN A GOOD GIRL, MADE YER PAPA PROUD WITH YER FUNGUS GARDEN--
GLANDEL!
KREEEE--!
SHLK

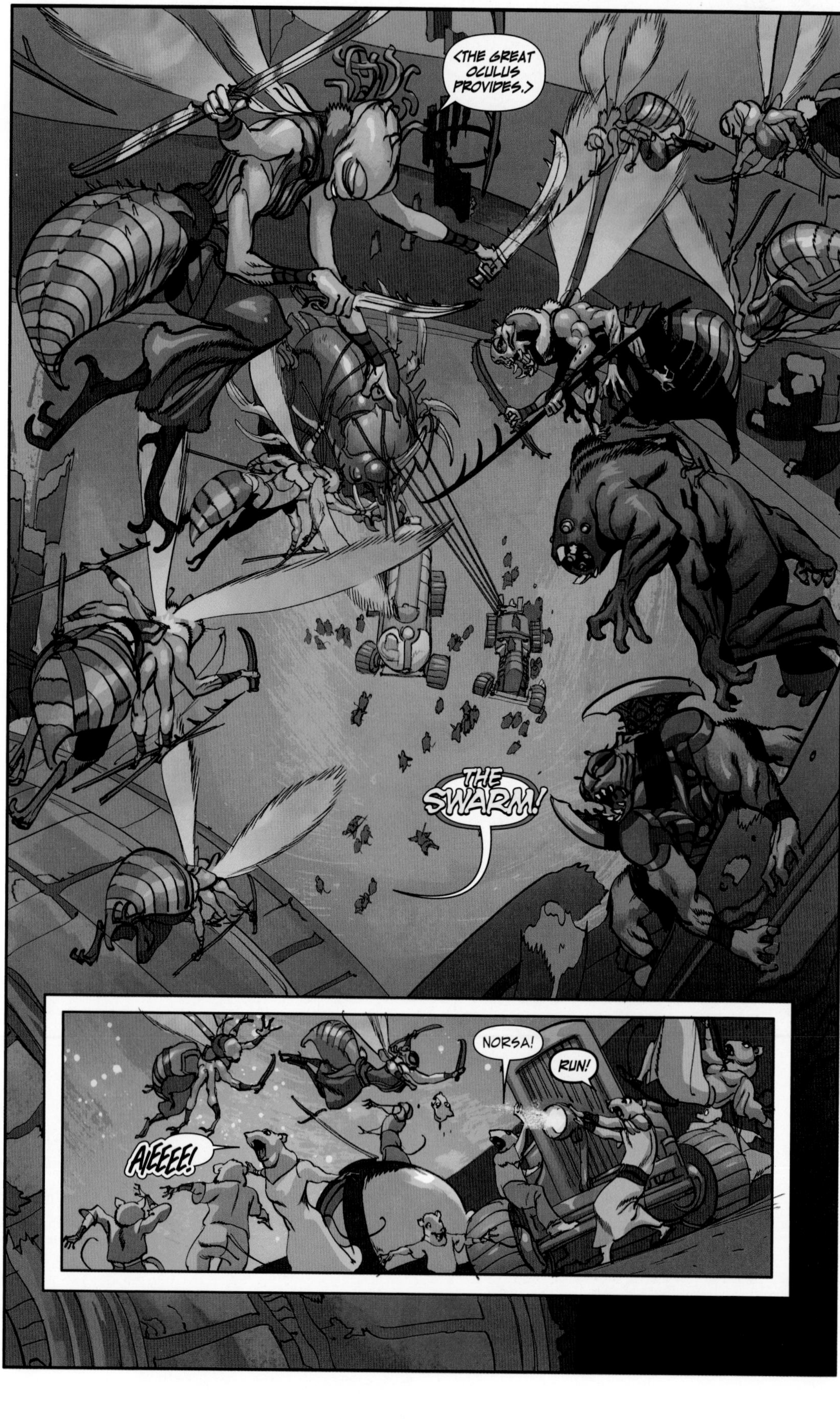
<THE GREAT OCULUS PROVIDES.>
THE SWARM!
NORSA!
RUN!
AIEEEE!

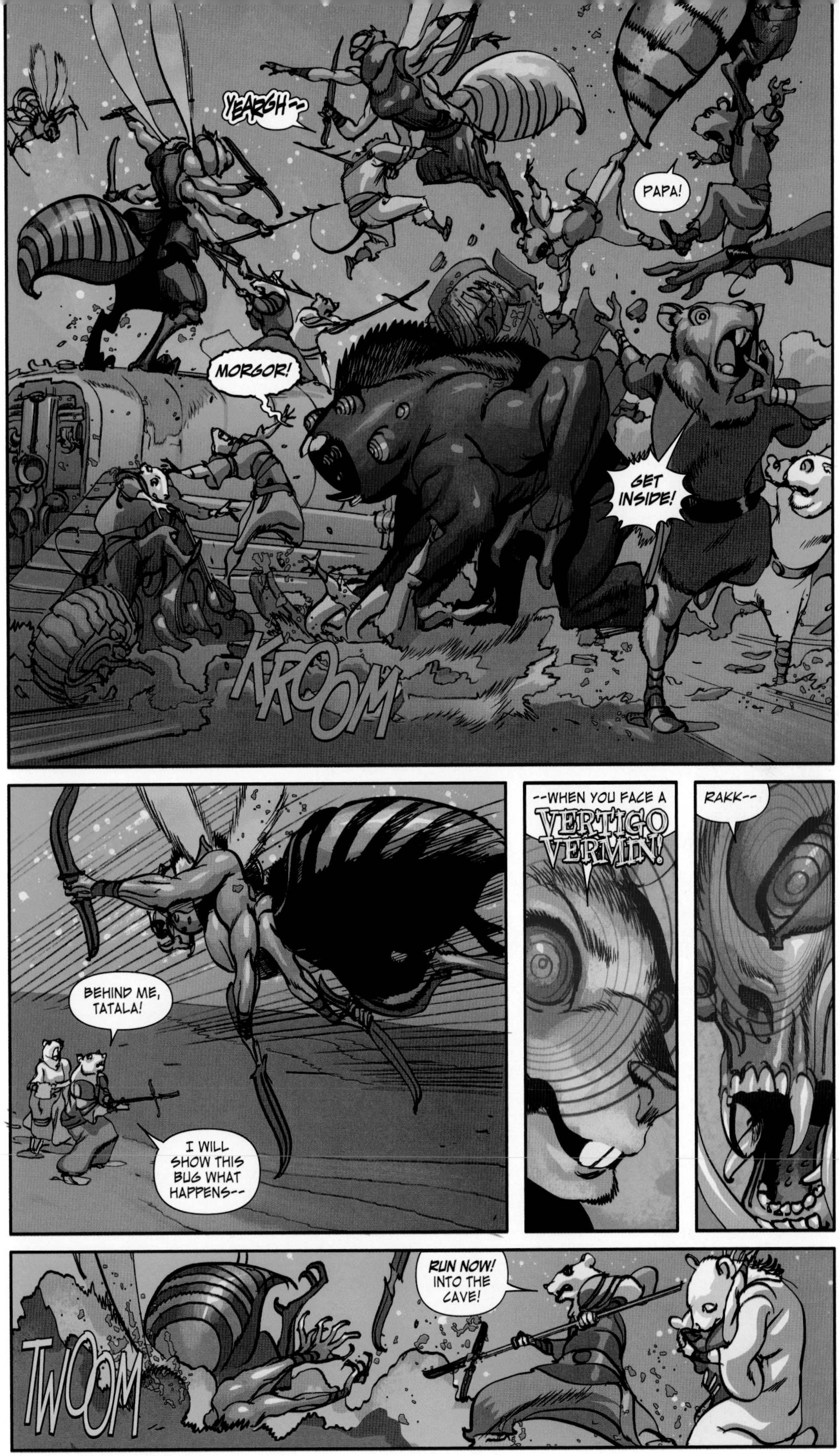

YEARGH--
PAPA!
MORGOR!
GET INSIDE!
KROOM
BEHIND ME, TATALA!
I WILL SHOW THIS BUG WHAT HAPPENS--
--WHEN YOU FACE A
VERTIGO VERMIN!
RAKK--
TWOOM
RUN NOW! INTO THE CAVE!

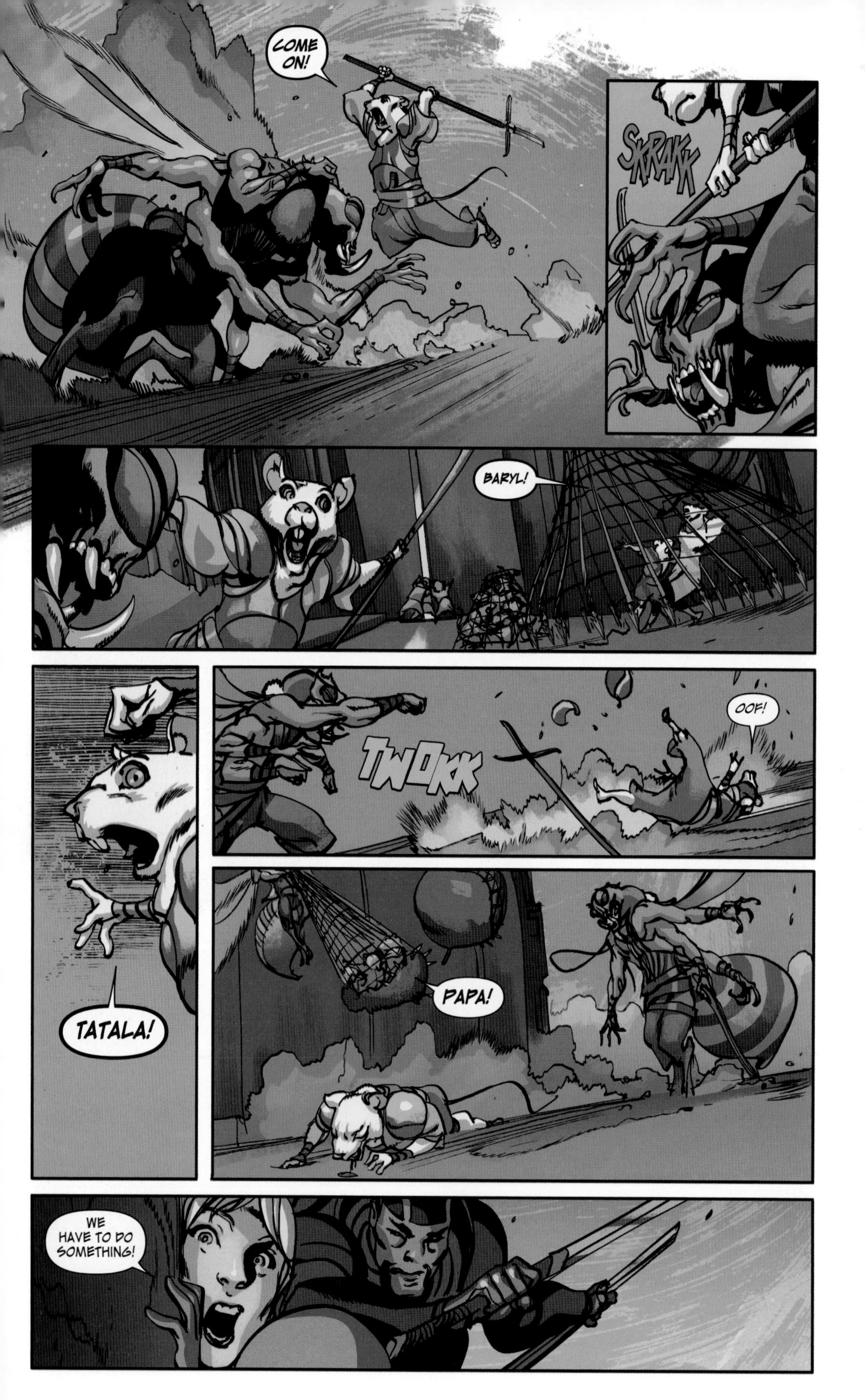
COME ON!
SKRAKK
BARYL!
TATALA!
TWOKK
OOF!
PAPA!
WE HAVE TO DO SOMETHING!

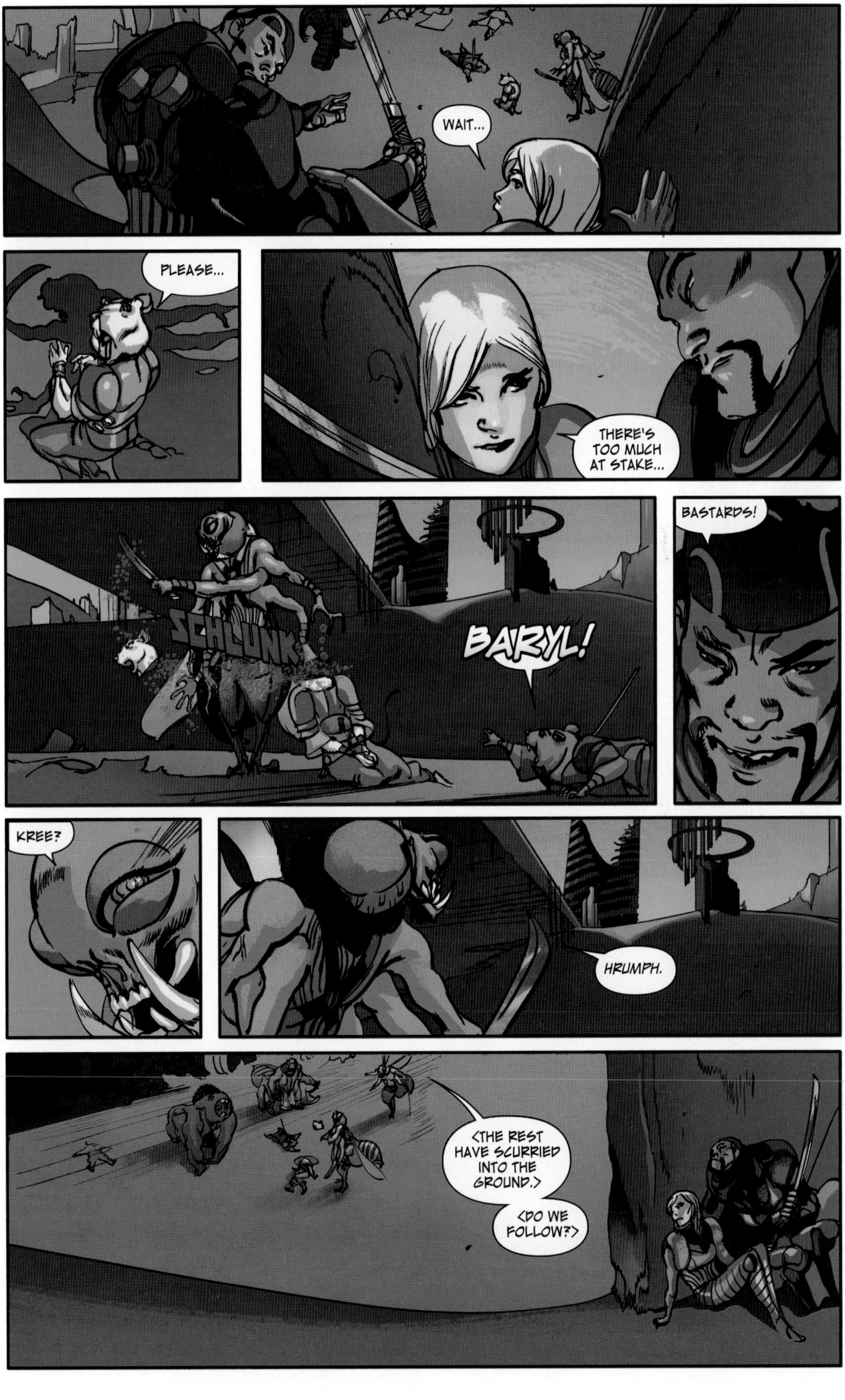
WAIT...
PLEASE...
THERE'S TOO MUCH AT STAKE...
SCHLUNK
BARYL!
BASTARDS!
KREE?
HRUMPH.
<THE REST HAVE SCURRIED INTO THE GROUND.>
<DO WE FOLLOW?>

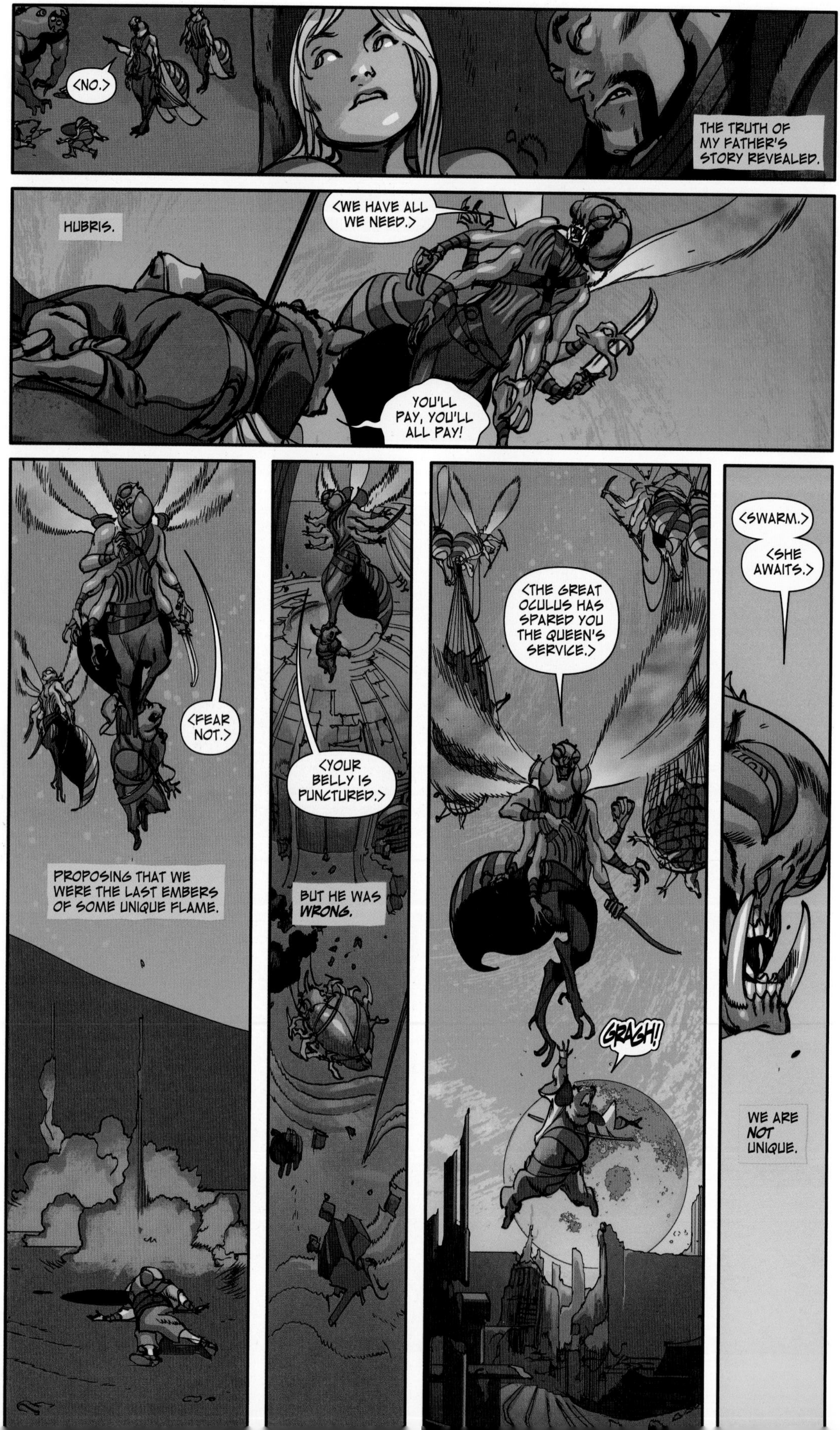
<NO.>
THE TRUTH OF MY FATHER'S STORY REVEALED.
HUBRIS.
<WE HAVE ALL WE NEED.>
YOU'LL PAY, YOU'LL ALL PAY!
<FEAR NOT.>
PROPOSING THAT WE WERE THE LAST EMBERS OF SOME UNIQUE FLAME.
<YOUR BELLY IS PUNCTURED.>
BUT HE WAS WRONG.
<THE GREAT OCULUS HAS SPARED YOU THE QUEEN'S SERVICE.>
GRAGH!
<SWARM.>
<SHE AWAITS.>
WE ARE NOT UNIQUE.

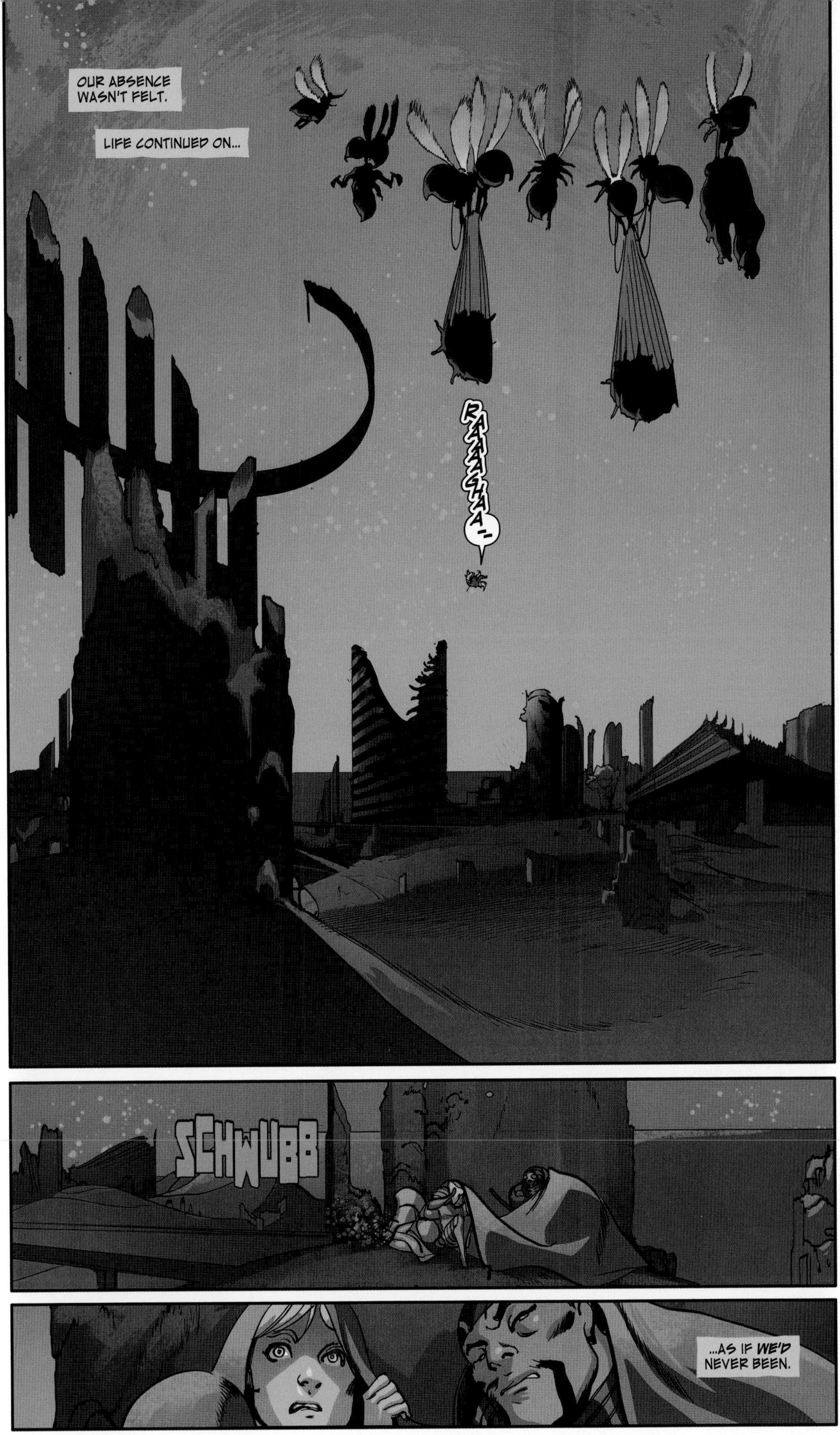
OUR ABSENCE WASN'T FELT.
LIFE CONTINUED ON...
RAAAAGHAA--
SCHWUBB
...AS IF WE'D NEVER BEEN.

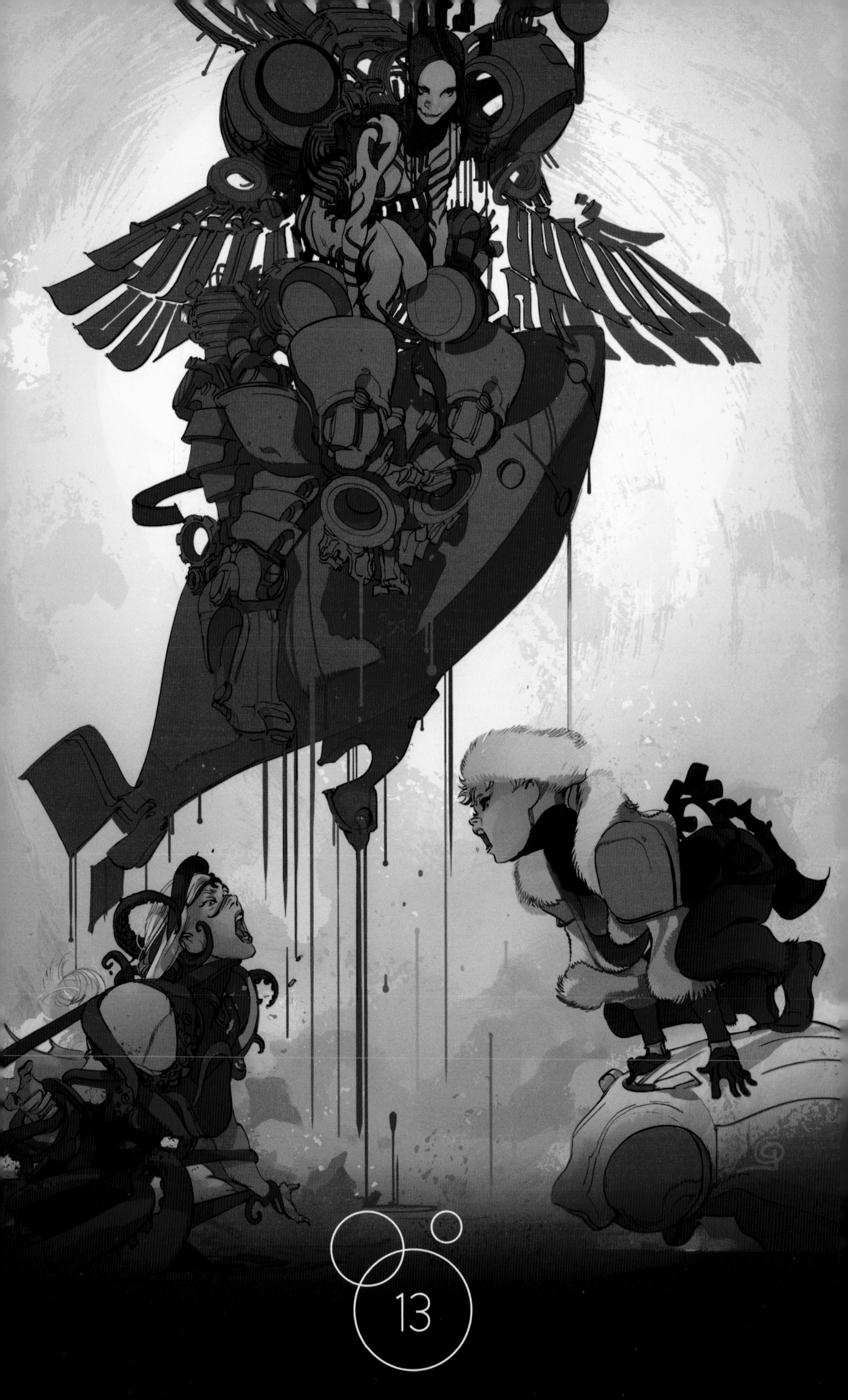
13

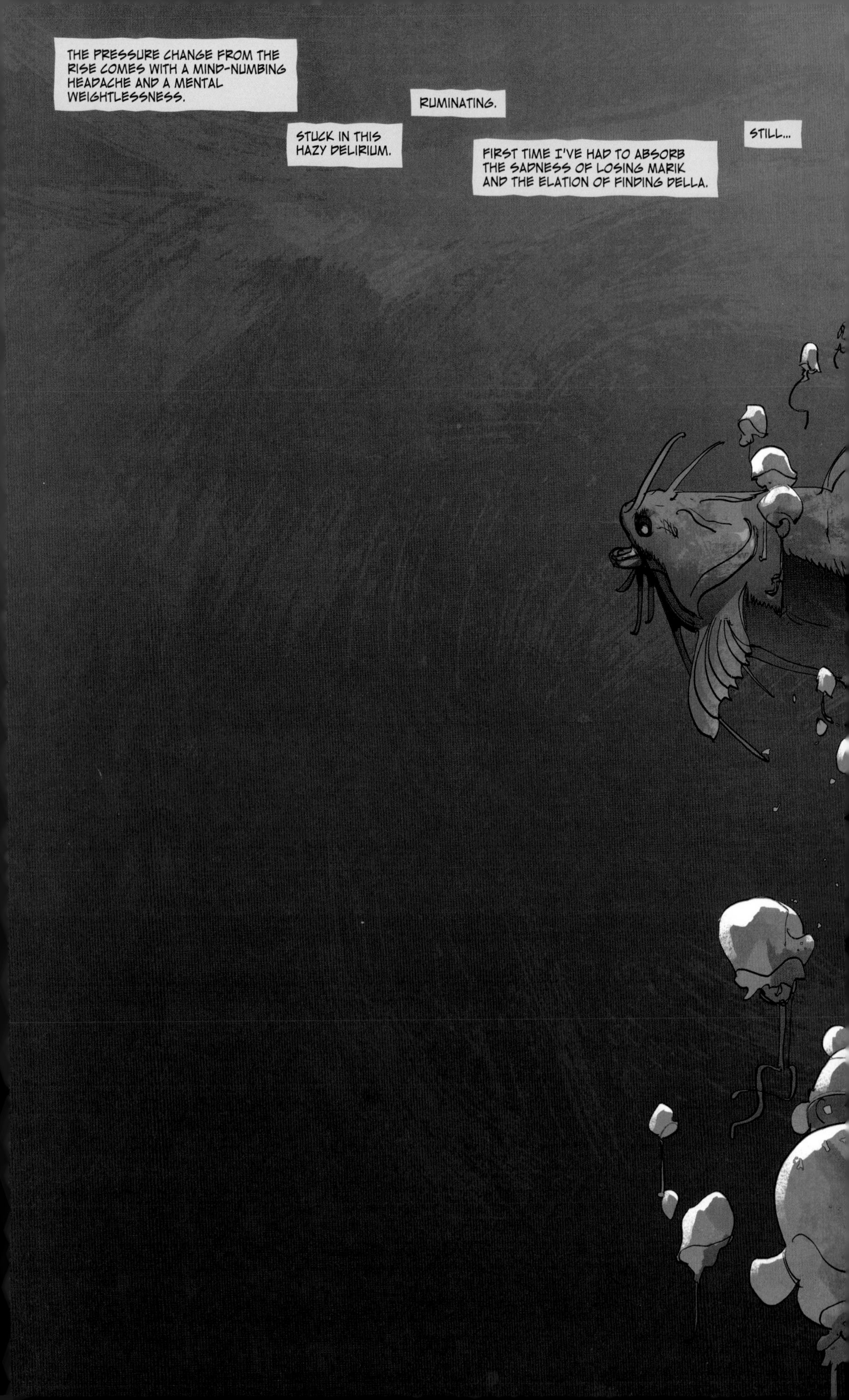
THE PRESSURE CHANGE FROM THE RISE COMES WITH A MIND-NUMBING HEADACHE AND A MENTAL WEIGHTLESSNESS.
RUMINATING.
STUCK IN THIS HAZY DELIRIUM.
FIRST TIME I'VE HAD TO ABSORB THE SADNESS OF LOSING MARIK AND THE ELATION OF FINDING DELLA.
STILL...

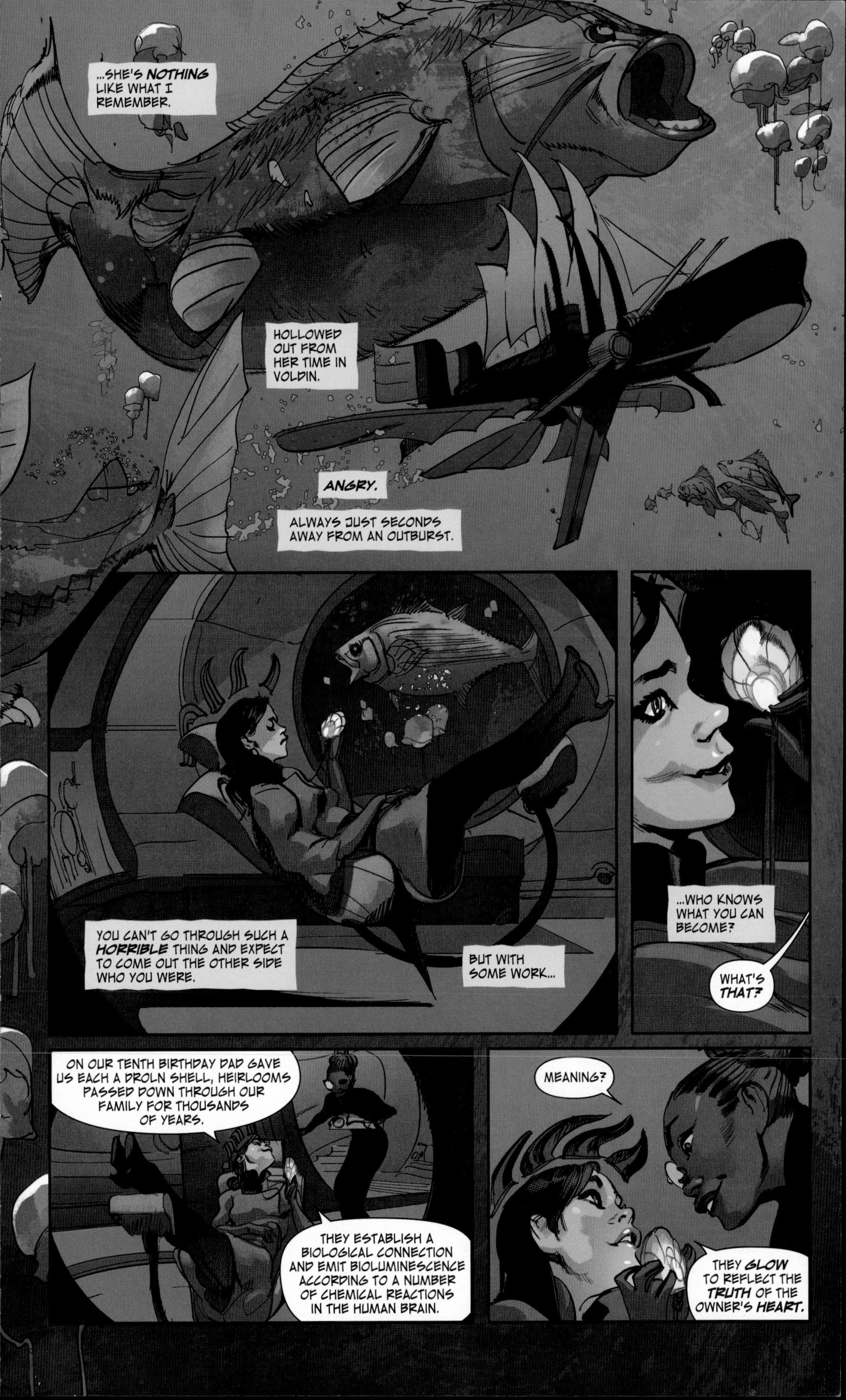

...SHE'S NOTHING LIKE WHAT I REMEMBER.
HOLLOWED OUT FROM HER TIME IN VOLDIN.
ANGRY.
ALWAYS JUST SECONDS AWAY FROM AN OUTBURST.
YOU CAN'T GO THROUGH SUCH A HORRIBLE THING AND EXPECT TO COME OUT THE OTHER SIDE WHO YOU WERE.
BUT WITH SOME WORK...
...WHO KNOWS WHAT YOU CAN BECOME?
WHAT'S THAT?
ON OUR TENTH BIRTHDAY DAD GAVE US EACH A DROLN SHELL, HEIRLOOMS PASSED DOWN THROUGH OUR FAMILY FOR THOUSANDS OF YEARS.
THEY ESTABLISH A BIOLOGICAL CONNECTION AND EMIT BIOLUMINESCENCE ACCORDING TO A NUMBER OF CHEMICAL REACTIONS IN THE HUMAN BRAIN.
MEANING?
THEY GLOW TO REFLECT THE TRUTH OF THE OWNER'S HEART.

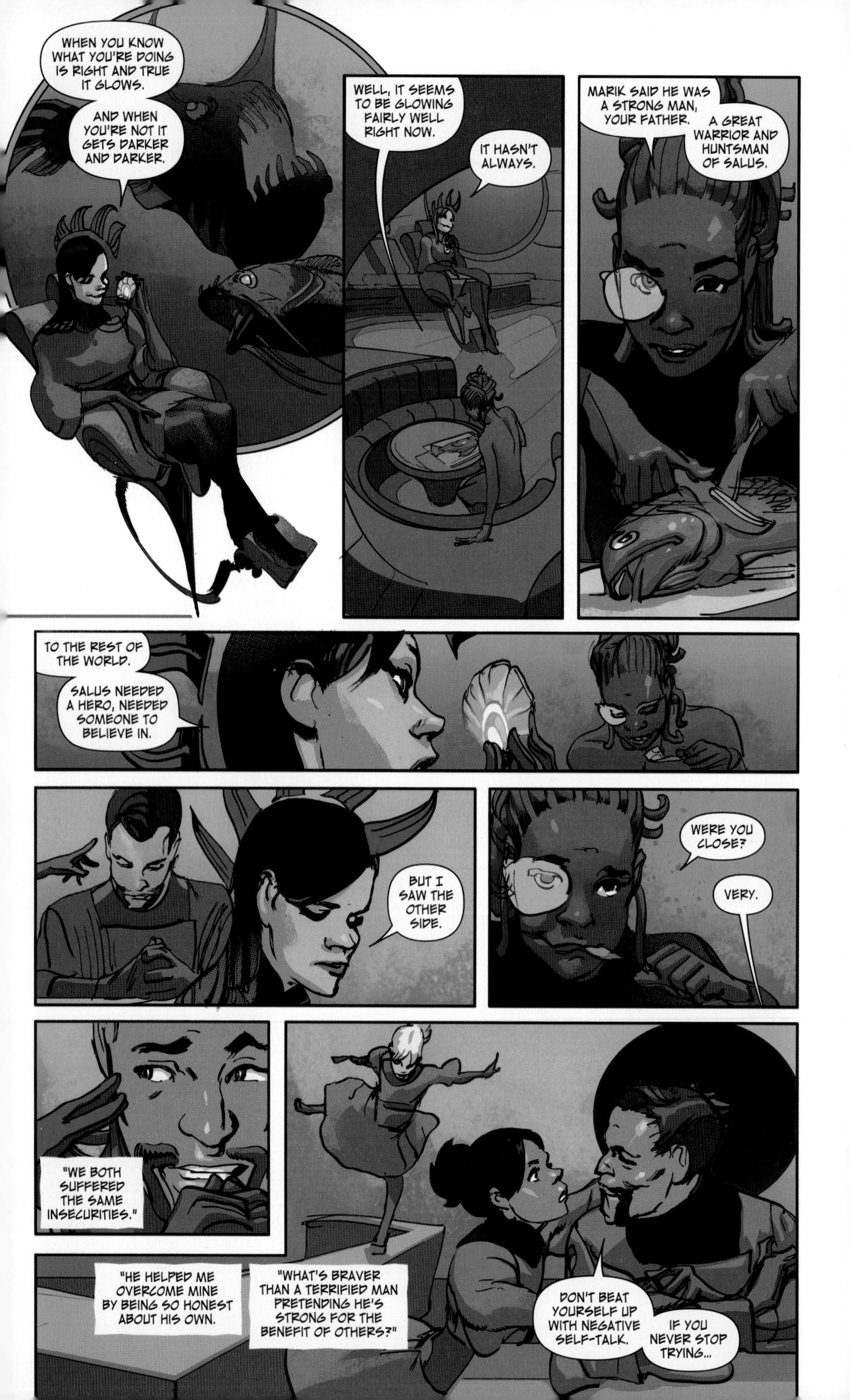
WHEN YOU KNOW WHAT YOU'RE DOING IS RIGHT AND TRUE IT GLOWS.
AND WHEN YOU'RE NOT IT GETS DARKER AND DARKER.
WELL, IT SEEMS TO BE GLOWING FAIRLY WELL RIGHT NOW.
IT HASN'T ALWAYS.
MARIK SAID HE WAS A STRONG MAN, YOUR FATHER.
A GREAT WARRIOR AND HUNTSMAN OF SALUS.
TO THE REST OF THE WORLD.
SALUS NEEDED A HERO, NEEDED SOMEONE TO BELIEVE IN.
BUT I SAW THE OTHER SIDE.
WERE YOU CLOSE?
VERY.
"WE BOTH SUFFERED THE SAME INSECURITIES."
"HE HELPED ME OVERCOME MINE BY BEING SO HONEST ABOUT HIS OWN.
"WHAT'S BRAVER THAN A TERRIFIED MAN PRETENDING HE'S STRONG FOR THE BENEFIT OF OTHERS?"
DON'T BEAT YOURSELF UP WITH NEGATIVE SELF-TALK.
IF YOU NEVER STOP TRYING...

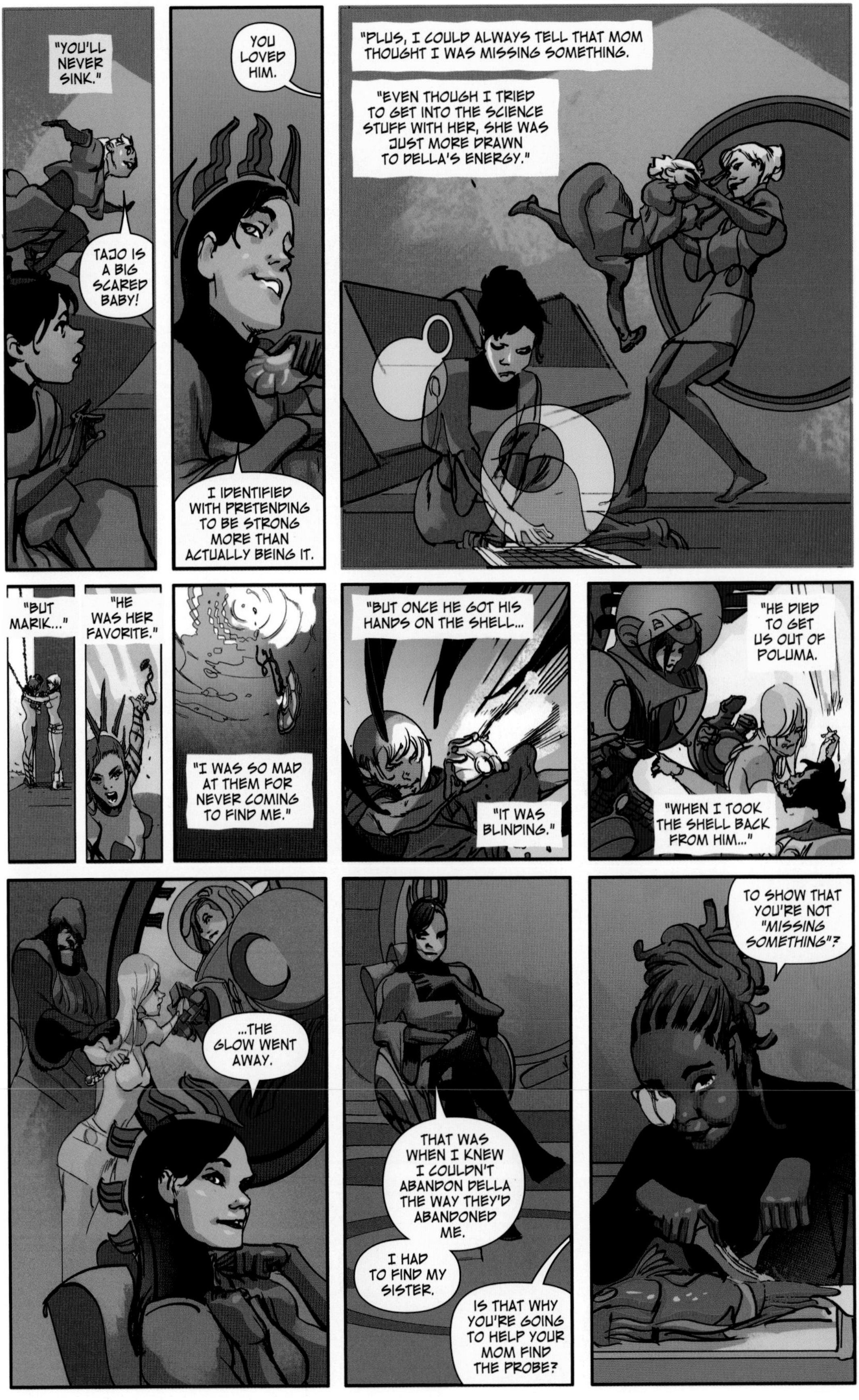
"YOU'LL NEVER SINK."
TAJO IS A BIG SCARED BABY!
YOU LOVED HIM.
I IDENTIFIED WITH PRETENDING TO BE STRONG MORE THAN ACTUALLY BEING IT.
"PLUS, I COULD ALWAYS TELL THAT MOM THOUGHT I WAS MISSING SOMETHING.
"EVEN THOUGH I TRIED TO GET INTO THE SCIENCE STUFF WITH HER, SHE WAS JUST MORE DRAWN TO DELLA'S ENERGY."
"BUT MARIK..."
"HE WAS HER FAVORITE."
"I WAS SO MAD AT THEM FOR NEVER COMING TO FIND ME."
"BUT ONCE HE GOT HIS HANDS ON THE SHELL...
"IT WAS BLINDING."
"HE DIED TO GET US OUT OF POLUMA.
"WHEN I TOOK THE SHELL BACK FROM HIM..."
...THE GLOW WENT AWAY.
THAT WAS WHEN I KNEW I COULDN'T ABANDON DELLA THE WAY THEY'D ABANDONED ME.
I HAD TO FIND MY SISTER.
IS THAT WHY YOU'RE GOING TO HELP YOUR MOM FIND THE PROBE?
TO SHOW THAT YOU'RE NOT "MISSING SOMETHING"?

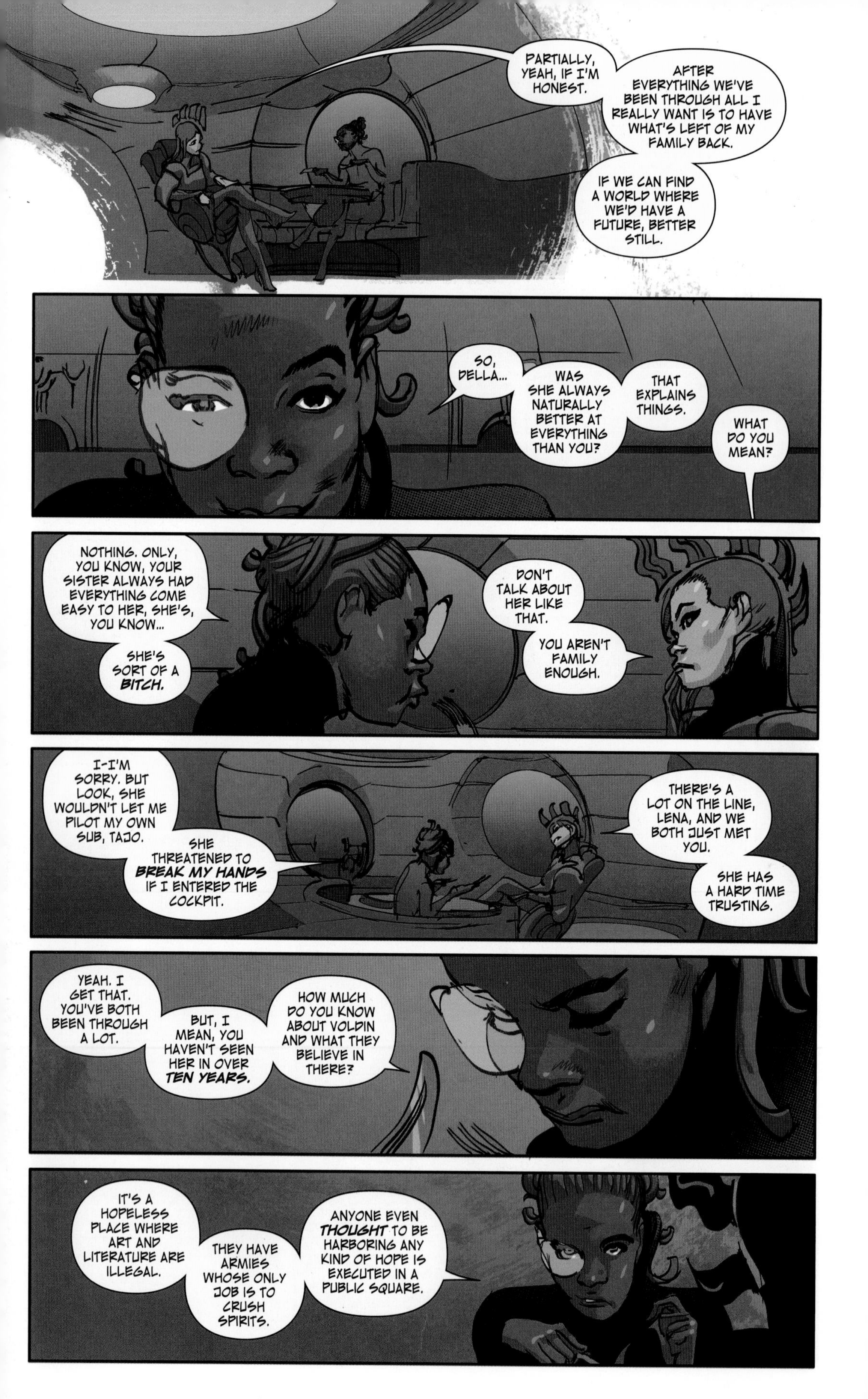
PARTIALLY, YEAH, IF I'M HONEST.
AFTER EVERYTHING WE'VE BEEN THROUGH ALL I REALLY WANT IS TO HAVE WHAT'S LEFT OF MY FAMILY BACK.
IF WE CAN FIND A WORLD WHERE WE'D HAVE A FUTURE, BETTER STILL.
SO, DELLA...
WAS SHE ALWAYS NATURALLY BETTER AT EVERYTHING THAN YOU?
THAT EXPLAINS THINGS.
WHAT DO YOU MEAN?
NOTHING. ONLY, YOU KNOW, YOUR SISTER ALWAYS HAD EVERYTHING COME EASY TO HER, SHE'S, YOU KNOW...
SHE'S SORT OF A ***BITCH.***
DON'T TALK ABOUT HER LIKE THAT.
YOU AREN'T FAMILY ENOUGH.
I-I'M SORRY. BUT LOOK, SHE WOULDN'T LET ME PILOT MY OWN SUB, TAJO.
SHE THREATENED TO ***BREAK MY HANDS*** IF I ENTERED THE COCKPIT.
THERE'S A LOT ON THE LINE, LENA, AND WE BOTH JUST MET YOU.
SHE HAS A HARD TIME TRUSTING.
YEAH. I GET THAT. YOU'VE BOTH BEEN THROUGH A LOT.
BUT, I MEAN, YOU HAVEN'T SEEN HER IN OVER ***TEN YEARS.***
HOW MUCH DO YOU KNOW ABOUT VOLDIN AND WHAT THEY BELIEVE IN THERE?
IT'S A HOPELESS PLACE WHERE ART AND LITERATURE ARE ILLEGAL.
THEY HAVE ARMIES WHOSE ONLY JOB IS TO CRUSH SPIRITS.
ANYONE EVEN ***THOUGHT*** TO BE HARBORING ANY KIND OF HOPE IS EXECUTED IN A PUBLIC SQUARE.

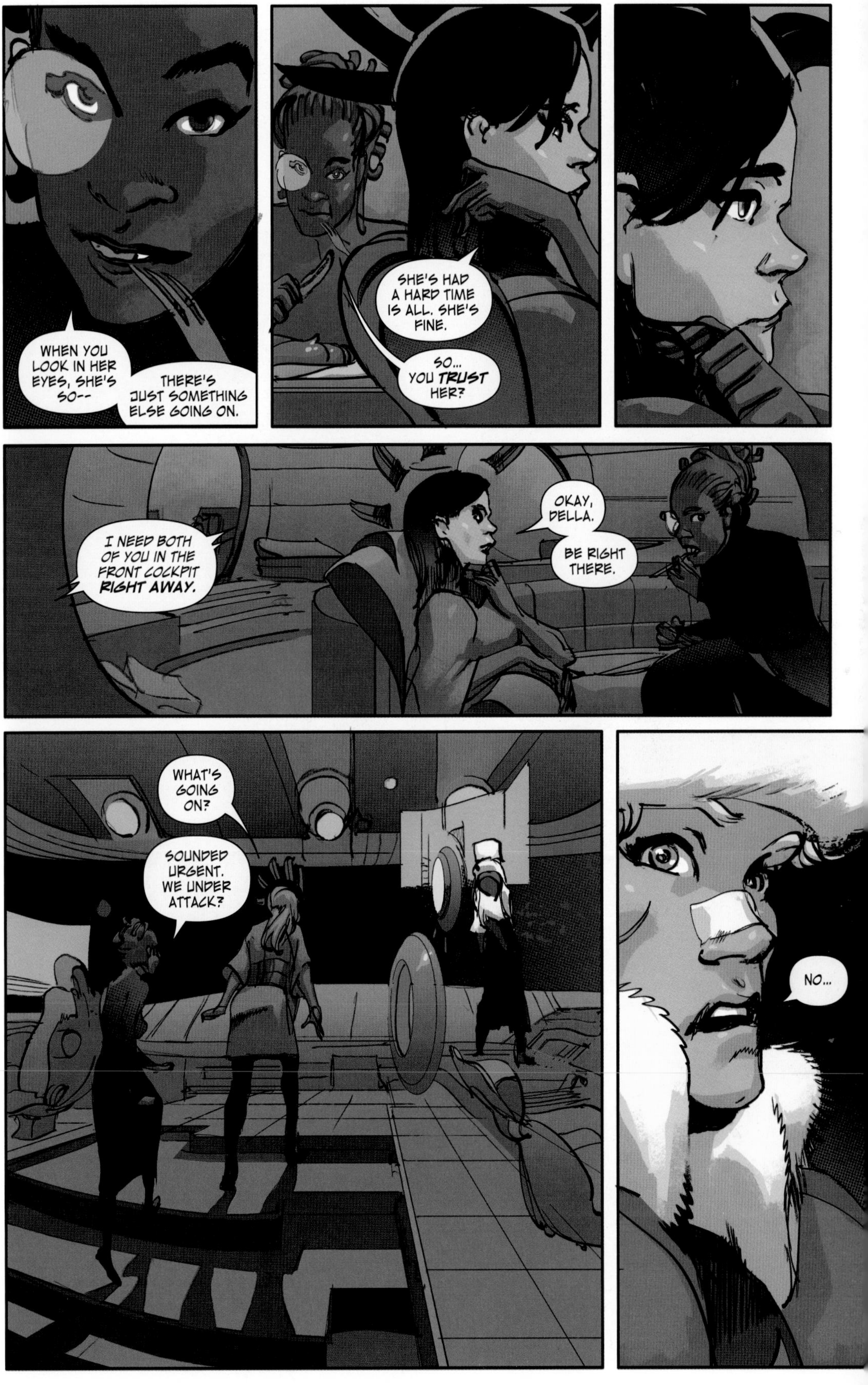

WHEN YOU LOOK IN HER EYES, SHE'S SO--
THERE'S JUST SOMETHING ELSE GOING ON.
SHE'S HAD A HARD TIME IS ALL. SHE'S FINE.
SO... YOU TRUST HER?
I NEED BOTH OF YOU IN THE FRONT COCKPIT RIGHT AWAY.
OKAY, DELLA.
BE RIGHT THERE.
WHAT'S GOING ON?
SOUNDED URGENT. WE UNDER ATTACK?
NO...

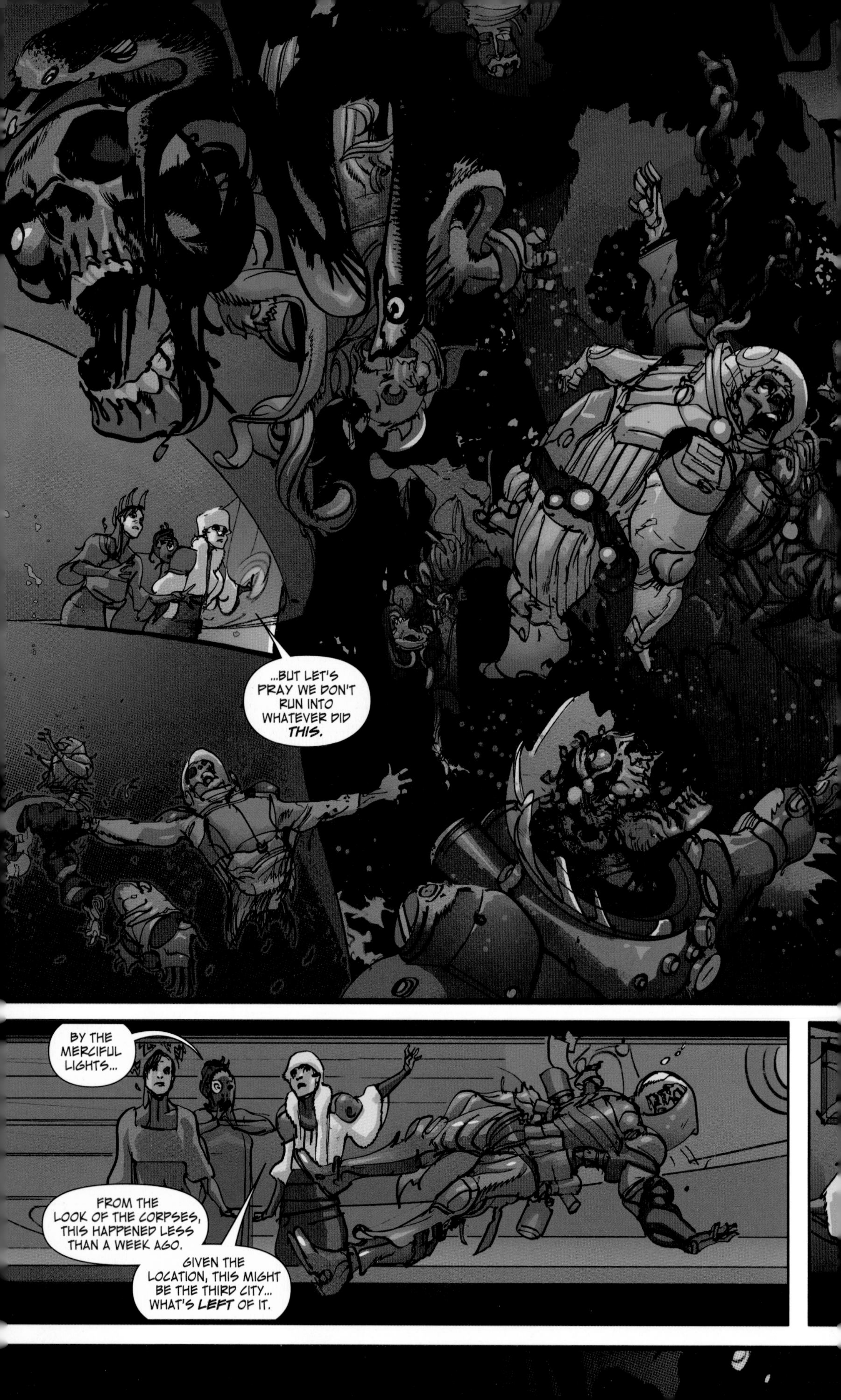
...BUT LET'S PRAY WE DON'T RUN INTO WHATEVER DID *THIS.*
BY THE MERCIFUL LIGHTS...
FROM THE LOOK OF THE CORPSES, THIS HAPPENED LESS THAN A WEEK AGO.
GIVEN THE LOCATION, THIS MIGHT BE THE THIRD CITY... WHAT'S *LEFT* OF IT.

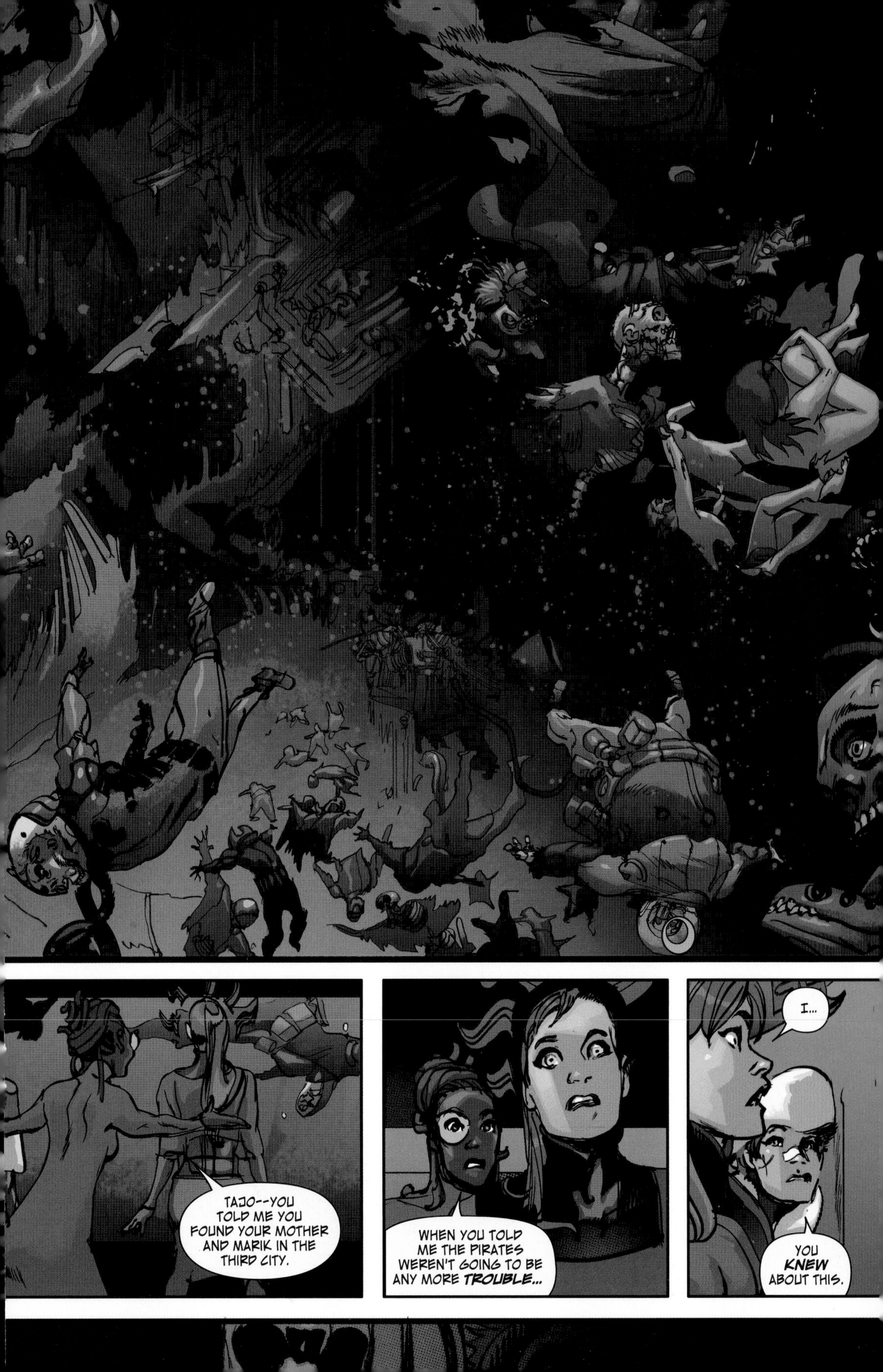
TAJO--YOU TOLD ME YOU FOUND YOUR MOTHER AND MARIK IN THE THIRD CITY.
WHEN YOU TOLD ME THE PIRATES WEREN'T GOING TO BE ANY MORE TROUBLE...
I...
YOU KNEW ABOUT THIS.

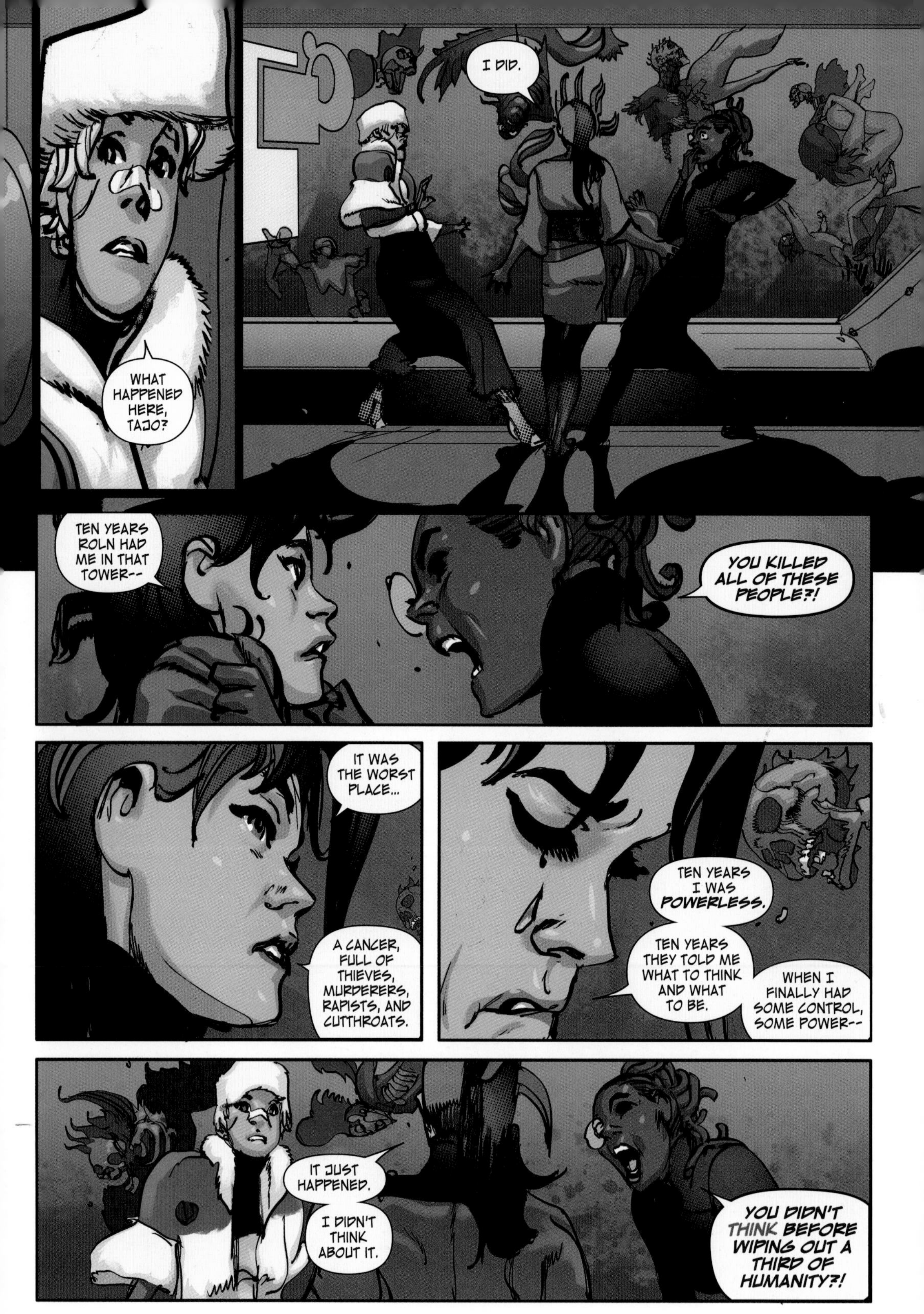
WHAT HAPPENED HERE, TAJO?
I DID.
TEN YEARS ROLN HAD ME IN THAT TOWER--
YOU KILLED ALL OF THESE PEOPLE?!
IT WAS THE WORST PLACE...
A CANCER, FULL OF THIEVES, MURDERERS, RAPISTS, AND CUTTHROATS.
TEN YEARS I WAS POWERLESS.
TEN YEARS THEY TOLD ME WHAT TO THINK AND WHAT TO BE.
WHEN I FINALLY HAD SOME CONTROL, SOME POWER--
IT JUST HAPPENED.
I DIDN'T THINK ABOUT IT.
YOU DIDN'T THINK BEFORE WIPING OUT A THIRD OF HUMANITY?!

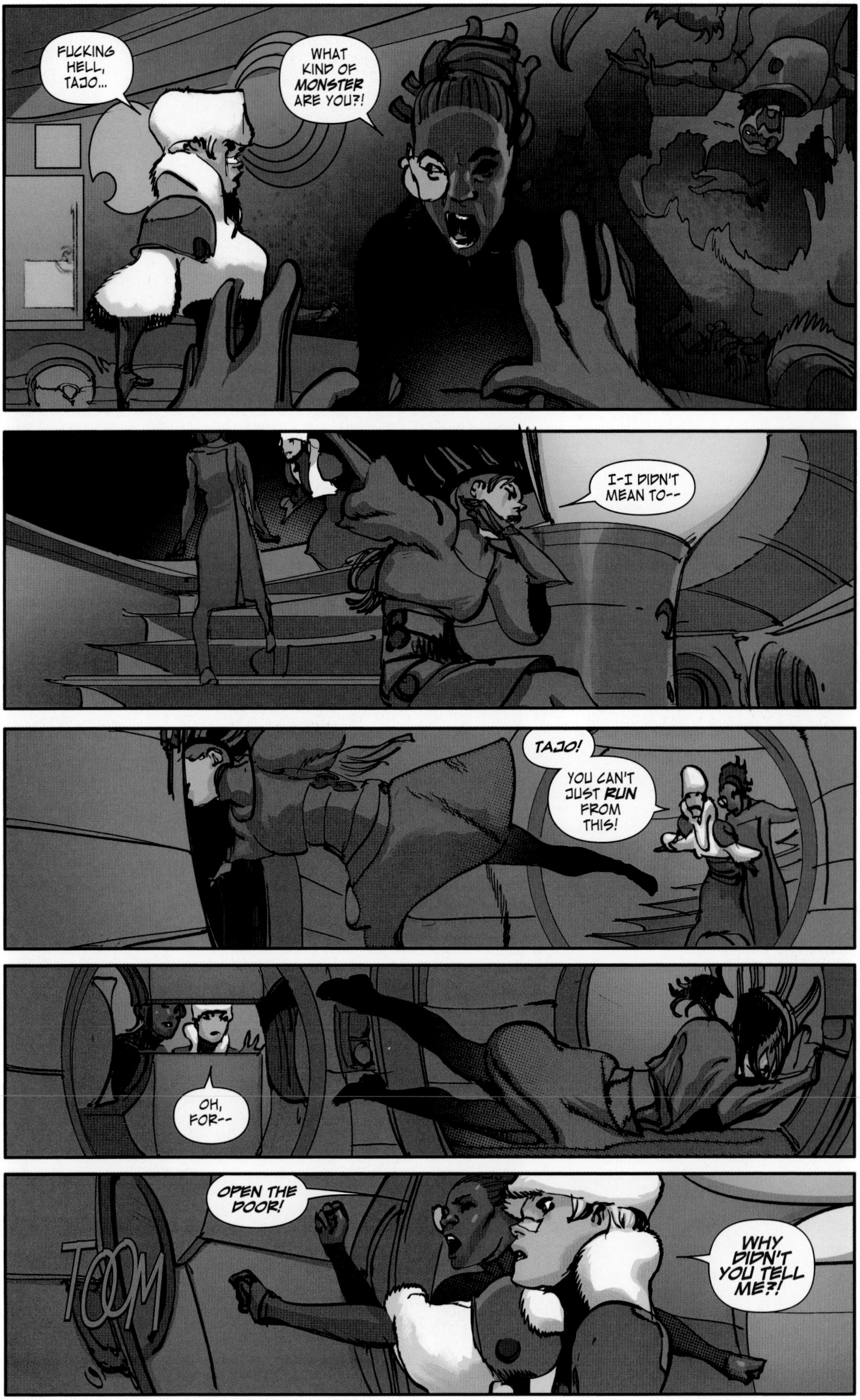
FUCKING HELL, TAJO...
WHAT KIND OF MONSTER ARE YOU?!
I-I DIDN'T MEAN TO--
TAJO!
YOU CAN'T JUST RUN FROM THIS!
OH, FOR--
OPEN THE DOOR!
TOOM
WHY DIDN'T YOU TELL ME?!

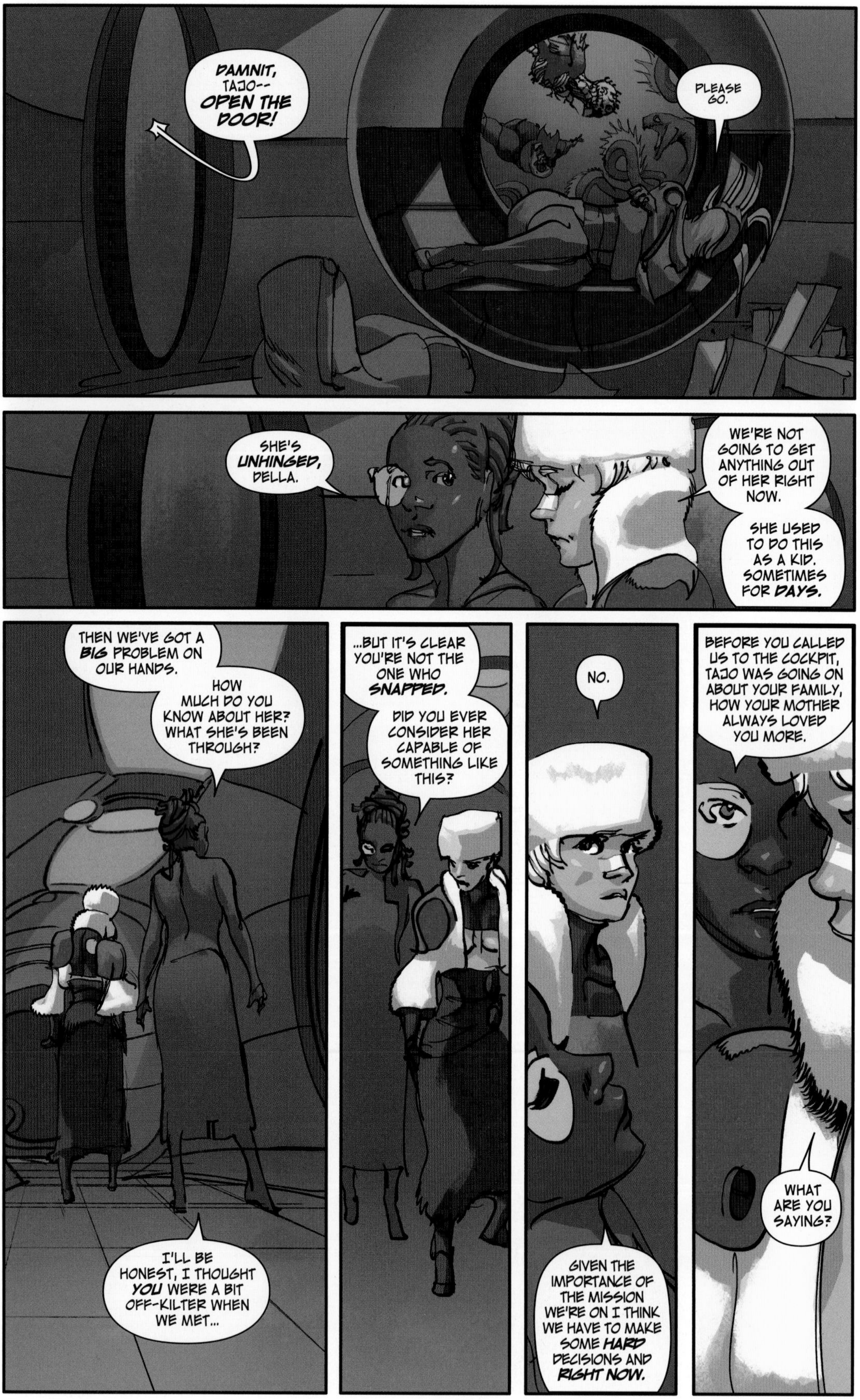
DAMNIT, TAJO-- OPEN THE DOOR!
PLEASE GO.
SHE'S UNHINGED, DELLA.
WE'RE NOT GOING TO GET ANYTHING OUT OF HER RIGHT NOW.
SHE USED TO DO THIS AS A KID. SOMETIMES FOR DAYS.
THEN WE'VE GOT A BIG PROBLEM ON OUR HANDS.
HOW MUCH DO YOU KNOW ABOUT HER? WHAT SHE'S BEEN THROUGH?
I'LL BE HONEST, I THOUGHT YOU WERE A BIT OFF-KILTER WHEN WE MET...
...BUT IT'S CLEAR YOU'RE NOT THE ONE WHO SNAPPED.
DID YOU EVER CONSIDER HER CAPABLE OF SOMETHING LIKE THIS?
NO.
GIVEN THE IMPORTANCE OF THE MISSION WE'RE ON I THINK WE HAVE TO MAKE SOME HARD DECISIONS AND RIGHT NOW.
BEFORE YOU CALLED US TO THE COCKPIT, TAJO WAS GOING ON ABOUT YOUR FAMILY, HOW YOUR MOTHER ALWAYS LOVED YOU MORE.
WHAT ARE YOU SAYING?

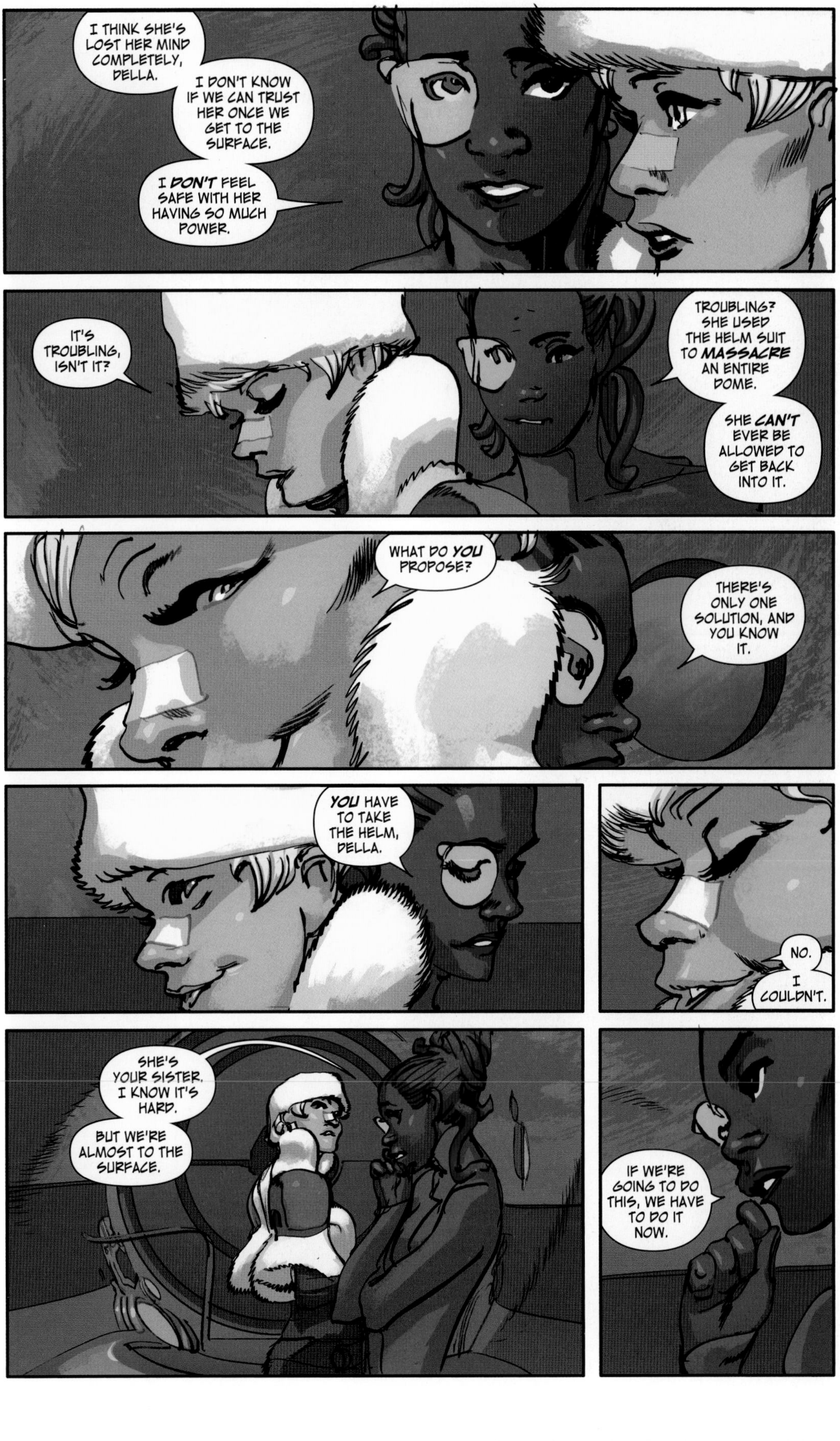
I THINK SHE'S LOST HER MIND COMPLETELY, DELLA.
I DON'T KNOW IF WE CAN TRUST HER ONCE WE GET TO THE SURFACE.
I DON'T FEEL SAFE WITH HER HAVING SO MUCH POWER.
IT'S TROUBLING, ISN'T IT?
TROUBLING? SHE USED THE HELM SUIT TO MASSACRE AN ENTIRE DOME.
SHE CAN'T EVER BE ALLOWED TO GET BACK INTO IT.
WHAT DO YOU PROPOSE?
THERE'S ONLY ONE SOLUTION, AND YOU KNOW IT.
YOU HAVE TO TAKE THE HELM, DELLA.
NO.
I COULDN'T.
SHE'S YOUR SISTER. I KNOW IT'S HARD.
BUT WE'RE ALMOST TO THE SURFACE.
IF WE'RE GOING TO DO THIS, WE HAVE TO DO IT NOW.

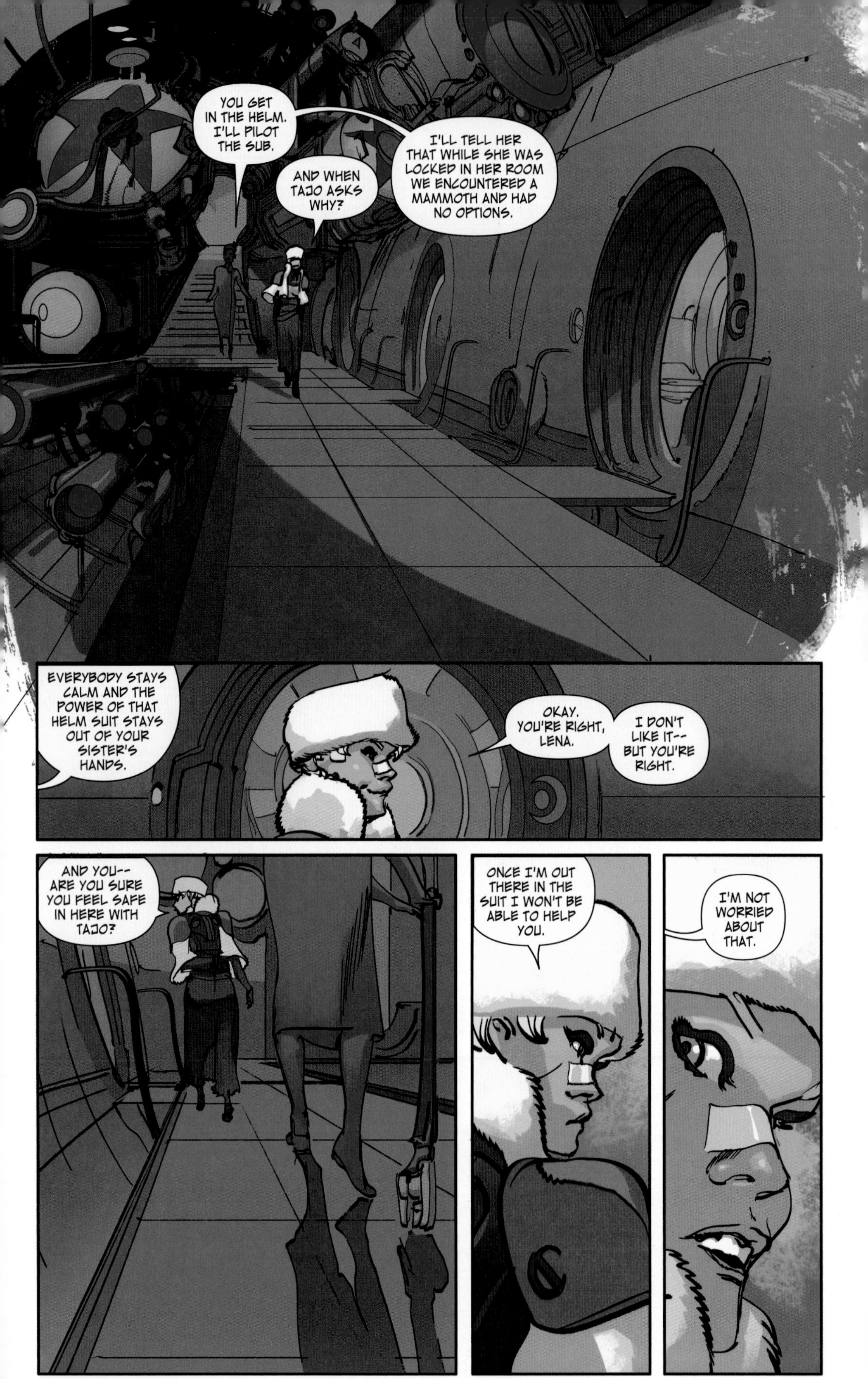
YOU GET IN THE HELM. I'LL PILOT THE SUB.
AND WHEN TAJO ASKS WHY?
I'LL TELL HER THAT WHILE SHE WAS LOCKED IN HER ROOM WE ENCOUNTERED A MAMMOTH AND HAD NO OPTIONS.
EVERYBODY STAYS CALM AND THE POWER OF THAT HELM SUIT STAYS OUT OF YOUR SISTER'S HANDS.
OKAY. YOU'RE RIGHT, LENA.
I DON'T LIKE IT-- BUT YOU'RE RIGHT.
AND YOU-- ARE YOU SURE YOU FEEL SAFE IN HERE WITH TAJO?
ONCE I'M OUT THERE IN THE SUIT I WON'T BE ABLE TO HELP YOU.
I'M NOT WORRIED ABOUT THAT.

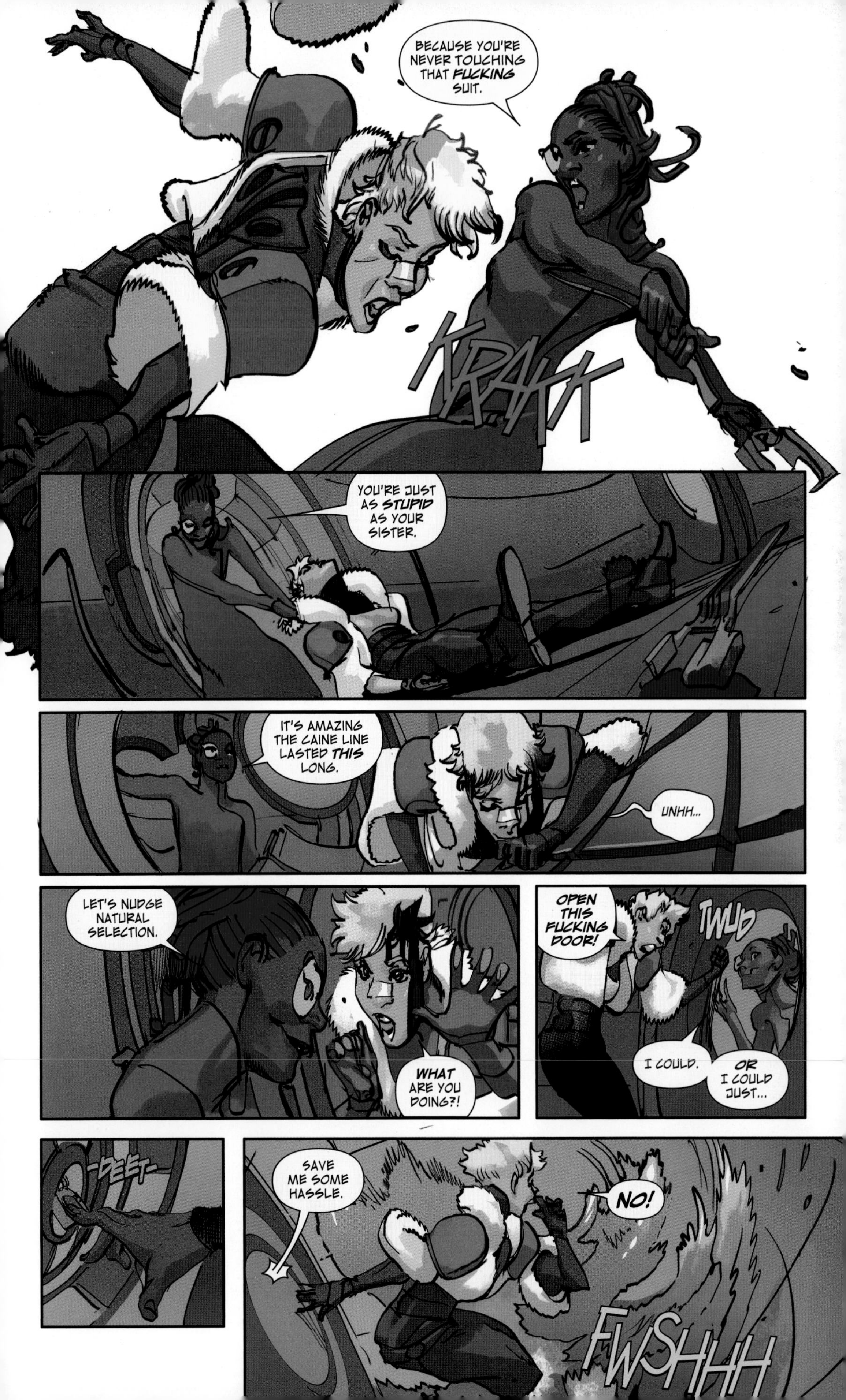
BECAUSE YOU'RE NEVER TOUCHING THAT FUCKING SUIT.
KRAKK
YOU'RE JUST AS STUPID AS YOUR SISTER.
IT'S AMAZING THE CAINE LINE LASTED THIS LONG.
UNHH...
LET'S NUDGE NATURAL SELECTION.
WHAT ARE YOU DOING?!
OPEN THIS FUCKING DOOR!
TWUD
I COULD.
OR I COULD JUST...
-DEET-
SAVE ME SOME HASSLE.
NO!
FWSHHH

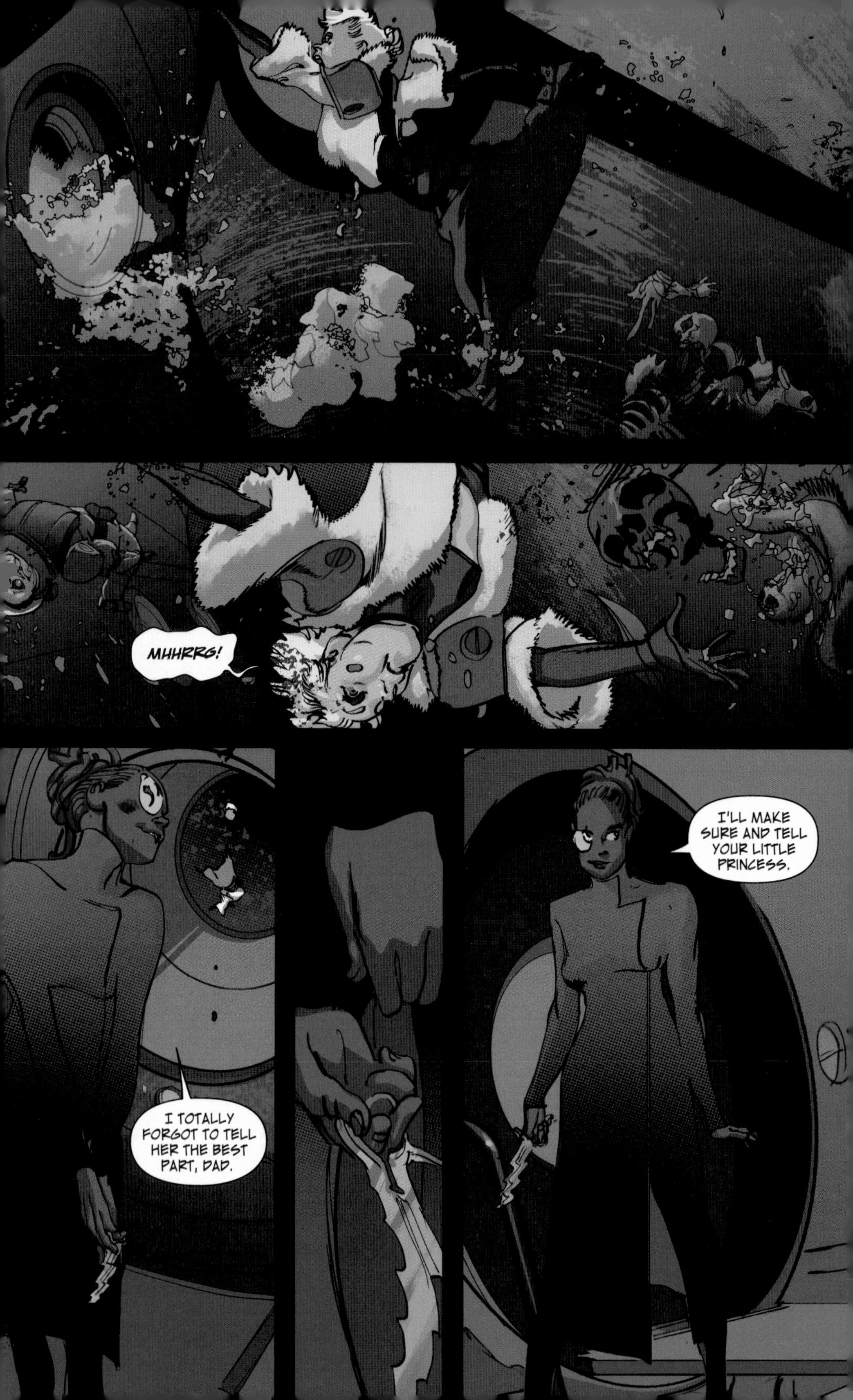
MHHRRG!
I TOTALLY FORGOT TO TELL HER THE BEST PART, DAD.
I'LL MAKE SURE AND TELL YOUR LITTLE PRINCESS.

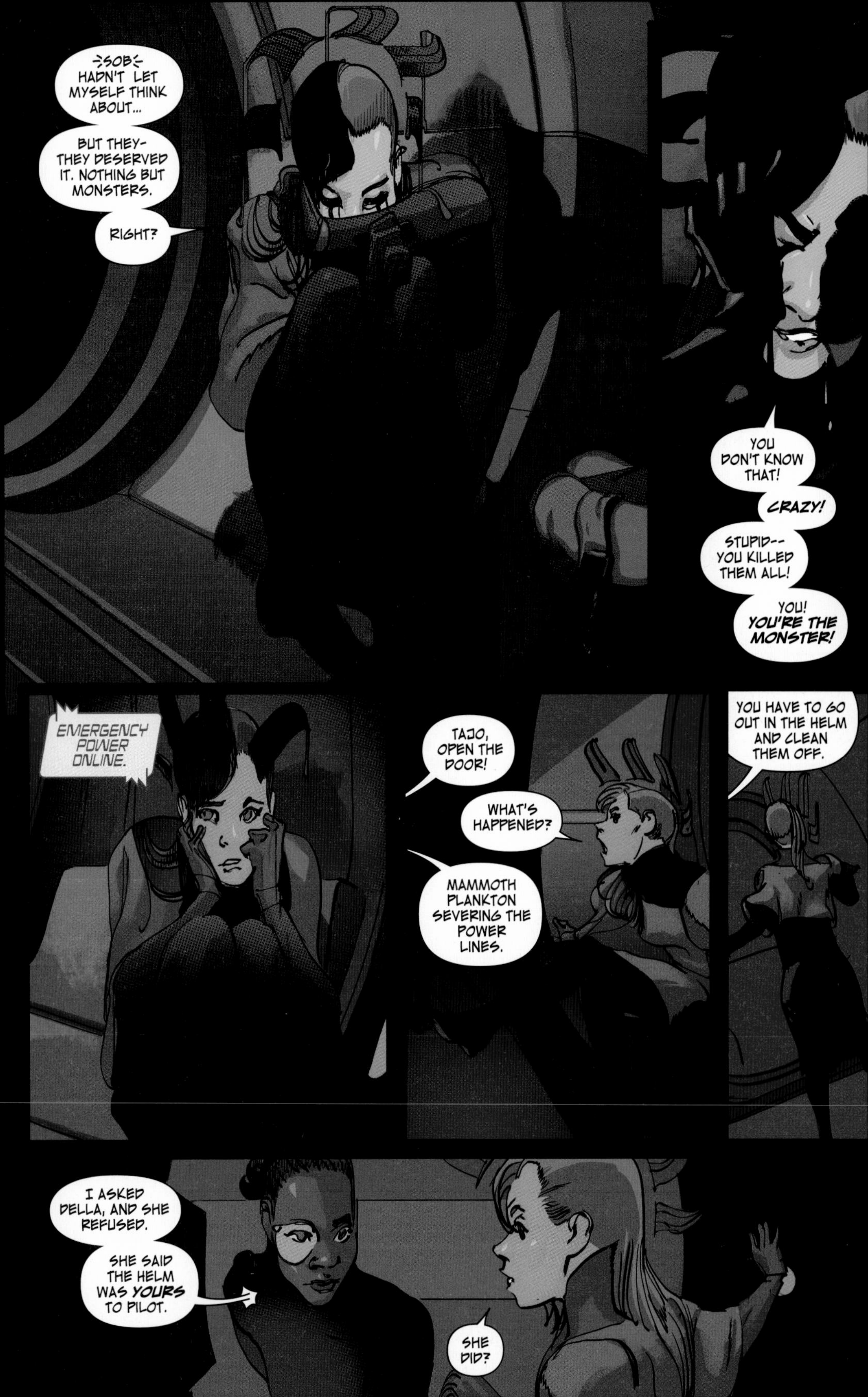

=SOB=
HADN'T LET MYSELF THINK ABOUT...
BUT THEY- THEY DESERVED IT. NOTHING BUT MONSTERS.
RIGHT?
YOU DON'T KNOW THAT!
CRAZY!
STUPID-- YOU KILLED THEM ALL!
YOU! YOU'RE THE MONSTER!
EMERGENCY POWER ONLINE.
TAJO, OPEN THE DOOR!
WHAT'S HAPPENED?
MAMMOTH PLANKTON SEVERING THE POWER LINES.
YOU HAVE TO GO OUT IN THE HELM AND CLEAN THEM OFF.
I ASKED DELLA, AND SHE REFUSED.
SHE SAID THE HELM WAS YOURS TO PILOT.
SHE DID?

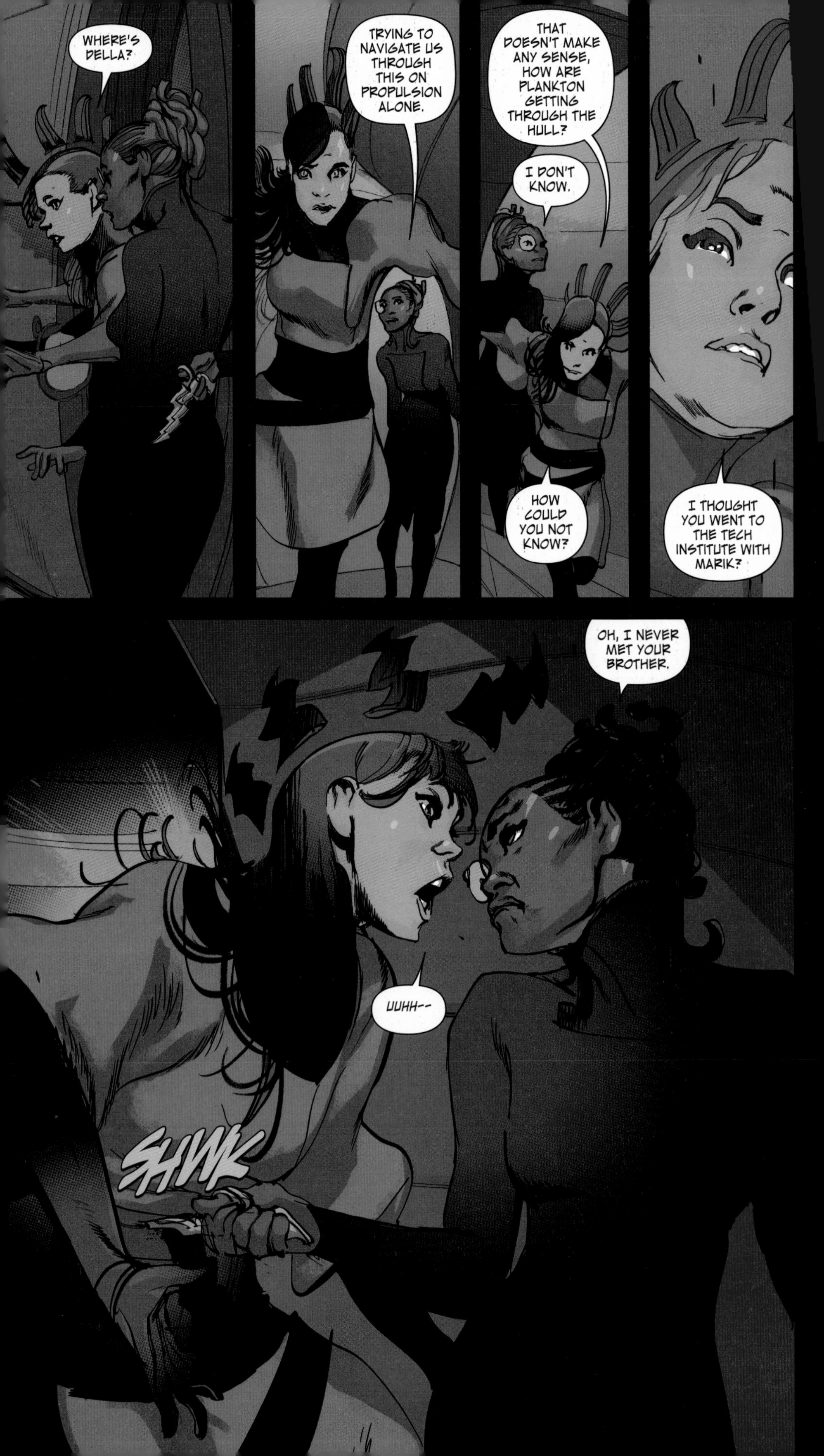
WHERE'S DELLA?
TRYING TO NAVIGATE US THROUGH THIS ON PROPULSION ALONE.
THAT DOESN'T MAKE ANY SENSE, HOW ARE PLANKTON GETTING THROUGH THE HULL?
I DON'T KNOW.
HOW COULD YOU NOT KNOW?
I THOUGHT YOU WENT TO THE TECH INSTITUTE WITH MARIK?
OH, I NEVER MET YOUR BROTHER.
UUHH--
SHNK

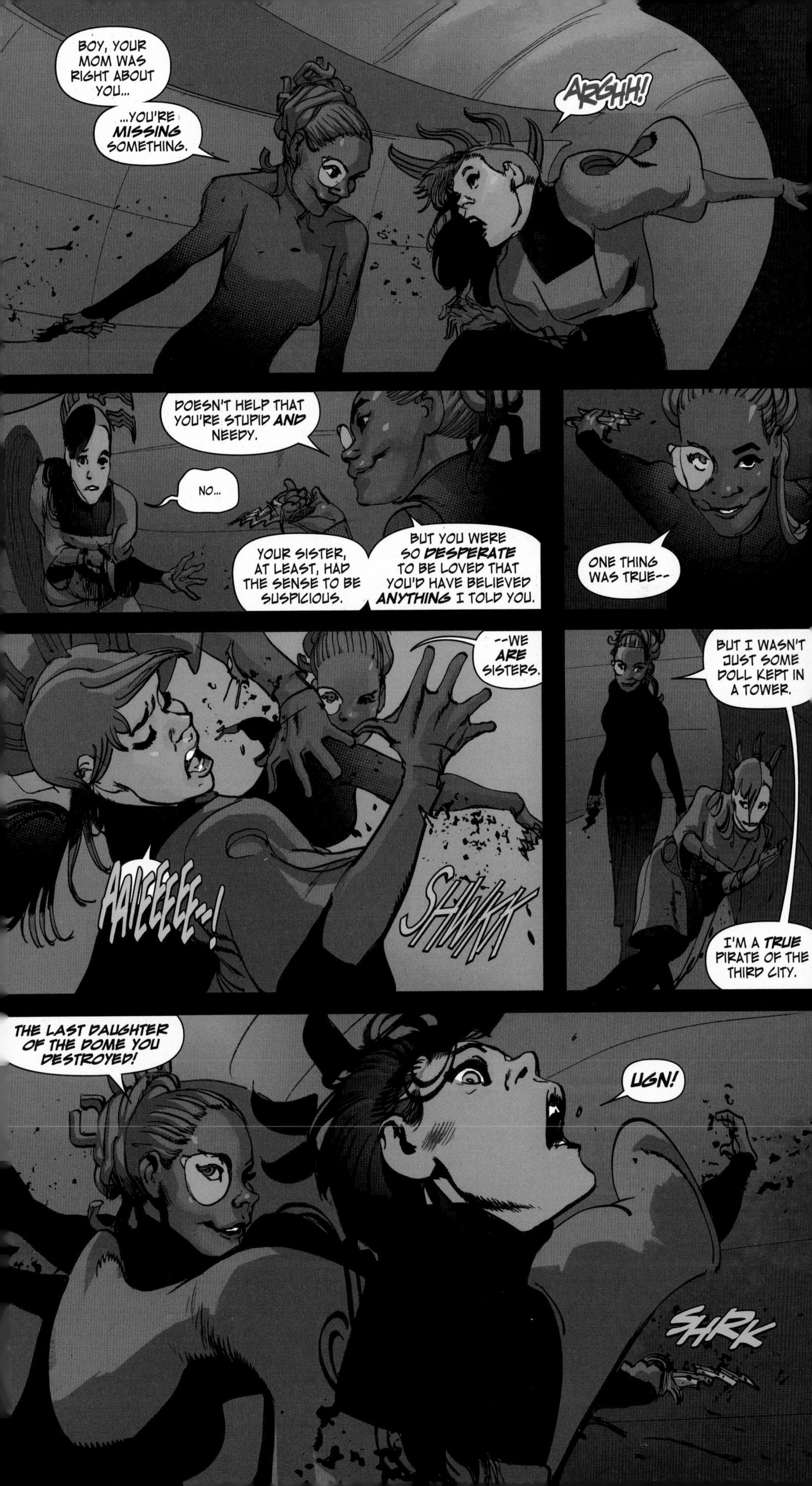
BOY, YOUR MOM WAS RIGHT ABOUT YOU...
...YOU'RE **MISSING** SOMETHING.
ARGHH!
DOESN'T HELP THAT YOU'RE STUPID **AND** NEEDY.
NO...
YOUR SISTER, AT LEAST, HAD THE SENSE TO BE SUSPICIOUS.
BUT YOU WERE SO **DESPERATE** TO BE LOVED THAT YOU'D HAVE BELIEVED **ANYTHING** I TOLD YOU.
ONE THING WAS TRUE--
--WE **ARE** SISTERS.
AAIEEEEEE--!
SHUKK
BUT I WASN'T JUST SOME DOLL KEPT IN A TOWER.
I'M A **TRUE** PIRATE OF THE THIRD CITY.
THE LAST DAUGHTER OF THE DOME YOU DESTROYED!
UGN!
SHRK

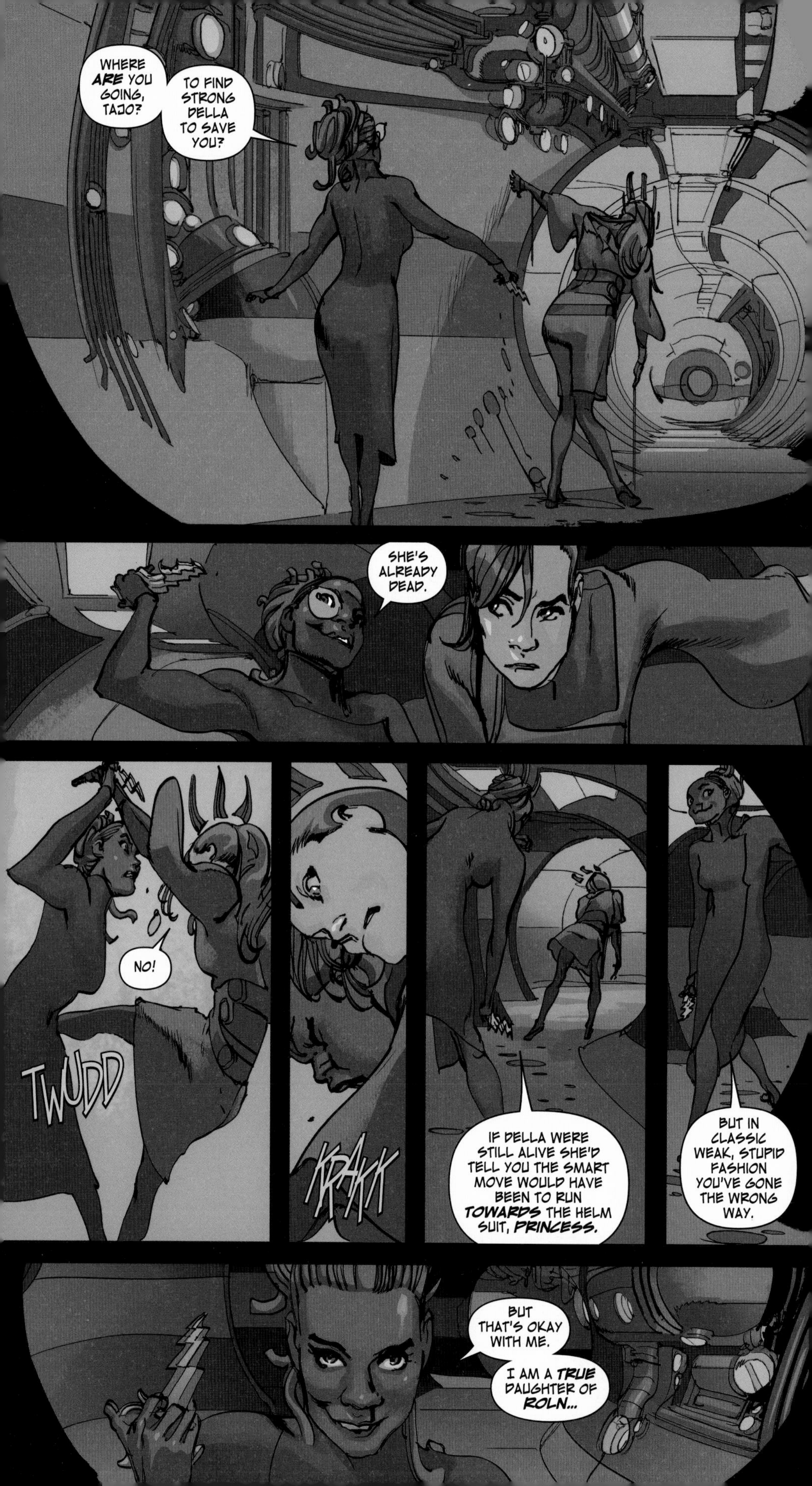
WHERE ARE YOU GOING, TAJO?
TO FIND STRONG DELLA TO SAVE YOU?
SHE'S ALREADY DEAD.
NO!
TWUDD
KRAKK
IF DELLA WERE STILL ALIVE SHE'D TELL YOU THE SMART MOVE WOULD HAVE BEEN TO RUN TOWARDS THE HELM SUIT, PRINCESS.
BUT IN CLASSIC WEAK, STUPID FASHION YOU'VE GONE THE WRONG WAY.
BUT THAT'S OKAY WITH ME.
I AM A TRUE DAUGHTER OF ROLN...

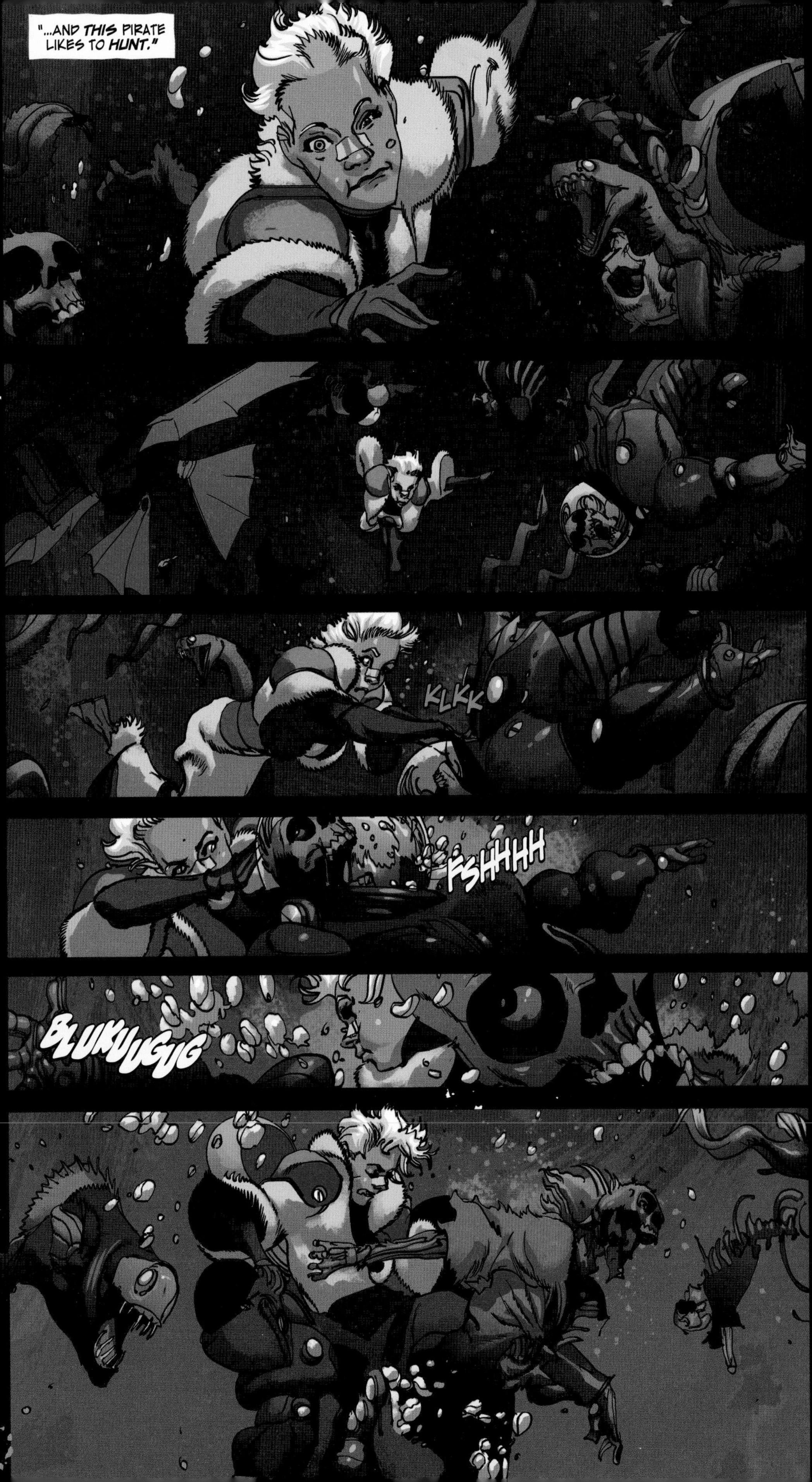
"...AND THIS PIRATE LIKES TO HUNT."
KLKK
FSHHHH
BLUKUUGUG

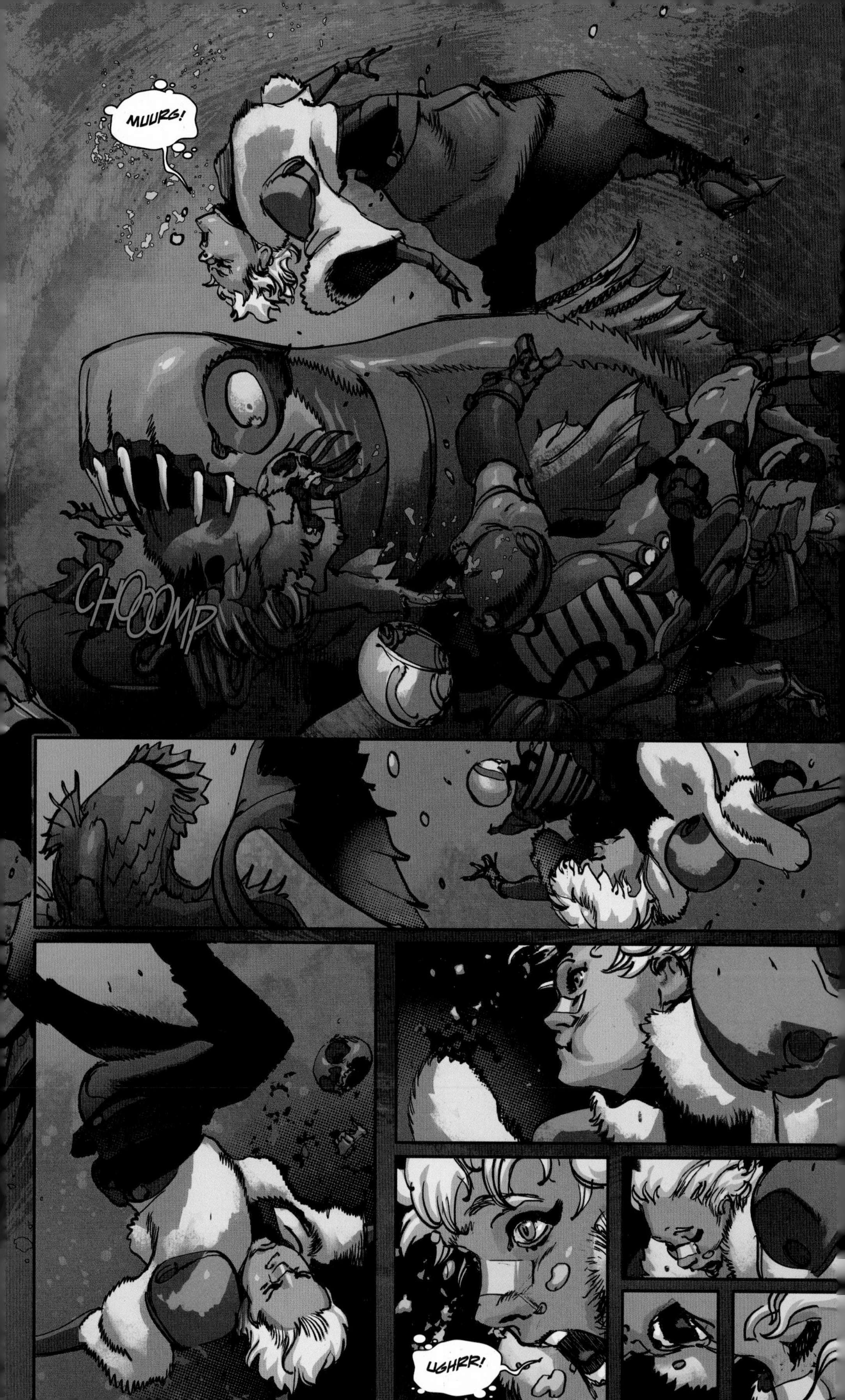
MUURG!
CHOOOMP
UGHRR!

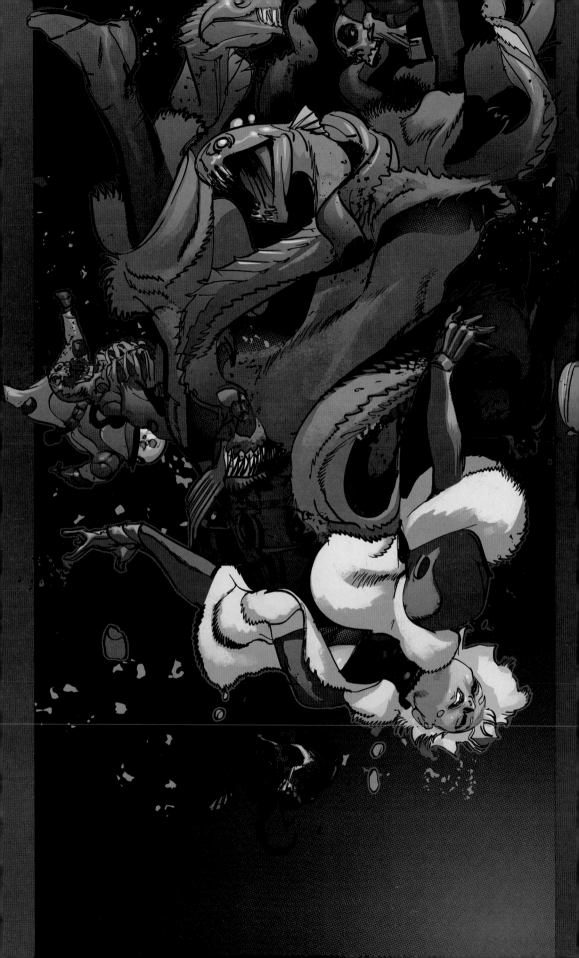

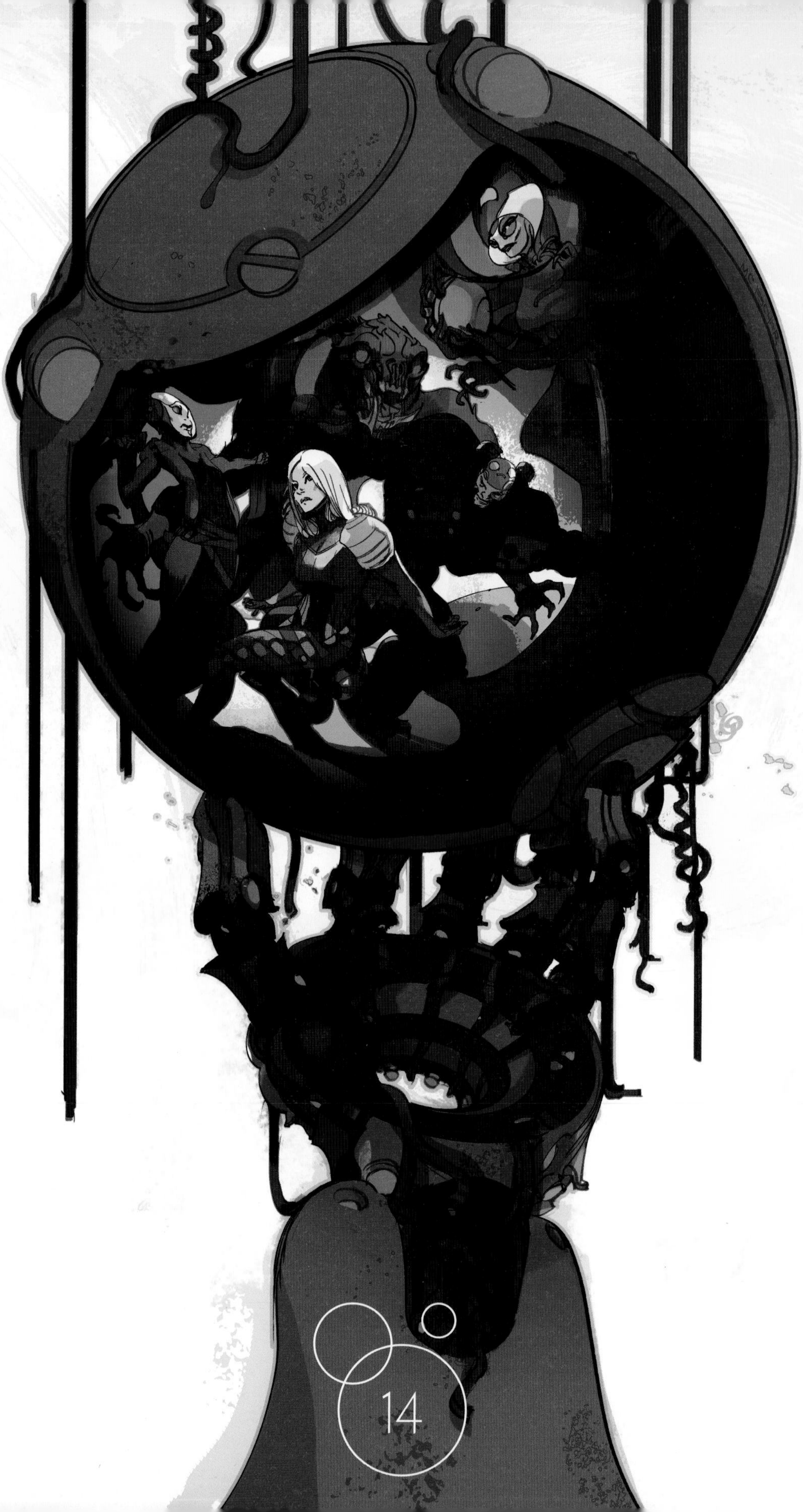
14

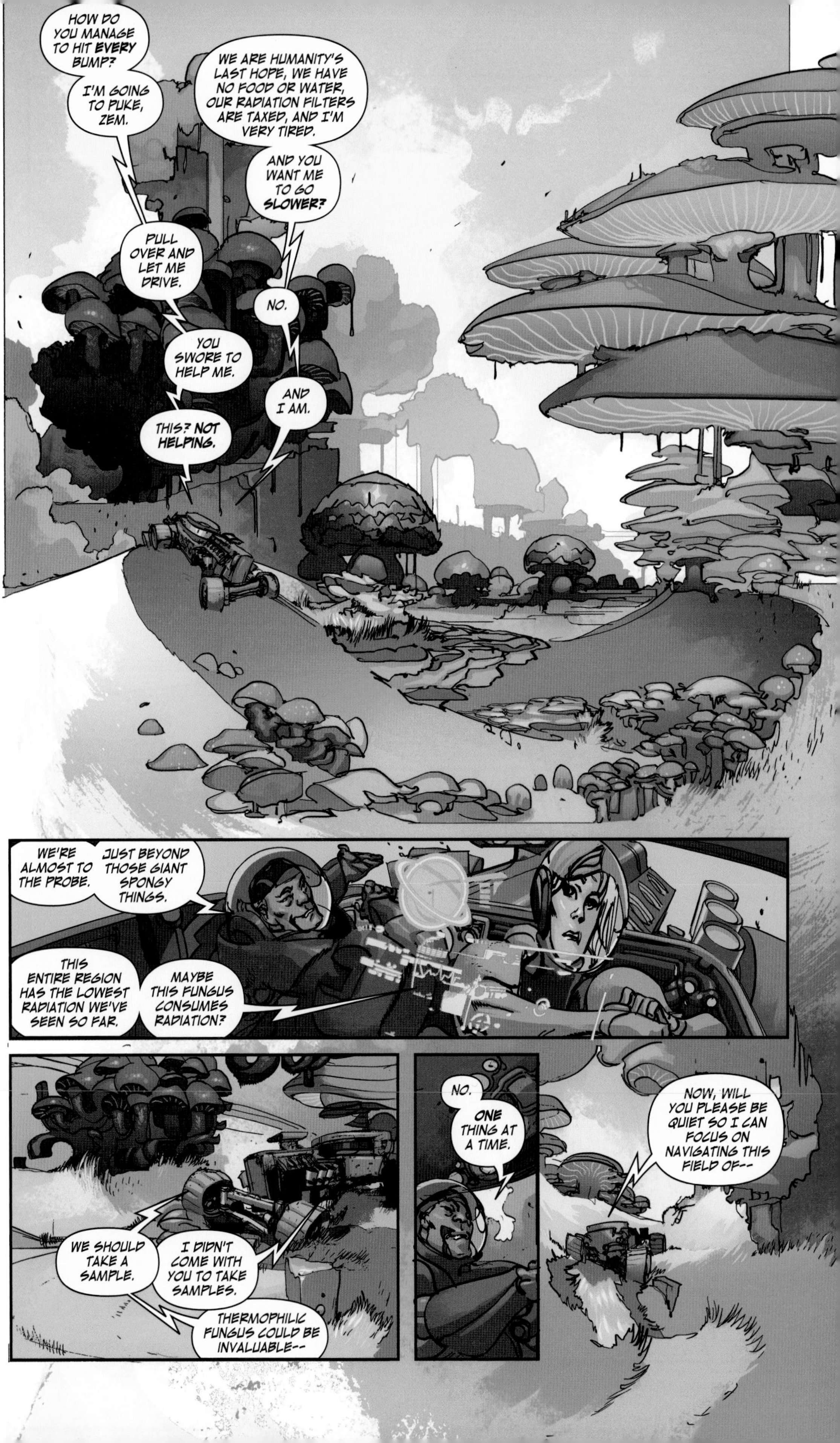
HOW DO YOU MANAGE TO HIT EVERY BUMP?
I'M GOING TO PUKE, ZEM.
WE ARE HUMANITY'S LAST HOPE, WE HAVE NO FOOD OR WATER, OUR RADIATION FILTERS ARE TAXED, AND I'M VERY TIRED.
AND YOU WANT ME TO GO SLOWER?
PULL OVER AND LET ME DRIVE.
NO.
YOU SWORE TO HELP ME.
AND I AM.
THIS? NOT HELPING.
WE'RE ALMOST TO THE PROBE.
JUST BEYOND THOSE GIANT SPONGY THINGS.
THIS ENTIRE REGION HAS THE LOWEST RADIATION WE'VE SEEN SO FAR.
MAYBE THIS FUNGUS CONSUMES RADIATION?
WE SHOULD TAKE A SAMPLE.
I DIDN'T COME WITH YOU TO TAKE SAMPLES.
THERMOPHILIC FUNGUS COULD BE INVALUABLE--
NO.
ONE THING AT A TIME.
NOW, WILL YOU PLEASE BE QUIET SO I CAN FOCUS ON NAVIGATING THIS FIELD OF--

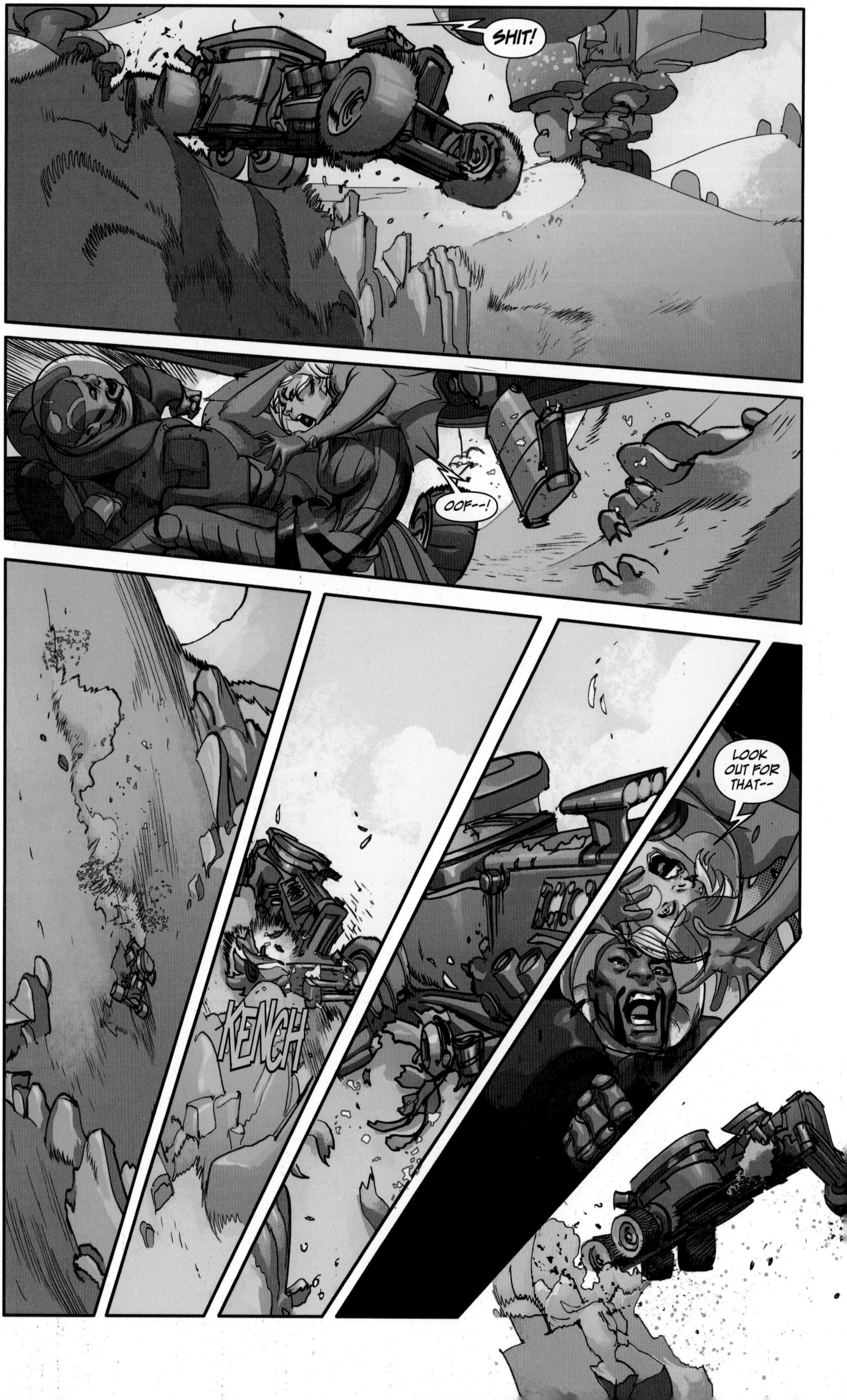
SHIT!
OOF--!
KENCH
LOOK OUT FOR THAT--

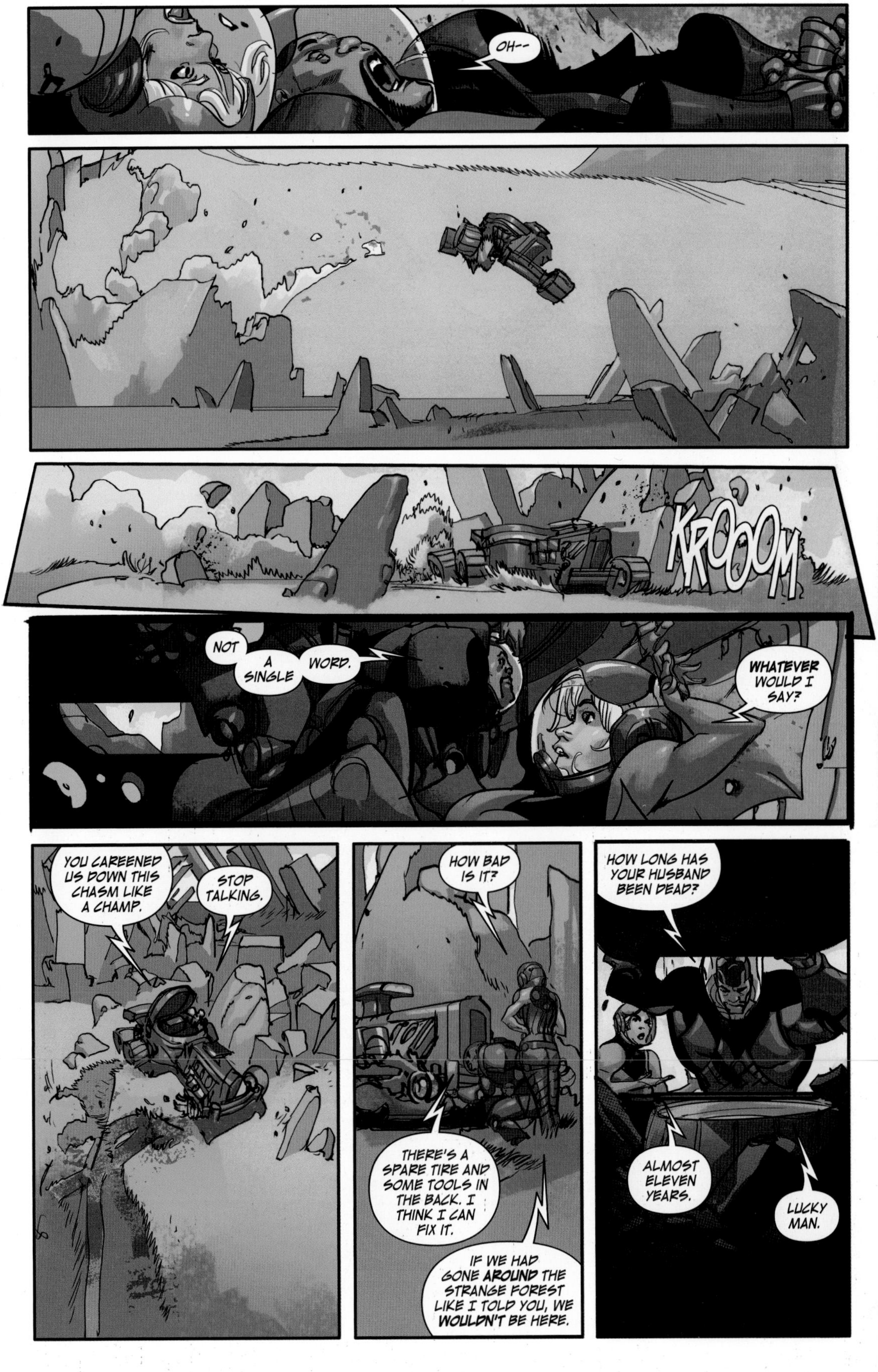
OH--
KROOOM
NOT A SINGLE WORD.
WHATEVER WOULD I SAY?
YOU CAREENED US DOWN THIS CHASM LIKE A CHAMP.
STOP TALKING.
HOW BAD IS IT?
THERE'S A SPARE TIRE AND SOME TOOLS IN THE BACK. I THINK I CAN FIX IT.
IF WE HAD GONE AROUND THE STRANGE FOREST LIKE I TOLD YOU, WE WOULDN'T BE HERE.
HOW LONG HAS YOUR HUSBAND BEEN DEAD?
ALMOST ELEVEN YEARS.
LUCKY MAN.

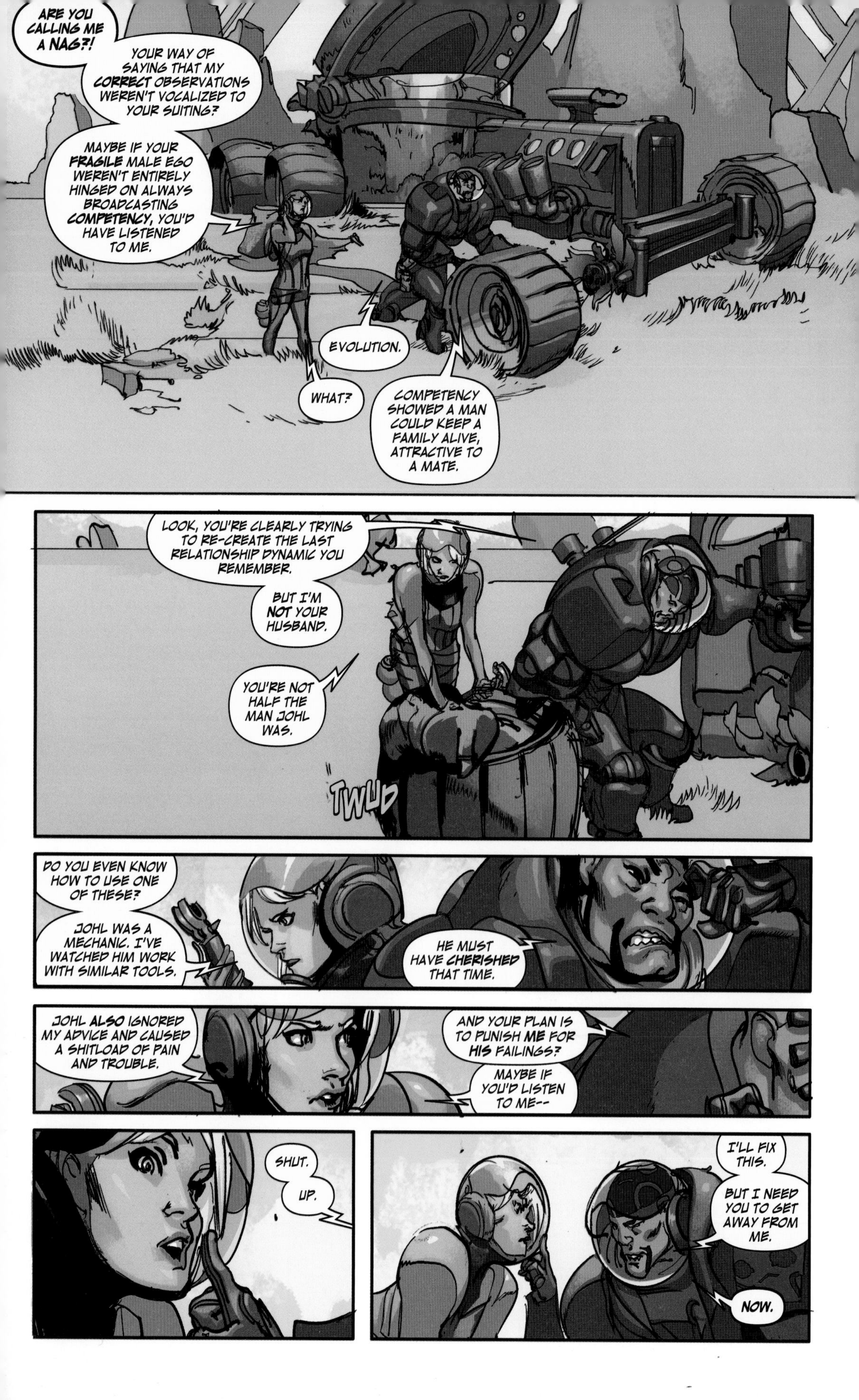
ARE YOU CALLING ME A NAG?!
YOUR WAY OF SAYING THAT MY CORRECT OBSERVATIONS WEREN'T VOCALIZED TO YOUR SUITING?
MAYBE IF YOUR FRAGILE MALE EGO WEREN'T ENTIRELY HINGED ON ALWAYS BROADCASTING COMPETENCY, YOU'D HAVE LISTENED TO ME.
EVOLUTION.
WHAT?
COMPETENCY SHOWED A MAN COULD KEEP A FAMILY ALIVE, ATTRACTIVE TO A MATE.
LOOK, YOU'RE CLEARLY TRYING TO RE-CREATE THE LAST RELATIONSHIP DYNAMIC YOU REMEMBER.
BUT I'M NOT YOUR HUSBAND.
YOU'RE NOT HALF THE MAN JOHL WAS.
TWUD
DO YOU EVEN KNOW HOW TO USE ONE OF THESE?
JOHL WAS A MECHANIC. I'VE WATCHED HIM WORK WITH SIMILAR TOOLS.
HE MUST HAVE CHERISHED THAT TIME.
JOHL ALSO IGNORED MY ADVICE AND CAUSED A SHITLOAD OF PAIN AND TROUBLE.
AND YOUR PLAN IS TO PUNISH ME FOR HIS FAILINGS?
MAYBE IF YOU'D LISTEN TO ME--
SHUT.
UP.
I'LL FIX THIS.
BUT I NEED YOU TO GET AWAY FROM ME.
NOW.

I'M GOING TO COLLECT FUNGUS.

AS LONG AS THE FUNGUS IS AWAY FROM ME, I DON'T GIVE ANY SHIT.

GO FUCK YOURSELF.

NOBODY TELLS ME TO SHUT UP, YOU GIANT SHITTY DRIVER ASSHOLE!

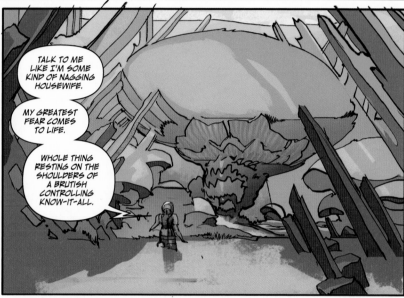

TALK TO ME LIKE I'M SOME KIND OF NAGGING HOUSEWIFE.

MY GREATEST FEAR COMES TO LIFE.

WHOLE THING RESTING ON THE SHOULDERS OF A BRUTISH CONTROLLING KNOW-IT-ALL.

THIS IS WHO I GET STUCK WITH?!

LAST MAN ON THE FACE OF EARTH IS AN ILLITERATE MISOGYNIST!

CALM DOWN.

IMAGINE SOMETHING DIFFERENT.

SWWSH

YOU THINK ABOUT FOOD AND SALIVATE.

YOU THINK ABOUT NEGATIVITY, YOU FALL TO DESPAIR.

WHAT YOU THINK DEFINES THE WORLD YOU LIVE IN.

NOTHING TAKES SHAPE UNTIL YOU VIEW IT.

AND WHAT YOU EXPECT TO SEE...

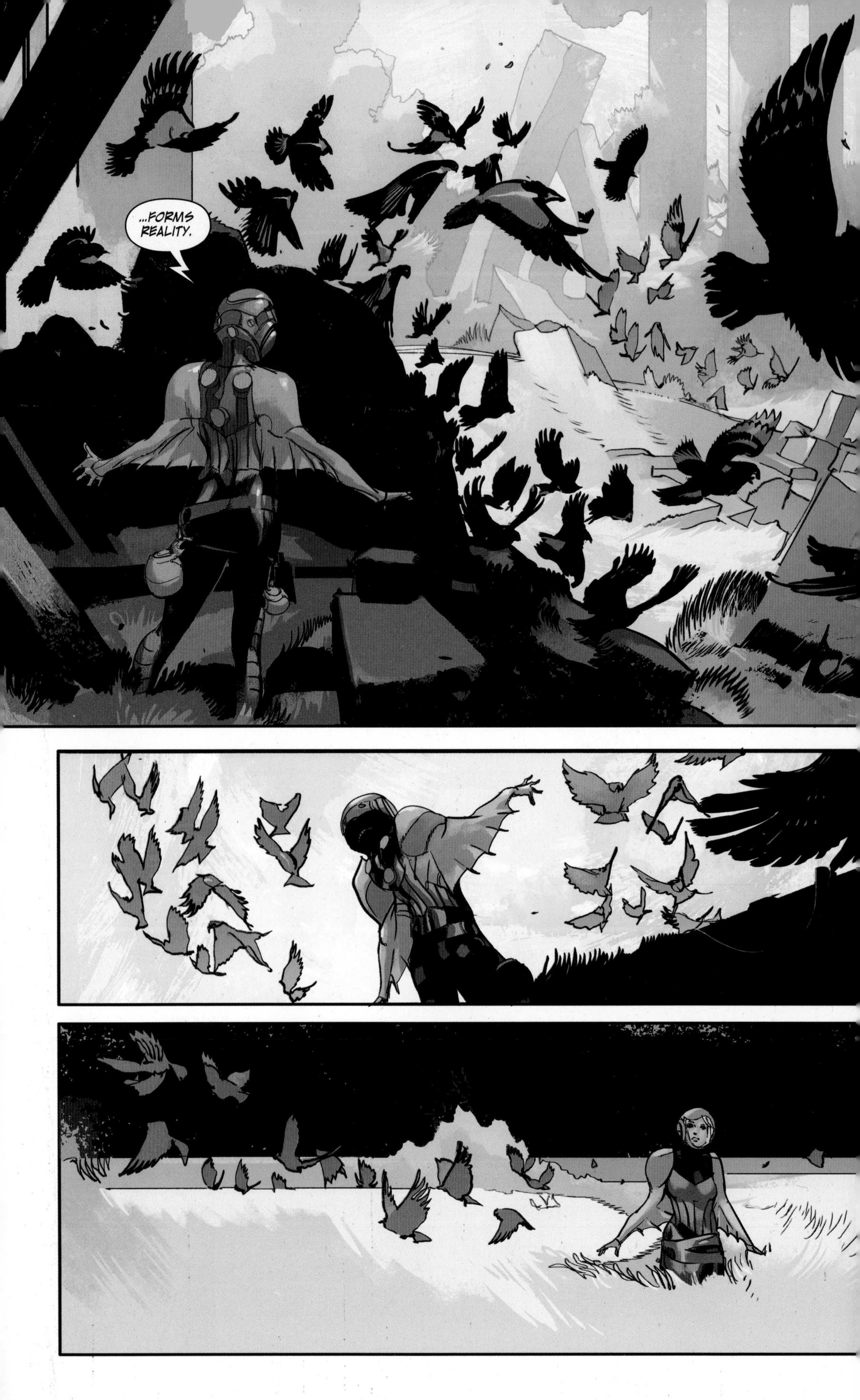
...FORMS REALITY.

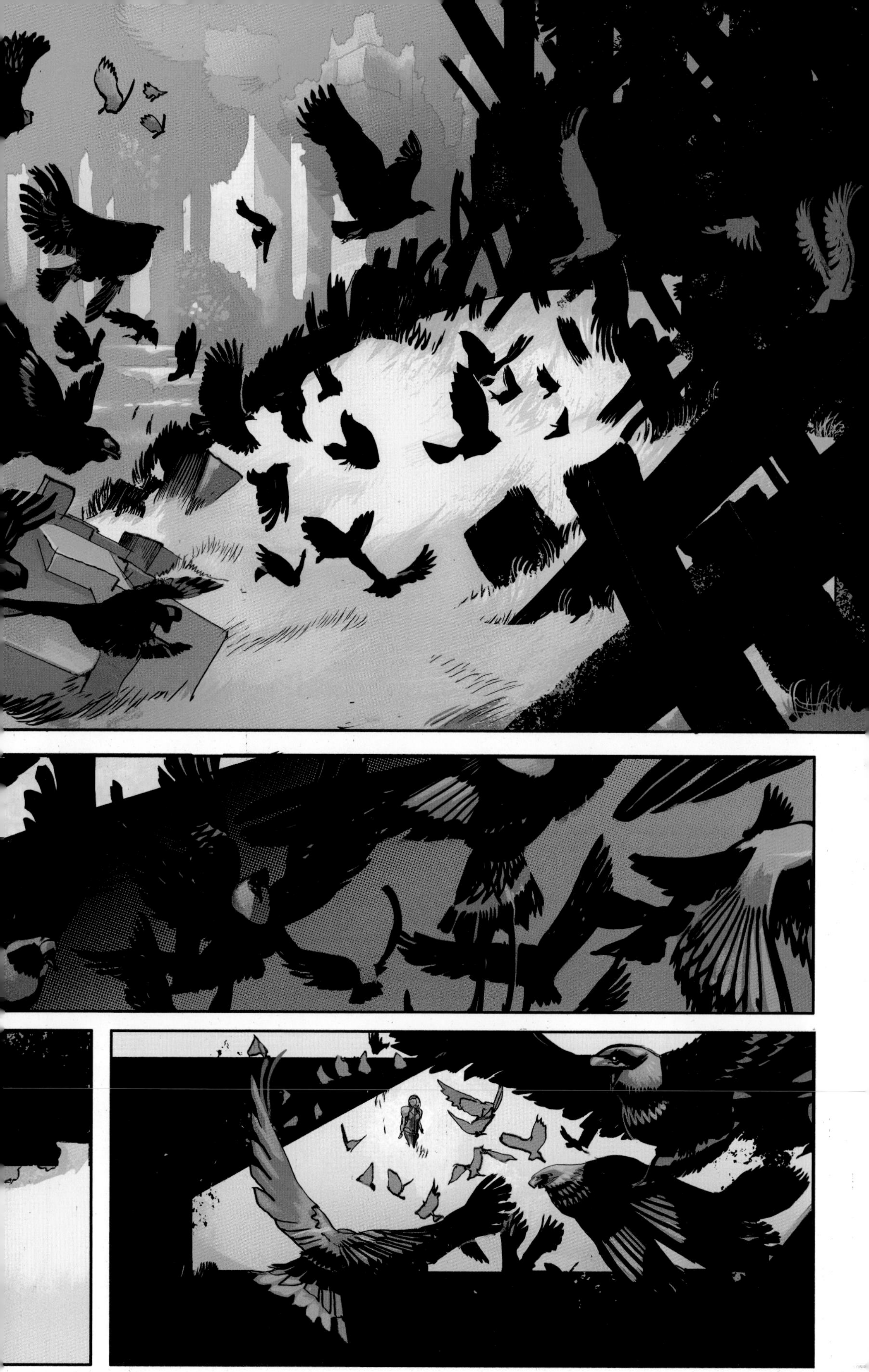

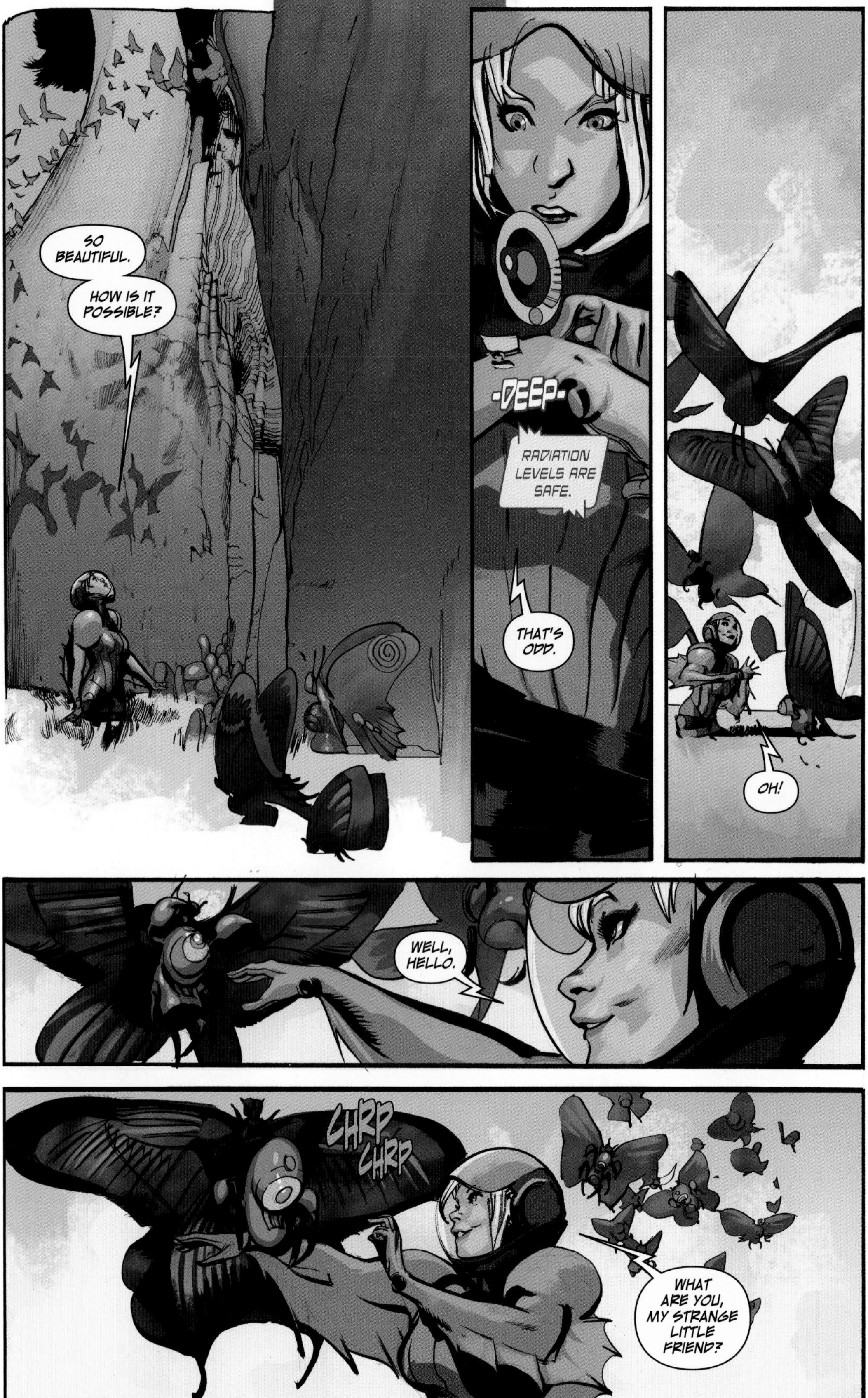
SO BEAUTIFUL.
HOW IS IT POSSIBLE?
-DEEP-
RADIATION LEVELS ARE SAFE.
THAT'S ODD.
OH!
WELL, HELLO.
CHRP CHRP
WHAT ARE YOU, MY STRANGE LITTLE FRIEND?

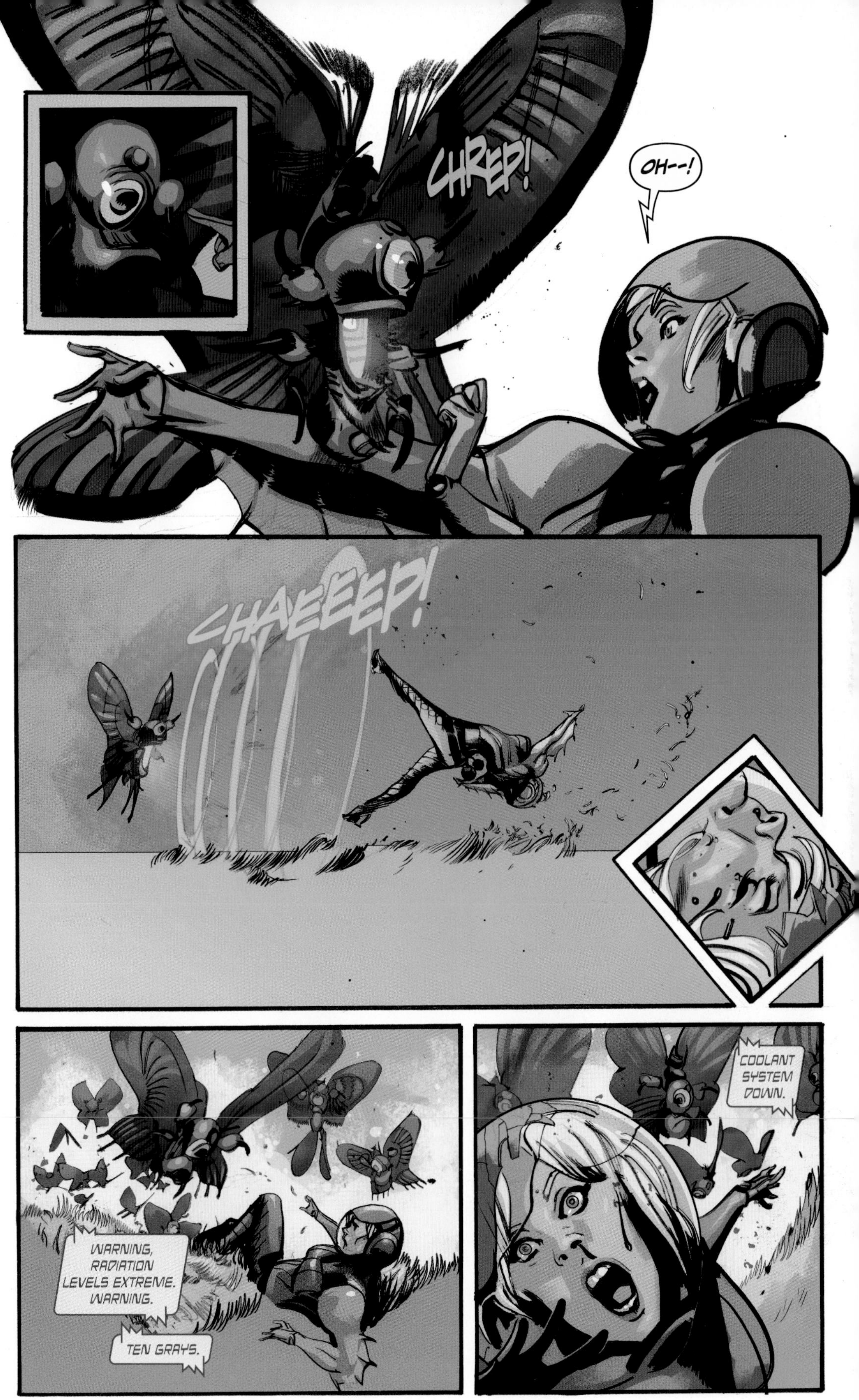
CHREP!
OH--!
CHAEEEP!
WARNING, RADIATION LEVELS EXTREME. WARNING.
TEN GRAYS.
COOLANT SYSTEM DOWN.

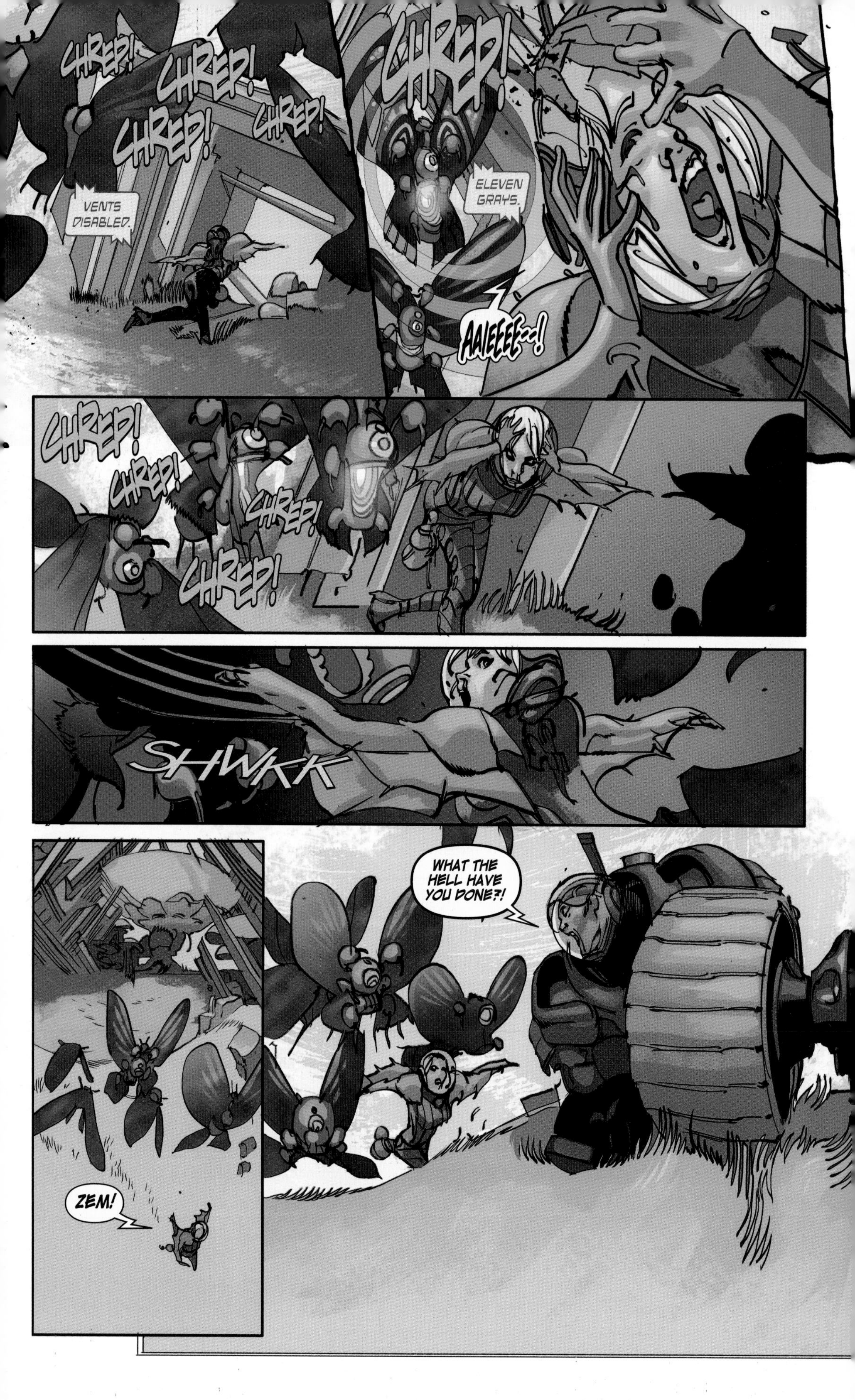
CHREP!
CHREP!
CHREP!
CHREP!
VENTS DISABLED.
CHREP!
ELEVEN GRAYS.
AAIEEEE--!
CHREP!
CHREP!
CHREP!
CHREP!
SHWKK
WHAT THE HELL HAVE YOU DONE?!
ZEM!

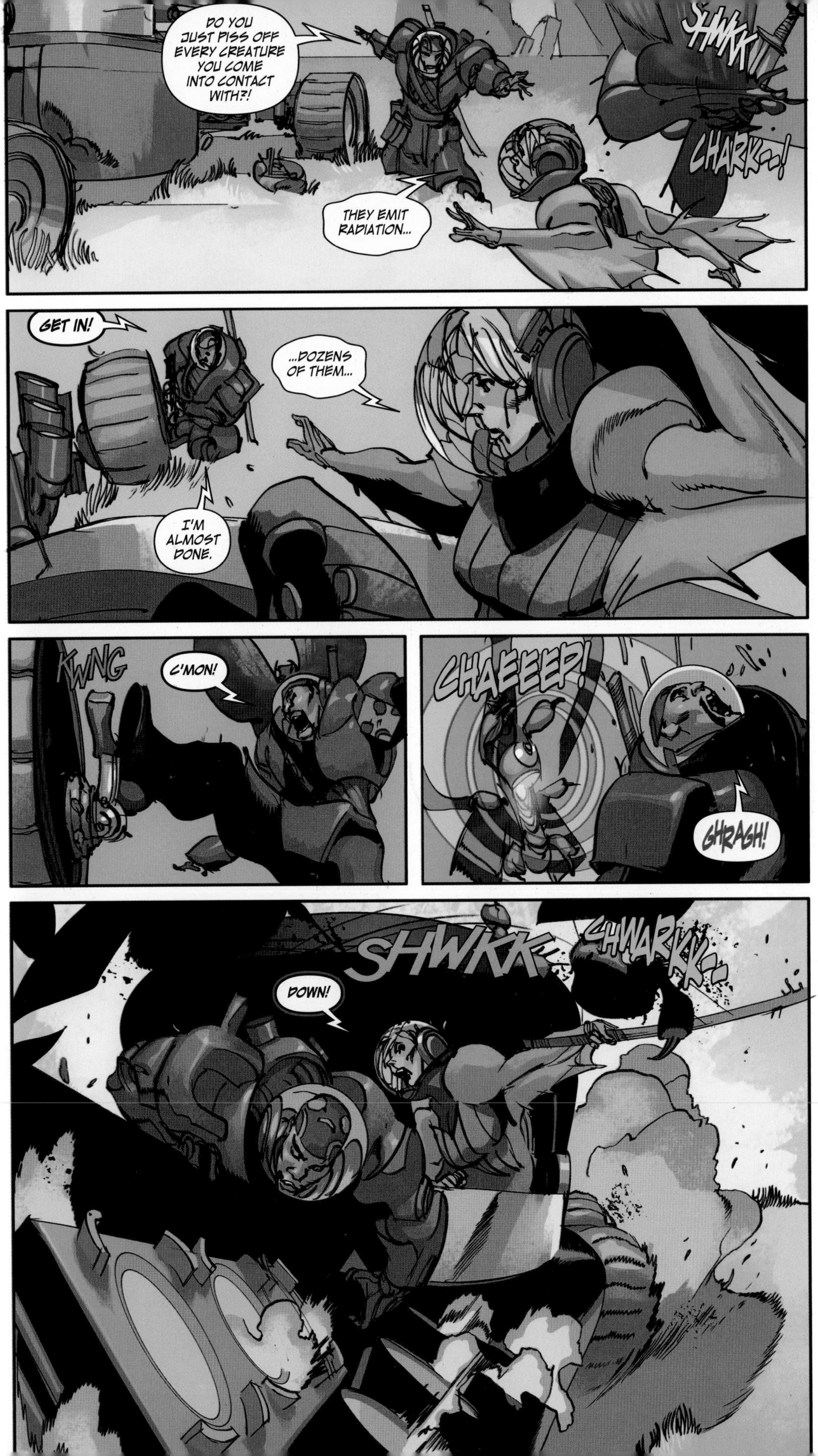
DO YOU JUST PISS OFF EVERY CREATURE YOU COME INTO CONTACT WITH?!
SHWKK
CHARK..!
THEY EMIT RADIATION...
GET IN!
...DOZENS OF THEM...
I'M ALMOST DONE.
KWNG
C'MON!
CHAEEEP!
GHRAGH!
SHWKK
CHWARKK..
DOWN!

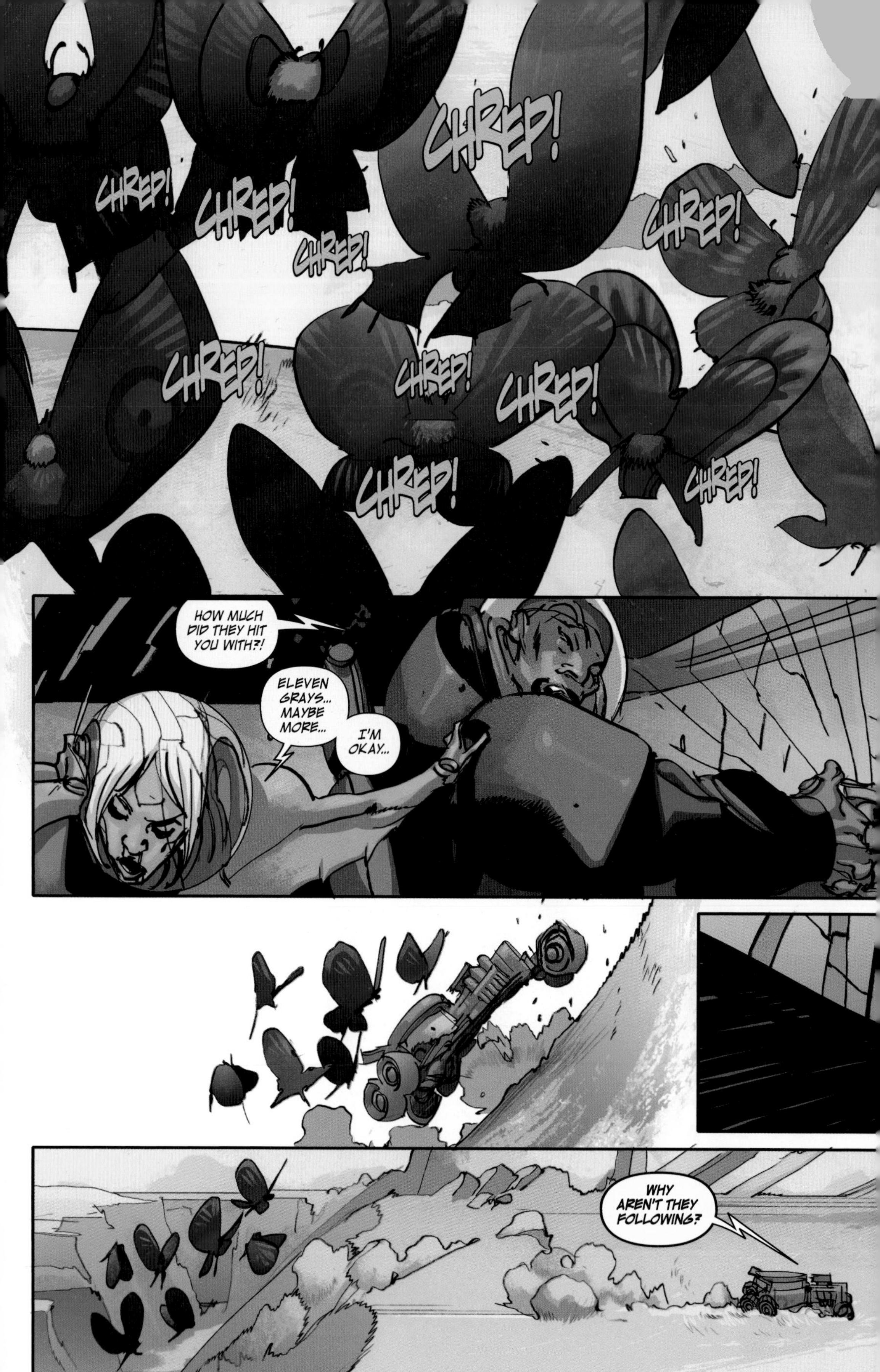
CHREP!
CHREP!
CHREP!
CHREP!
CHREP!
CHREP!
CHREP!
CHREP!
CHREP!
CHREP!
HOW MUCH DID THEY HIT YOU WITH?!
ELEVEN GRAYS... MAYBE MORE...
I'M OKAY...
WHY AREN'T THEY FOLLOWING?

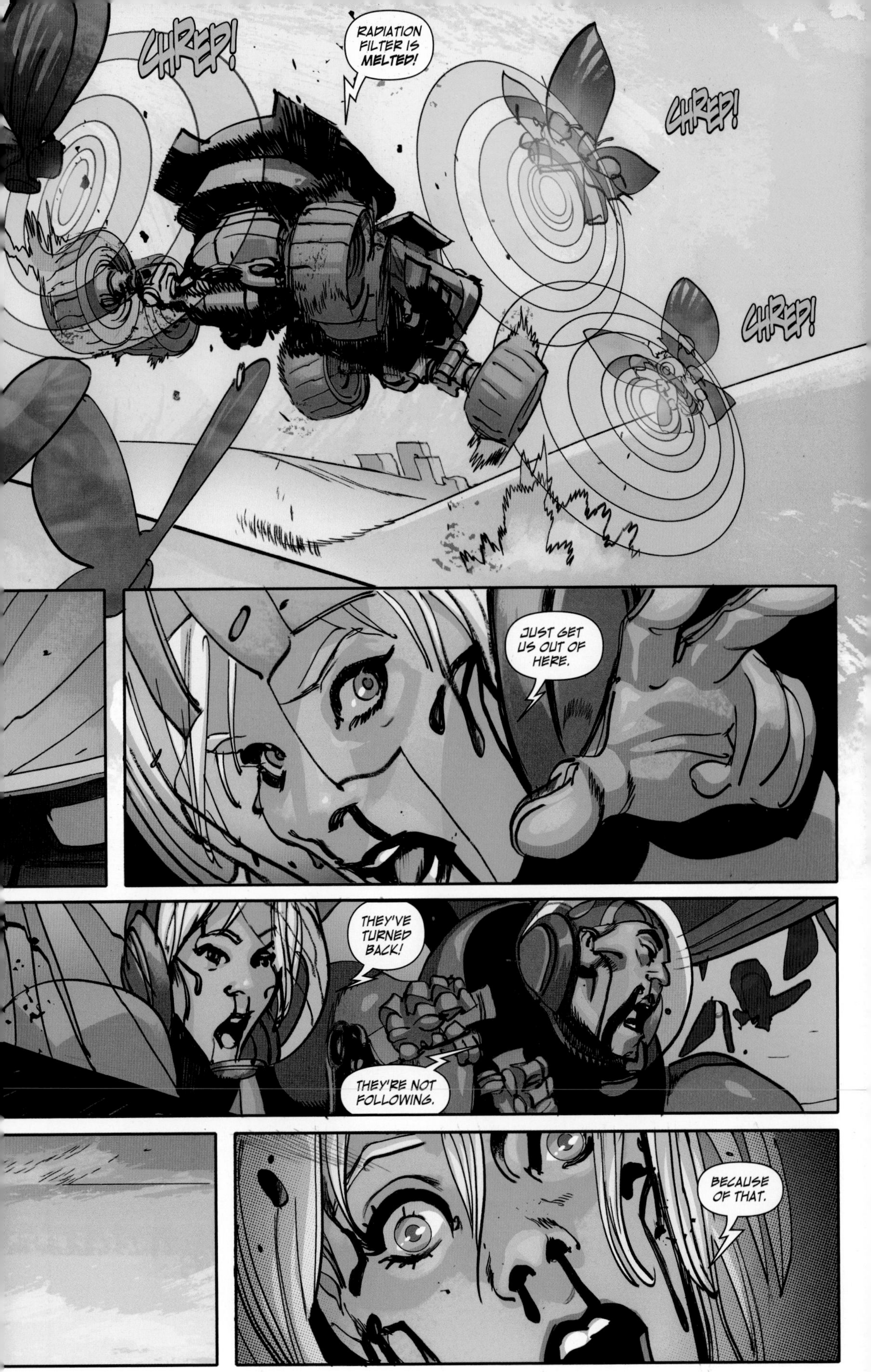

CHREP!
RADIATION FILTER IS MELTED!
CHREP!
CHREP!
JUST GET US OUT OF HERE.
THEY'VE TURNED BACK!
THEY'RE NOT FOLLOWING.
BECAUSE OF THAT.

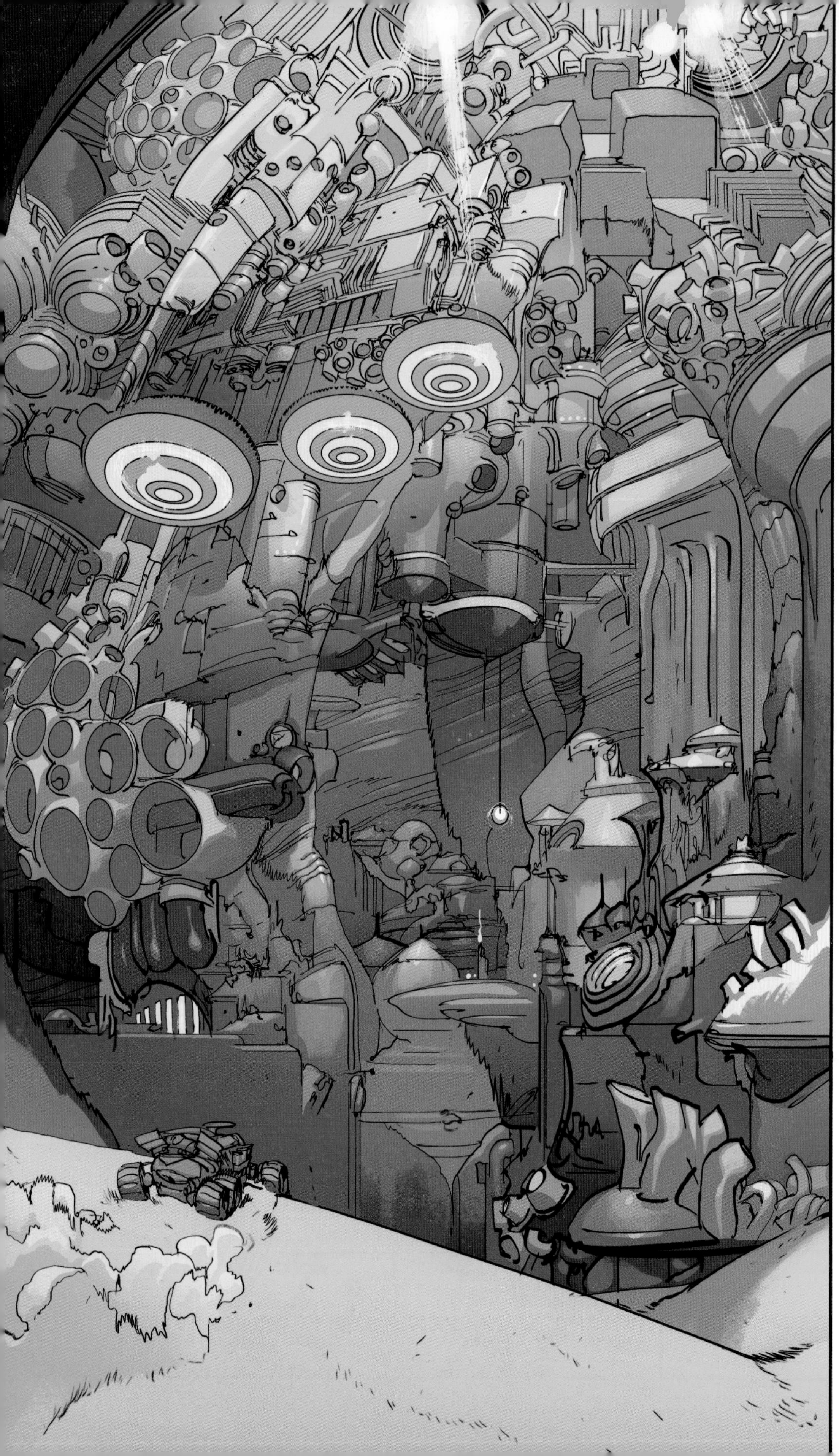

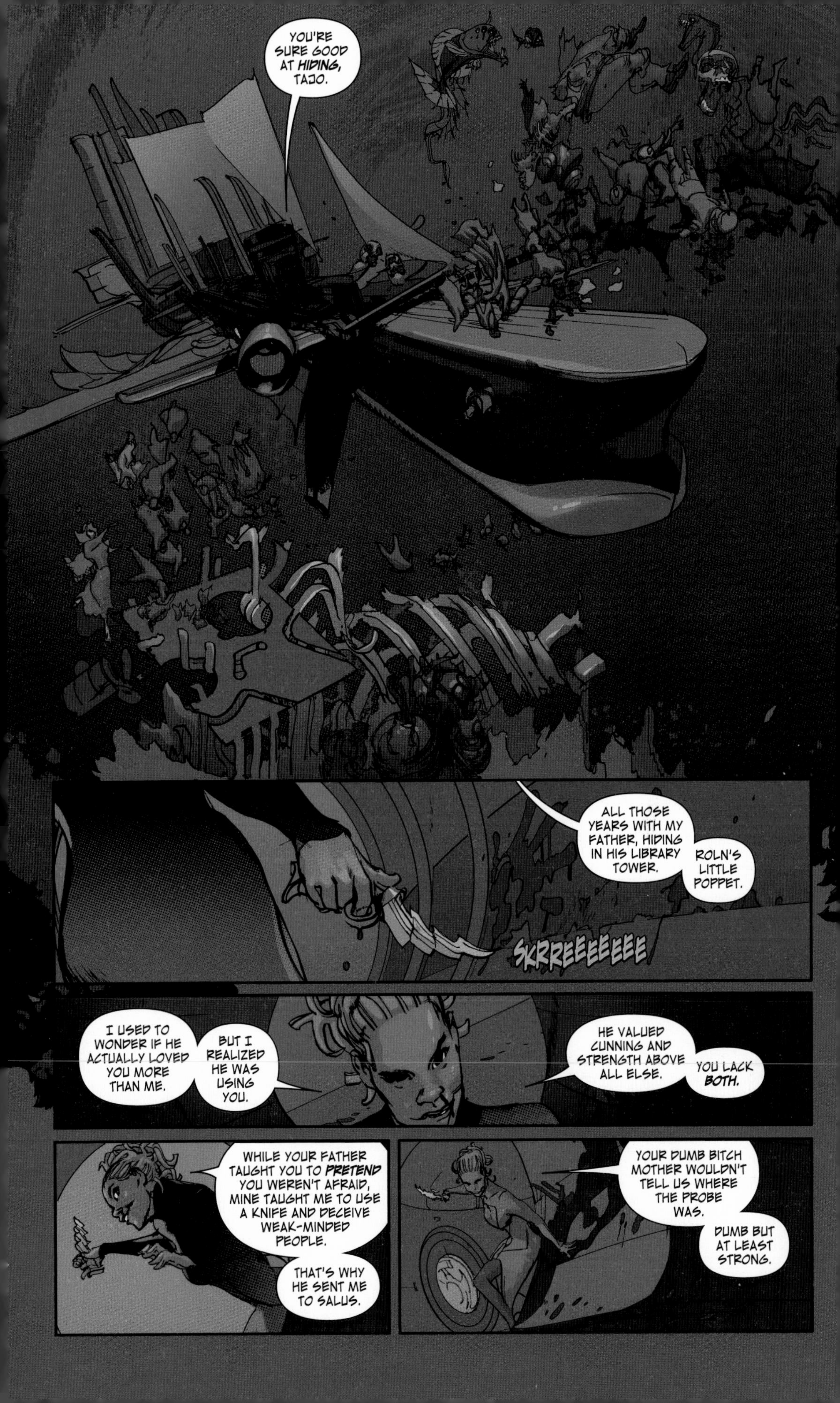
YOU'RE SURE GOOD AT *HIDING*, TAJO.
ALL THOSE YEARS WITH MY FATHER, HIDING IN HIS LIBRARY TOWER.
ROLN'S LITTLE POPPET.
SKRREEEEEEE
I USED TO WONDER IF HE ACTUALLY LOVED YOU MORE THAN ME.
BUT I REALIZED HE WAS USING YOU.
HE VALUED CUNNING AND STRENGTH ABOVE ALL ELSE.
YOU LACK *BOTH*.
WHILE YOUR FATHER TAUGHT YOU TO *PRETEND* YOU WEREN'T AFRAID, MINE TAUGHT ME TO USE A KNIFE AND DECEIVE WEAK-MINDED PEOPLE.
THAT'S WHY HE SENT ME TO SALUS.
YOUR DUMB BITCH MOTHER WOULDN'T TELL US WHERE THE PROBE WAS.
DUMB BUT AT LEAST STRONG.

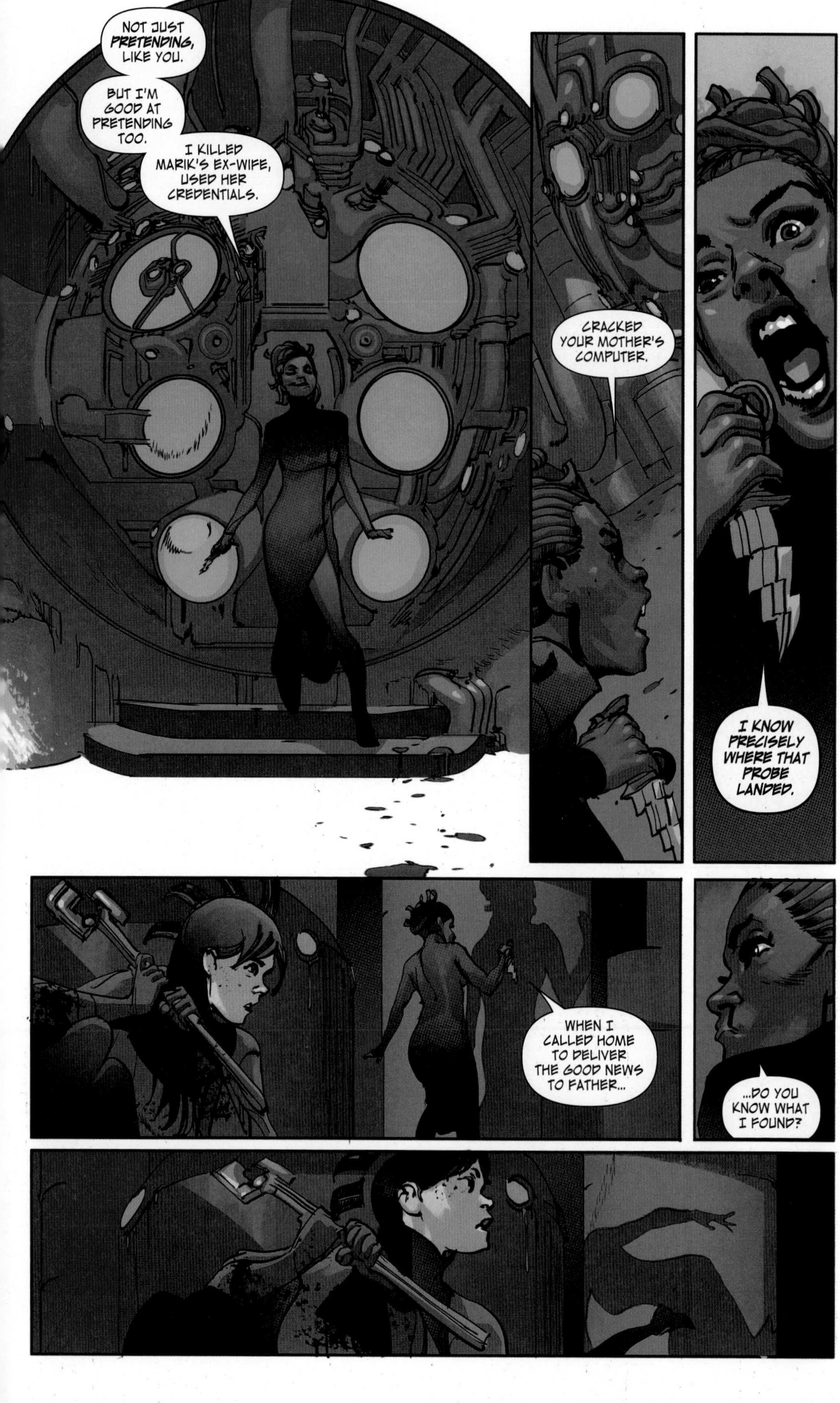
NOT JUST PRETENDING, LIKE YOU.
BUT I'M GOOD AT PRETENDING TOO.
I KILLED MARIK'S EX-WIFE, USED HER CREDENTIALS.
CRACKED YOUR MOTHER'S COMPUTER.
I KNOW PRECISELY WHERE THAT PROBE LANDED.
WHEN I CALLED HOME TO DELIVER THE GOOD NEWS TO FATHER...
...DO YOU KNOW WHAT I FOUND?

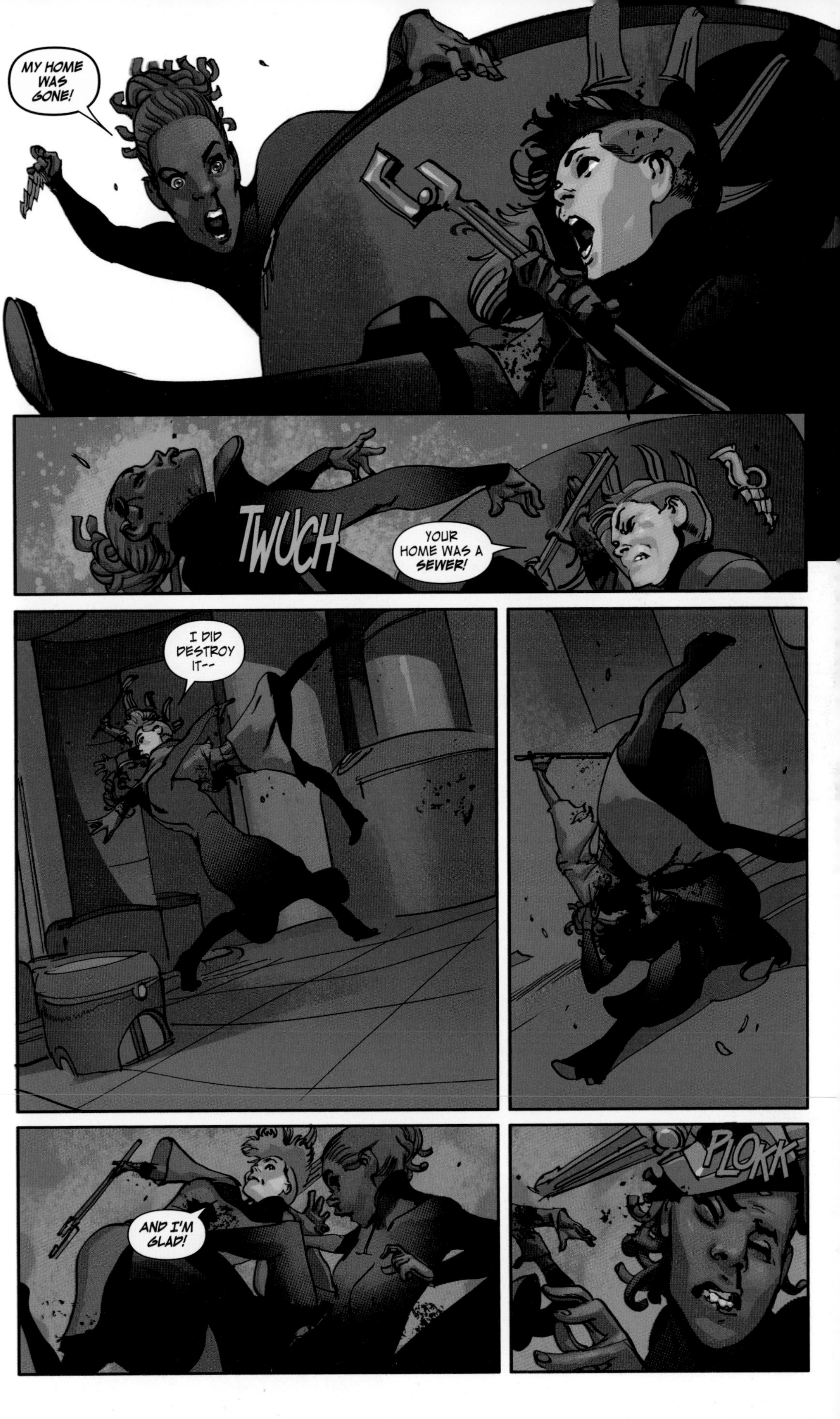
MY HOME WAS GONE!
TWUCH
YOUR HOME WAS A SEWER!
I DID DESTROY IT--
AND I'M GLAD!
PLOKK

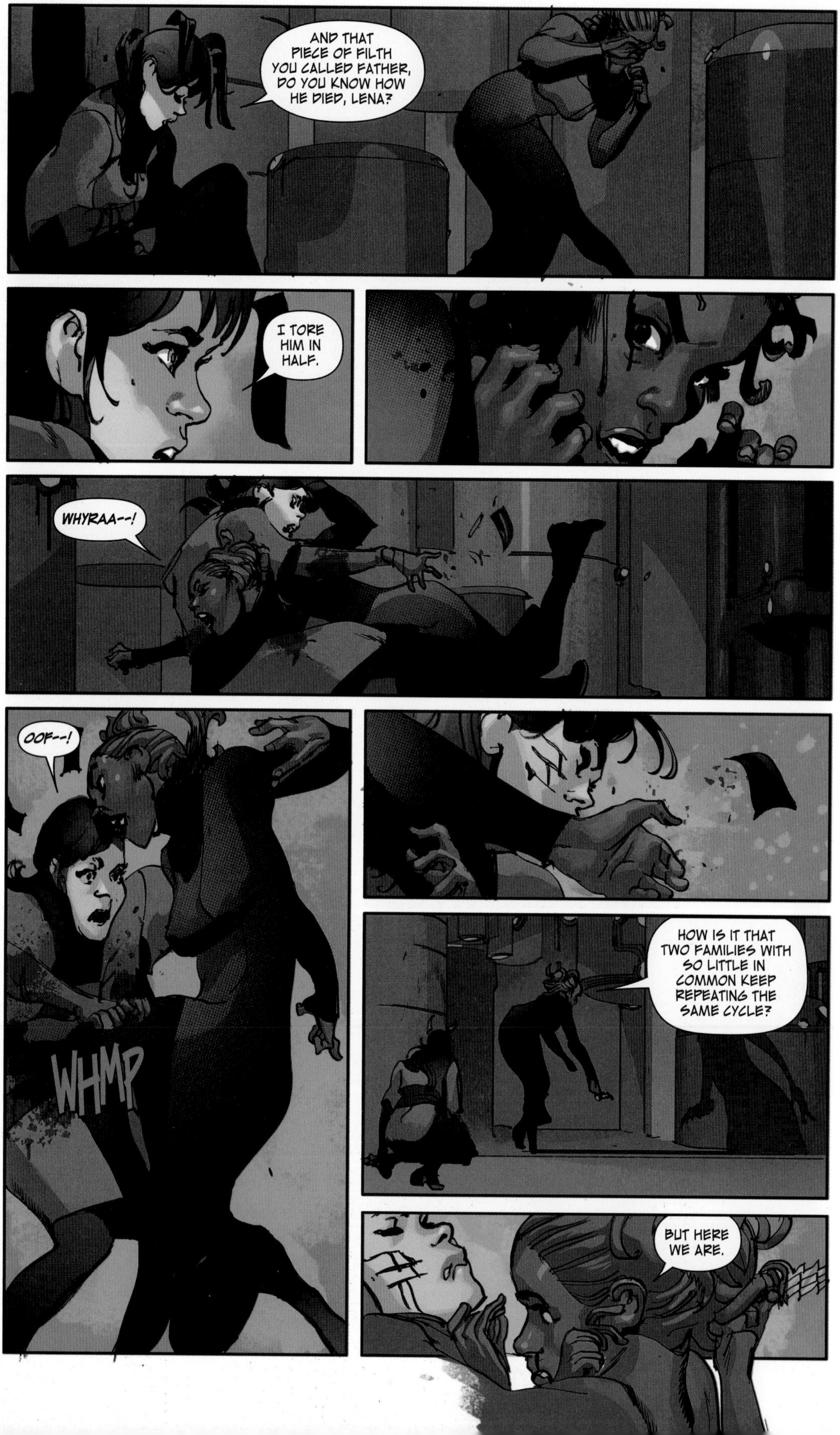
AND THAT PIECE OF FILTH YOU CALLED FATHER, DO YOU KNOW HOW HE DIED, LENA?
I TORE HIM IN HALF.
WHYRAA--!
OOF--!
WHMP
HOW IS IT THAT TWO FAMILIES WITH SO LITTLE IN COMMON KEEP REPEATING THE SAME CYCLE?
BUT HERE WE ARE.

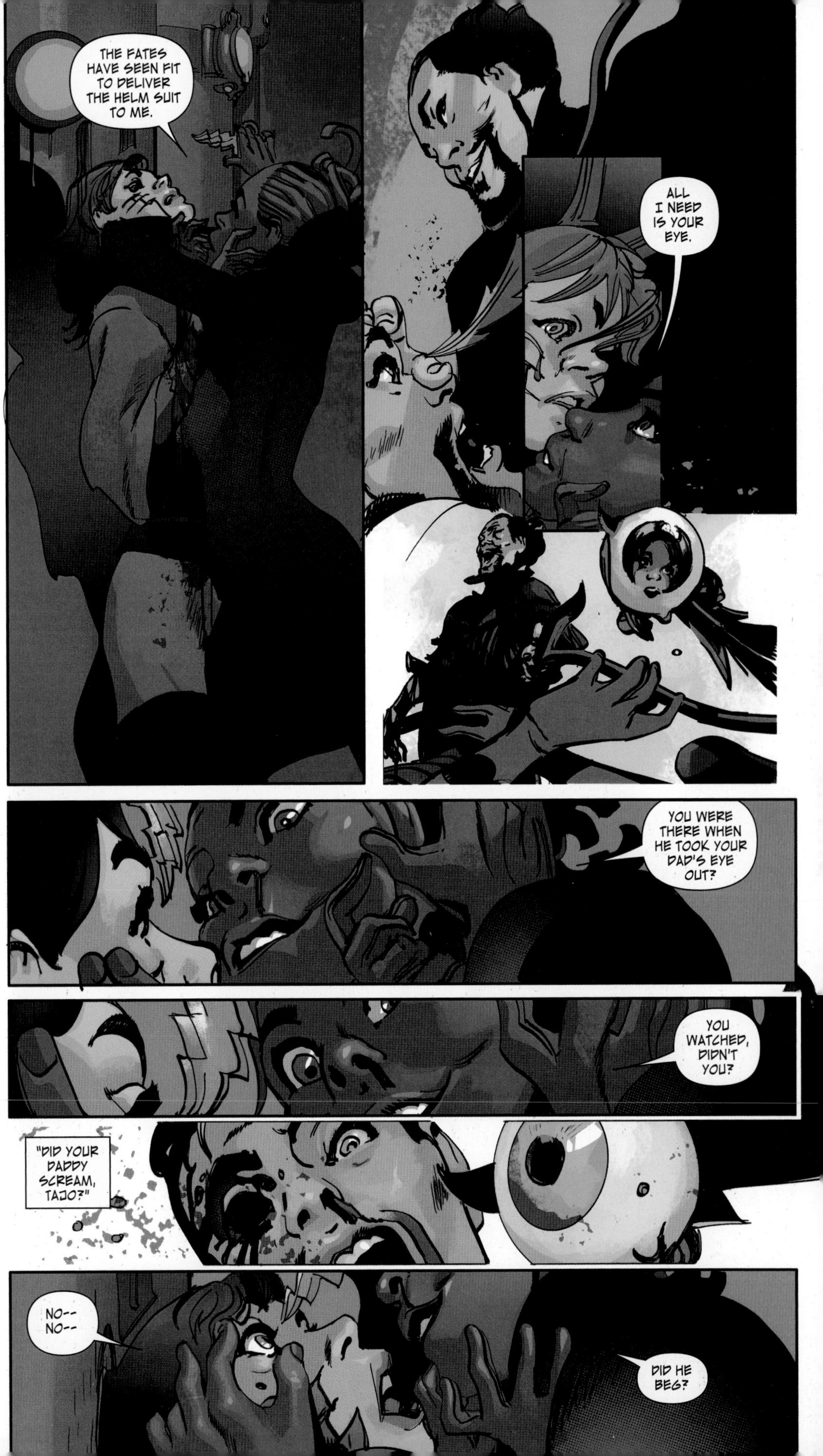
THE FATES HAVE SEEN FIT TO DELIVER THE HELM SUIT TO ME.
ALL I NEED IS YOUR EYE.
YOU WERE THERE WHEN HE TOOK YOUR DAD'S EYE OUT?
YOU WATCHED, DIDN'T YOU?
"DID YOUR DADDY SCREAM, TAJO?"
NO-- NO--
DID HE BEG?

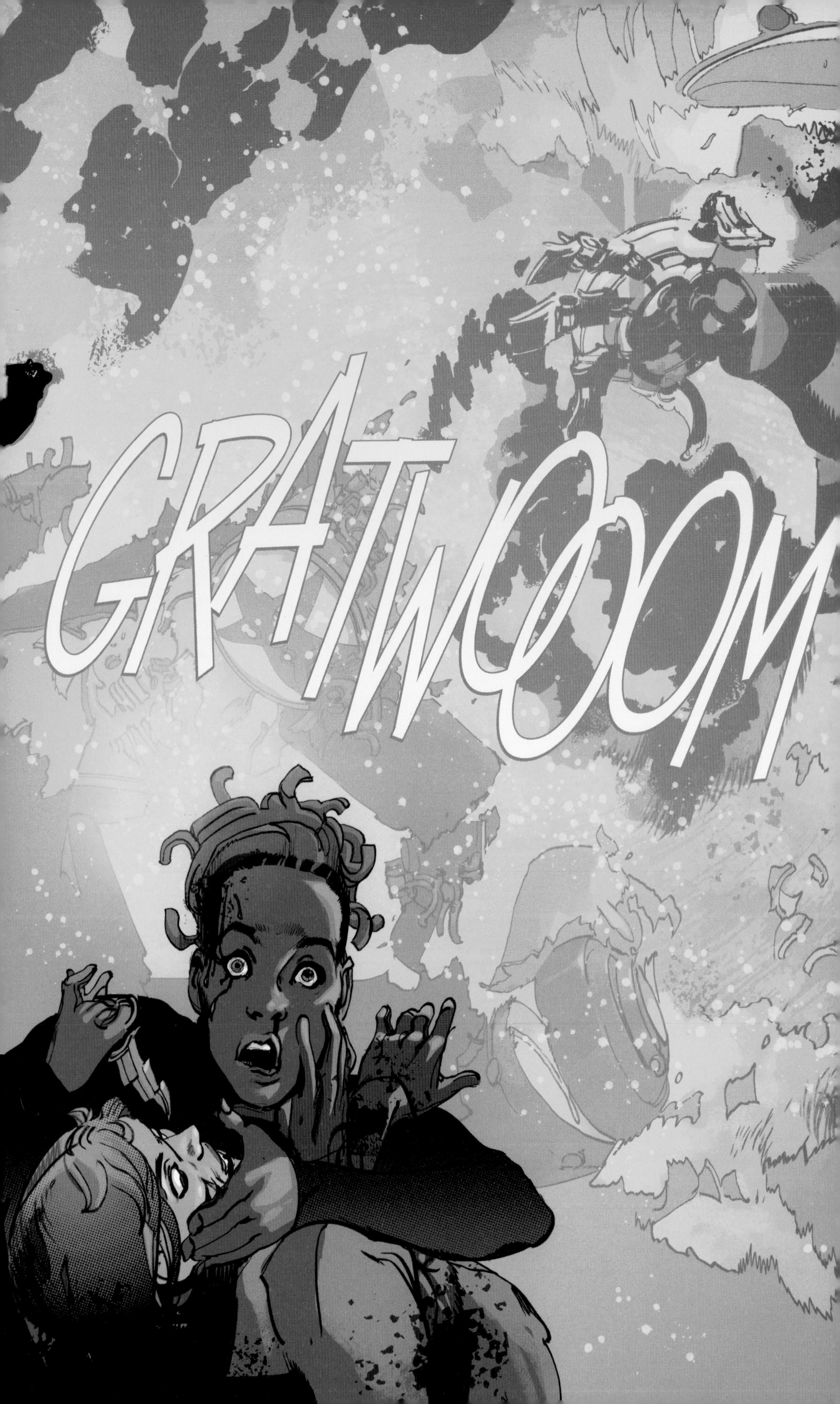
GRATWOOM

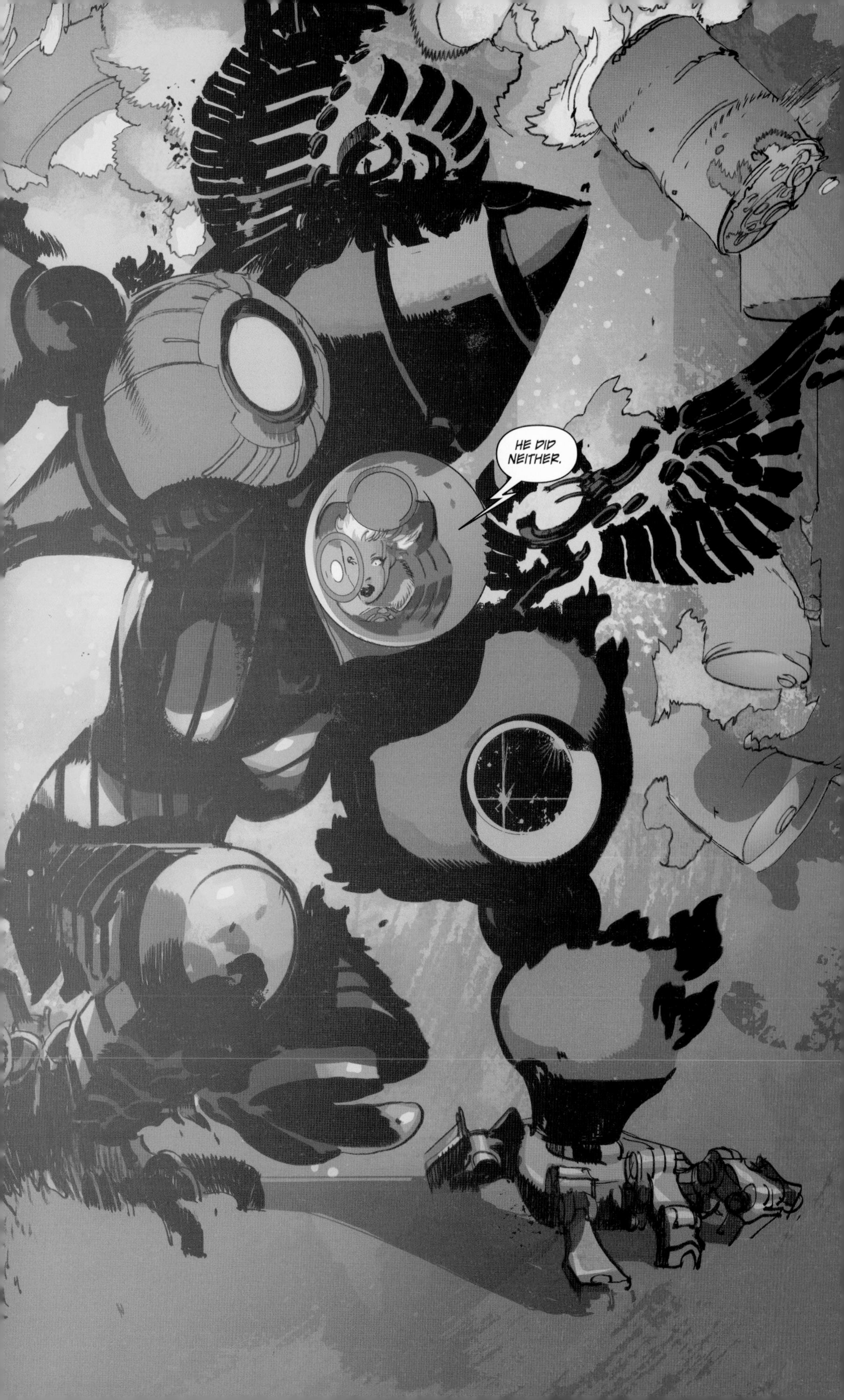
HE DID NEITHER.

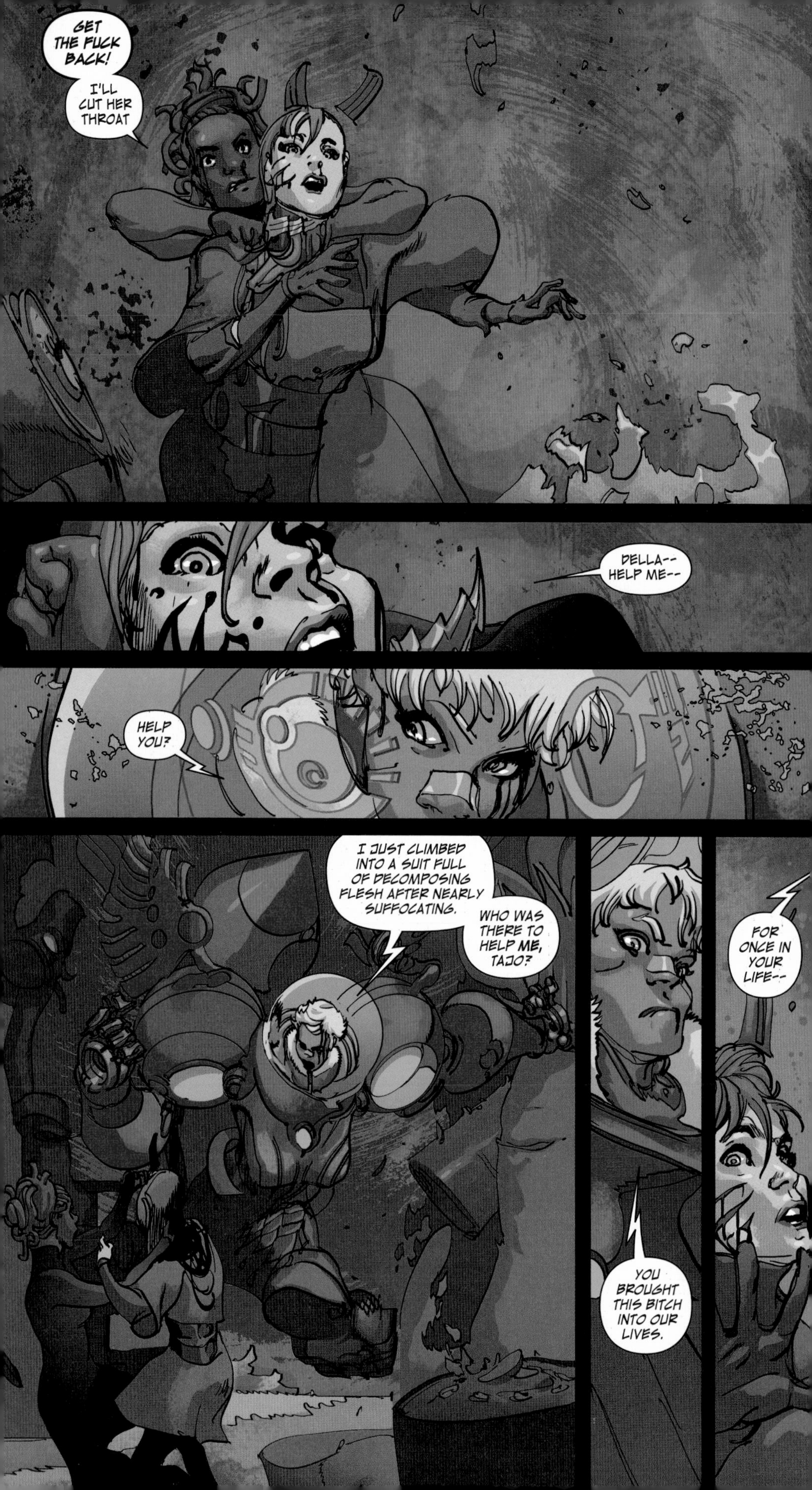
GET THE FUCK BACK!
I'LL CUT HER THROAT
DELLA-- HELP ME--
HELP YOU?
I JUST CLIMBED INTO A SUIT FULL OF DECOMPOSING FLESH AFTER NEARLY SUFFOCATING.
WHO WAS THERE TO HELP ME, TAJO?
FOR ONCE IN YOUR LIFE--
YOU BROUGHT THIS BITCH INTO OUR LIVES.

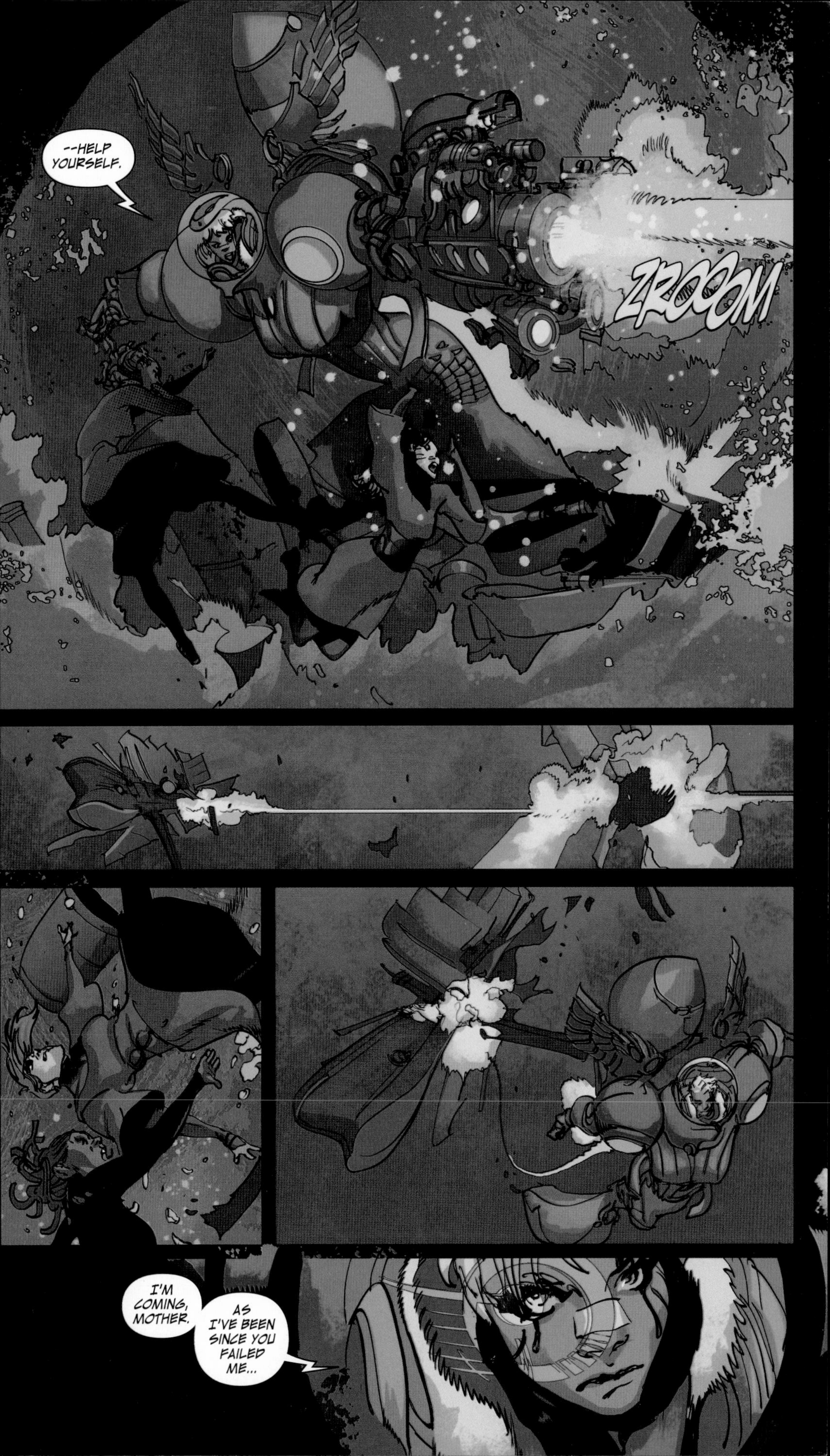
--HELP YOURSELF.
ZROOOM
I'M COMING, MOTHER.
AS I'VE BEEN SINCE YOU FAILED ME...

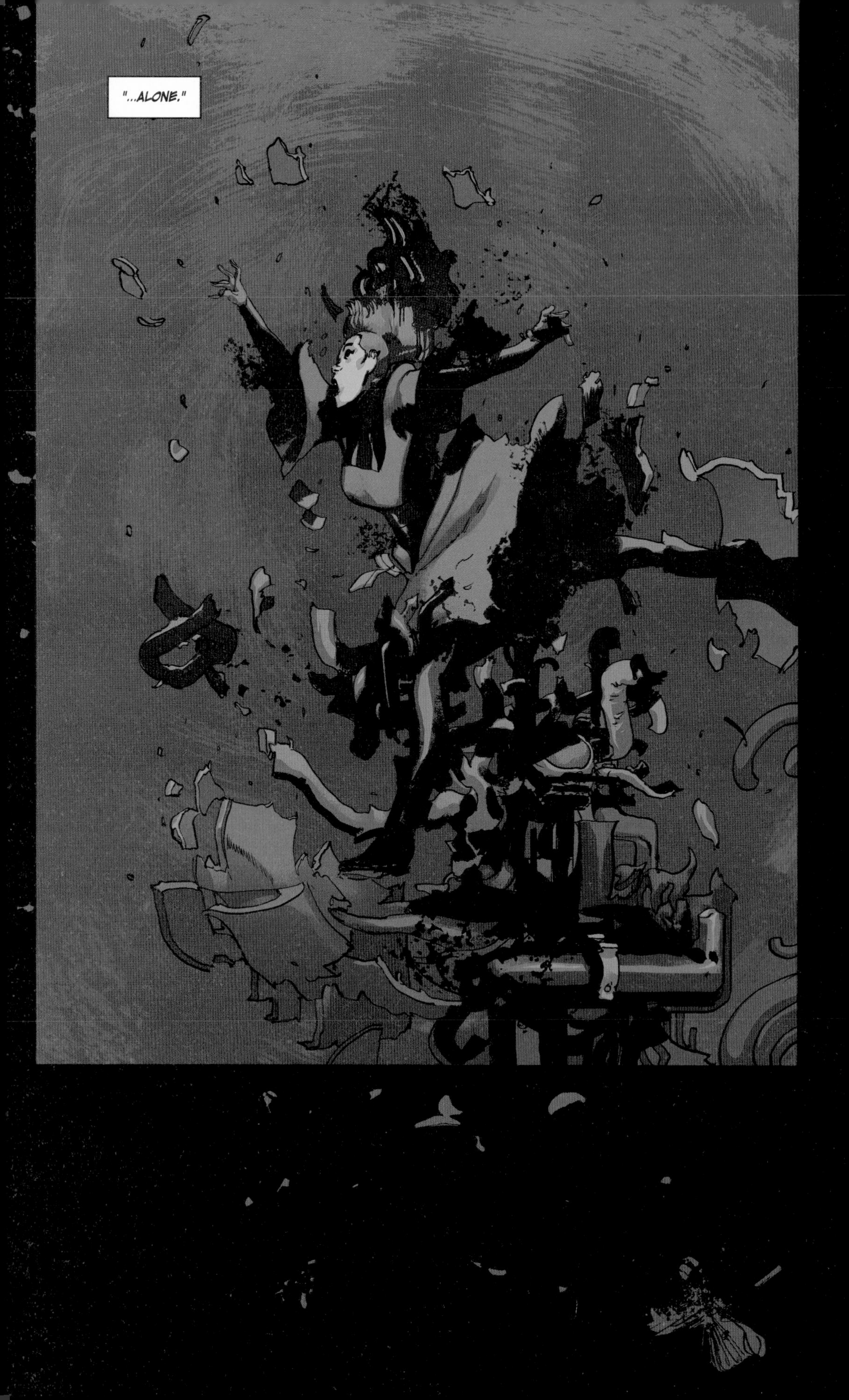
"...ALONE."

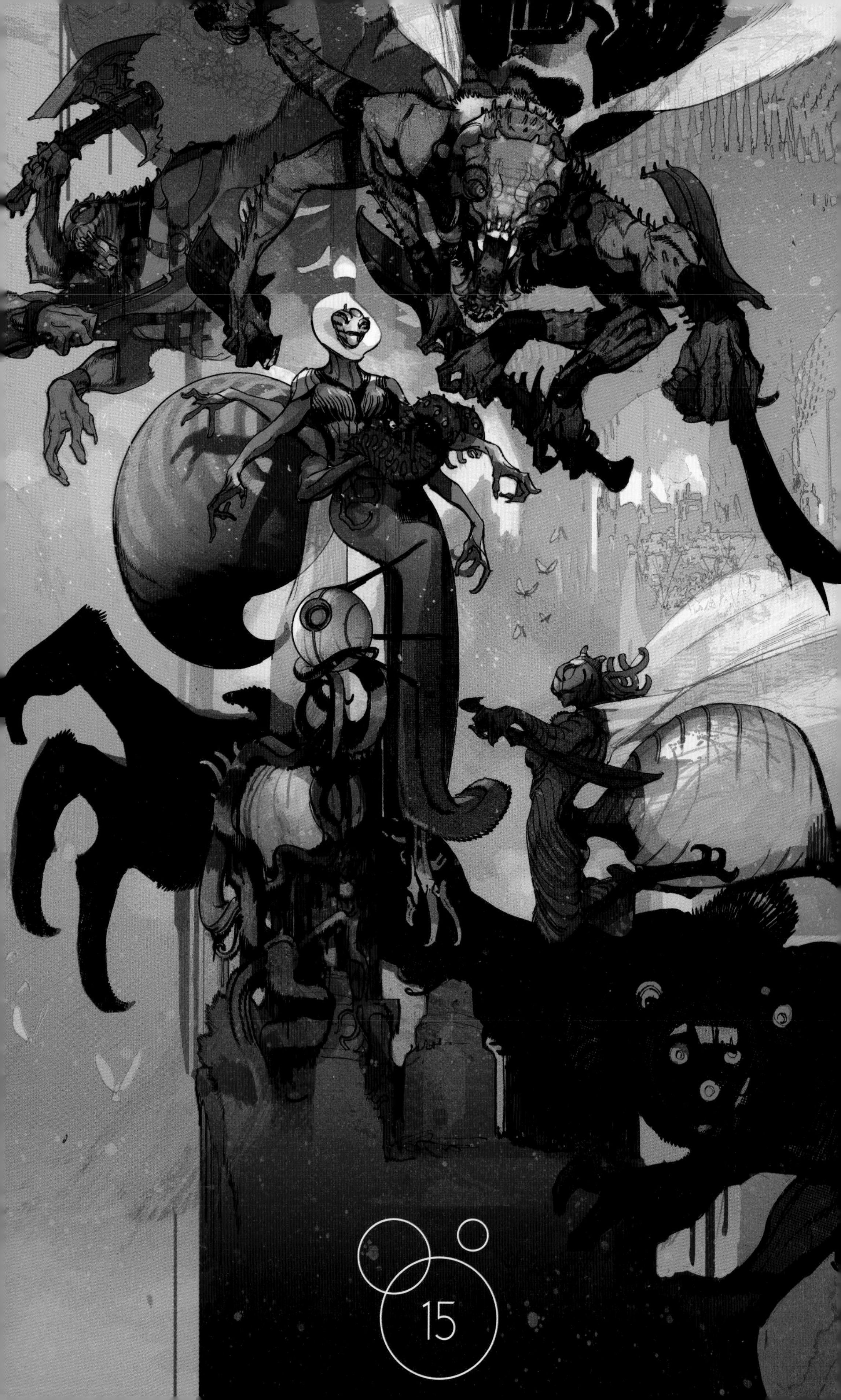
15

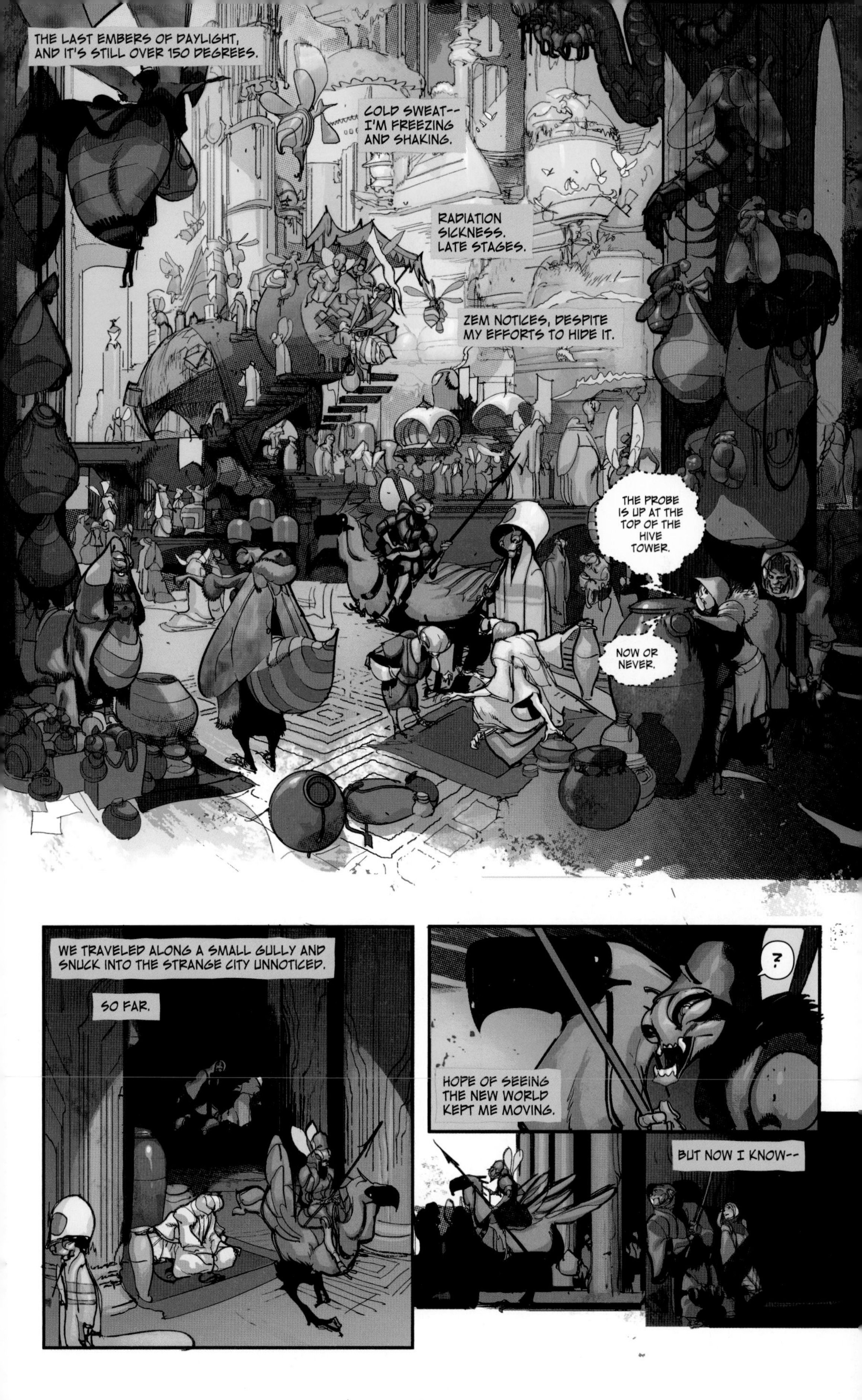
THE LAST EMBERS OF DAYLIGHT, AND IT'S STILL OVER 150 DEGREES.
COLD SWEAT-- I'M FREEZING AND SHAKING.
RADIATION SICKNESS. LATE STAGES.
ZEM NOTICES, DESPITE MY EFFORTS TO HIDE IT.
THE PROBE IS UP AT THE TOP OF THE HIVE TOWER.
NOW OR NEVER.
WE TRAVELED ALONG A SMALL GULLY AND SNUCK INTO THE STRANGE CITY UNNOTICED.
SO FAR.
?
HOPE OF SEEING THE NEW WORLD KEPT ME MOVING.
BUT NOW I KNOW--

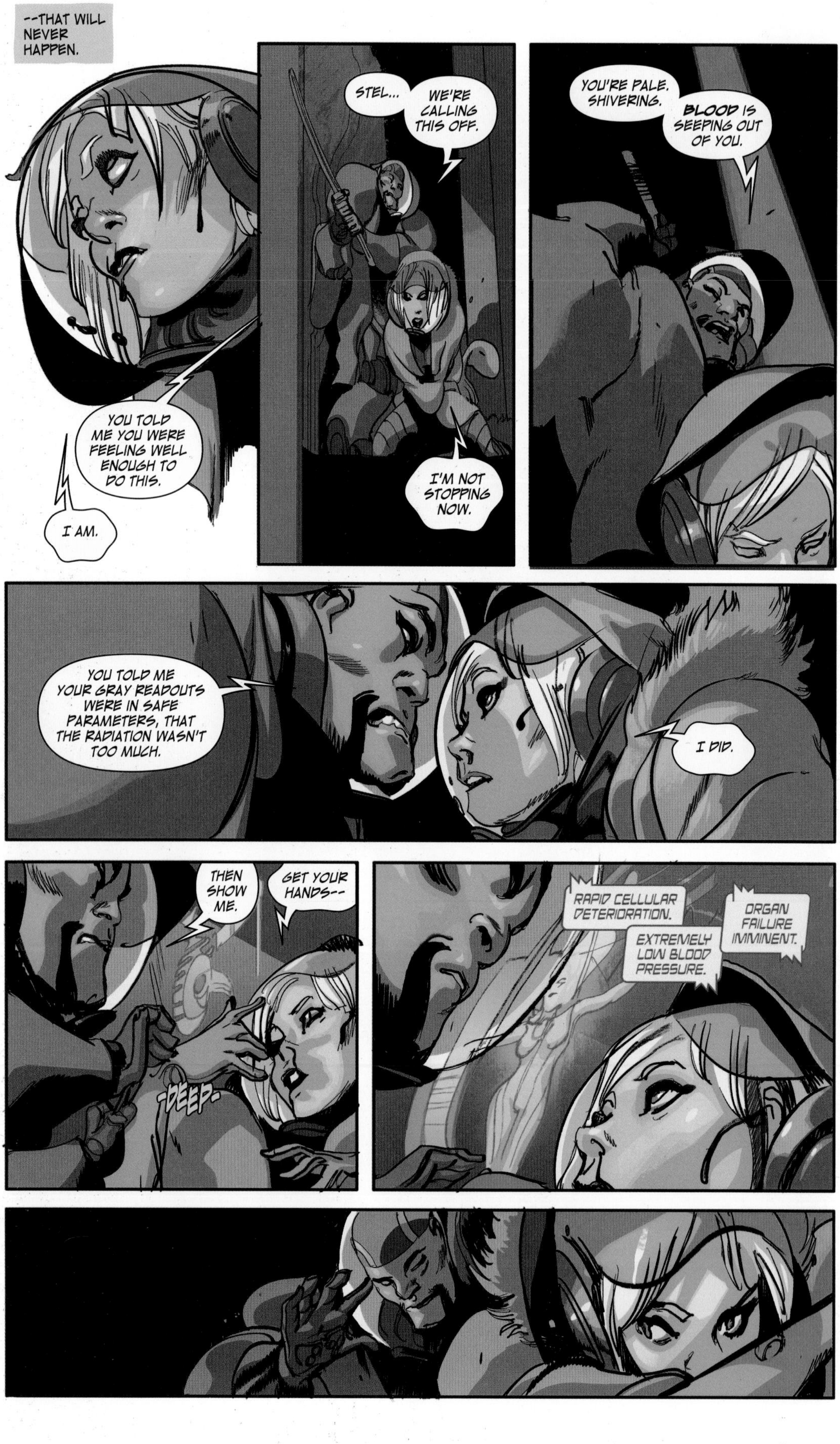

--THAT WILL NEVER HAPPEN.
STEL...
WE'RE CALLING THIS OFF.
YOU'RE PALE. SHIVERING.
BLOOD IS SEEPING OUT OF YOU.
YOU TOLD ME YOU WERE FEELING WELL ENOUGH TO DO THIS.
I AM.
I'M NOT STOPPING NOW.
YOU TOLD ME YOUR GRAY READOUTS WERE IN SAFE PARAMETERS, THAT THE RADIATION WASN'T TOO MUCH.
I DID.
THEN SHOW ME.
GET YOUR HANDS--
-DEEP-
RAPID CELLULAR DETERIORATION.
EXTREMELY LOW BLOOD PRESSURE.
ORGAN FAILURE IMMINENT.

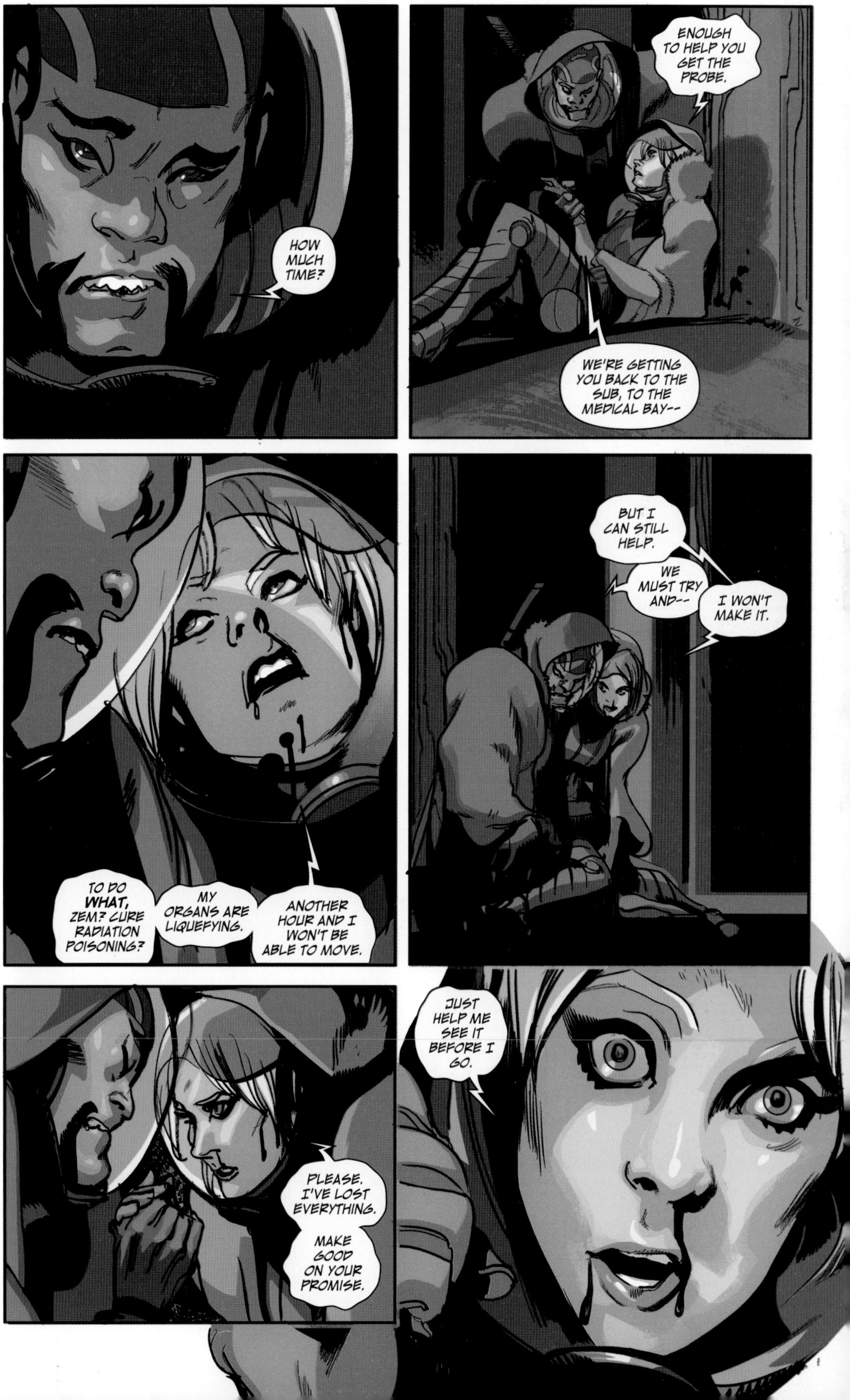
HOW MUCH TIME?
ENOUGH TO HELP YOU GET THE PROBE.
WE'RE GETTING YOU BACK TO THE SUB, TO THE MEDICAL BAY--
ANOTHER HOUR AND I WON'T BE ABLE TO MOVE.
MY ORGANS ARE LIQUEFYING.
TO DO WHAT, ZEM? CURE RADIATION POISONING?
BUT I CAN STILL HELP.
WE MUST TRY AND--
I WON'T MAKE IT.
PLEASE. I'VE LOST EVERYTHING.
MAKE GOOD ON YOUR PROMISE.
JUST HELP ME SEE IT BEFORE I GO.

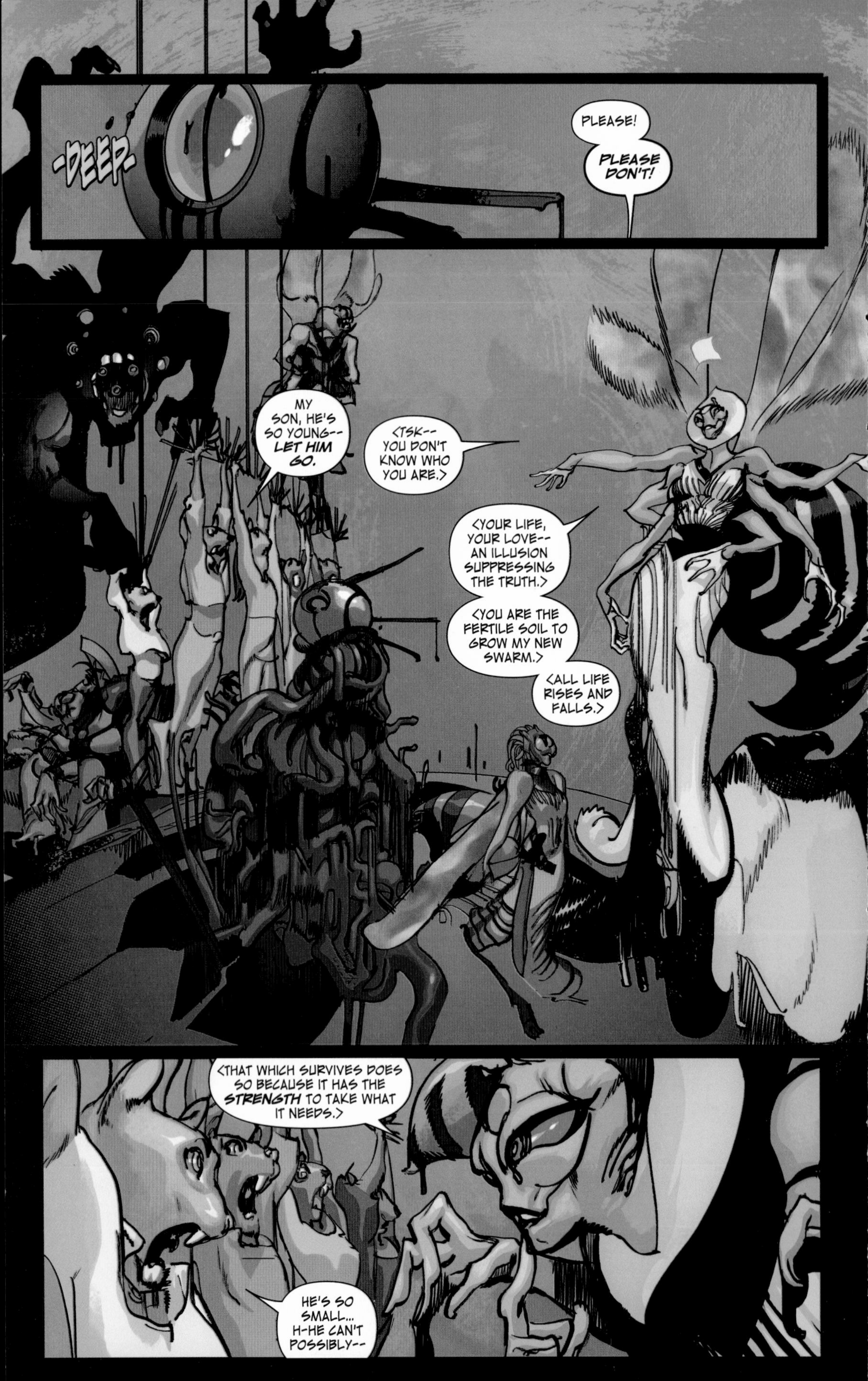
-DEEP-
PLEASE!
PLEASE DON'T!
MY SON, HE'S SO YOUNG-- LET HIM GO.
<TSK-- YOU DON'T KNOW WHO YOU ARE.>
<YOUR LIFE, YOUR LOVE-- AN ILLUSION SUPPRESSING THE TRUTH.>
<YOU ARE THE FERTILE SOIL TO GROW MY NEW SWARM.>
<ALL LIFE RISES AND FALLS.>
<THAT WHICH SURVIVES DOES SO BECAUSE IT HAS THE STRENGTH TO TAKE WHAT IT NEEDS.>
HE'S SO SMALL... H-HE CAN'T POSSIBLY--

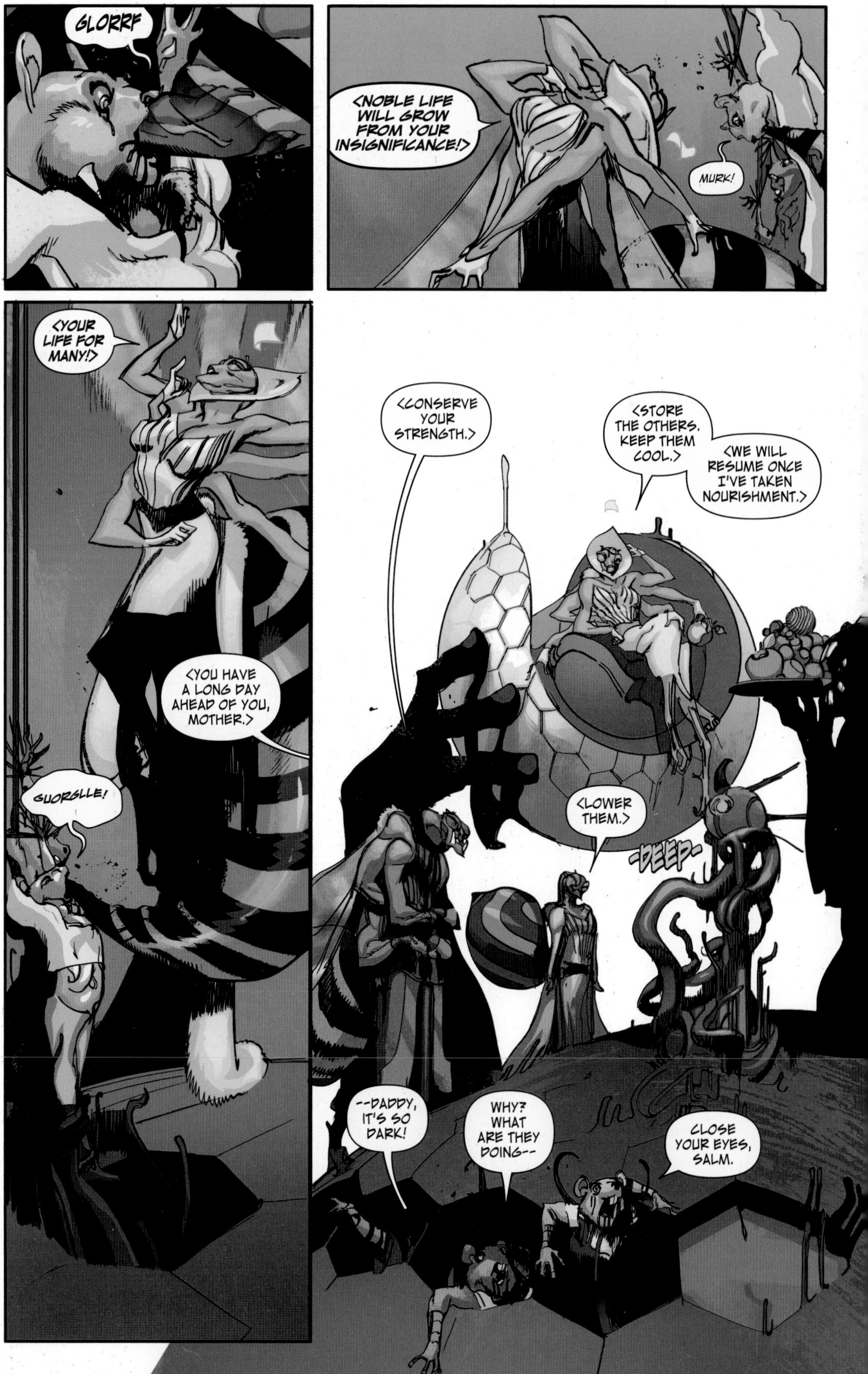
GLORRF
<NOBLE LIFE WILL GROW FROM YOUR INSIGNIFICANCE!>
MURK!
<YOUR LIFE FOR MANY!>
<YOU HAVE A LONG DAY AHEAD OF YOU, MOTHER.>
GUORGLLE!
<CONSERVE YOUR STRENGTH.>
<STORE THE OTHERS. KEEP THEM COOL.>
<WE WILL RESUME ONCE I'VE TAKEN NOURISHMENT.>
<LOWER THEM.>
-DEEP-
--DADDY, IT'S SO DARK!
WHY? WHAT ARE THEY DOING--
CLOSE YOUR EYES, SALM.

TOO MANY.
TOO BIG.
NOT A FIGHT WE CAN WIN.
NO WAY TO THE PROBE WITHOUT FACING THEM.
THAT'S NOT A VERY PIRATE-LIKE ATTITUDE.
I NEED A PIRATE TO HELP ME PLUNDER THAT PROBE.
SORRY FOR THE ALLITERATION.
HOW ARE YOU?
NOT AS SICK AS YOU, BUT NOT READY FOR THIS.
I'M NOT GETTING ANY MORE READY.
STEL...
YOU'RE **WRONG.** THIS IS--
DON'T.
IF YOU **THINK** YOU'RE GOING TO FALL, YOU **WILL.**
PLEASE.
I DON'T HAVE THE STRENGTH TO BE HOPEFUL FOR BOTH OF US.

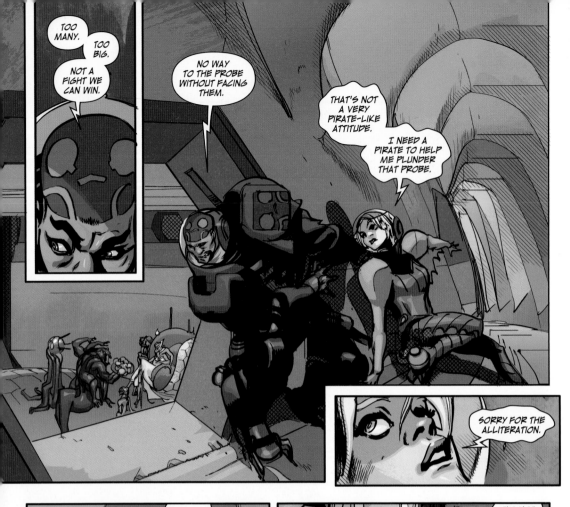

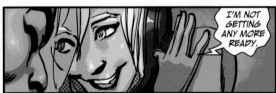

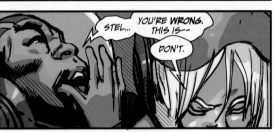

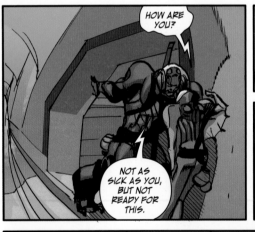

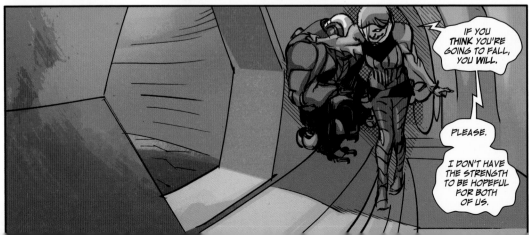

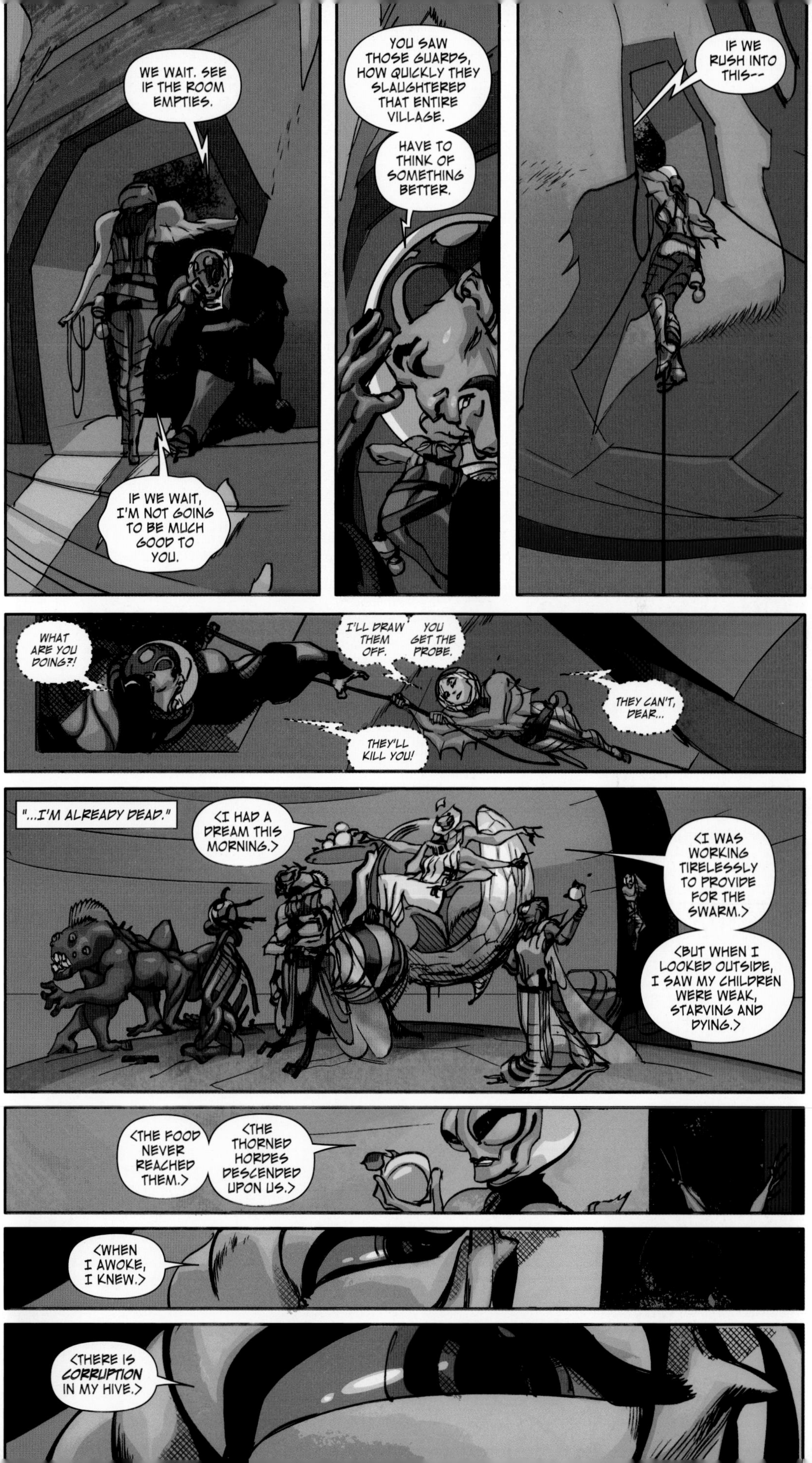
WE WAIT. SEE IF THE ROOM EMPTIES.
IF WE WAIT, I'M NOT GOING TO BE MUCH GOOD TO YOU.
YOU SAW THOSE GUARDS, HOW QUICKLY THEY SLAUGHTERED THAT ENTIRE VILLAGE.
HAVE TO THINK OF SOMETHING BETTER.
IF WE RUSH INTO THIS--
WHAT ARE YOU DOING?!
I'LL DRAW THEM OFF.
YOU GET THE PROBE.
THEY'LL KILL YOU!
THEY CAN'T, DEAR...
"...I'M ALREADY DEAD."
<I HAD A DREAM THIS MORNING.>
<I WAS WORKING TIRELESSLY TO PROVIDE FOR THE SWARM.>
<BUT WHEN I LOOKED OUTSIDE, I SAW MY CHILDREN WERE WEAK, STARVING AND DYING.>
<THE FOOD NEVER REACHED THEM.>
<THE THORNED HORDES DESCENDED UPON US.>
<WHEN I AWOKE, I KNEW.>
<THERE IS CORRUPTION IN MY HIVE.>

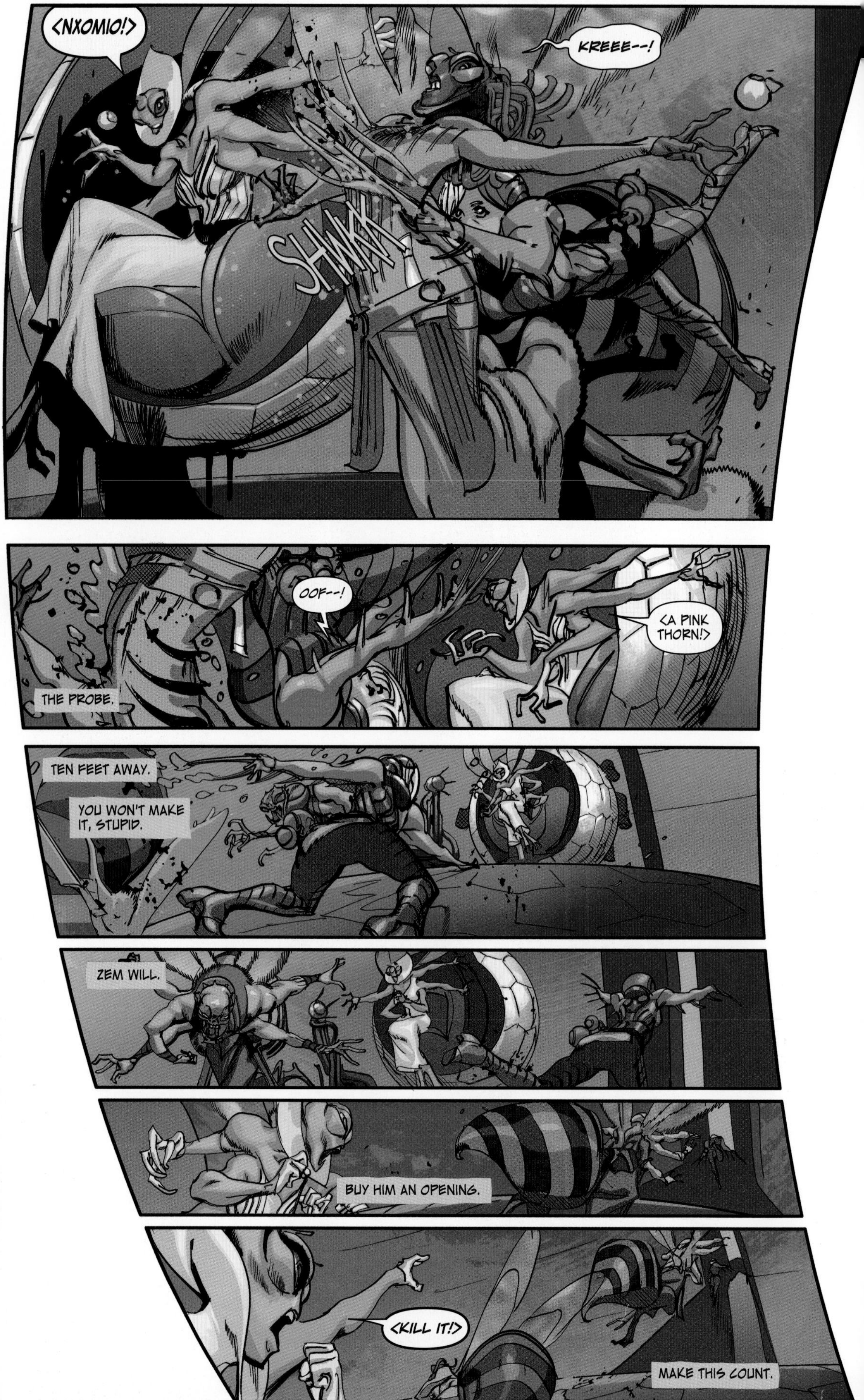
<NXOMIO!>
KREEE--!
SHKK
OOF--!
<A PINK THORN!>
THE PROBE.
TEN FEET AWAY.
YOU WON'T MAKE IT, STUPID.
ZEM WILL.
BUY HIM AN OPENING.
<KILL IT!>
MAKE THIS COUNT.

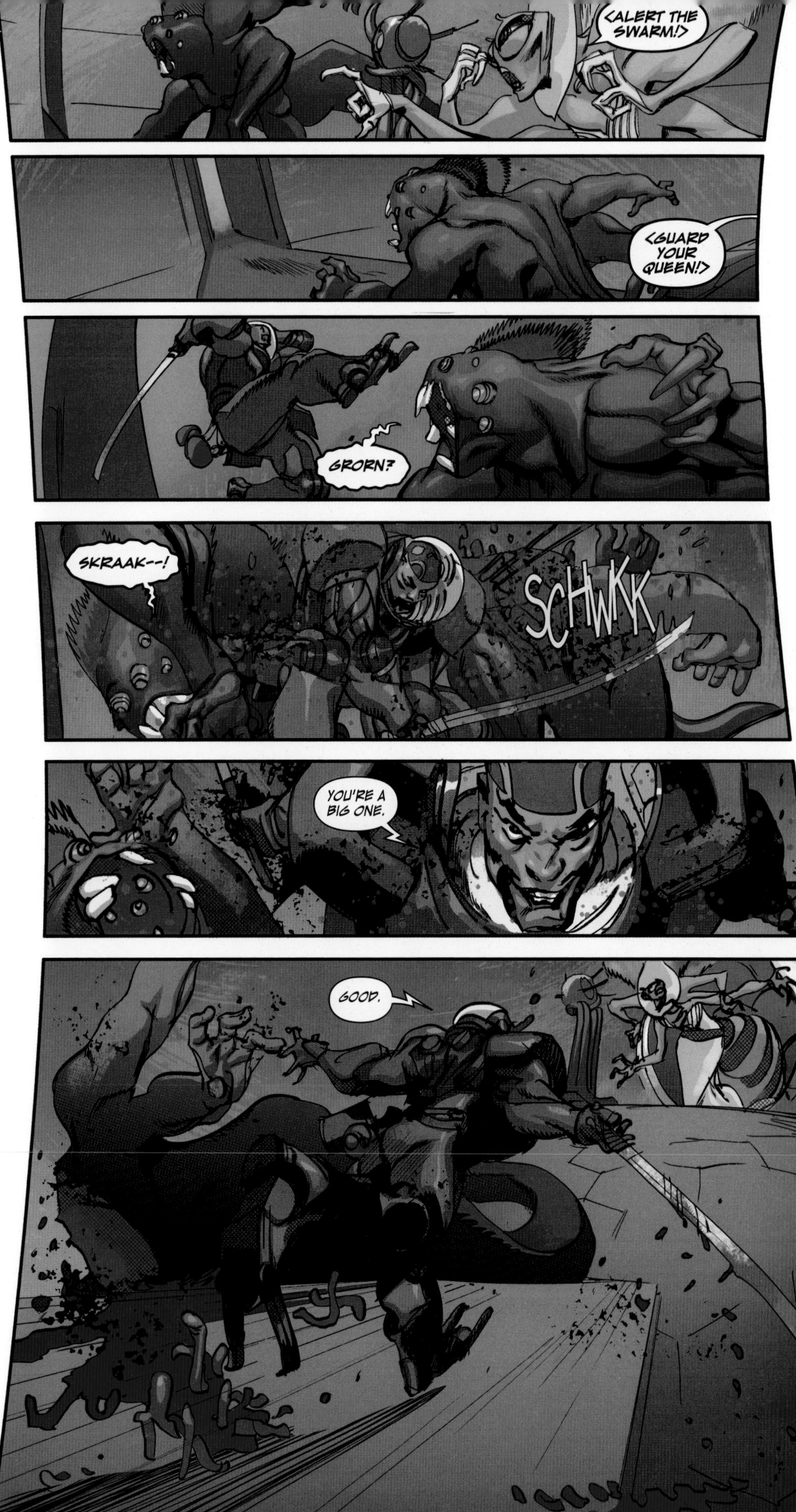
<ALERT THE SWARM!>
<GUARD YOUR QUEEN!>
GRORN?
SKRAAK--!
SCHWKK
YOU'RE A BIG ONE.
GOOD.

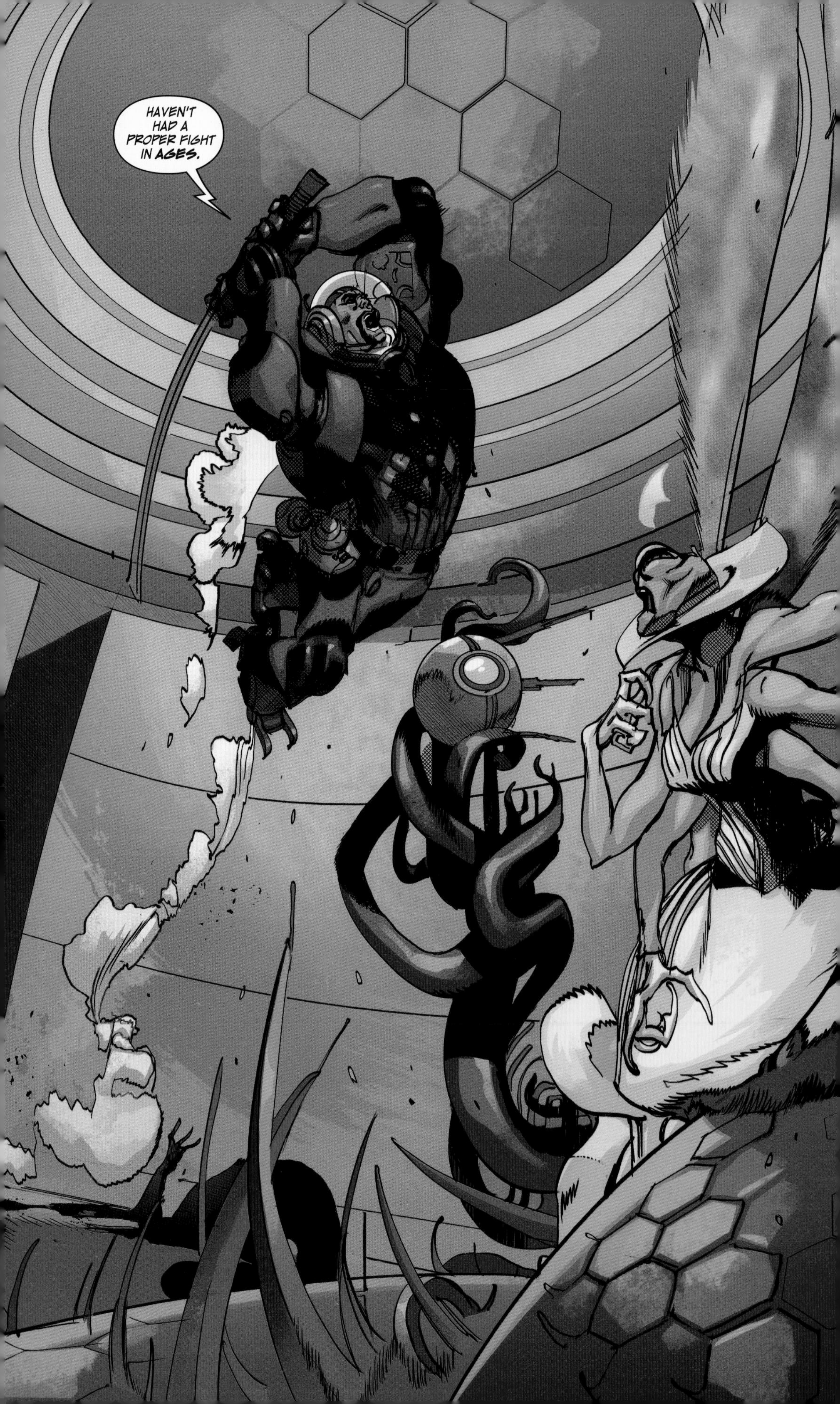
HAVEN'T HAD A PROPER FIGHT IN AGES.

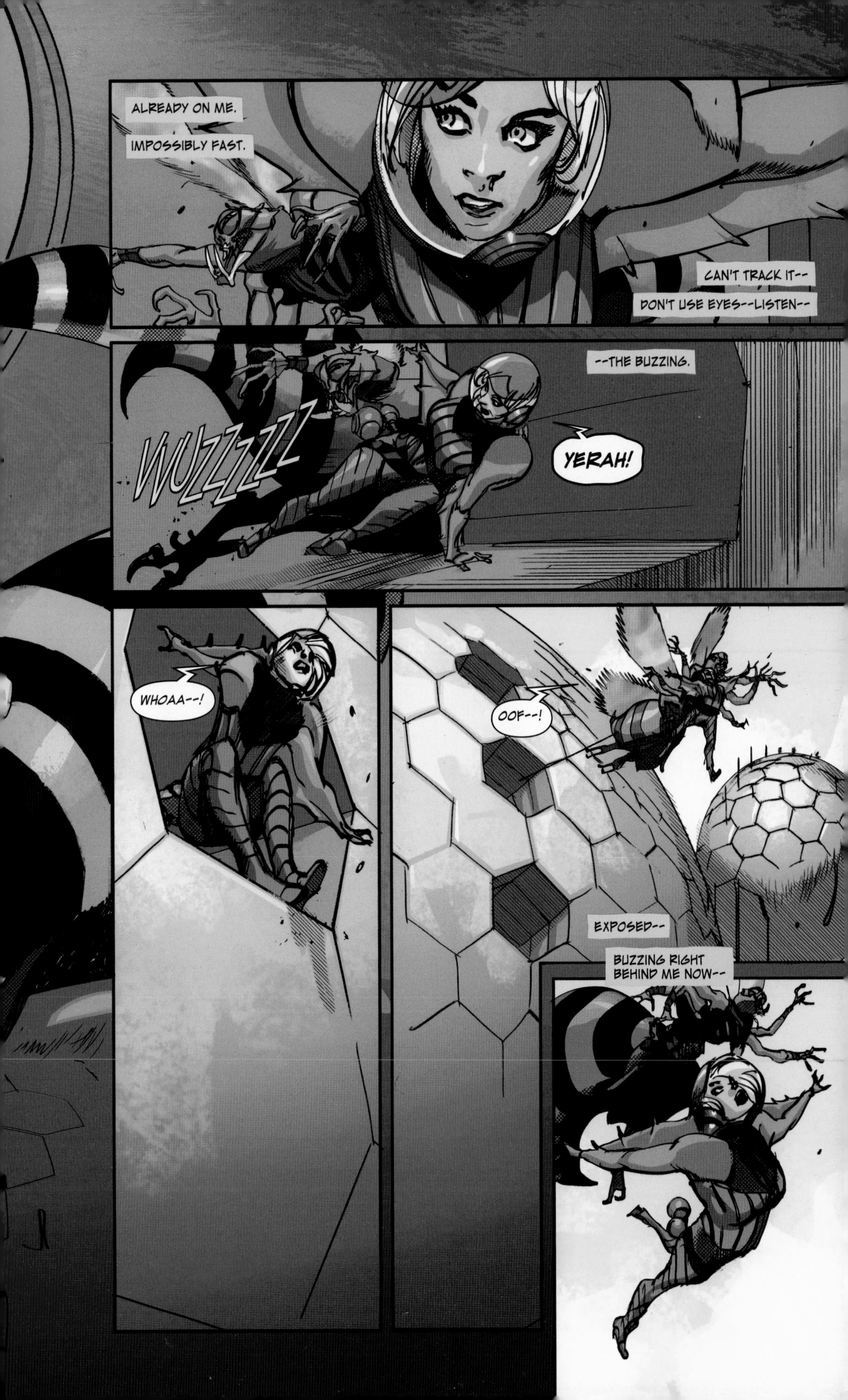
ALREADY ON ME.
IMPOSSIBLY FAST.
CAN'T TRACK IT--
DON'T USE EYES--LISTEN--
--THE BUZZING.
WUZZZZZZ
YERAH!
WHOAA--!
OOF--!
EXPOSED--
BUZZING RIGHT BEHIND ME NOW--

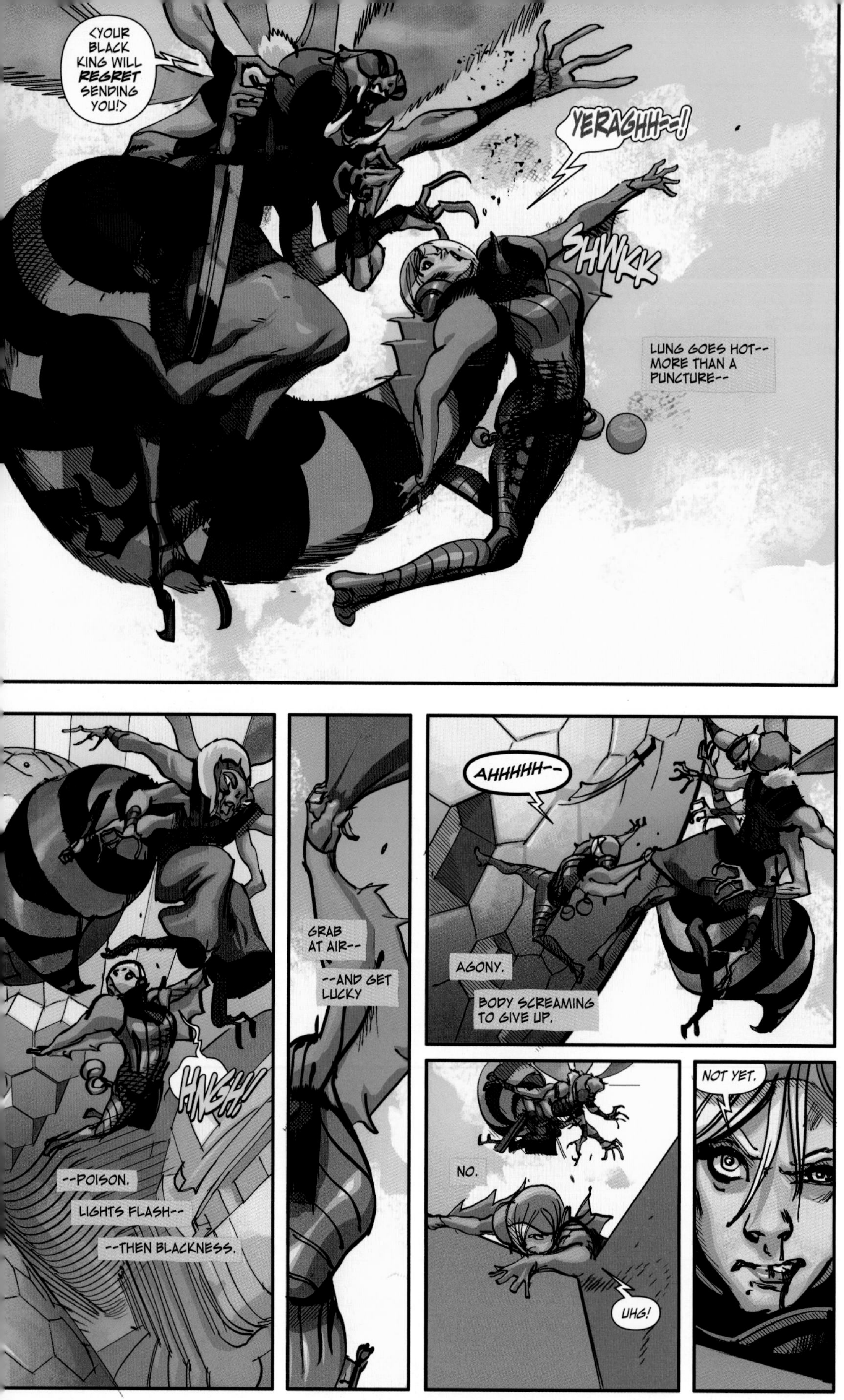
<YOUR BLACK KING WILL REGRET SENDING YOU!>
YERAGHH--!
SHWKK
LUNG GOES HOT-- MORE THAN A PUNCTURE--
HNGH!
--POISON.
LIGHTS FLASH--
--THEN BLACKNESS.
GRAB AT AIR--
--AND GET LUCKY
AHHHHH--
AGONY.
BODY SCREAMING TO GIVE UP.
NO.
UHG!
NOT YET.

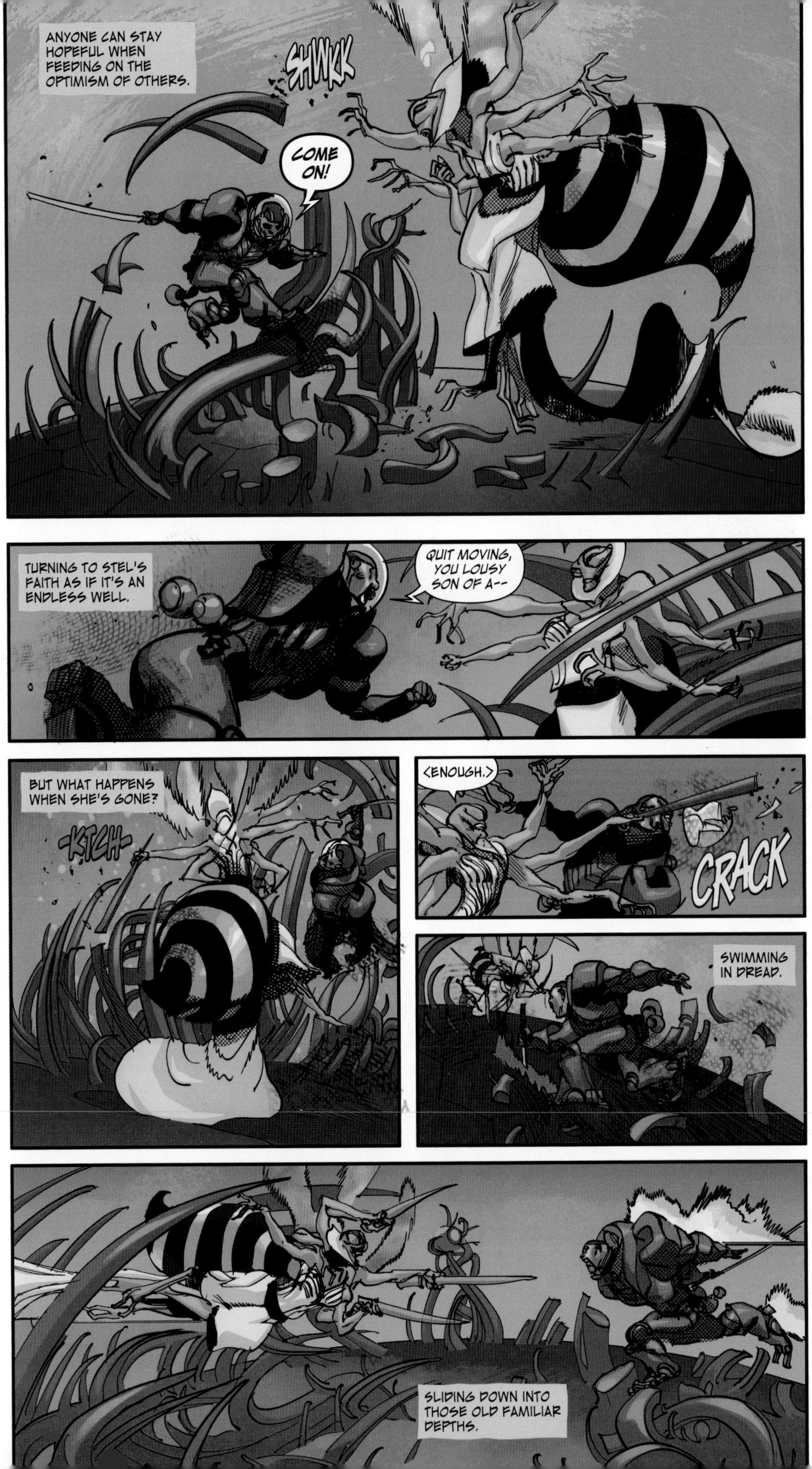
ANYONE CAN STAY HOPEFUL WHEN FEEDING ON THE OPTIMISM OF OTHERS.
SHWKK
COME ON!
TURNING TO STEL'S FAITH AS IF IT'S AN ENDLESS WELL.
QUIT MOVING, YOU LOUSY SON OF A--
BUT WHAT HAPPENS WHEN SHE'S GONE?
KTCH
<ENOUGH.>
CRACK
SWIMMING IN DREAD.
SLIDING DOWN INTO THOSE OLD FAMILIAR DEPTHS.

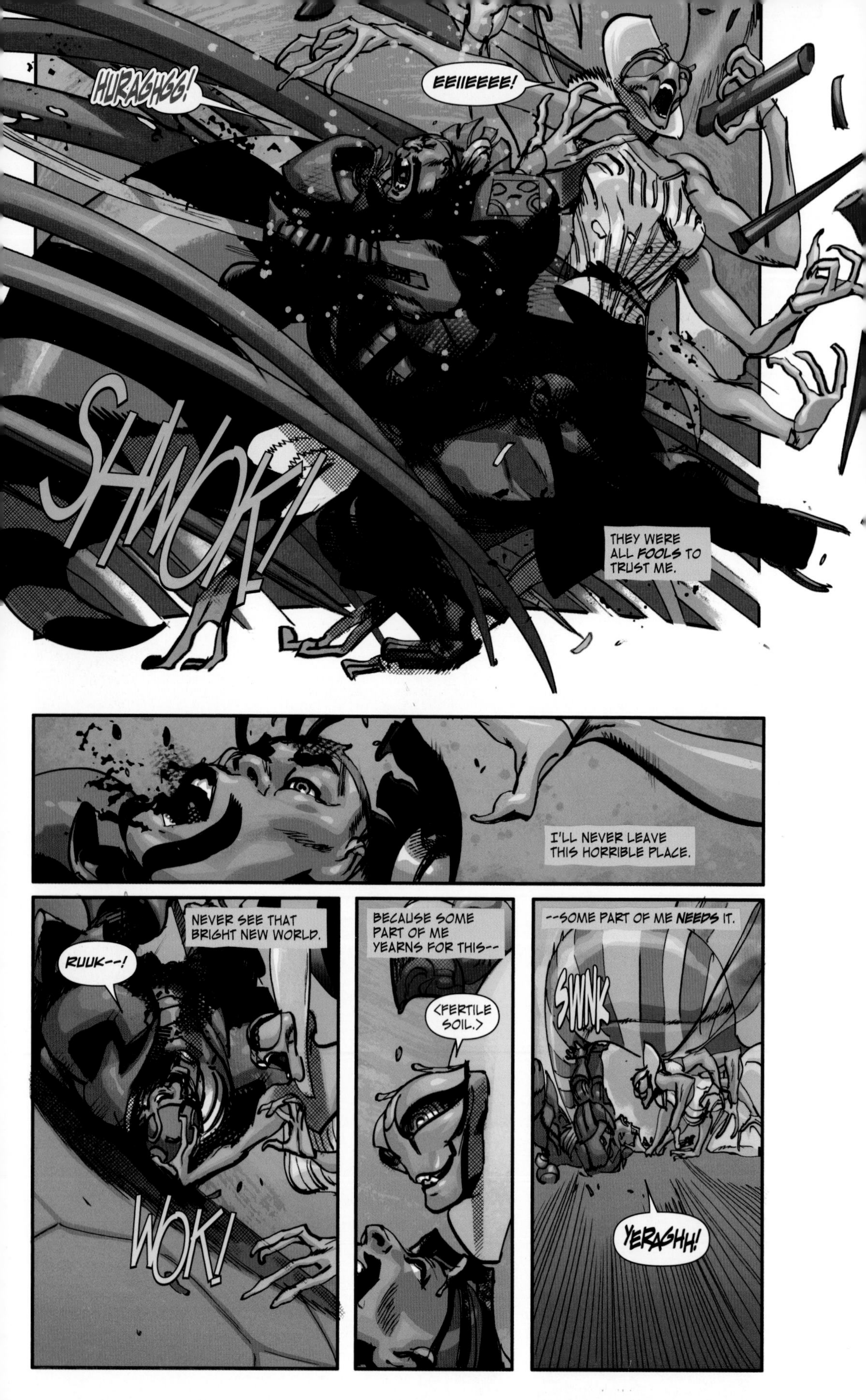
HURAGHGG!
EEIIEEEE!
SHWOK!
THEY WERE ALL FOOLS TO TRUST ME.
I'LL NEVER LEAVE THIS HORRIBLE PLACE.
NEVER SEE THAT BRIGHT NEW WORLD.
RUUK--!
WOK!
BECAUSE SOME PART OF ME YEARNS FOR THIS--
<FERTILE SOIL.>
--SOME PART OF ME NEEDS IT.
SWINK
YERAGHH!

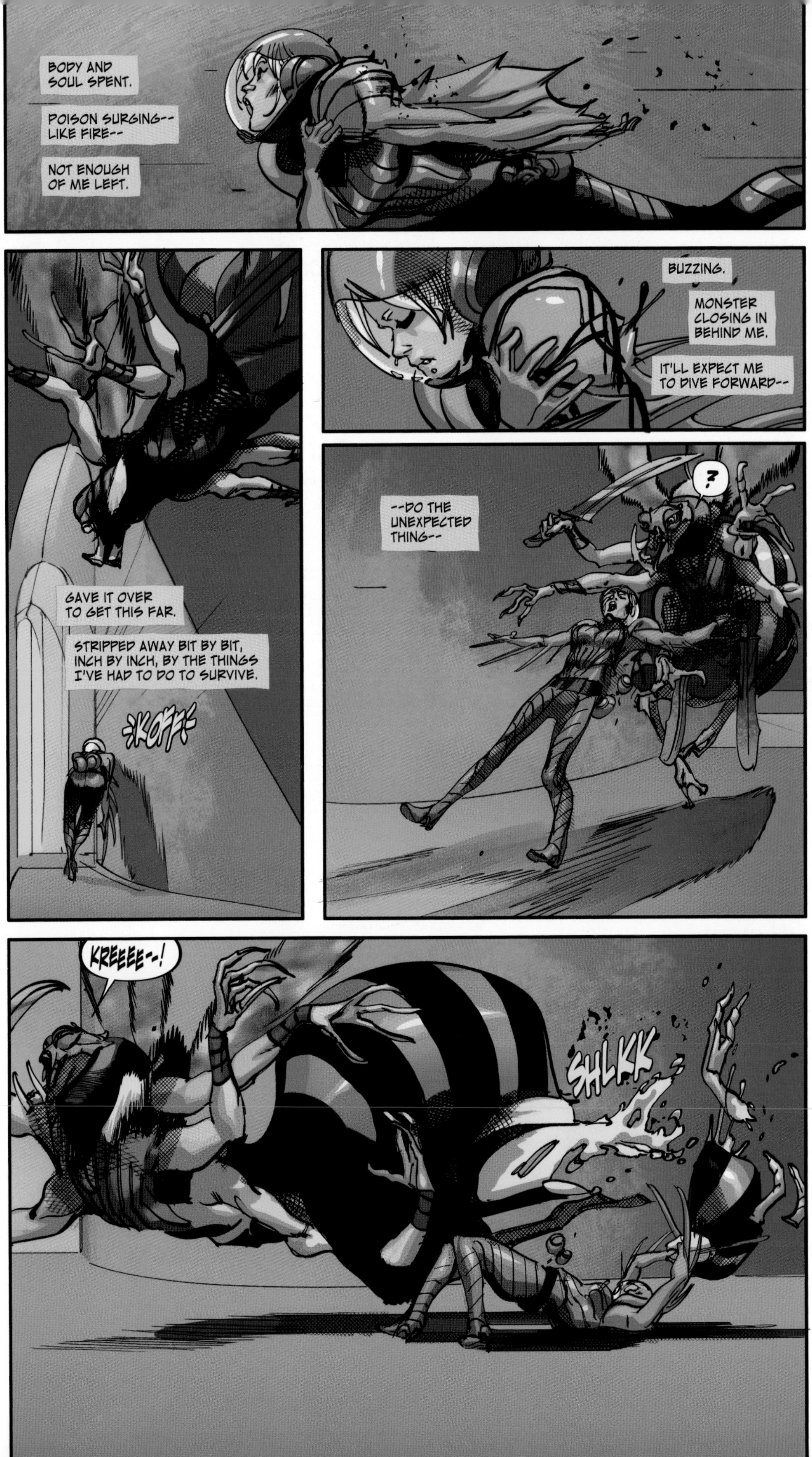
BODY AND SOUL SPENT.
POISON SURGING-- LIKE FIRE--
NOT ENOUGH OF ME LEFT.
GAVE IT OVER TO GET THIS FAR.
STRIPPED AWAY BIT BY BIT, INCH BY INCH, BY THE THINGS I'VE HAD TO DO TO SURVIVE.
KOFF!
BUZZING.
MONSTER CLOSING IN BEHIND ME.
IT'LL EXPECT ME TO DIVE FORWARD--
--DO THE UNEXPECTED THING--
?
KREEEE--!
SHLKK

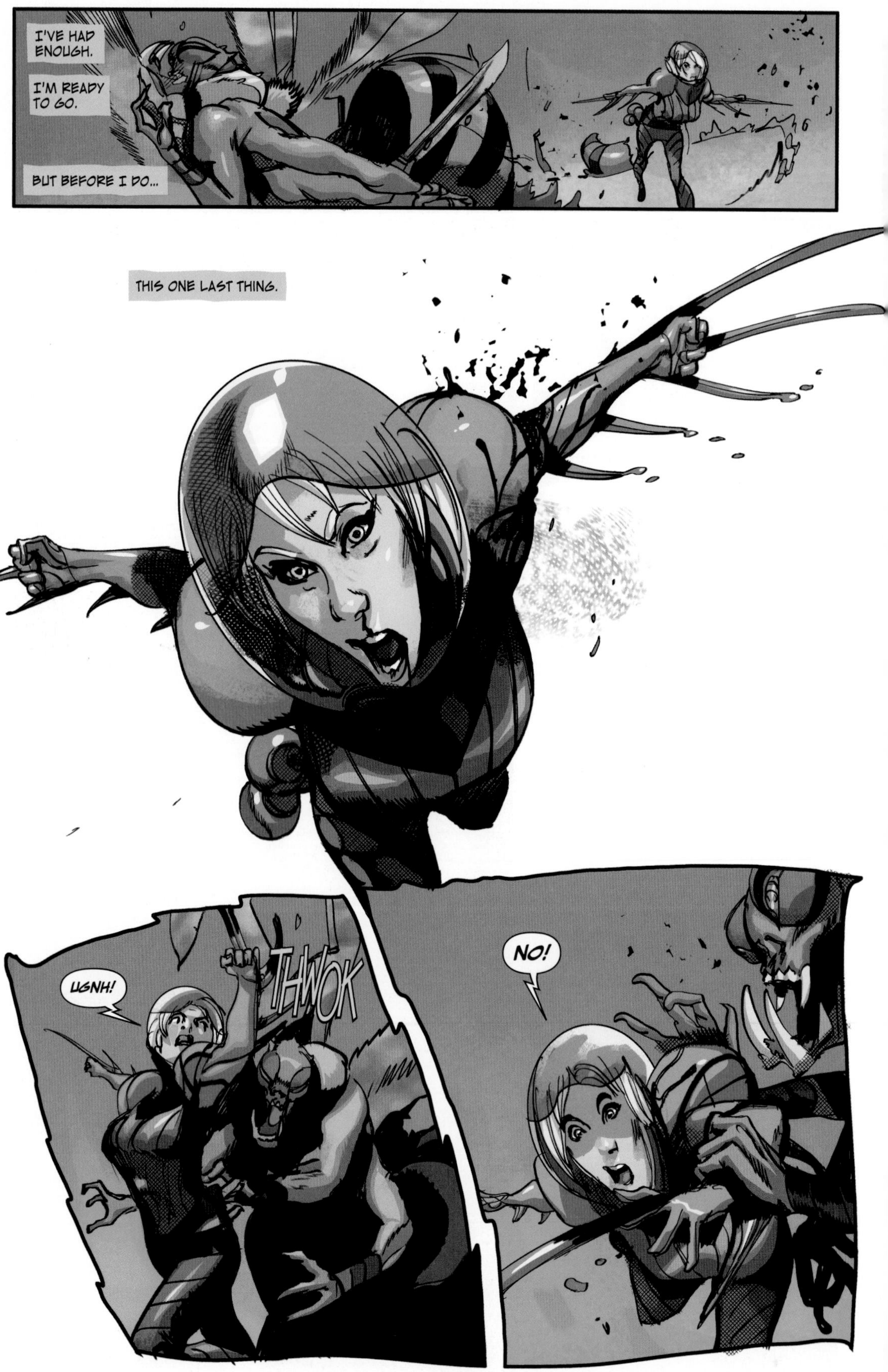
I'VE HAD ENOUGH.
I'M READY TO GO.
BUT BEFORE I DO...
THIS ONE LAST THING.
UGNH!
THWOK
NO!

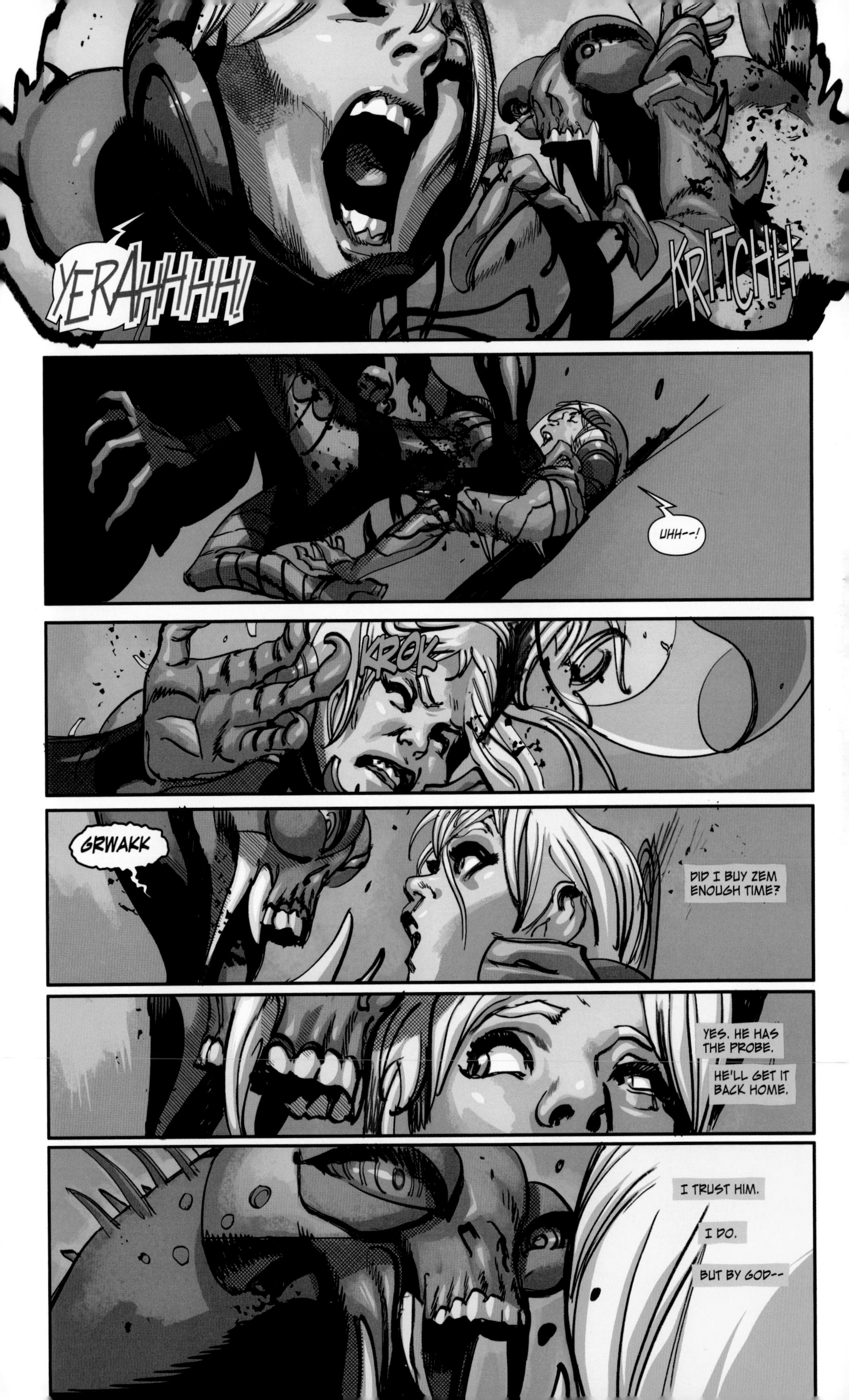
YERAHHHH!
KRITCHH
UHH--!
KROK
GRWAKK
DID I BUY ZEM ENOUGH TIME?
YES. HE HAS THE PROBE.
HE'LL GET IT BACK HOME.
I TRUST HIM.
I DO.
BUT BY GOD--

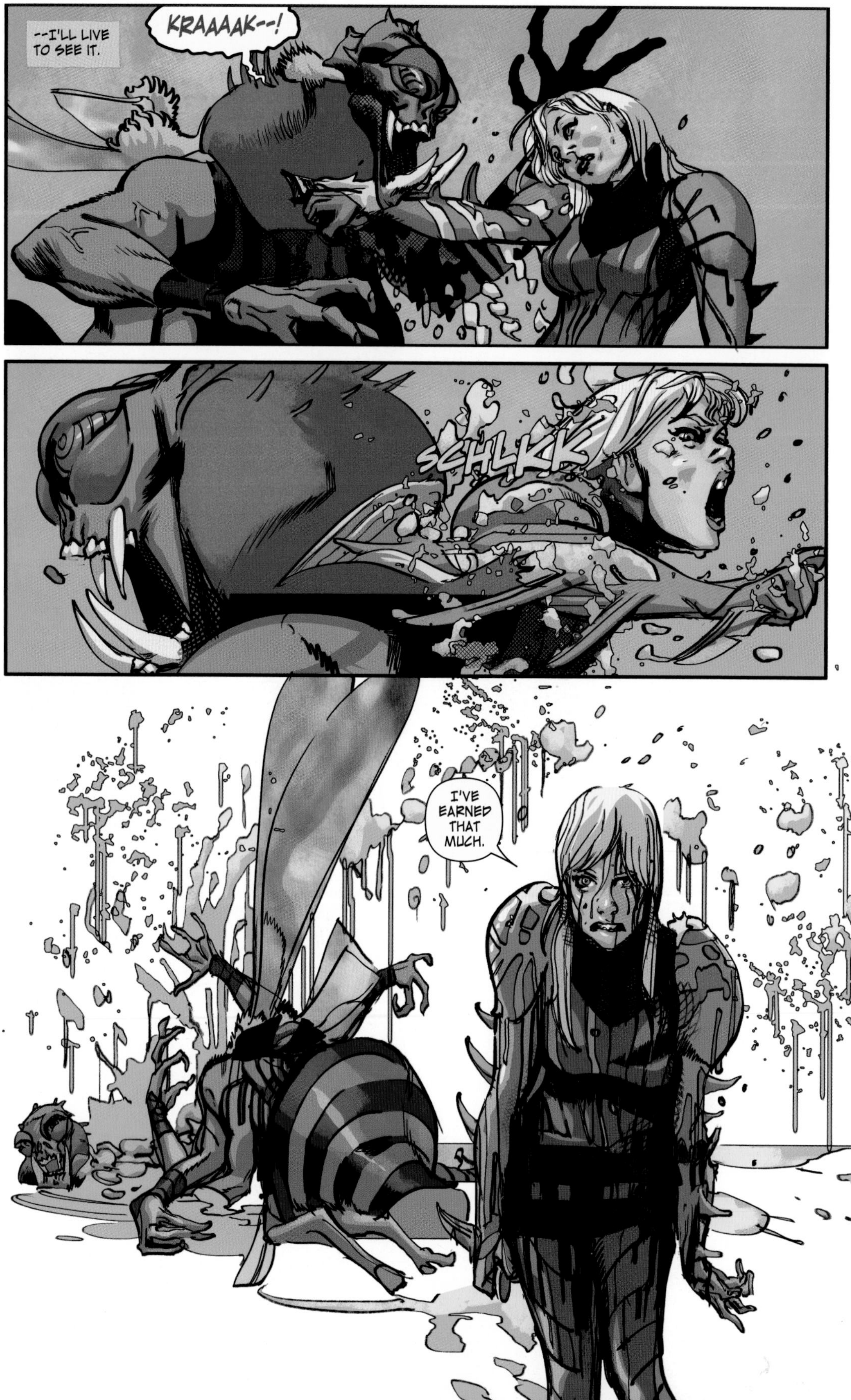
--I'LL LIVE TO SEE IT.
KRAAAAK--!
SCHLKK
I'VE EARNED THAT MUCH.

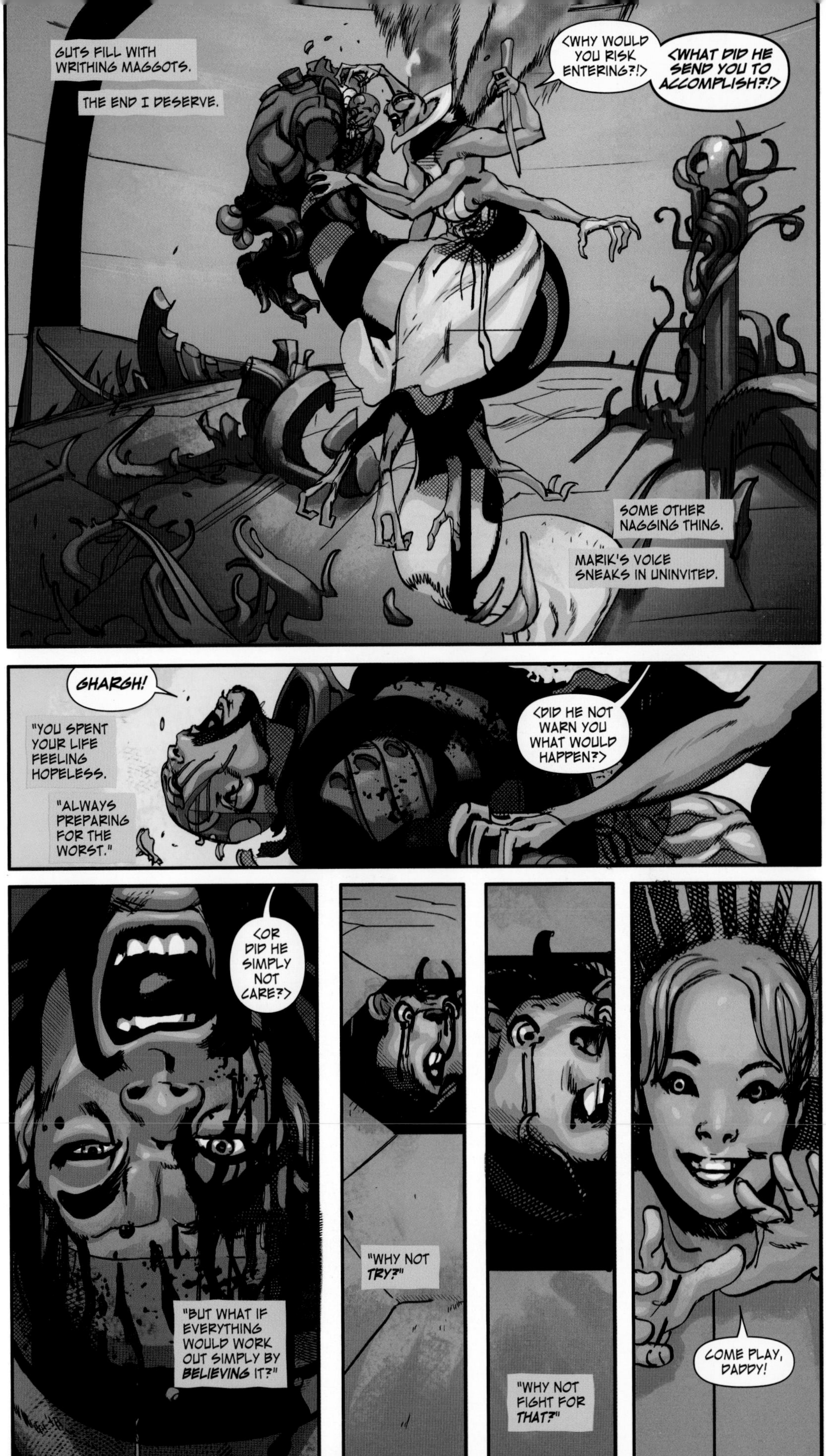
GUTS FILL WITH WRITHING MAGGOTS.
THE END I DESERVE.
<WHY WOULD YOU RISK ENTERING?!>
<WHAT DID HE SEND YOU TO ACCOMPLISH?!>
SOME OTHER NAGGING THING.
MARIK'S VOICE SNEAKS IN UNINVITED.
GHARGH!
"YOU SPENT YOUR LIFE FEELING HOPELESS.
"ALWAYS PREPARING FOR THE WORST."
<DID HE NOT WARN YOU WHAT WOULD HAPPEN?>
<OR DID HE SIMPLY NOT CARE?>
"BUT WHAT IF EVERYTHING WOULD WORK OUT SIMPLY BY BELIEVING IT?"
"WHY NOT TRY?"
"WHY NOT FIGHT FOR THAT?"
COME PLAY, DADDY!

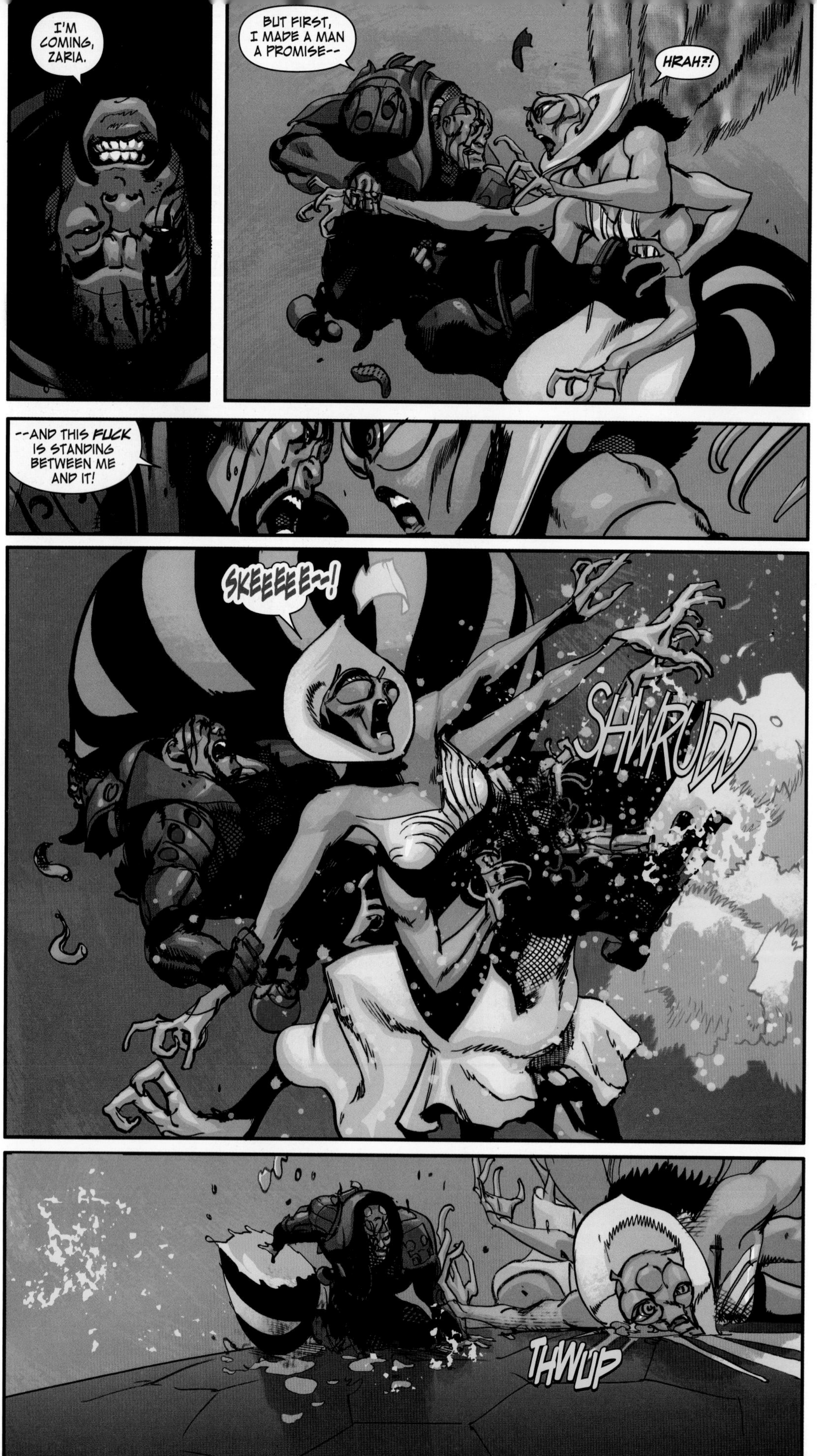
I'M COMING, ZARIA.
BUT FIRST, I MADE A MAN A PROMISE--
HRAH?!
--AND THIS FUCK IS STANDING BETWEEN ME AND IT!
SKEEEEEE--!
SHWRUDD
THWUP

I-- WILL--

TRY!

JOHL USED TO SAY THERE IS NO SUCH THING AS A HAPPY ENDING.

TIME CHIPS AWAY EVERYTHING YOU LOVE.

KILLING IT OFF ONE PIECE AT A TIME.

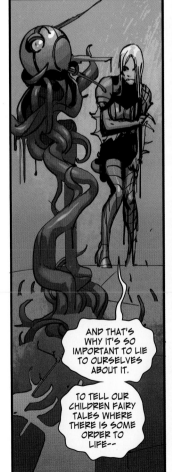

AND THAT'S WHY IT'S SO IMPORTANT TO LIE TO OURSELVES ABOUT IT.

TO TELL OUR CHILDREN FAIRY TALES WHERE THERE IS SOME ORDER TO LIFE--

BECAUSE EVERYTHING WE LOVE WILL BE TAKEN AWAY FROM US.

EITHER WE'RE LEFT ALONE TO BEAR ITS ABSENCE...

BEEP.

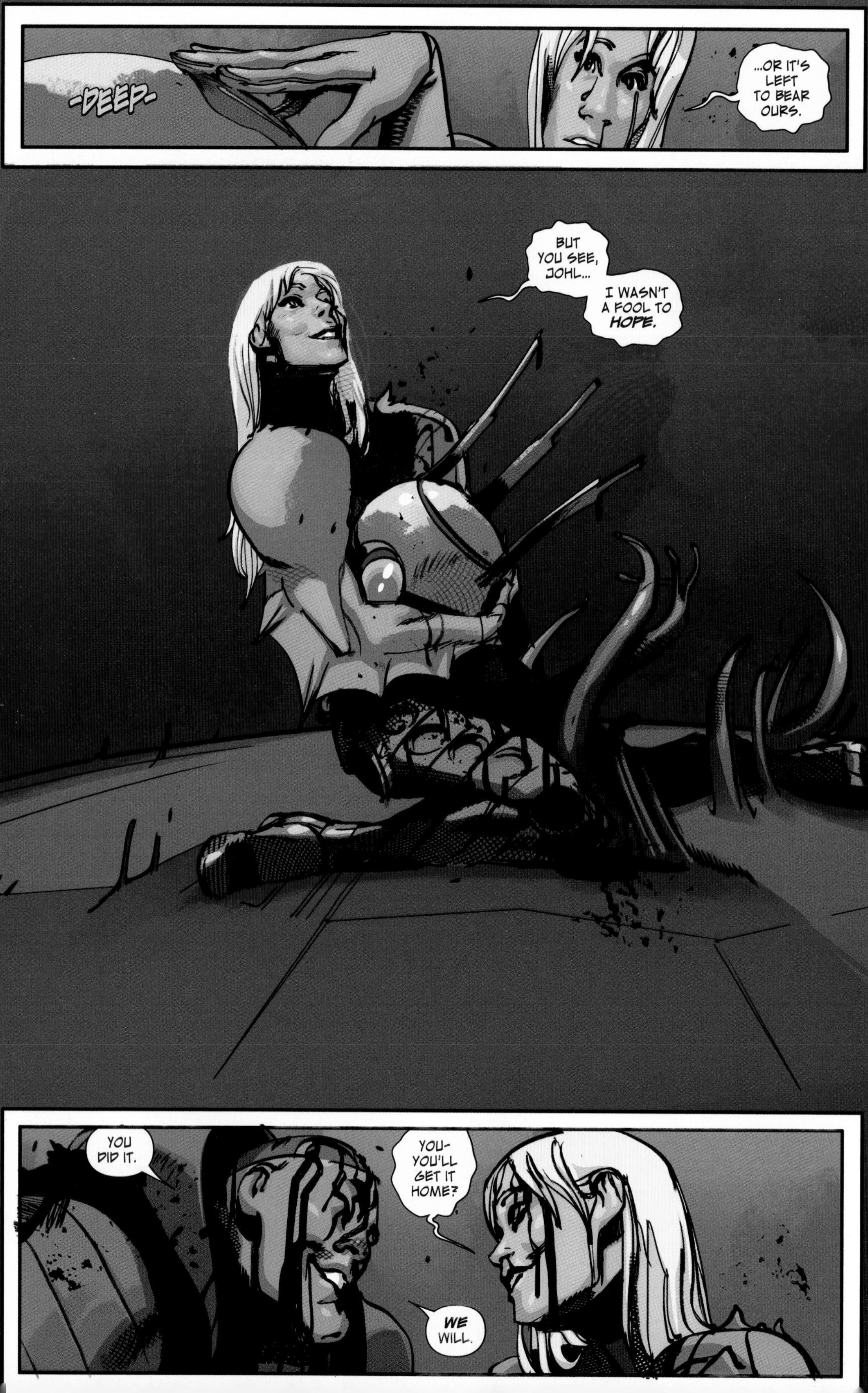
-DEEP-
...OR IT'S LEFT TO BEAR OURS.
BUT YOU SEE, JOHL...
I WASN'T A FOOL TO HOPE.
YOU DID IT.
YOU- YOU'LL GET IT HOME?
WE WILL.

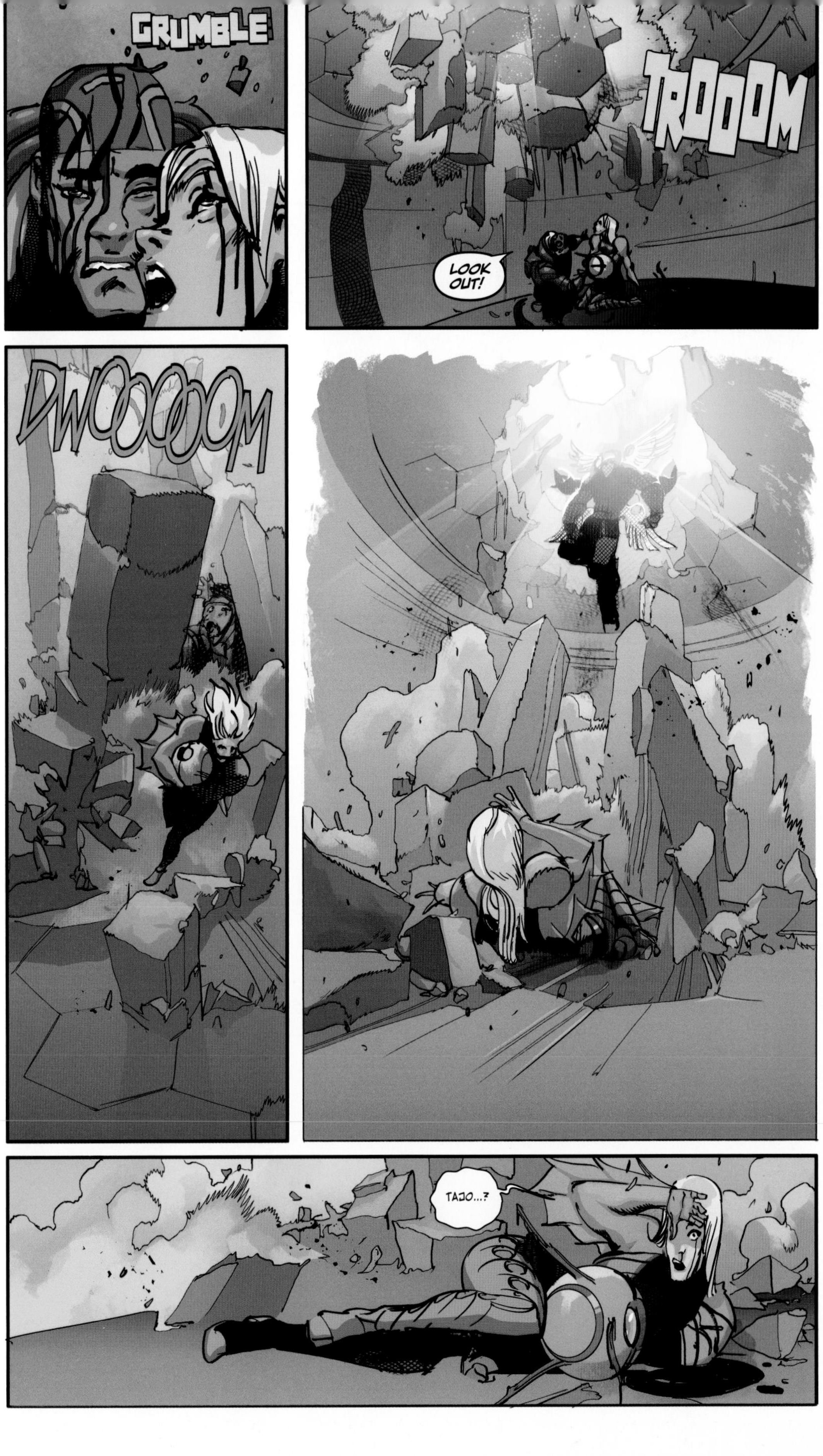
GRUMBLE
TROOOM
LOOK OUT!
DWOOOOOOM
TAJO...?

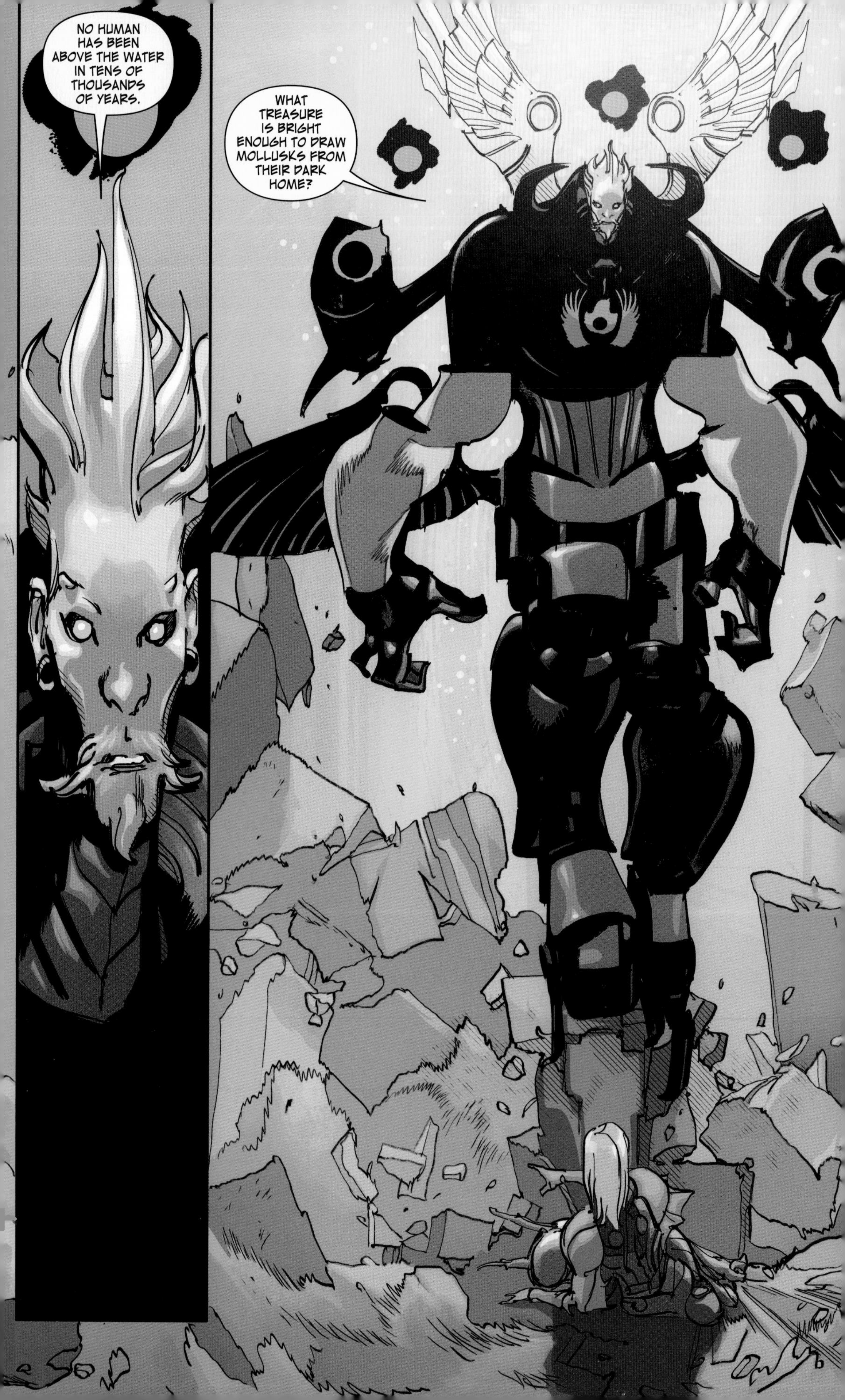
NO HUMAN HAS BEEN ABOVE THE WATER IN TENS OF THOUSANDS OF YEARS.
WHAT TREASURE IS BRIGHT ENOUGH TO DRAW MOLLUSKS FROM THEIR DARK HOME?

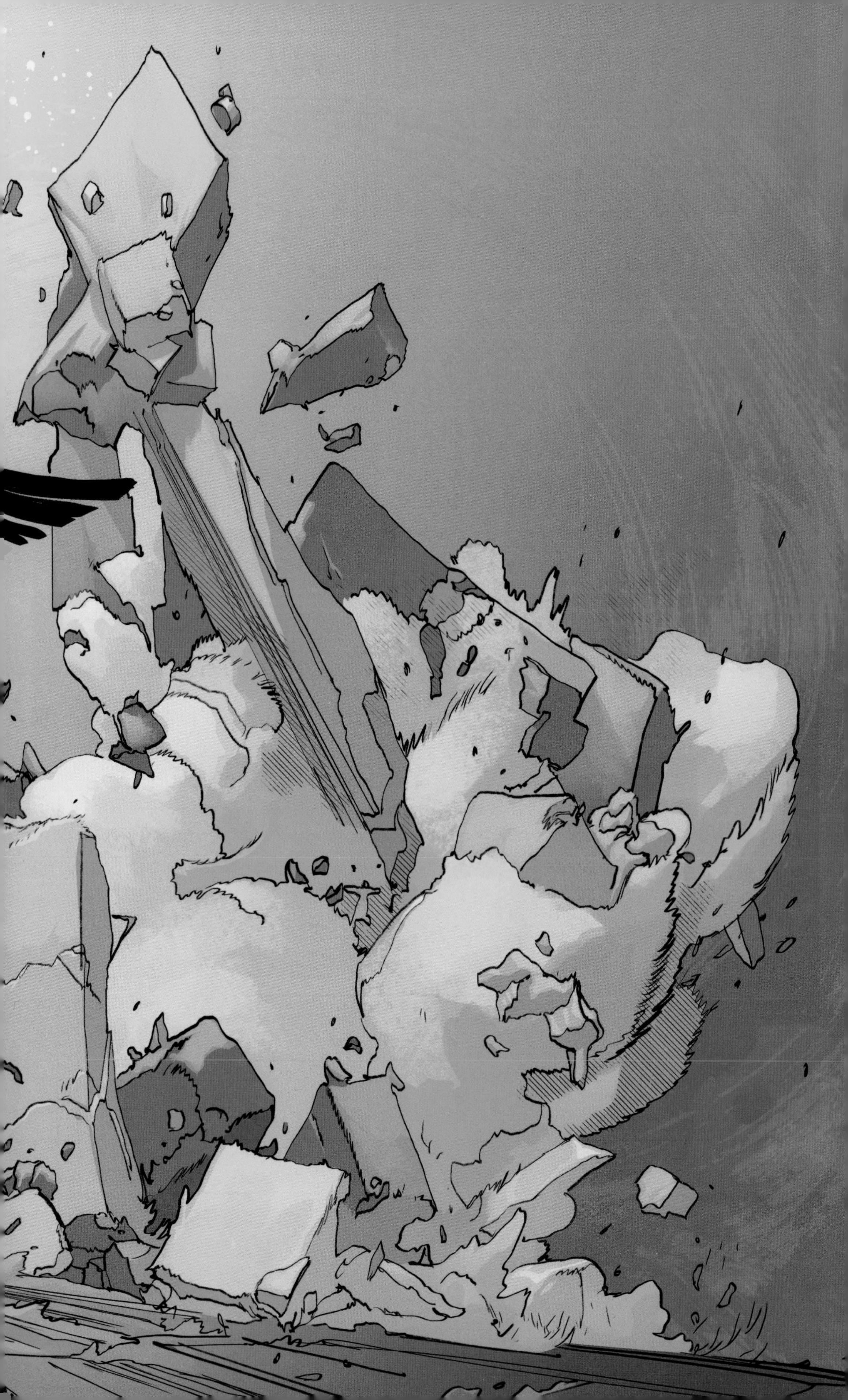

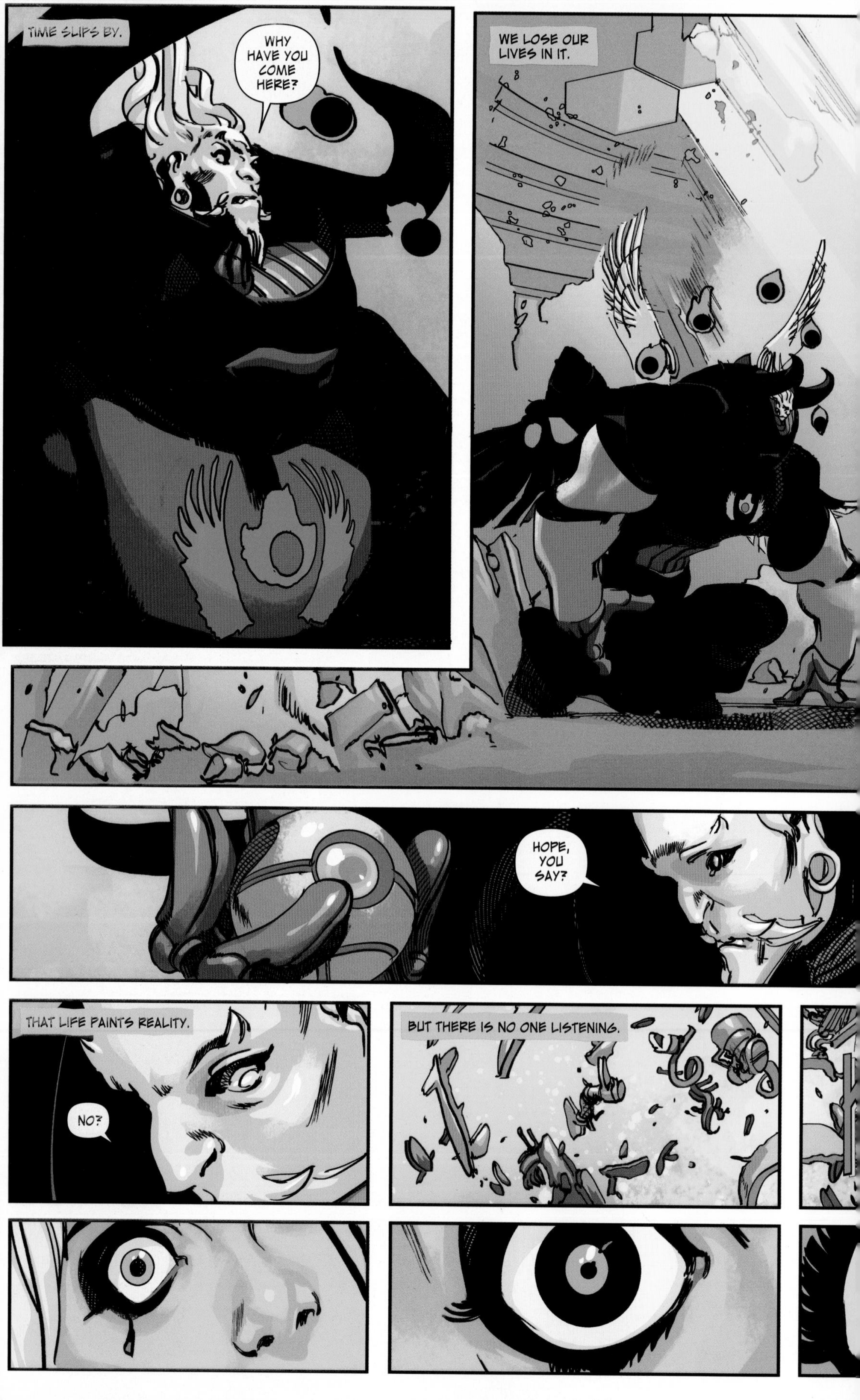
TIME SLIPS BY.
WHY HAVE YOU COME HERE?
WE LOSE OUR LIVES IN IT.
HOPE, YOU SAY?
THAT LIFE PAINTS REALITY.
NO?
BUT THERE IS NO ONE LISTENING.

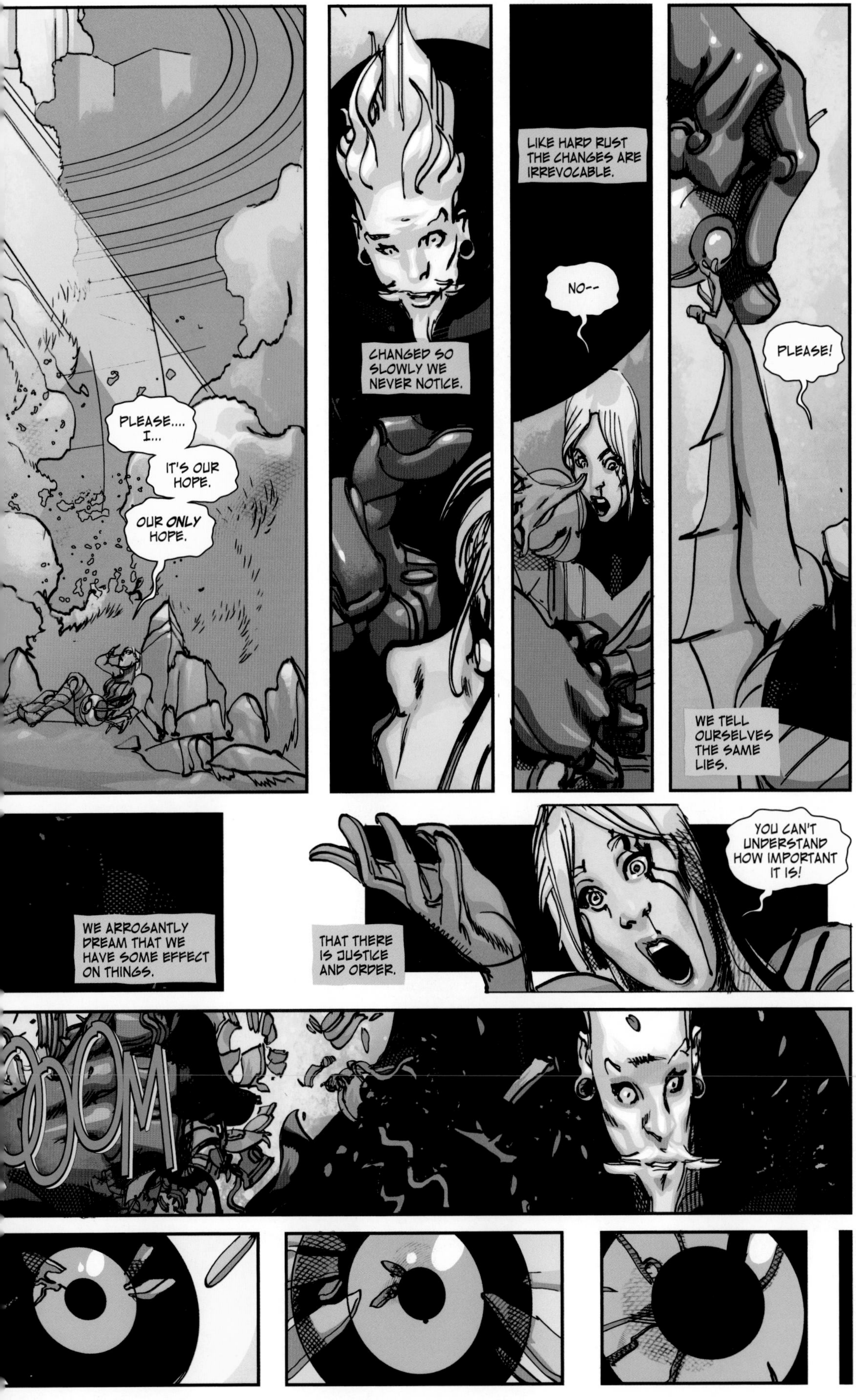
PLEASE.... I...
IT'S OUR HOPE.
OUR ONLY HOPE.
CHANGED SO SLOWLY WE NEVER NOTICE.
LIKE HARD RUST THE CHANGES ARE IRREVOCABLE.
NO--
PLEASE!
WE TELL OURSELVES THE SAME LIES.
WE ARROGANTLY DREAM THAT WE HAVE SOME EFFECT ON THINGS.
THAT THERE IS JUSTICE AND ORDER.
YOU CAN'T UNDERSTAND HOW IMPORTANT IT IS!
OOOM

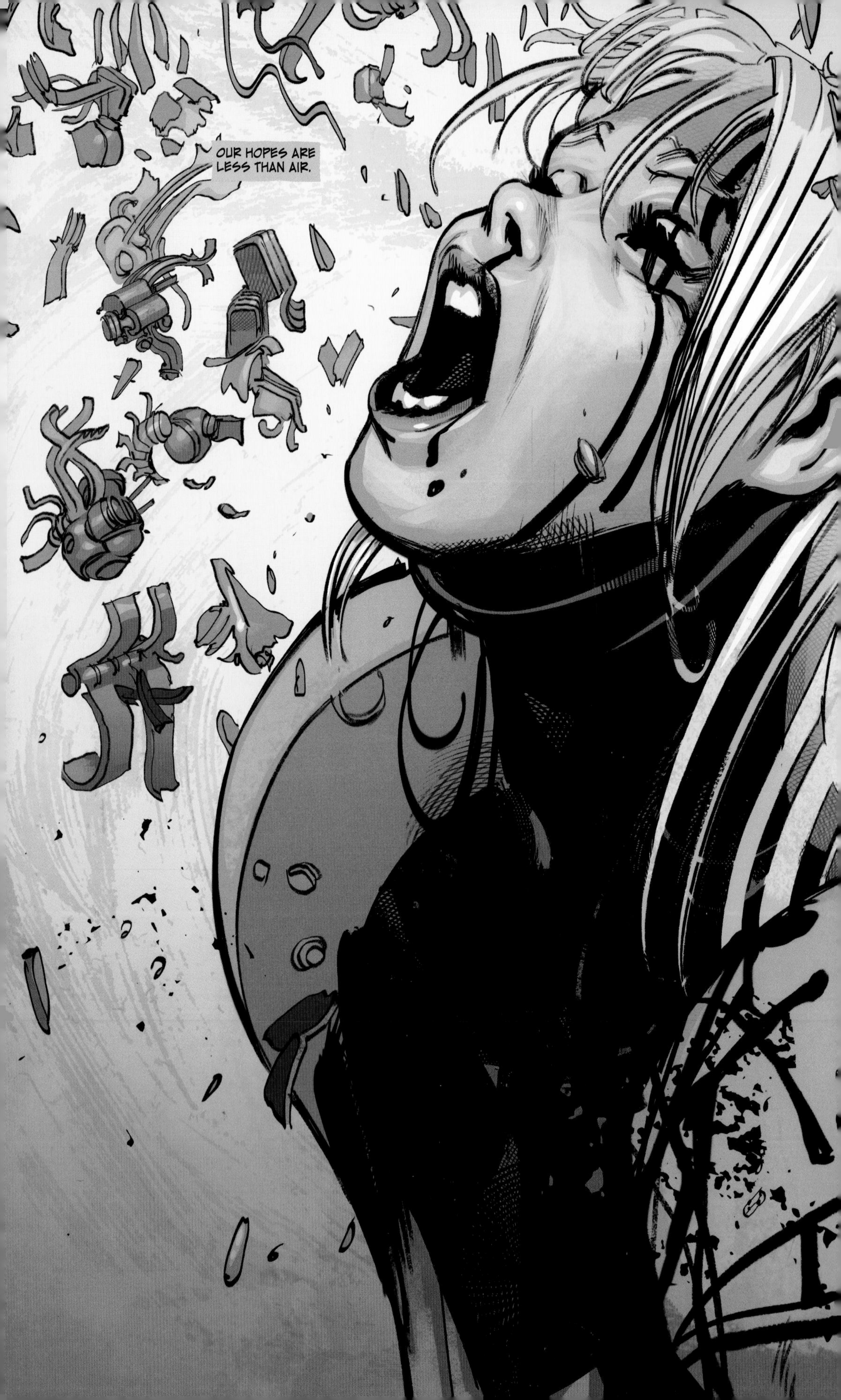
OUR HOPES ARE LESS THAN AIR.

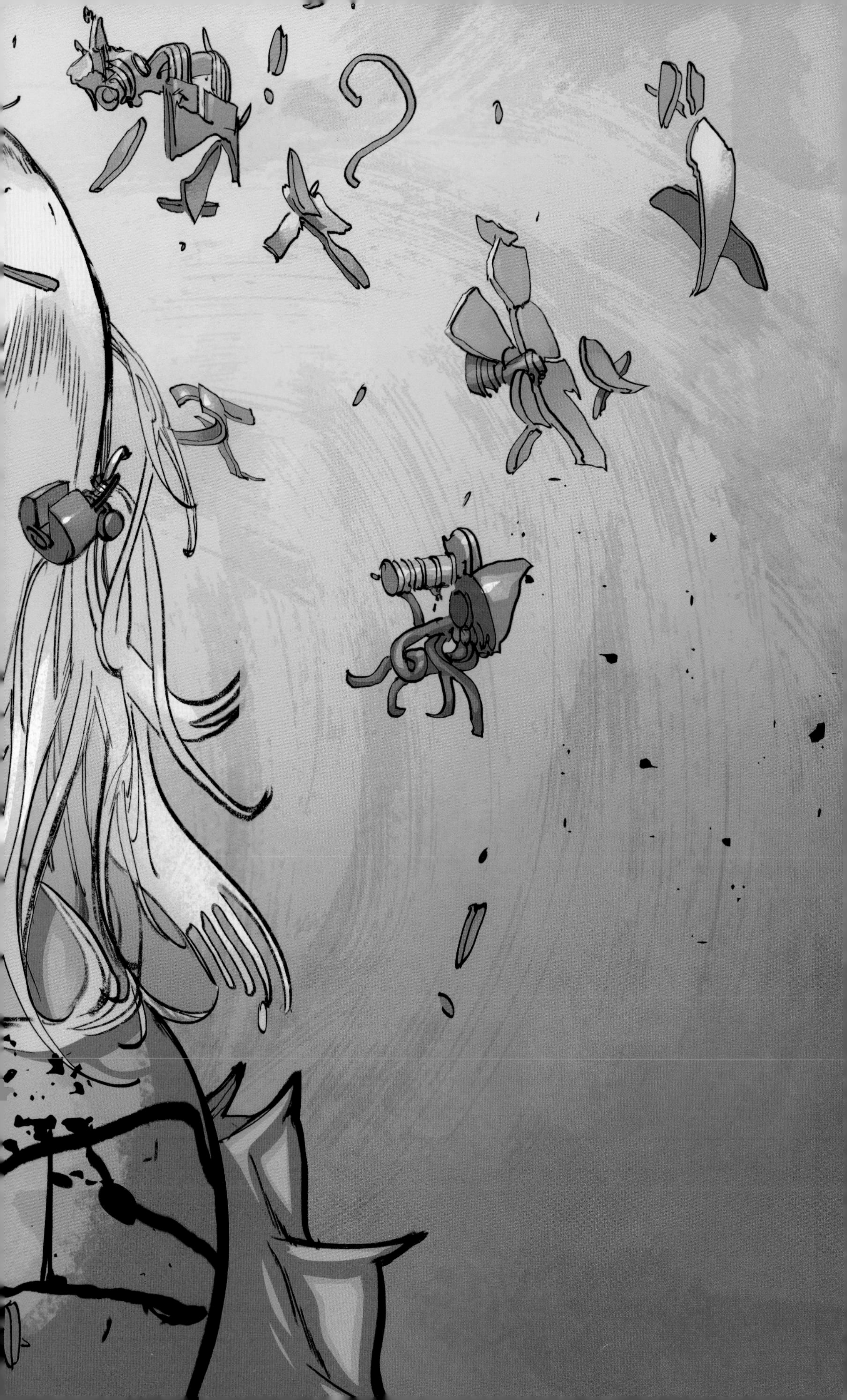

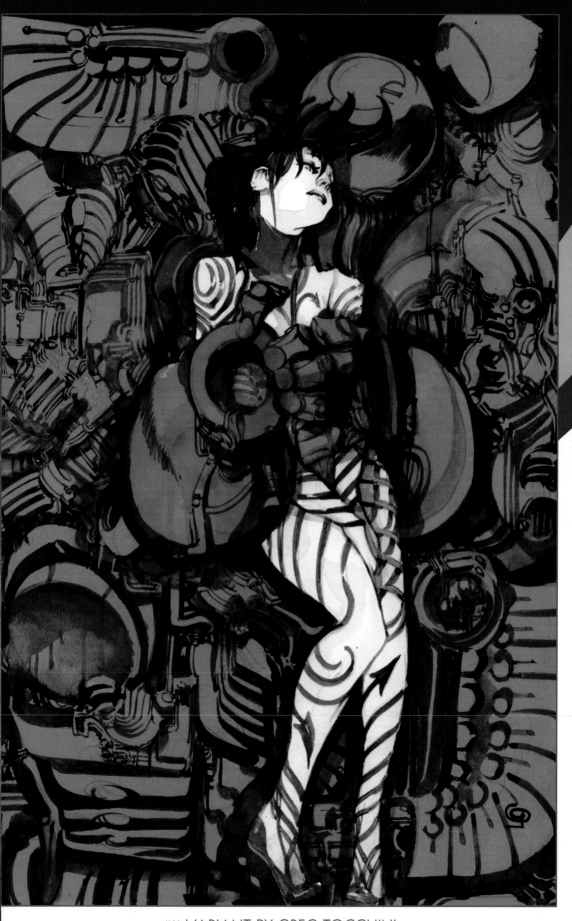

#11 VARIANT BY GREG TOCCHINI

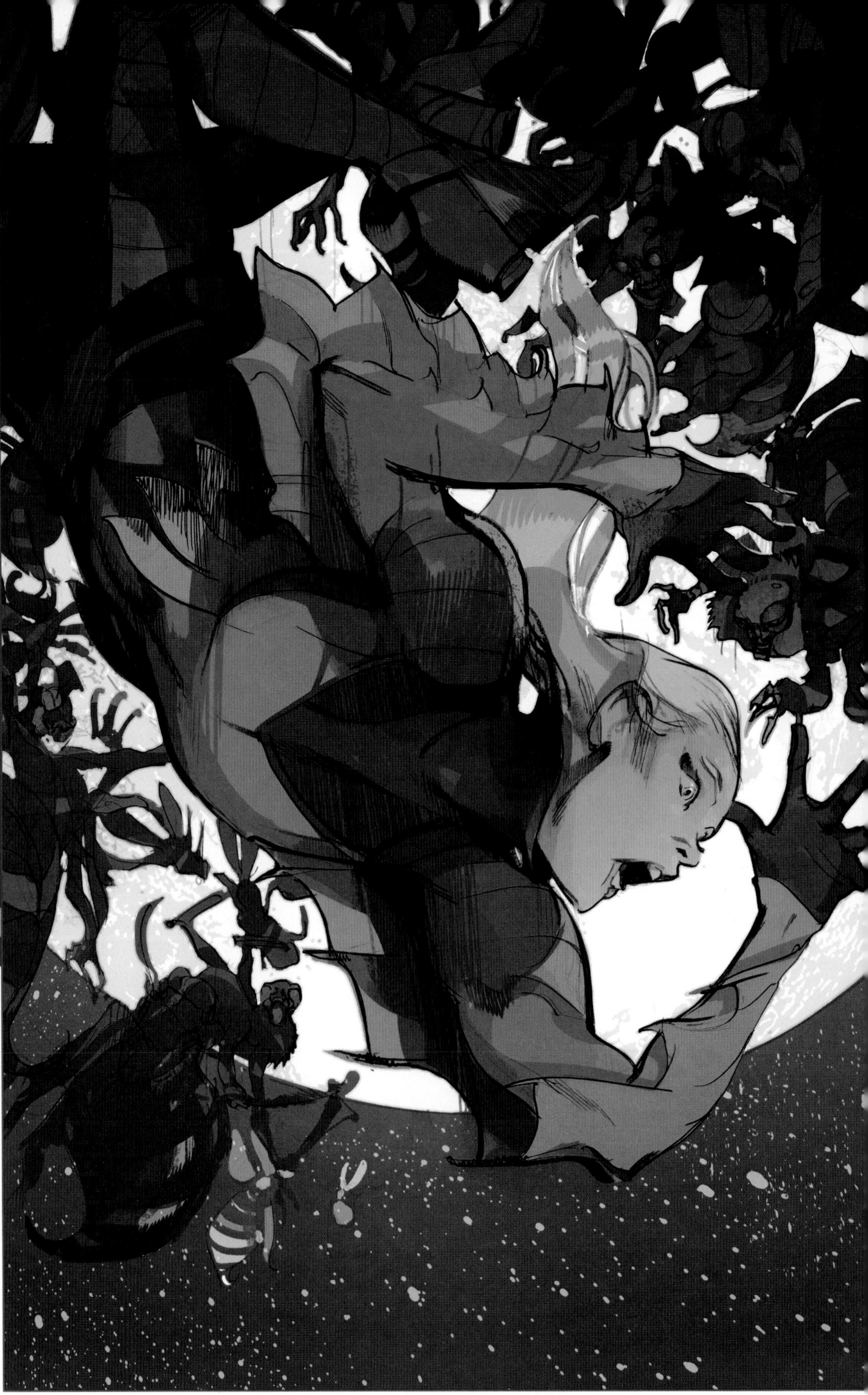

#12 VARIANT BY GREG TOCCHINI

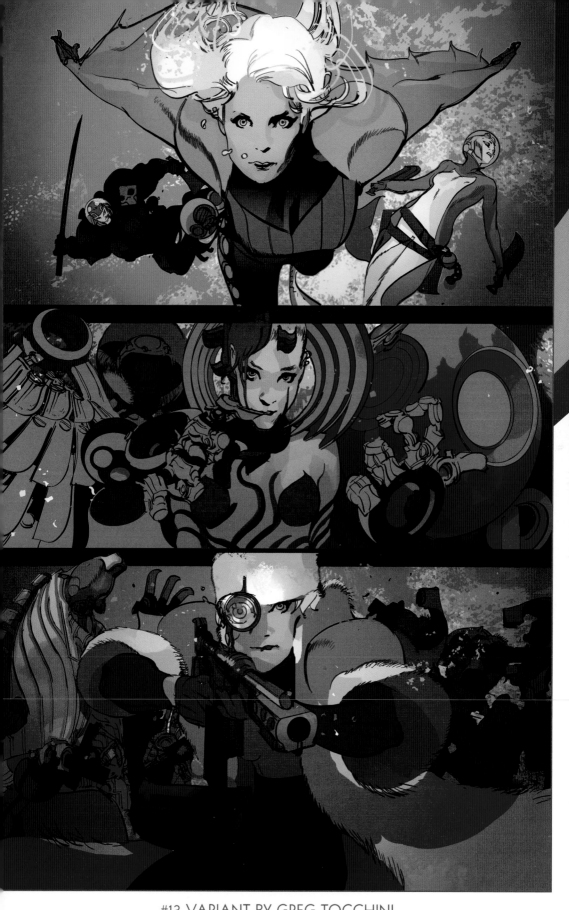

#13 VARIANT BY GREG TOCCHINI

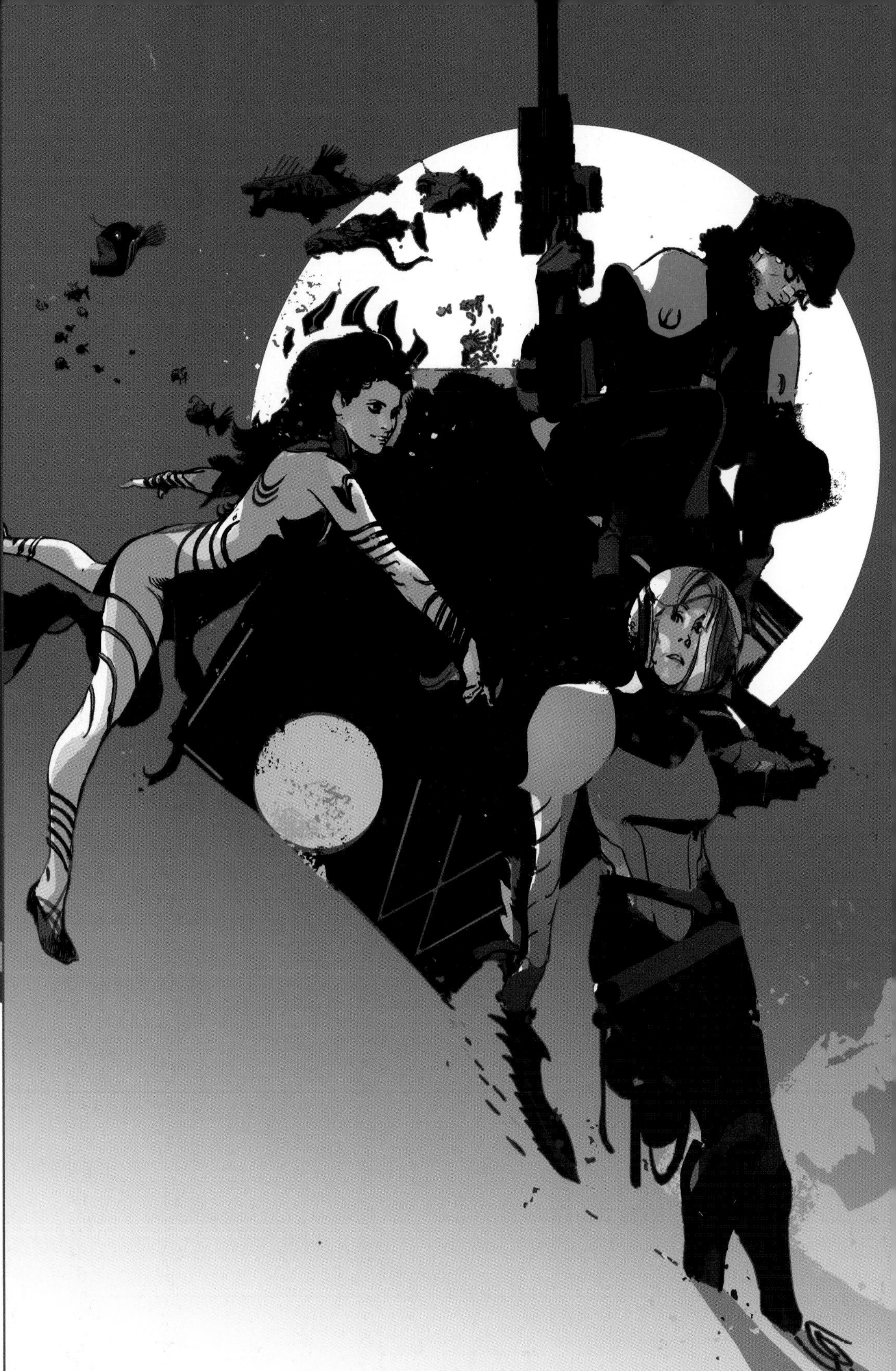

#14 VARIANT BY GREG TOCCHINI

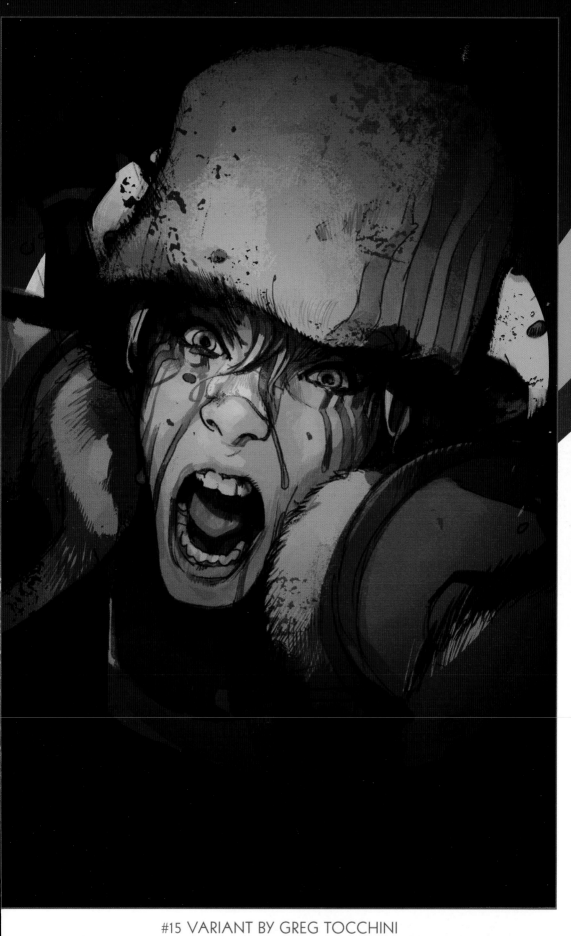

#15 VARIANT BY GREG TOCCHINI

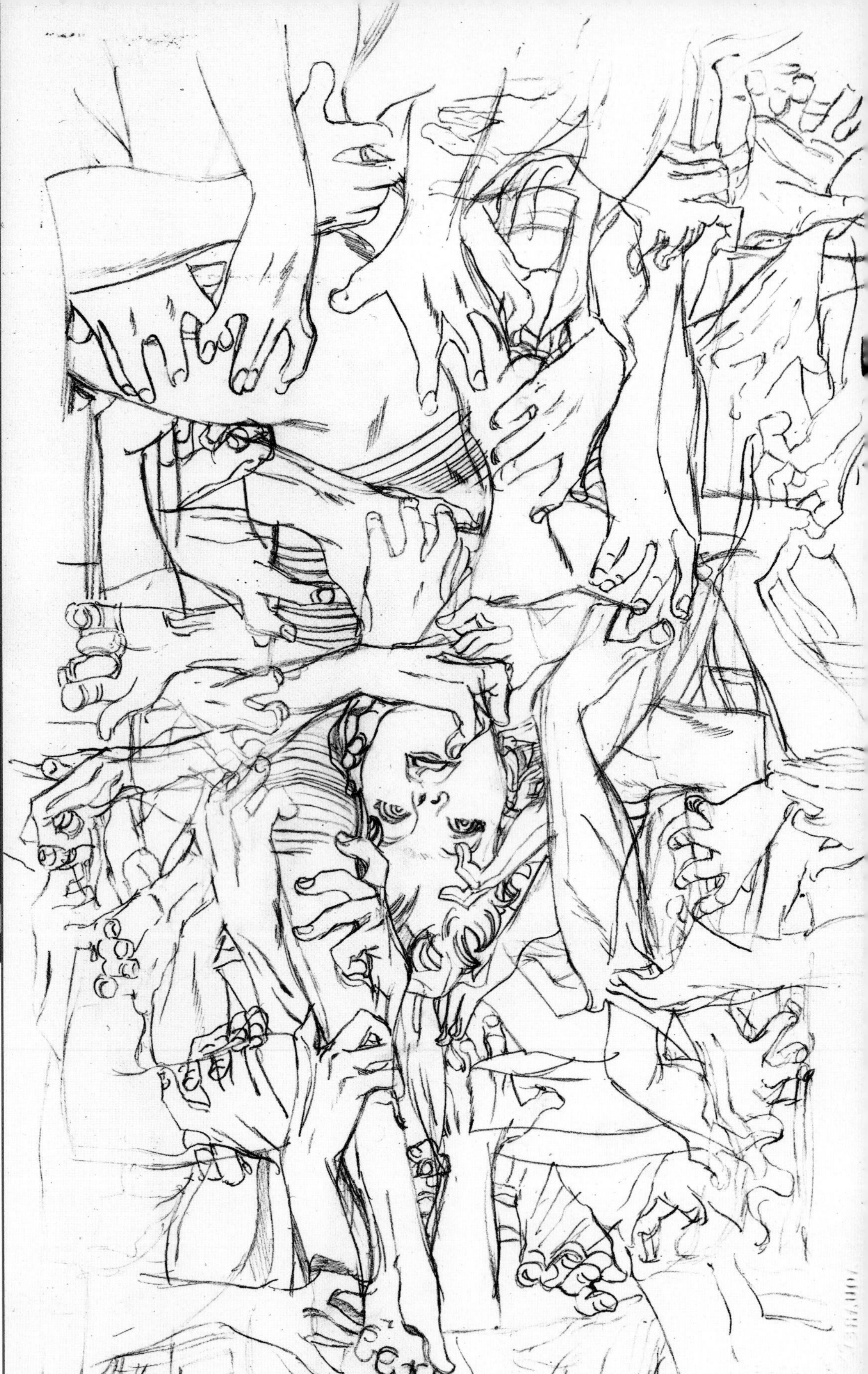

#11 COVER PENCILS BY GREG TOCCHINI

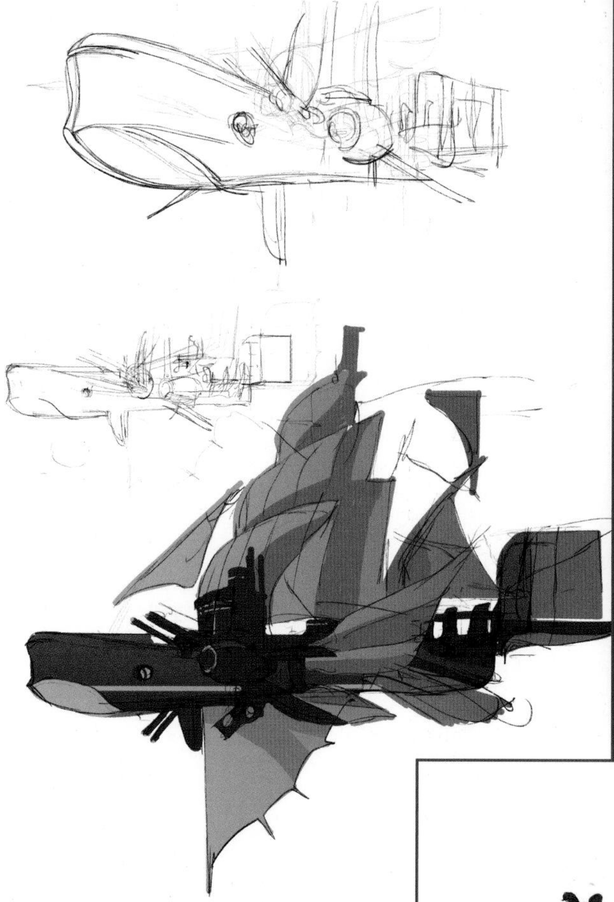

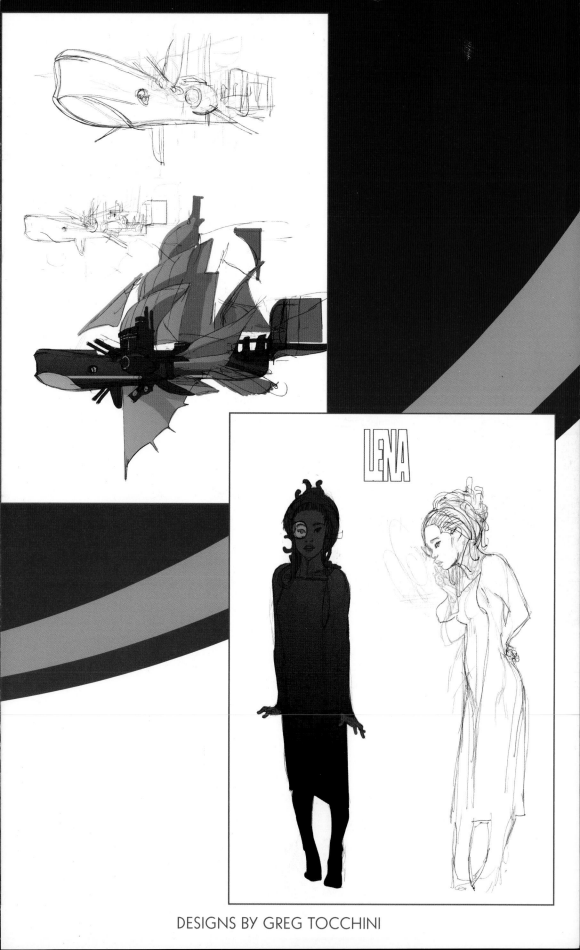

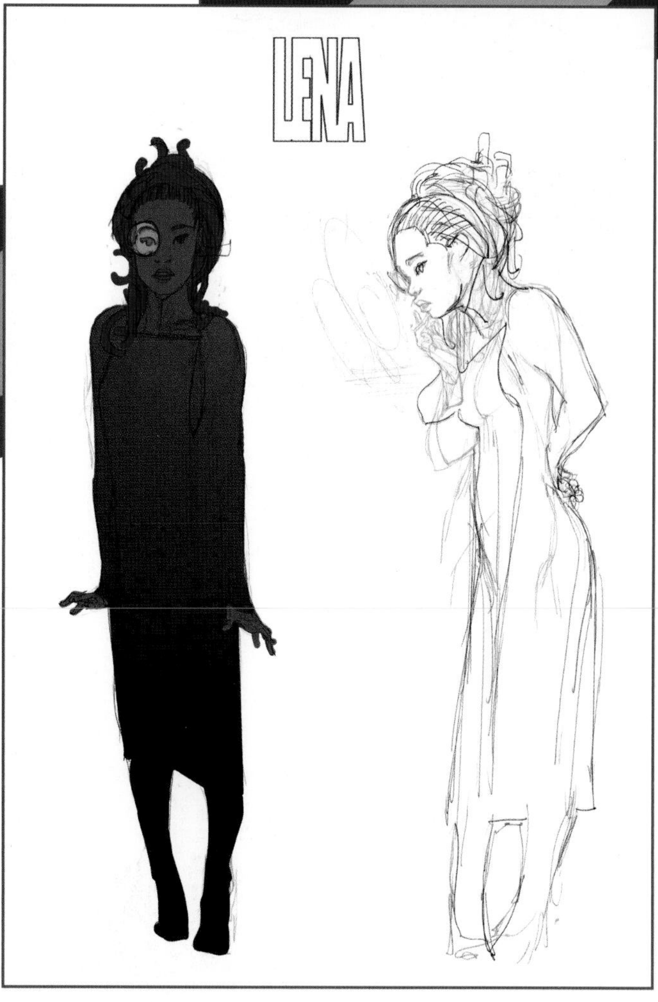
LENA

DESIGNS BY GREG TOCCHINI

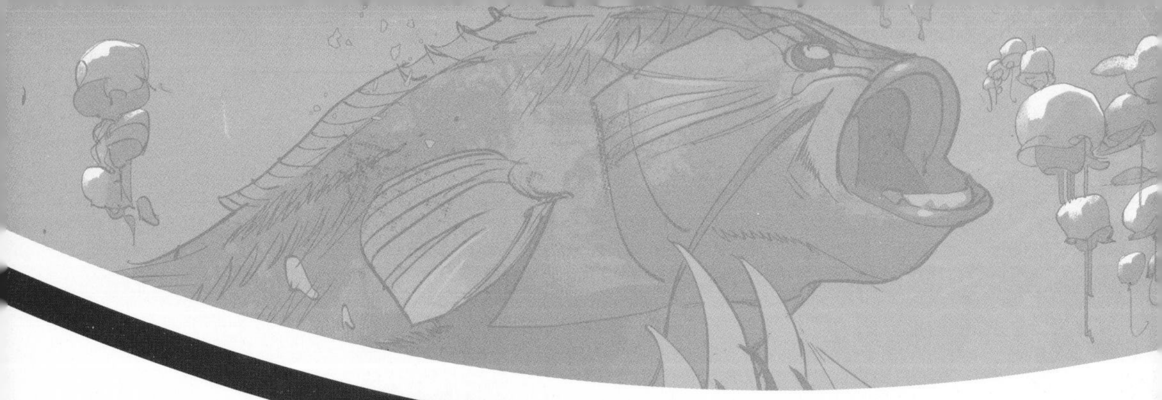

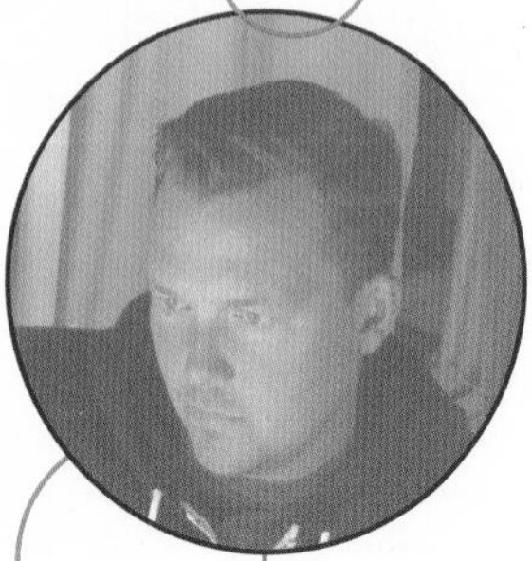

RICK REMENDER is the writer/co-creator of comics such as *Deadly Class*, *Fear Agent*, *Tokyo Ghost*, and *Black Science*. For Marvel he has written titles such as *Uncanny Avengers*, *Captain America*, *Uncanny X-Force*, and *Venom*. He's written video games such as *Bulletstorm* and *Dead Space*, and worked on films such as *The Iron Giant*, *Anastasia*, and *Titan A.E.* He and his tea-sipping wife, Danni, currently reside in Los Angeles raising two beautiful mischief monkeys.

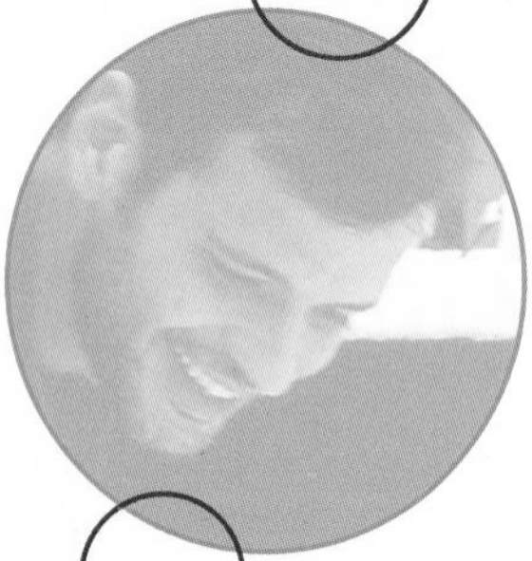

GREG TOCCHINI was born in 1979, in São Paulo, Brazil.

Since 2002 his work has been published internationally by companies such as Marvel and DC Comics (USA) and Le Lombard (France). Some titles include, *The Odyssey*, *Wolverine: Father*, *Fantastic Four*, *Thor: Son of Asgard*, *Captain America*, *Spider-Man*, *1602: A New World*, *ION*, *Batman and Robin*, *Uncanny X-Force*, *Infinity Section*, and many others.

He was the artist on the mini-series *The Last Days of American Crime* written by Rick Remender, with whom he recently co-created the science fiction series *Low*, currently being published by Image Comics. His independent label Dead Hamster Comics published his graphic novel *Sequence Shot* as well as works by various Brazilian artists.

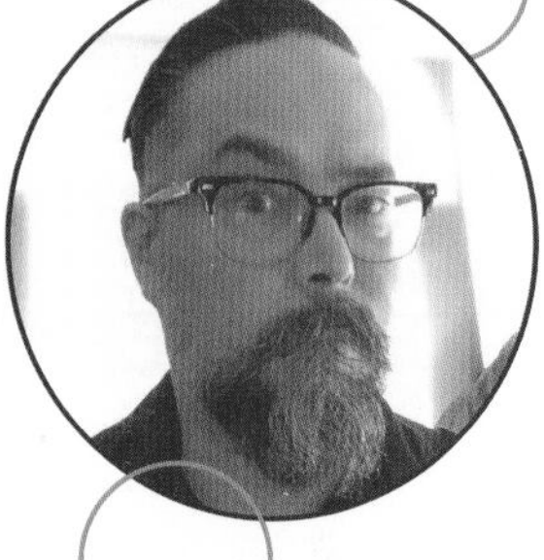

DAVE McCAIG is an Inkpot and Emmy award-winning colorist for comics and animation. He's known for coloring *Superman: Birthright*, *Nextwave*, *American Vampire*, *Northlanders*, and his work as lead color on *The Batman* animated series. He lives in New York with his two humans and two cats.